Then the third
burning like a tor
rivers and spring

and a third of the waters became wormwood, and many
people died from the water, because it became so bitter.

Revelation 8:9–11

WORMWOOD

• • •

MICAH ACKERMAN

ISBN: 1497329531
ISBN 13: 9781497329539
Library of Congress Control Number: 2014905109
CreateSpace Independent Publishing Platform
North Charleston, South Carolina

ACKNOWLEDGMENTS:

This book is dedicated to my family; my beautiful wife Patty, My incredible daughter Emma, My right hand man Timothy and My little shadow Micah Jr. Love is not a big enough word to describe how I feel about you guys.

I couldn't have done this without my Aunt Janet Ackerman, she gave me a gift that I will never forget. Thank you a million times, thank you.

I would like to thank my first readers and best critics
Steve Ackerman, Don Ackerman, Ben Ackerman, Dennis Perkins and Rich Cote.

And to my parents who have been supportive throughout every second of my life, I love you and couldn't have done this without you.

Please check out The Megapods sci-fi and horror podcast www.themegapods.com

To my readers: I hope this book finds you well wherever you are and that you will continue to read my stories. I appreciate every single one of you.

You can find out more about me and my new releases at www.MicahAckerman.com

Author's Note: All characters appearing in this work are fictitious. Any resemblance to real persons, living or dead, is purely coincidental. I have attempted to be accurate when describing locations in Connecticut, but I did take some liberties for continuity. The town of Middlebrook is fictional, but is based on my hometown in Connecticut. Although some actual town names were used in the surrounding areas all descriptions are a creation of my imagination.

1

THE IDES OF APRIL

"Shut up…just shut up," Nate said out loud, even though there was no one else in the car. He was trying to tell his own mind to stop. "Please, God, make it go away!" Nate was in the midst of another panic attack, and one of his rituals for dealing with an attack was trying to talk himself out of it. He felt dizzy; his heartbeat pounded like a heavy metal drummer's foot on the double bass pedal. "Just shut up; you're acting crazy. You're not normal," he said out loud again. He knew the trigger of the anxiety was what he had just heard on the radio, but he couldn't bring himself to shut the damn thing off. He was having enough trouble concentrating on the road. He couldn't breathe, he couldn't swallow, and his vision was cloudy. Nate wondered why this always happened to him. It was silly: the more he tried to make it go away, the more his own thoughts would betray him. "Please, please, please, just stop." He looked up into the rearview mirror, into his own green eyes, and said, "Just stop thinking." He knew if he had to pull over to the side of the road, he'd never make it to work and would spend another day sitting on the side of the road talking to himself. How had he let this happen again?

Nathan had always hated April, when the snow had melted away, exposing the wreckage of winter. That's what Nate felt like—his exterior had been peeled away, exposing the layers of raw nerves. Even the singing birds and the earthen smell made Nate cringe. Something evil was always happening in April, some faraway tragedy or catastrophic world event. It seemed history despised April as well— whether it was the Lincoln assassination, the *Titanic* sinking, Chernobyl, or James Earl Ray killing Martin Luther King Jr. All of these had happened in April. It seemed the changing of seasons and the spring flowers brought out the worst karma could offer.

Nathan always thought the world was ending every time he turned on the TV, surfed the Internet, or in this case listened to the radio. It seemed to be a hereditary fault, a Wilder family trait that had been passed down from his father like a genetic disposition to cancer or male pattern baldness. There was something masochistic about it, like stopping to watch a car crash. It was partially why he had entered the medical field in the first place. Yes, he liked helping people, but he loved having inside knowledge of infections and diseases. He had never done all that well in school, but he found the road of least resistance at the local community college, where he had gotten his certification in phlebotomy.

Drawing blood was like being the eyes and ears of the clinic. Every piece of information came through Nathan. Every patient, no matter the prognosis (even the healthy ones), needed blood work eventually. He was the middleman between the patients and the doctors, and he spent his day interacting with couriers, receptionists, lab techs, and IT crews. He was a pipeline of information, both good and bad.

This particular Saturday in April, Nate was driving into work, listening to a talk radio station out of New York, when a breaking news bulletin caught his attention.

North Korea had been antagonizing the United States since February, when they had tested two nuclear devices. The US government's policy had always been to ignore loose cannon dictatorships, turning its back and hoping the problem would go away. In North Korea, a new leader was stretching his wings, flexing his muscles, whatever metaphor you wanted to use. He seemed unstable, but in the past Korea's bark had always been far worse than its bite. Nate hoped the new dictator's bravado would play out the same way as that of his father, Kim Jong Il—a lot of bluster and threats, but no serious action. Nate thought this report sounded different, though, maybe even more severe. And the fact that it was April weighed heavily on his mind. Something in his gut told him to pay close attention, but the more he listened, the more his mind revolted against his body.

The North had already test-fired three rockets capable of carrying weapons of mass destruction over the ocean. They had also moved medium-range Madu Dan missiles toward the coast, putting them in the range of Hawaii and Japan. The news anchor spoke as if this was an everyday occurrence, just another boring bit of trivia, following this information with the latest celebrity fuckup. Nate was flabbergasted—typical New York radio, a tidbit of serious news followed by an hour of gossip. He flipped to National Public Radio, a more dependable source for this type of news. His timing was impeccable—they had just begun a segment on the "escalation." He tried to control his breathing as he listened.

Nate knew enough about the basics of the North Korean situation to make him more anxious, but not enough to flip out completely...or feel secure either. North Korea had always had an economy and society based on war. They had nearly a million troops stationed along the South Korean border, known as the Demilitarized Zone since the Korean conflict. North Korea had been pushing the limits since UN resolutions had isolated them from the rest of the world. They were always building, building, building. Whether it was more tanks, more guns, bigger bombs, or longer-range missiles, it seemed they never stopped. North Korea seemed to believe that the only way of getting the world's attention was matching the strength of other countries with firepower—or trying to at least. They acted like the ugly, molested stepchild, never getting enough attention and always craving a hug from Dad.

Today's news was different, however, in actions as well as words. The North Korean chief of staff was quoted as saying, "We will burn the aggressors out of our lands. We will wield our sacred sword and remove their stain from our homeland." Nate listened to the recording and then listened as the analytical news anchor's voice tore the quote apart. The *aggressors* were assumed to be the United States and South Korea, and the *sacred sword* may have referred to a weapon of mass destruction. Nate slammed his hands into the steering wheel. Why didn't they just say that?

As Nate listened to the broadcast, he was flung back to a time in his youth when missile silos were as common as state parks and the Berlin Wall was still a symbol of the "Quiet War" being waged between us and them—the Communists against the good guys. It was a time when fallout shelters, school drills, and supersonic spy planes were the torment of a generation. How many times had they come to the brink in the forty-year Cold War? But it never came to blows. It wouldn't happen with a tiny rogue regime like North Korea. It couldn't.

Nate kept driving toward work on that warm April morning, thoughts of the broadcast still replaying in his mind. Only residual palpitations remained from his panic attack and the resulting scattered thoughts...of another conflict, another car crash, a bigger wreck, this year's spring disaster.

Nate pulled up to the familiar white concrete building, which was actually two identical structures separated by a narrow alley. On one side was the blood draw facility and adjoining lab. It was a self-contained diagnostic center where blood could be drawn, processed, and resulted all at the same location. The building next door was the urgent care health clinic, a small walk-in doctor's office where people who had everything from broken bones to the flu could go for treatment. Both buildings were white cinder block with automatic sliding glass doors.

Nate parked his car at the back of the parking lot, which served both the blood facility and the clinic. He took a deep breath before walking in and checked the mirror again to make sure he didn't look flustered. He had hoped it wouldn't be busy, but he could tell by the line of people standing outside that it would be another slammer. It always amazed Nate how many customers had nothing better to do at eight o'clock in the morning on a Saturday than have their blood drawn. The line of senior citizens outside the glass doors reminded Nate of the scene from the movie *Dawn of the Dead* where the zombies come to the mall because it was an important place in their lives. Nate walked up the smooth asphalt and overheard two patients talking about the precarious "North Korean pickle." The line of eight to ten people buzzed like a beehive in a flower garden. *They sure are full of spunk for being in the latter stages of life,* Nate thought whimsically.

He slid his key into the lock and turned on the automatic doors, allowing the deluge of humans to pour into the blood draw station. Nate walked in and flipped on the bank of lights, illuminating the lobby, which was set up like a typical physician's waiting room. The decor was tame, with plush carpeting, a small coffee table for magazines, some vanilla paintings on the wall, and a small television fixed to the ceiling in one corner. The square room at least had color on the walls, which were forest green with brown fake wood trim. At the far end of the waiting room, there was a glass window in the center of the wall. On weekdays a receptionist would be seated behind the glass, registering patients as they entered, but on Saturdays, Nate was on his own.

"If everyone could please sign in, that'd be great," Nate announced to the crowd. He tried not to show his annoyance as he walked behind the reception desk and turned on all the computers. The reception area was a small cubicle that contained the computer and phone systems. The entire area was sterile white and smelled of camphor. Next to the reception area was a door that led from the waiting room back to the actual blood draw section of the facility. The blood draw area consisted of three separate stalls with curtains for privacy bordering a long hallway that served as the phlebotomist's workstation.

Lately, Saturdays at work had become a nightmare. In addition to it being Nate's usual day off, there was no receptionist on duty. This meant Nate had to register, draw blood, and enter the tests from every patient who visited the clinic all day. It was a time-consuming process that added to the customers' wait time and stressed their patience. That would mean some pain-in-the-ass complainers for Nate to deal with.

He walked into the back and opened the door to the lab that was adjacent to the blood draw areas. The lab was a big square room with huge spinning processing machines against all four walls. The walls had an aseptic whiteness that was almost blinding. Down the center were three connected tables with centrifuges that separated the blood that was to be tested.

The blood would then be passed to an area in the rear corner, where microscopes were lined up next to a computer station. The medical technologists operated the machines and microscopes and logged the results.

Sitting behind the computer station was the day-shift med tech, Jeannette Leach. Nate had always had a puppy-dog crush on Jeannette; she was tall and athletic with shoulder-length brown hair and penetrating brown eyes. Her skin was the color of almonds and had the soft look of silk. She was beautiful in that girl-next-door kind of way. Her biggest asset was how she carried herself: she was smart, very smart—too smart to work as a med tech at such a small facility. Her one flaw was her left hand, which was crumpled and fused and noticeably smaller than her right, a genetic defect. Nate didn't think it was a defect, though; in fact, it endeared her to him even more. He had always assumed it was what had kept her out of the city hospitals and what had brought her here to backass Middlebrook. In that way it was a gift, a gift like her perfect eyes or her perky breasts. Jeannette was immaculate in every way, but she never made anyone else feel inferior, and that was part of what Nate admired about her. Her hand never held her back, even though it drew the occasional stares from coworkers. She could have been a doctor if she had wanted, but thankfully for Nate, fate had dropped her here in Connecticut.

He walked over to exchange his usual good morning pleasantries. "Hey, Jeannette," he said, trying feebly to sound casual. He would have been mortified if she ever picked up on his infatuation.

"Hey, Nate," she said without even a glance up from her work.

It was torture to have a schoolboy's crush on a woman and yet be so petrified to show it that he didn't even stumble when he spoke anymore. His words came out in one quick syllable, almost like a caveman from the cartoons: "Me man. You woman." Nate had felt this torture for over a year and had never got much past wisecracks and good mornings with Jeannette. His extensive history with women had boiled down to a few one-night fucks with women after parties in college. The next day was customarily filled with regret and disappointment, both from his own conscience and from whomever he had woken up next to. Love? What's love to a guy who is always consumed by a sense of dread and forced to breathe into a paper bag every other day? Nathan Wilder didn't have the heart to bring someone else into his miserable future when he was convinced the future would be full of damage and ruin.

Nate walked back to the blood draw room, berating himself for not being more social. He started taking in patients, one after the other. The process of performing a blood test was pretty simple. First he would bring the patient in, register him or her, and begin entering the tests into the computer. The patient sat in the blood draw chair and chattered on about the weather while Nate worked on the computer. Once all the basic check-in procedures had been completed, he would find a vein and select the proper needle and blood tubes that corresponded with the requested tests. Then he would puncture the vein. Veins could be small and spindly or huge like firehoses. Some veins rolled, some veins were below three inches of fat and flesh, and some veins spidered out like a cluster of worms in a bait can. As an empathetic listener, Nate also needed to pay attention to the patients, who tended to confess to him like he was a bartender at a brothel. Nate had heard countless variations on the classic blood draw jokes: patients liked to say that they had come to visit the vampire, or some would ask him whether he had left them enough blood to make it home with. Nate felt his job was the worst paid and least respected in the medical field. Here he was, sticking a needle in someone's vein, and he was paid like a janitor. Some patients would jump when he stuck them or squirm out of the way; if the needle happened to slip out of the skin, he was at risk of a needlestick and might contract hepatitis or HIV. All that, and still Nate took home just over minimum wage. Sometimes it didn't seem worth it.

It was close to ten o'clock before Nate had a moment to himself without a patient breathing down his neck. Being a phlebotomist wasn't extremely difficult, but it took exactly the right kind of person and required an immense amount of responsibility. He had to make sure that the blood was labeled with the correct patient's name, and he also had to make sure it was sent to the correct processing lab. A lot could go wrong, and it often did.

Nate logged on to the Internet around ten thirty and started browsing the hardcore news sites. The blogosphere was buzzing with differing theories about the North Korean Missile Crisis, as the reporters were now calling it. Nate was particularly interested in finding out if that horse's ass President Everett had even addressed the issue yet. Steven Everett, the president of the United States, was a Republican hawk only elected due to superb historical timing. Two months before the last presidential election, four Syrian nationals had been caught trying to smuggle an eighteen wheeler full of fertilizer explosives across the Mexican border. The ammonium nitrate explosives would have been powerful enough to flatten an entire city block. The nation's attention was instantly turned away from the floundering economy and placed squarely on homeland security. Knowing full well that the American public has the attention span of a gnat, Everett kept them focused on terrorism through the debates right up to the election. Everett was a war hero, having risked his own life to save his platoon in Iraq, and his campaign played that card until the entire deck was exhausted. The Democrat who campaigned against Everett was a spineless peacenik who had dodged the draft back in Vietnam and had probably smoked dope with Bob Dylan while burning the flag.

Nate finally found what he had been searching for as his cursor scrolled to the headline "US President Responds to Escalating North Korean Tension." He read:

Today in Washington, DC, President Steven Everett spoke to White House correspondents in the Rose Garden about recurring claims by North Korea that their country is now a fully functional nuclear state. The president answered back with a stern edict for the North Korean dictatorship.

"The United States and the world will not be held hostage by this puppet regime; we refuse to be bullied by a coward hiding behind his own people as he continues to lead them down a path of destruction."

The president has pushed forward with his policy of supporting UN sanctions against the rogue nation.

"Until North Korea agrees to abandon its nuclear aspirations, we will continue to encourage the United Nations to impose crippling economic sanctions. All options are on the table; we will not stand idly by while this paper lion threatens his neighbors."

North Korea remains headstrong in the face of worldwide multilateral pressure. The small country's economy has ground to a startling halt beneath the weight of some of the strictest sanctions in the United Nation's storied history. All imports and exports, including, for the first time, humanitarian aid, have been blocked. The stranglehold is being kept in place by the Seventh Fleet of the US Navy. Intelligence analysts have stated that even with UN sanctions in place, North Korea continues operating at least three separate nuclear reactors, designed with the sole intent of producing fissile material for multiple weapons. They also continue production of the new Musudan-2 rockets, capable of carrying multiple tipped warheads over three thousand kilometers. This would put the west coast of the US mainland within range.

As Nate continued to read, his head began spinning like a dreidel on Chanukah. This was like an acute version of the Cold War all over again—two sides with missiles pointed at each other. North Korea had to understand that launching a missile would be suicidal. The United States still had more than seven thousand nuclear weapons in its arsenal. Some of them were 1970s Cold War relics, but they would do the job in a pinch. Just one ten-megaton B-61 gravity bomb would be hundreds of times more powerful than Korea's six-to-eight-kiloton firecrackers. The United States had cruise missiles, stealth bombers—hell, they had ICBMs capable of hitting a thimble thousands of miles away. Nate wondered what exactly North Korea was thinking. What was their play here?

He continued with his shift, occasionally stopping to check the Internet for news and, of course, sneak a peek at Jeannette. It was disheartening being so close to a woman who outclassed him in every way. Jeannette was intelligent and perfectly proportioned, whereas Nate was out of shape, anxious, and not much to look at. He was average in every way—average height, average weight, average looking, and, in Nate's own opinion, of average intelligence. Jeannette knew how to handle herself with the exact balance of intellect and charm. She was a uniquely crafted sculpture, whereas Nate felt like a brown lump of clay. Nate sat daydreaming of slipping off Jeannette's blouse and cupping her perky, just-a-handful breasts. He imagined her smiling and whispering in his ear, only to be sharply drawn back to reality by a patient in the waiting room calling, "Hello, hello? Is anyone working today?"

THE DEAR LEADER

The North Korean leader Kim Jong Un had run short of options. His people were starving. That in itself didn't bother him, but now his mighty army was crumbling like a Chinese building during an earthquake. Forces were breaking down, soldiers were deserting—more than his generals could handle and most likely more than they would admit. He couldn't execute them all...well he could, but that would only exacerbate the problem. The soldiers were going AWOL to try and feed their own families. Things were getting bad even for the families of his beloved military. The soldiers would leave the army and attempt to beg, borrow, or steal enough food to keep their families alive. This was a problem. It weakened morale, and rebellion was only a spark away from that dry, crisp kindling. National grain and rice stockpiles were almost completely exhausted. There was only so much he could milk from the homeland. It had been a hard winter, and the fields lay fallow—most of the crops that had come in this year were blighted and scanty. Selling missile technology and hardware to Iran, Syria, and Nigeria had been a source of income, but the devil's sanctions were making that impossible. He thought and thought to come up with an answer, a solution to this dilemma that threatened his mighty grasp on the nation. What would the old man do? The Dear Leader...his father.

His father, the great leader Kim Jong Il, had been dead two years now. His father had always seemed to have the solution to any problem. The son was young and inexperienced in the art of international manipulation. His generals didn't trust him; they thought him prostrate, afraid to stand up to the imperialist aggressors. Kim couldn't figure out what exactly the military commanders wanted from him. He had already defied the whole world by building this new holy fire that they had so desperately needed and spent every resource at his disposal to strengthen their ranks and improve their weaponry. He had invested millions, perhaps billions, in the rockets and technology. He had even risked everything by hiring (if you could call it that) fourteen French expert hackers to create General Su-chen's cyber virus. Of this he understood little, but he had shown faith in his commanders. The French students, Kim thought with a giggle—Western mutants with their tattoos and body piercing. They were all so cocksure and arrogant; they were actually excited to be in this exotic land behind the "bamboo curtain," enjoying the grand adventure of it all. If they only knew that they'd never leave. Kim would dispose of them once they had served their purpose like a well-worn condom, used once then flushed away.

The next move on the chess board would need to be a bold one. The time for deliberation had passed. Kim couldn't allow a military coup to build to fruition. No people's rebellion would dethrone this Dear Leader. Desperate times called for desperate measures. Kim needed something to coalesce his people behind a solitary goal. He would need to leverage his newfound nuclear might. He made a mental note: if he couldn't reach out to the world for help, then the world would need to come to him...on its knees. What he needed was a sign, a sign from God, a sign from his dead father, something to direct him down the correct path. After hours of contemplating just what to do, he made his decision. The instigators needed to be made an example of. He would take the

South, reunify the Koreas. The South had sold out to the capital-
ists long ago. Like some ancient Roman emperor, Kim believed
that if his own land couldn't produce what his people needed to
survive, he would simply take someone else's. Invade, pillage,
plunder, dominate—it was the nature of this world that the strong
shall gobble up the weak. What of the South's partner in crime,
though, the great imperialists from the West? The South had
snuggled up so close to the Americans that any incursion would
draw the wrath of their smart bombs, drones, and other coward-
ice by remote control.

There would need to be a way to take the Americans out of the
picture, to leave the South alone on an island. He needed a great
distraction—the old bait and switch. Something that would keep
the Americans so preoccupied that they had no choice but to look
the other direction. If only the Americans had an equal, someone to knock the bully on its ass. Even the mighty North Korean
Army was no match for the American capitalist military, funded
by Wall Street and subsidized by Silicon Valley. The lesson that
could be learned from the People's Republic of Vietnam as well
as from Iraq was that the American public had no stomach for
blood. A war on foreign soil would bring them to the streets like
spoiled children.

Kim called in his chief advisor, Secretary Chan, who had
been his closest confidant since the Academy. "It's coming to a
head, Chan," said Kim, standing behind his desk in the great palace. Tapestries of the great leaders of the war hung on the walls.
Paintings of glories past watched over them like history judging
the present.

"I agree, Dear Leader," the tall, thin secretary said, fixing a
pin on the lapel of his neatly pressed uniform.

"What can we do to bring honor to this great nation of ours?
What avenue will in one fell swoop feed the masses, bring the
people behind us, and defeat our enemies?"

"It is quite the problem, my Dear Leader," Chan said, meeting the gaze of his superior.

"Have a seat, my friend," Kim said to his most trusted ally.

"Sir, there can be no moral victories this time. We need to strike a crushing blow to the West, something to rally our own people and even the world to our cause." Chan cleared his throat.

Kim paced behind his desk, looking up at the great portrait of his father that hung on the wall. "Yes, a great and swift crushing blow to the imperialists." Kim poured himself a glass of tea from the kettle on his desk. "There can be no victory without blood this time."

"Yes, my Dear Leader, there can be no success without sacrifice. The generals must be shown that you have the fortitude to confront our enemies." With that, the two men concocted a scheme laced with vengeance: a plan for the ages that would bring the two Koreas together and thrust a knife through the hearts of their enemies.

2

BEFORE FAILSAFE

Nate only had a couple of hours to go before his shift was due to be over, but the last thing on his mind was work. He could feel a knot in his stomach. Anxiety and paranoia go hand in hand like french fries and ketchup. Nate had suffered panic attacks his whole life. He had been through psych evaluations and had even had tried medications like Valium and Xanax; nothing seemed to erase the dread that constantly seeped into his daily routine. A psychiatrist had once explained to him, "Panic and anxiety are simply the body's natural fight-or-flight response kicking in when you don't need it. It's your brain making something benign into a life and death situation." Nate always made Mount Everest out of a molehill, but this time he felt different—if anything, it seemed more rational, like he had been having déjà vu about something bad that had actually come to fruition. The North Korean Missile Crisis was pounding the walls inside his head like a demolition team with an arsenal of sledgehammers.

How many times had this happened to him in the past? A national event—something entirely outside of his control—dominating his every thought? He remembered the year of the nationwide outbreak of H1N1, otherwise known as swine flu. Nate was convinced that it was the new bubonic plague and would lead to an extinction event. He bought cases of hand sanitizer and washed his hands incessantly, like some eccentric germaphobe with obsessive compulsive disorder. He had studied up on the influenza pandemic of 1918, when one quarter of the world's population had perished. He had started taking all sorts of holistic herbs and spices in an effort to boost his immune system. Nate also remembered stocking up on batteries, canned food, and bottled water in case the nation's infrastructure collapsed. He had also worn a surgical mask at work, even once it had become uncomfortable and claustrophobic to himself and his patients. Nate had never been a germaphobe before—hell, he worked with blood and needles everyday—but he nad been convinced that this was the epidemic that was going to bring down society like some old testament pestilence. He also remembered following every news media website (like he was doing now) and counting the numbers of swine flu cases across the country. Nate had even made a chart using Microsoft Excel and logged the severity and location of every infected person he could find. Then one morning, he had woken up with a simple sinus headache. He went to see his doctor, who diagnosed him with a minor cold. Nate recalled feeling betrayed and almost disappointed that he wasn't more sick, like the doctor was concealing the truth of his real sickness from him like some cancer patient who only had months to live. This time, though, Nate was prepared; it wasn't exaggeration. This time some schism was coming, some cataclysmic event. He was sure of it.

Nate, beaten down and exhausted, longed to be finished with work, to be home on the couch drinking a beer and watching his beloved Red Sox. No matter how many times the Sox let him down, they were always there for him, like a security blanket calming his nerves in a time of crisis. The day dragged on whether or not he had patients to deal with. This was the only job that he had ever had where the busier he was the slower time seemed to move. In most cases, when a person is immersed in work it makes the hours fly by. Being busy generally accelerates the clock. But not here...not today. The last few patients of the day were always the worst, especially on a Saturday. They always acted like the phlebotomists had been placed on the earth solely for their needs. Like Nate was a serf sitting there all day simply waiting for them to enter his life.

The last patient on this Saturday was a real doozy. It was a woman with a two-page gynecological requisition full of obscure hormonal tests. And even though she had entered the facility five minutes before closing, she was bitchy and wanted her blood drawn "now, not later, now!" When Nate explained to her that it would take some time to enter her tests in the computer and this was hardly a process that she would want rushed, she refused to wait. Nate tried to work as quickly as possible, but he still received an earful of good cheer while she was sitting in the draw chair as he drew her blood.

The one silver lining to this otherwise very dark cloud was that one of the samples he had to draw required ice and immediate processing. This was an excuse to see Jeannette. So after the blood was drawn, Nate slipped the tubes into a red biohazard bag, grabbed a handful of ice to add to the pouch, and strolled into the connecting lab. He found her sitting in her little corner of the room, typing into her desktop computer. She looked so serious and truly Junoesque, librarian chic right down to the glasses teetering on her nose. Nate slowed his pace and stood watching her for a moment. Her hair was slightly askew where she had haphazardly brushed it off her face with the back of her forearm. She felt his presence and looked up from her computer. Nate blushed, having been caught staring. "Jeannette, I have a present for you," he said, holding up the biohazard bag that contained the ice and the tube of blood.

"Oh, gee thanks, Nate, just what I always wanted," she said with a sarcastic smile. That little smile always melted Nate, and he could feel his heart pounding in his ears. He walked over sheepishly, trying to play it cool and collected. He handed her the sample and hovered for a moment, trying to think of something clever to say.

"So, Jeannette, what do you think about this North Korea situation?" It was the first thing to enter his mind, beyond her. Jeannette gave Nate a surprised look; it was probably the first time he had ever broached a serious subject with her. It was a mile beyond the usual talk about work or the weather he was so accustomed to.

"Well, Nate," she said, as if she were being quizzed by a college professor in one of her civics classes, "I think nothing good can come of it. North Korea is a country on the edge of starvation. They are dangerous, like a cornered animal protecting a cub...Yet I don't think they want a war; I don't think they could afford one. I think they are trying to scare the world into feeding them. Perhaps they want to trade peace for sustenance." She paused, breaking away from her workstation's gravitational pull for the first time. "No matter how technologically advanced they've become, I doubt they could get a missile to the mainland of the United States." She thought about it for a moment longer before continuing. "I think we have some sort of missile defense as well, not that it would ever come to that, but I remember something about missile defense from the first Gulf War. Remember, we shot down those missiles over Israel?" Jeannette took the specimen from Nate and began to feed the tube into the centrifuge closest to her.

"You mean the SCUDS?" Nate asked.

"The what?" Jeannette asked, confused.

"The SCUD missiles that Saddam Hussein shot at Israel during the first Gulf War?"

"Yes, those," Jeannette answered as she pressed the power button down and the machine started spinning.

Again, Nate was mesmerized. Jeannette could probably talk circles around Nate on any subject, but she made him feel smart and included. It was really a gift she had.

Nate attempted to run with the conversation to stretch the feeling of warmth he was getting as long as he could. "I assume you're right, but it just seems different, at least to me, this time." Nate could hear that he sounded paranoid, and he attempted to justify the statement. "I remember back in '94, North Korea made the same kind of vague threats, but this time they seem more desperate, even a bit crazed. You have that new dictator over there, you know the guy whose dad looked like the Korean Elvis?"

"Yup, I know what you mean; that kid is probably out to prove something." Jeannette made Nate feel saner just by agreeing.

Nate sensed Jeannette's distraction at being drawn into this conversation while she was trying to work and decided to quit while he was ahead. He was beginning to feel a small glimmer of confidence, but he didn't want to push any further or, worse yet, annoy her while she was concentrating on resulting samples. "OK, Jeannette, I have to get back to closing up the shop for the day. I'll see you on Monday...have a good rest of the weekend." Jeannette gave Nate a puzzled look; perhaps she wasn't ready to give up the conversation.

"Sure, Nate, you too, see ya Monday. I'm sorry we couldn't talk longer. I'm just so busy, and if I ever want to get out of here I need to finish this shit up," Jeannette said with a sigh. She finished by blowing her hair out of her eyes, a maneuver that on anyone else would look like an annoying tick but on Jeannette just added to her allure.

Nate skulked back to the blood draw room and started cleaning up his work area with sanitized wipes. The day hadn't been as bad as he had worried it would be work wise, but it hadn't been a good one either. Nate couldn't remember his last really good day at work—or good day in general. At least he had been able to talk with Jeannette for a bit and hadn't made a complete ass out of himself. He started to daydream again about what it would be like to have someone like Jeannette as a girlfriend... her olive skin, dark hair, and soothing chestnut-brown eyes. He had never had anyone that he could really care for, be romantic with, or even lust after. Nate was a social misfit. People like Jeannette weren't meant to be with people like Nate. Her voice fluttered around in Nate's head like a moth bouncing against a lightbulb.

He snapped back to reality and looked quickly back on the Internet for more news. It was everywhere, like a brushfire across all the sites he scanned. North Korea planned to increase their troop buildup along the DMZ. The United States had responded by moving two new aircraft carriers into the region. They would be stationed off the north coast of Japan, within striking distance of Pyongyang. International news was rarely a hot Internet topic—only occasionally when something interesting was happening. Usually Nate would really need to search for it, but today it was dominating every message board. It was at the top of even the more mainstream sites like Yahoo, AOL, MSN, and there was even a crawl on Google! He felt a little bit vindicated for his earlier anxiety. Two of Nate's favorite sites for news, the Huffington Post and the Boston Globe, both had the story scrolling at the top of their pages with hourly updates. It was an ominous omen that a subject that rarely sells was smashing its way into even the entertainment sites. It was almost as if the entire Internet was starting to feed Nate's paranoia. With each word he read, the knot in Nate's stomach drew tighter, like a noose around his neck. He had to physically force himself up and away from the computer. It was time to go home; he pushed himself back, took a breath, and got up to lock the front sliding glass doors.

As Nate walked out to his car, he started making mental notes of all the things he would need in the event of a nuclear attack. If it ever got that bad, his location in central Connecticut would be a benefit. North Korea would hardly choose Connecticut out of all the possible targets in this country. If they did target Connecticut, the closest high-profile military outpost would be the submarine base and Coast Guard Academy in New London, which was about forty miles away from Nate as the crow flies. The closest civilian target would probably be New York, which was always at the top of every attacker's list, especially if the goal was to dismantle the US financial markets. If you made a triangle on a map of the northeastern United States, Nate would be at the apex, while New York City and New London, Connecticut, would be at the bottom corners. New York was a bit farther away from Nate, though, at around one hundred miles. Boston would be another population target, but probably of lesser importance to North Korea. The town of Middlebrook, where Nate had moved as a teenager from northwest Connecticut, sat about ninety miles from Boston. Nate didn't think North Korea had the firepower to reach all three targets, but New York City was the most attractive. All things considered, Nate had to feel relatively safe; even if the North Koreans could hit NYC, he should be far enough away from the blast that he wouldn't be directly affected. These locations and a map of the East Coast flashed in his mind—the big cities covered with large yellow and black nuclear symbols. It was another of his mental health quirks, the minutia playing out on a loop. The concerns for Nate would be nuclear fallout, any EMP effect, and general civil unrest. He could prepare—he could stockpile food, water, and ammunition—but he could never be completely safe. The more Nate thought about it, the more items he identified as essentials: nonperishable food, potable water, weapons, flashlights, batteries, and most of all shelter. A method for measuring radiation would be ideal also, but where could he get a Geiger counter?

Finding a suitable shelter soon rushed to the top of his mental list. He would need something to protect him from fallout and a place that would be away from any looters, or at least secure enough to keep them out. Nate paused as he started his car, laughing to himself over his compulsiveness in going so far over something that would likely never occur. Did Nate *want* something cataclysmic to happen? Nate needed something major to change his stagnant life, but a slow death by radiation sickness didn't appeal to him. He had always thought that he could survive without society if need be. He had grown up in the outdoors and figured he could get by without modern creature comforts. The one useful thing Nate's father had taught him was how to catch fish and hunt game. Nate's dad would take him on weekend camping trips to the mountains or woods, and they would often pretend that they could only eat what they had caught or killed. Trips to the supermarket or restaurants weren't allowed on those weekends. He would show Nate what berries were safe to eat, what mushrooms weren't toxic, and how to clean and gut fish, deer, and other small game.

Did Nate hope something would happen? The question lingered in the back of his mind. No, Nate was fairly comfortable in his rut of a life, despite the anxiety. He despised the idea of pain and death, and he had spent his adulthood caring for his fellow man, even if it was simply drawing blood. He had seen a lot of good in humanity from his little blood draw station in this small town. In the event of a nuclear war, thousands if not millions of people would be killed—that was too big of a disaster, even for Nate.

He pulled out of the parking lot and headed toward his apartment, past the center of town. Middlebrook was the smallest of the small when it came to tiny New England towns. The only reason they even had a blood lab and health clinic was because they were affiliated with a large university hospital and served the entire county. It was literally a one-stoplight town, and the light was right at the center of town. The town center was the only developed area, with municipal buildings and a few restaurants. The majority of the berg consisted of rural suburbia and farmland; most of the residents commuted to work in bigger cities. Nate drove, thinking of Jeannette's face and that shy little smile. If only he had the balls. The sun's warmth felt comforting through the windshield, the kind of warmth where you want to find a big picture window and nap and bask in the radiance.

STRATEGO

The North Korean Leader shuffled the pile of topological maps in front of him. He sat at the head of a long, black glossy hardwood table; the table dominated an enormous amount of space in the situation room of the North Korean government. It resembled a board meeting at a Fortune 500 company, with men seated up and down both sides His generals, national ministers, and most trusted advisors had all been called to order to put in motion his strategy for bringing the first world to its knees. Kim had devised a genius plan that would be spoken of for generations like a battle formation from Sun Tzu. His great nation couldn't afford to take the blows from standing toe to toe with the Americans. They simply had too many weapons; a nuclear exchange would bring far too much destruction to the homeland, and one cannot enjoy the fruits of one's labor when one is beneath a pile of rubble. As much as he wanted to strike at the heart of his great nemesis, the time called for a more subversive plan of action. "How do you knock a bully off the block?" he asked no one in particular. "You find a bully from a different neighborhood and trick him into destroying your bully." Kim smiled at his own cleverness; the analogy was perfect. "And if the bully will not come to you, how do you get his attention? You find the bully's best friend and punch him in the nose."

A revelation had come to Kim that he wouldn't fight the Americans. No, he would instigate a fight between the Americans and the only country with the firepower to match theirs...the hibernating bear, the Russians. The Dear Leader had deliberated about this for days; he had thought long and hard about a solution to his quagmire. He described the way forward to all his commanders in eloquence. His plan was three-faced, like a great trident capable of striking down some mythical beast. The first phase would be to draw the Americans in by detonating a small but effective nuclear package in Tokyo Harbor. This, of course, would incite the Americans to strike. Japan had been America's bitch since tasting the heat of the atom at Hiroshima and Nagasaki. The Dear Leader had already ordered the construction of a missile base in the North, outside the town of Onsong. It would be a decoy, a facade—old missiles, new recruits, and an older, well-used, and outdated nuclear reactor. This base would glow red for the American satellites. It would not only contain enough nuclear fuel and waste to leave a footprint for the Americans to hone in on, but it would also allow enough contamination to spread into Siberia. The Onsong reactor would be a dumping ground for as much contaminate as they could find. Between the bomb in Japan and Onsong, that would be an enormous amount of radiation for the wind to set adrift toward Russia. Phase two would initiate once the Russians were drawn in, presumably incensed at the contamination of their people and of their soil. Kim would then strike with his French guests, the hackers here on sabbatical. After setting the bait and letting it fester, the hackers would wreak havoc among the Russian and American early warning systems around the globe. The two countries would be alerted of a massive imminent incoming nuclear strike from the opposing side. The chaos-creating hackers would blind them and disrupt their communications with a virus to shut down their technology. They would have no choice but to fire on each other in earnest. With America ablaze with hellfire, phase three would begin. North Korean troops would stream across the DMZ like water through a broken dam. "We will unify the homeland," the dictator shouted to his now standing subordinates. "It was my father's dream and his father's before him. Hell all around and a unified Korea left standing alone at the top." He walked to the huge picture windows looking out over Kim II Sung square and looked out at his great country.

After the fires of war had died down, the dictator would turn to his old friends in China. Yes, they had turned their backs on him in recent years, but old alliances would be restored. Trade would resume, and the people of Korea would finally prosper, allowing Kim to take his place in history next to his father and grandfather. The military commanders began to applaud and cheer; Kim turned from the window and smiled.

3

THE YOSSARIAN

Nate sat in front of his computer in his tiny one-bedroom efficiency. His home was sparsely decorated with posters of bands and some furniture his mother had left him when she passed away three years ago. For a thirty-two-year-old, Nate had become a specialist at avoiding the maximum amount of responsibility. His apartment didn't even have enough room to become messy; he had one set of dishes, so he had very little washing to do. He wore scrubs at work and even most of the time at home, and he used the coin-operated laundry down the street to wash them. His apartment building was a two-story brick structure in the center of Middlebrook. He had lived in town since college, but he knew next to no one; even his patients were strangers to him, more than half of them hailing from neighboring towns. The only relationships he had bothered to foster were at work, and they were meager at best. Nate was the definition of a lone wolf, and for the most part he liked it that way.

He typed quickly, creating an immaculately organized spreadsheet of items he would need in the event of a nuclear attack. Nate was trying to skirt the line between listing practical items that he could use in the likelihood that nothing happened and stocking up like some Michigan militiaman survivalist. The Unabomber was one of those survivalists, and he didn't want to associate himself with that style of paranoid doomsday prepper. Nate needed to decide what materials he had already (not much) and what he would need to buy. Money was always an issue with Nate because his irresponsibility showed no bounds, especially when it came to due dates on bills. The reason he liked his job so much was that there was no "homework." He hated deadlines.

The most difficult item for Nate to find would also be the most important, and that was shelter. The dingy, cramped cellar of his apartment building was out of the question. It had a dirt floor that flooded in a drizzle, and it was too easily accessible from the outside. It was also quite drafty, and there was always the chance that the old lady who lived below Nate would try to shelter there. The thought of spending any time with her sent a shiver down Nate's spine. He didn't want anyone with him, especially any panicked nutballs he'd have to babysit. He thought about the irony of that. He would need to find a relatively clean, ventilated, secure fallout shelter shut off from the rest of the world, but far from a trap or a prison. This was a very tall order indeed. Finding the ideal shelter would take some time, and fortifying it and making it habitable would be beyond Nate's means. He needed a place where he could come and go as he pleased without drawing attention. He searched the Internet, but every page was about building your own bunker, and he was neither an architect nor a carpenter.

Beyond shelter, Nate wasn't sure where to begin. He knew the basics—food, water, weapons, and light. The immediate concern would be identifying how much of each he would need to stockpile. Nate minimized his spreadsheet and clicked over to a search engine. He found a few sites that described surviving a nuclear attack, mostly leftover nostalgia from the eighties. After reading through a plethora of useless theoretical information, he found what he was seeking: a scientific site about the likelihood of surviving a nuclear winter and what the atmospheric conditions would look like. On the sidebar was what Nate had been hoping for. It spoke of distances and rads, information that Nate had only heard of in movies. If there was a nuclear explosion within thirty miles, depending on the strength, it would take about ten days for the fallout to dissipate enough for limited exposure. Thirty days would be enough time for enough electron decay to take place to actually go outside and venture around without glowing in the dark. Sixty days and the atmosphere would be safe to remain in indefinitely, as long as he didn't drink contaminated water, eat contaminated food, or even burn contaminated wood, which could redistribute the particles back into the air and thus into the lungs.

Nate also found some information on a secondary characteristic of nuclear explosions, the EMP or electromagnetic pulse effect. An EMP occurs when a nuclear device detonates at high altitudes within the atmosphere. It wreaks havoc on all electrical circuitry, trashing the grid and shutting off electricity—cars, planes, and anything else with sophisticated wiring or computers is rendered useless. Every word Nate read drove his blood pressure a few ticks higher; he was working himself into quite a lather thinking about the real-life consequences of the grid shutting down.

In the bottom corner of one page, Nate found his first truly useful item to purchase. There was a smartphone app that would convert the phone into a Geiger counter. The app was actually a memory card that, when installed in the phone, would convert the phone's camera into a receiver that measured radiation. The same link also contained instructions for protecting the phone from an EMP. He could buy a box, designed by the military, that would protect a laptop or cell phone from almost any damaging effects, including high temperature, water, and electronic disturbances such as a lightning strikes or magnetic pulses. Nate rifled through his wallet and pulled out his one and only credit card. He ordered the smartphone card and the protective case and checked the box for overnight delivery via FedEx.

Nate stood up, stretched, and walked over to the tall metal cabinet in the far corner of his living room. The cabinet had been his father's and looked out of place in the nearly empty apartment. It had served as Nate's gun safe since he had moved out of his parents' house when he was eighteen. Many times he had thought about pawning his father's guns, but he had never had the heart to do it. Nate opened the cabinet and inventoried the contents. There was a semiautomatic 30-06 deer rifle with a scope, a very accurate gun. It had been Nate's father's favorite rifle when they used to deer hunt every November. Just seeing the gleaming walnut stock unleashed a flood of memories from Nate's youth. He remembered sitting in a tree stand while his father walked the forest hoping to push a deer toward his son. It was always so cold, and Nate had no patience for being uncomfortable...or for his dad in general. It had been five years since Nate had been hunting. His father had died only a year after his mother, and Nate couldn't bring himself to hunt without the old man. That was Nate's father's thing; hunting would have been too hard, and the wounds were still painful and cut too deep. The last year of his dad's life consisted of days in a deep depression. Nate understood depression, but it was too hard to talk to the man who had passed so many unwelcome feelings on to his son. His dad was simply killing time waiting to die and join his wife. For all intents and purposes, Nate's father had died the same day his mother had. They had been so devoted to each other—married for twenty-nine years, the constant vigil at her deathbed—that Nate remembered feeling like the cancer was eating them both alive. Nate's father never left his mother's side in those final days; even a trip to the convenience store was too much to ask. She had put up with so much shit and enabled him for so long that he probably felt like it was the least he could do. A year later, when Nate's father had a massive heart attack, it was almost a relief. Nate was devastated, but at least his father was free from the pain of being alone. His dad had never had any major heart problems, but depression can be a terminal illness too.

Nate thought about this absurd situation, and for the first time he was glad he was an orphan. He had been an only child, born late in his parents' lives, probably spoiled and sheltered because of it. Now it finally seemed like having no family and no attachments might be a blessing. Whether this was a real calamity boring down on him or some primal concoction of his mental illness, it was better that he didn't have to worry about his parents while it was happening.

Nate scanned the rest of the contents of the safe. There was a Mossberg pump action shotgun with a rifled barrel for shooting slugs. This was the gun he had used while deer hunting. At the bottom of the safe were a few boxes of ammunition and a hard plastic case. Nate grabbed the hard case and opened it. This was the last Christmas present he had received from his father before he died. Inside the case was a brand new Glock nine-millimeter handgun. Nate had only fired the pistol at the local target range once, two weeks after it was given to him. Nate's father had always believed in personal protection and felt that every young man should have a firearm. He never had the heart to tell his father that the town of Middlebrook was hardly a hotbed of crime. Nate set the handgun box at the bottom of the cabinet. He picked through the ammo, opening each box to make sure it was full. There was more ammunition than Nate had originally thought. He had at least thirty rounds for each firearm.

Nate sat back down at the computer and began entering each gun and the amount of ammunition into a column labeled Assets. The next stop would have to be the grocery store; he'd need sixty days of food and water. His bedroom closet was full of camping supplies. He didn't even need to look, though it had been a while since he had opened the door. He had a sleeping bag, a portable gas stove, a hunting knife, and a few fishing rods, all of which he entered into the spreadsheet. Organizing everything this way made Nate feel more secure. Within an hour, Nate had a finalized printout of what he would need to get and what he already had. He could be prepared within days for an event that he figured would almost certainly never come.

Nate gave up and retreated to his bed, which he pulled from his sofa like a transforming children's toy. He stood thinking about his lonely existence and turned to the television, which he flipped on out of habit just so he could hear a voice other than his own in his head. He tossed an armful of blankets onto the bed, grabbed the remote control, and lay down with a thud. He danced through the channels for an hour or so, never really settling on anything. He was still obsessing over the last few supplies he needed. The next day would be Sunday, and he could get anything he wanted then. Nate stopped searching for something to keep his mind busy and let a benign reality show blare while he closed his eyes.

He could see the storm coming. It was gigantic; the sky was black with an orange rim. The ground was littered with charred human forms half buried along the roadside, limbs and torsos mixing together to look like a human spider. The grass was brown and wilted, the trees were sagging and broken, the lowest limbs had thick empty rope nooses hanging from them. Nate walked away toward the area he had last seen the sun, but he could feel the storm gaining ground, creeping up behind him like some practical joke. He picked up the pace, jogging now, trying to put some distance between himself and the smell. God, the smell. It was rancid, like bloody, maggot-infested meat. He could taste the air—it was metallic, coppery. An electric charge, something in the atmosphere, was making the hair on his arms stand on end. He glanced back over his shoulder and saw that the storm was swirling, wispy clouds like tentacles extended out, grabbing, biting. Nate started to run now. He could hear the storm's teeth chattering like someone shaking a bag of marbles. If he could only reach the warmth then he wouldn't be so cold, so damn cold. He could feel safety just over the next rise. Just a couple more steps. He could see a silhouette up ahead; it was beautiful like light and long like a fluorescent bulb, pale against the dark sky. It was the outline of his mother—or was that just what he wanted to see? Nate was sprinting now...sweating, but so cold. His legs felt frozen, like they were binding up at the joints. It had been like running in deep mud, each step harder than the last. He turned again looking over his shoulder...and there he was.

Nate woke to a late-night infomercial, something about how to treat stubborn acne. His heart was racing; it seemed to be beating too fast. It couldn't be healthy to have a heartbeat that fast. If he could just control his breathing he might be able to calm down. "Just stop thinking about it!" he shouted to the empty room, but he knew he was trying to talk to his own thoughts. He grabbed the remote control and changed the channel to CNN; they were having a round table discussion about the "International Tensions in North Korea." For some strange reason, this gave Nate some peace. His heartbeat returned gradually to normal, and his mind was lost in the conversation on the screen. During the next commercial, he got out of bed and went to the refrigerator to grab a beer; he thought the alcohol might help him sleep. Three deep slugs and the beer was empty. He placed the bottle on the counter, enjoying the quick head rush as he stumbled a little on the way back to bed. Thankfully, sleep came shortly after his head touched the pillow.

Nate rolled out of bed, gargled some water, and threw on his typical Sunday attire: jeans and a T-shirt. Most of his Sundays were spent fighting off hours of boredom. Occasionally in the summer Nate would spend the day fishing or take a long walk. He figured he would do his best to ignore the news, because the Sunday talk shows were always filled with blowhards who loved to hear themselves talk. Today was going to be constructive, with motivation and determination to finish the mission at hand; Nate pulled on his sneakers and grabbed his keys and wallet.

Walking down to his car, Nate glanced up at the overcast skies. His dream came flooding back and he thought to himself, *What the fuck was that about anyway?* He wondered briefly what the sky would look like after a nuclear war. Would it be like that? Or would it be the textbook "nuclear winter," with gray particles drifting down from the heavens? Nate imagined it would look similar to this, milky silver clouds with no definition. Some predictions on various websites indicated that an all-out nuclear war would block out the sun and cause another ice age. Others predicted extreme heat caused by thousands of pounds of ash and debris in the atmosphere holding in the heat and creating a greenhouse effect. Trapped geothermal heat could raise the temperatures to near tropical conditions. The thought of it made Nate claustrophobic.

Nate started his car and drove two towns over to the nearest Walmart. Nate always laughed to himself at Walmart, as if he was in on some inside joke that no one but him understood the punch line to. Walmart always met the stereotype—grubby-looking kids clinging to their frazzled and sometimes abusive mothers, lonely seniors, morbidly obese people in their little scooters when nothing would be better for them than to walk. They were all people buying shit they didn't need, for people who wouldn't want them, with money they didn't have. To some extent, this was what society had become: disposable junk for disposable people, reason 496 why terrorists hated this country: the miracle of capitalism, instant gratification with items that would be used up or break so you could turn around and buy more, on credit of course.

Nate ambled through the automatic doors, nodded to the greeter, and grabbed a shopping carriage. He pushed quickly, keeping his head down. He found that he was afraid to make eye contact and wondered if he might be having a small dose of agoraphobia. His first stop would be the canned and dried food section. The most bang for his buck would come from protein and carbs, which would be easy to store and versatile. Nate scoffed at the price of beef jerky; he'd go broke trying to survive on that. Canned meats and beans wouldn't taste great, but this theoretically would be survival—taste would be pretty far down the list of concerns. Nate pulled can after can off the shelves and dropped them into his carriage with a clank. He also needed to get fruits and vegetables, which Nate usually avoided like a case of smallpox. Just like a child, Nate had to be forced to eat his veggies, but it would be ironic to survive a nuclear strike yet succumb to rickets, scurvy, or some other malnutrition disorder. The idea of where he'd go and fortify and where he'd call home if things went down like he imagined dominated the thoughts clinging to the back of his head.

Nate remembered when he was a kid, back in the eighties, every few houses had a basement fallout shelter. It was the height of the Cold War, and the Soviet Union had everyone scrambling from paranoia just like Nate was now.

The next stop would be batteries and light. He added a plastic battery-operated lantern, a ten-pack of flashlights, and multiple cases of different-sized batteries. He also included two cell phone batteries. Following the row of shelves down to the hardware section, he also grabbed some rope, fishing line, matches, and some white gas for his camp stove. His shopping carriage was nearly full, and as he rolled into the checkout line he tried to add up the cost of this little endeavor. The clerk scanned the bulk cases of batteries over the barcode reader and asked with a giggle, "Are we getting a storm?"

"Just in case," Nate responded, trying to conceal his embarrassment. Wasn't everyone getting ready for the apocalypse?

Nate loaded up his silver Honda Accord, knowing full well that most of these supplies would clutter his trunk for a month, maybe more. He drove home, shaking his head at the level of compulsiveness it took to max out his only credit card on crap that would only soothe his nerves for a short time. He had wasted the majority of his Sunday, and by the time he pulled onto his road he felt emotionally and physically drained. He keyed the lock to his apartment and flipped the TV back on, hoping for more news. Watching the broadcasts became like scratching an itch or picking a scab—it felt good for a minute or two, but it always left you bleeding afterward. How much warning would he even have if the shit did hit the fan—were the old civil defense systems still functioning? The eighties were thrust back in his face through memories of the Big Red Menace with thousands of missiles pointed in his direction. Thankfully, at worst it would be a handful of nukes with only one or two pointed in his direction this time, he thought sarcastically.

Back in his early twenties, Nate had tried a variety of anti-depressant medications when his anxiety had become this bad. Nothing really improved his condition, however. The pills only led to troubled erections and more vivid dreams. He had learned breathing techniques and yoga, but these just made him feel self-conscious and lacking willpower. Sedatives would lead to self-medicating; Nate knew himself well enough to know he was susceptible to addiction. Maybe all of this was easily explained by a weak constitution, or possibly it was genetics, but most likely it was a combination of all of the above. Mental illness is funny like that. What does the cause really matter, in the end you still feel like a piece of shit even if you are able to get small doses of relief. It's like being a mixed martial arts cage fighter, only your opponent in every match is yourself.

THE SHOT HEARD AROUND THE WORLD

Kim paced along the length of the table looking up and down at the faces. Did they trust him? Would they undermine him? He had assembled a general from every branch of his military and experts from nuclear power, the department of the interior, and agriculture. He had even called in a meteorologist.

"I have been blessed with a strategy, blessed from my father, blessed from my people. This strategy will bring great glory to the homeland while erasing the great Satan from this region." *He paused at the head of the table, staring down at the flag in its centerpiece. "We will bait the Americans into attack, and then we will dupe the sleeping Soviets into a counterstrike in our stead." Kim was putting on a show for his subordinates, like a great actor on a medieval stage. After all, what are politics, but theater and delicate persuasion? He sat back down, allowing his guests to*

respond for the first time. The first to stand was the great naval admiral Cho Singh So.

"We have disguised a freighter as a cruise junk carrying refugees who wish to defect to Japan. Onboard will be a six-kiloton device, similar to the ones we tested underground last year. It is an inefficient hulk of a thing and far too bulky to be carried by a missile or dropped from a bomber. It must be delivered by ship, you see, and in that fashion it suits our needs perfectly. The ship will enter Tokyo Bay from the Pacific side to help conceal its origin. Once the ship is docked in Tokyo Harbor, agents aboard the ship will detonate the weapon." Cho abruptly sat back down.

"Japan is not our enemy, at least not directly. Why waste a precious device there?" Interior Secretary Sin Chieng interrupted. He was squirrelly man with enormous front teeth and wire rim glasses.

"It is the only way to guarantee an American strike against the homeland without dividing our assets," the North Korean dictator snapped at Chieng, not hiding his annoyance.

The commander of the air force and ballistics stood up. "We have assembled a small stockpile of Mundong missiles and Silkworm antiship rockets on portable launchers at the Onsong reactor, my Dear Leader. The old facility still had enough waste material to create quite a mess, but in addition we have transported all waste that is radioactive, including civilian and medical from Pyongyang, and deposited it on the site. It should easily throw up a red flag for the American satellites." The commander finished speaking and quickly sat down.

The state-sponsored meteorologist stood and spoke as if he was reading lines from a teleprompter. "If we time our initial attack correctly, the American counterstrike will spread a radioactive cloud across the Tumen River into Russia. Fortunately, the prevailing winds at this time of year are very favorable for this effect. Fate is on our side, Dear Leader."

Sin Chieng stood again. "Forgive me, Dear Leader, but the Russians have been a friend to our country throughout the years. Without their friendship, victory over the South never would have been possible. We could have never forced the armistice if—"

Kim shouted from his seat, interrupting the appalling boldness of the dissenter, "Do you not think we have considered this matter? Doesn't the end justify the means?" He had never been questioned like this before. It was clear that even his generals and trusted confidants no longer respected his authority or opinion. This would never have taken place while his father was alive, nor would his father have stood for such arrogance in his government chambers. He didn't need to qualify his plans, but he did so for the sake of the others. "The only harm from the radioactive fallout will be to the Russian radar array and the forgotten house of friendship! The surrounding area is mountainous and sparsely populated! The greatest impact will be felt symbolically. The Americans will not take into account our proximity to the Russian border as they attack Onsong. We will leave obvious breadcrumbs so that the weapon in Japan can be traced to that reactor. The Americans will be blinded by their hatred; they will strike at Onsong and attempt to decapitate Pyongyang. We have seen it before in Afghanistan, Syria, and Iraq!" The Korean dictator was frothing at the mouth. "After phase one is complete, the Russians' hatred of the West will be reinvigorated by the Americans. Phase two will be our opportunity to use our most advanced weapon, far ahead of even the American technology." He paused for effect. "Are the French visitors properly motivated?" he asked the room.

A short man stood at the far end of the chamber against the wall. "Our young French wards have assured us that anything can be hacked. They have already run many test viruses on the DOD server. They feel the Russian early warning systems will be even easier to infiltrate. Shutting down the communication lines between Moscow and Washington will only involve disabling one link-up satellite. The years of complacency have made both countries vulnerable to this kind of sabotage. Only one member of the French entourage had to lose his life for the remainder to be properly motivated, my dear leader." Steven Yui, an American-born man of North Korean heritage, finished his update for the dictator and took his seat. Yui had been a data analyst in South Korea before heroically returning to his homeland to serve. He was a favorite of Kim's.

It all lined up: the winds, the computers, the Russians, even the Japanese had their place, and Kim took this to mean that divine grace had allowed the stars to line up in the homeland's favor.

"We will be the fly buzzing around the elephant's head; they will destroy each other in charcoal and fire and when all is over they will come to us for aid, not war. We shall be the great humanitarians and help the world rebuild. After we have taken what is rightfully ours, a unified Korea, we will be generous." He cleared his throat and ceremoniously raised his voice. "Korea will stand alone atop the mountain, one unified, true superpower!" He was really rolling now; everyone in the room rose in thunderous applause that echoed off the walls like an explosion in a metal can. Kim ushered his commanders out to set the wheels spinning.

A series of calls from the generals and two short days later, a freighter was steaming across the Sea of Japan with one armed nuclear package. It would make its way through the Tsugaru Strait unchecked. No suspicions would be raised; it was flying a South Korean flag. Its cover as a South Korean ship full of refugees from the North worked as designed.

As night fell, the ship docked just outside of Tokyo, where it sat waiting for the signal.

4

THE NASTY IS COMING

Nate drove to work thinking about what it would prove if his paranoia turned out to be justified—would that make him feel a little less crazy? Would it be prudence, intuition, or just coincidence? When he arrived at work he was surprised to discover that the electricity was out. He called his supervisor from his cell phone to determine what was going on; maybe they didn't pay the bill because of an oversight, maybe it was a transformer that blew out. Luck was on Nate's side, as there were no patients waiting to have their blood drawn.

Nate's supervisor always treated him like a two-year-old, and even though Nate had been working there for years she always acted like he was the new guy. Part of that was because Nate was quiet and antisocial and never really got to know his boss. She explained to him that an HVAC crew had been working on the heating unit on Sunday. They always took care of maintenance on Sundays to avoid bothering patients. His boss figured the crew must have inadvertently tripped a breaker on the lower level. This came to a surprise to Nate, who hadn't even realized there was a lower level. According to his boss, there was no elevator—just a hidden back staircase through the rear door of one of the supply rooms. The sunlight flooding in through the windows gave him enough light to move around. Inside the supply room Nate found a set of shining hinges on the far wall; they had been totally obscured by the boxes of biohazard containers stacked to eye level. Nate turned sideways to squeeze through the line of boxes that was blocking the door. He had a small Maglight on his keychain, which he shined into the darkness searching for the knob on the hidden door. Nate slid the boxes forward to create a space big enough for the door to swing open. The door had been almost completely invisible; if he hadn't known what to look for he never would have found it. In fact, he had taken supplies from that room countless times and hadn't even had an inkling that there was a door on the opposite wall. The areas farther from the windows on the main floor had been half lit by emergency lights that were fixed to exit signs at regular intervals. As he swung open the door to the stairwell, he was amazed at how pitch black it looked down there. There wasn't light from anywhere, not even small cracks of sunlight to penetrate the darkness. The work crew must have shut off all the lights on their way out and slid the boxes back in front of the door before leaving.

Nate found the top of the railing with his Maglight and felt his way down the narrow stairway. He had one hand on the railing and one hand on the opposite wall, and he held the flashlight between his teeth as he traversed the steep steps. At the bottom of the stairs, Nate stepped down onto a hard concrete floor. There was a small landing with another door straight ahead. He instinctively reached for the light switch next to the doorknob, but it flipped up and down with no result. Nate turned around and flashed the light back up the stairs; he hadn't noticed how long the stairway had been. At least twenty steps stretched up to the faint light filtering in from the supply room. A shiver started at his heels and rose up to where it settled at the back of his neck. Nate turned the knob, and the door opened onto a long corridor that appeared endless. He felt as though he were spelunking through some underground catacomb. The air was cold and dusty but otherwise surprisingly dry. Usually, a basement feels damp from condensation, but the walls looked freshly painted without any hint of mold or mildew. The air seemed as though it was still being circulated, even though the power was out. Nate didn't smell any staleness, only the faint smell of new paint and drywall.

He followed the long hallway to the far end; it must have run the entire length of the building. At the end of the corridor were three doors, one to the right, one to the left and one straight forward. It reminded him of a Choose Your Own Adventure book, the kind with the dragons and dark dungeon. He turned the knob on the door at his right, which opened into a small square room. The room was nearly empty and had been used for storage. Three dusty wheelchairs, two metal exam tables, and a gurney sat in the middle of the room. Two cardboard boxes with open lids sat against the wall, and next to the boxes was a metal No Parking sign leaning at an angle. Nate concentrated his small light on the walls, scanning for a breaker panel, but all he saw was more white, freshly painted plaster. He backed out of the room, closing the door behind him. He turned around 180 degrees to the opposite door, which he opened into a large water closet with a large, yellow plastic basin. The basin had two spigots, red for hot water and blue for cold. It was obviously used for rinsing mops and filling buckets. In front of the basin was a janitor's bucket on wheels with a long unused mop, still in the package, sticking out of the top. The basin and the bucket were perfectly clean and looked like they had never seen a day's work. Still no breaker panel. Nate backed out again and turned to the last door, the one that had been straight ahead when he came down the hallway. The door had a sign that read Employees Only, which struck him as extremely odd—why would a patient or customer come down here anyway?

Nate turned the knob and pushed, laughing to himself, "I wonder what fabulous prize is behind door number three, Bob."

The door swung open into the largest room. The door itself seemed much heavier than the other two, so heavy that Nate almost expected it to lead outside. The room was rectangular, elongated to the right side, and looked like it might have been someone's office at some point. There was a desk with several unfinished wooden shelves hanging on the wall above it. He could count six wheeled office chairs with blue padding. On the far end was a row of gigantic metal file cabinets, and on the floor in front of them were about a dozen cans of paint. Boxes of painting supplies and reams of paper were scattered about next to the cabinets. Nate found the fuse panel next to a bulking, silver furnace and hot water heater on his left. He walked over and opened the metal cover to the panel. Two long lines of black switches ran vertically inside. At the bottom were two larger switches, which Nate figured had to be the main breakers. He shined the light on the backside of the small cover, revealing a numbered schematic confirming this to be true. He flipped the two black switches, which seemed to swing together; they flipped over and snapped back. A huge roar arose from the furnace, and a bank of fluorescent lights illuminated the room with a buzz. The air began to smell slightly like diesel as the oil burner began to warm the room. In the light, the area looked even bigger than before, with a great deal of floor space. Nate could hear the mechanical hum and vibration of the lab equipment, which would put his position at the rear of the building. The floor of the lab had been sealed, both for soundproofing and to prevent the spread or growth of any bacterium. The soundproofing muted the majority of the mechanical chirps and alarms, but the dull rumbling of the centrifuges warming up was still audible even from below.

It didn't take Nate very long before he came to the conclusion that what he had just stumbled on would make an ideal fallout shelter. He had twenty-four-hour access to the space; the area was relatively well hidden; and it could be fortified if necessary. There was access to water and heat, but best of all it was almost completely hidden to the outside world.

Nate hurried back upstairs, feeling an excitement that couldn't be explained. Yes, he had found a huge piece to his personal enigma, but he'd only need it if a catastrophe and mass death were to occur. It was another pacifier—a treatment for his anxiety that no breathing exercises or medication could give him. Nate spent the rest of the day taking care of demanding patients and occasionally chatting up Jeannette. Patients constantly tried to make conversation with him about the North Korean problem, which Nate would divert. Talking about the situation was like hearing about a recently deceased parent. It seemed too soon...the sting too fresh. One interesting old timer told him how "we're gonna kick their yellow asses just like we did back in '53." Nate felt like he was keeping a secret from the old man, like he had some inside information on what would happen.

At 5:30, Nate's shift ended, and he sat waiting for the building to empty out. He went outside and waited for the lights to dim at the urgent care clinic next door. Both buildings together could be considered a small strip mall. They belonged to the same company, under the same banner of a major local hospital that was trying to corner the ambulatory outpatient care market in the area. Each building looked identical; they had slightly differing hours, different functions, and a different security system. Nate possessed the door key and access card to the blood draw facility, and while the same access card could be used at the urgent care facility to disable the alarm, the keys were not the same. This allowed him unfettered access to the blood draw building, but he could only access the urgent care facility during open hours. He wanted to avoid prying eyes, so once the lights were down in both buildings, Nate headed to his car in the parking lot. The parking lot lights remained on all night for security reasons, which meant Nate could see what he was doing, but it also meant that anyone driving by would notice his actions. Not that what he was doing was wrong or illegal, but Nate wanted to avoid any questions or anything getting back to his boss. Nate unlocked his car and pulled a large duffel bag from the backseat. He started to fill the bag with the cans of food and other supplies. Nate made trip after trip down to the basement office.

By 8:00 p.m., Nate had unloaded all the supplies and had filled two file cabinets with the contents. If any employees were to happen across the items in the shelter, he hoped that while they might find them odd they would perhaps write them off as another hospital food drive that had been overlooked and mistakenly never taken to a soup kitchen. Nate would still need to get the weapons, clothing, and a few other items from his apartment, but for now he had eased his mind about the location of his shelter. Now the question was when, if ever, would he need to run there? He spent the rest of the evening cleaning up the location, making sure the doors had a good seal, and planning out how to finish making the bunker livable. Tired, sweaty, and dirty, he headed back to his apartment.

Arriving at his place around eleven o'clock, Nate was in a great mood. He had something to build upon and somewhere to go if need be. Nate went about packing up the canned food in the back of his cabinets. The guns and some pots and pans he placed in a large rucksack, and his clothing into black garbage bags. It was hardly an elegant choice for luggage, but Nate hadn't ever been a serious traveler and didn't even own a suitcase. He had just about finished with the odds and ends when he had a strange feeling that he'd been too disconnected from the news for too long. He turned on the television, hoping to catch the eleven o'clock news.

A bright red crawl of text had been scrolling across the bottom of the screen.

Breaking News: Unconfirmed reports from multiple sources indicate there has been a sizeable explosion just east of Tokyo, Japan. Stay tuned for updates as they come in.

The scroll kept repeating.

Nate blasted the volume; a very beautiful female news anchor was sitting behind the news desk reading off a teleprompter. Nate had turned on the television midsentence: "Eyewitness statements identified the explosion as a large, orange mushroom cloud in the center of the harbor area. Fires are still burning all over the area within the blast radius. We have been trying to confirm if this explosion is an accident or possibly a terrorist attack. Experts are currently analyzing video footage and trying to determine if this explosion could be nuclear in nature. They are testing the air for indications of radiation, poisonous gas, or other hazardous material. Speculation continues that this may have been a detonation of a dirty bomb of some kind."

Nate stood stunned, watching the words scroll across the bottom of the screen. He tried to read the news anchor's face, but she looked very stern, professional, and determined. There was no sign of fear or even worry.

"...There have been no reports of casualties at this time, but due to the size of the area affected and the population concentration in that area, the loss of life would have to be catastrophic. Local sources in the vicinity of the explosion are already reporting horrific scenes of panicked survivors and destruction of property. We are trying to pull up a live feed from the scene, and we'll have that to you as soon as we can. Let me repeat, if you are just joining us. A large explosion has occurred in Tokyo, Japan. At this time we are unsure of the cause or source of this explosion."

The anchor put her hand to her earpiece and paused before continuing. "OK, OK, we have a statement from Washington." Suddenly the presidential seal appeared on a podium in a room busy with the murmur of reporters. The female anchor, no longer in view, spoke into her microphone: "Press Secretary Kathleen Panella will be making a brief statement any minute."

A tall woman in her early fifties with short, graying brown hair took her place behind the podium. She wore a blue skirt suit with a white blouse and looked visibly tired and agitated. She began to speak in a slow, serious tone; her voice was very deep and didn't fit her feminine look. "About two hours ago, a nuclear device was detonated in Tokyo harbor." An audible gasp came from the reporters seated at the press conference, but the press secretary ignored it and continued speaking. "The explosion appears to have been intentional. I will say that again: this wasn't an accident. Our experts have come to that conclusion through meticulous review of satellite images." She paused, looking up into the flashbulbs that reflected on the wall behind her. "The US government is offering every possible resource to the people of Japan. We stand as one with our allies and condemn this act against humanity. Justice will be brought to those responsible, but for right now our thoughts must remain with the people in Japan and the first responders who are now risking their lives in rescue and recovery efforts. The United States has many, many resources currently on route. Thank you. We will have more for you soon, and our thoughts and prayers will reside with the Japanese people tonight."

She retreated offscreen as a roar of questions followed her from the throng of reporters now standing. The shot quickly returned to the original news anchor back in the studio. She began recapping everything Nate had heard from the beginning, now updated to include the phrases *nuclear device detonated* and *this wasn't an accident*.

Nate felt like he might lose consciousness. He slumped at the foot of his bed with his head in his hands; his throat seemed to be filled with cotton, and he couldn't swallow. He was starting to hyperventilate, and he stared blankly up at the television trying to control his breathing, which started to descend like an overfilled balloon deflating. The first thought to enter his mind was; *What rotten luck for the Japanese, nuclear weapons have been used three times on human populations and they've all hit Japan.* It was a strange thought, considering that the likelihood of a true exchange had just increased tenfold.

Nate sat dumbfounded watching the news all night, eventually drifting off to sleep at four in the morning. What a boon the twenty-four-hour news cycle is for insomniacs.

He hovered above a dream city of fire and slowly drifted to the ground, settling in a pile of rubble. Nate reached his arm out and his hand touched a corpse. He pulled the twisted, charred body on top of himself to hide from some unseen danger. He lay that way for a long time, playing dead and hoping and praying that he wouldn't be found. The entire time he was in the rubble, he could hear the distraught voice of a newswoman weeping softly as she read casualty figures off of a teleprompter. An alarm, a siren, civil defense is warning everyone...

Nate woke to the distant blaring beep of his bedroom clock radio. He stood up stiffly with a sharp, gnawing pain in the right side of his head and neck. It hurt just to hold his head up; it was like his neck couldn't support the weight of his enormous lead-filled skull. He could feel his pulse throbbing in his temples, like too much blood was flowing through veins that were far too narrow. Was it possible for sinuses and arteries to get clogged with anxiety? Nate felt like something had snapped in his brain, some crucial synapse that maintains balance or separates up from down.

He drove to work that morning with one eye open, stopping only to grab a Red Bull in hopes that the caffeine would make him feel human again. He flipped on the radio, dreading more news but unable to avoid it—he had always loved the car crash. Another New York talk show was in full-on panic mode. The host was taking live calls from listeners saying that the time had come to go to war with North Korea. Nate wondered how those listeners knew who was responsible for the Tokyo bomb. Moments later the host read an update and Nate had his answer. A container ship had been boarded in Tokyo Harbor with unknown cargo. UN sanctions had allowed for the search and seizure of any ship suspected of containing possible exports from North Korea. The Japanese customs agents had reported by walkie talkie that they were boarding the ship, preparing to search the cargo hold, when the explosion had rocked the harbor, cutting off all communications. The origin of the bomb had been that ship, and although it hadn't necessarily been from North Korea, it had at one point filed paperwork suggesting that it had either contained North Korean crew members or had been used for North Korean exports in the past.

Nate didn't understand this situation at all. North Korea had to know that attacking America was suicidal, so instead they nuke one of America's closest allies? America had occupied and rebuilt Japan after World War II. The Americans had nursed Japan back to health, and the Japanese constitution forbade the country from having a standing army or waging war on a foreign adversary. Japan's military could only be used for self-defense. The United States would surely come to Japan's aid, and that would mean a military action against North Korea. Maybe North Korea had never given up the grudge they had held for the Japanese occupation before World War II. It was actually the current leader of North Korea's great grandfather who had led the communist rebellion and pushed the Japanese out. That was how his family line had taken over as dictators of North Korea. Nate remembered taking a class on the lead-up to World War II, the War itself, and the aftermath. Perhaps, Nate thought, this all harkened back to some sixty-year-old vendetta. So maybe it *had* been personal. Still, they had to know that the American response would be devastating, even nuclear.

Nate wasn't sure if knowing that the United States would have to take out most if not all of North Korea's nuclear capabilities made him feel any safer. Or if it made him more worried to know that the nuclear envelope had been breached. A nuclear weapon hadn't been used in more than fifty years; now that glass ceiling had been broken, the genie was out of the bottle again...all he could think of was apt clichés. The US government, especially this president, had liked symbolism as much as any North Korean dictator. They would respond in kind by fighting fire with a bigger fire, which would probably mean more nukes would be tossed around.

Nate unlocked the blood draw facility and walked in; there were no patients waiting. Nate would have been surprised if any patients had come in at all today. After the September 11th attacks had happened, everyone had stayed home to watch the news. He had figured today would be the same—very slow.

He sat at his computer and stared blankly at the blue screen until his eyes buzzed with red, black, and white fuzzy spots. Finally, he blinked away the daze. He couldn't get the dream he had out of his skull—a great city skyline darkened by soot. Flames had been all around, and the ash had fallen like snow flurries.

Jeannette entered the blood draw area carrying an armful of log books, startling Nate from his stupor. She stopped by him and sat in front of his draw chair on a small doctor's stool on wheels that Nate used for hand draws. Then she abruptly stood up, looking confused; she hadn't even acknowledged Nate's presence. She set the log books on the counter, looking as though she had slept even worse than Nate had. She met Nate's eyes with hers and gave him a sad little smile, tilting her head slightly. Then without saying a word she burst into tears and tumbled into Nate's arms in a violent sob. It was an awkward, clumsy embrace, but Nate could feel her warmth against him. Her hair smelled of fresh pears, clean and sweet. Instantly his heart was broken with hers, he didn't even know why she was so distraught, other than the Japanese incident.

She pulled away in shock, a look of horror on her face. "Nate, I'm so sorry, I don't..." She was fighting back sobs, trying hard to swallow so she could finish her sentence.

"It's all right Jeannette, everything will be all right." Something changed in Nate; for the first time he felt confident and comfortable around her. He had been forced into action, and it unleashed something good in him. "I think everyone feels like you do, Jeannette; at least I know that I have felt like this all morning," he said, hoping she would collapse into his arms again.

She fought hard to compose herself, wiping her tear-streaked face on her white lab coat. "Nate, do you understand what's going on? Think about how many people are dead or will die." She spoke in starts and stops, pulling herself back every few words. "Those assholes are gonna destroy this planet!" The tears started to flow again. "I just, I don't know what to do with myself...I'm just so scared."

Nate tried his best to be the rational one, to comfort her. It was a strange and foreign role for him to play. "They'll contain this, whatever it is...they have to. They're sick, but not sick enough to start lobbing nukes all over the globe." Nate wanted to sound sturdy; he didn't want his own anxiety to upset her any further.

"You really think it will stop at one?" she asked, not pausing to listen to his answer. "They've already crossed a line that can't be uncrossed; it's easier for us to push the buttons now that someone else has done it first. When has this country ever walked away from a fight?" She sighed and blew the hair off her forehead with an extended lower lip. It was the gesture that Nate loved, but at that moment he would have done anything to see her smile. He cleared his throat and gathered up his balls. "Jeannette, do you want to have dinner with me tonight?" It was completely out of character for Nate, who had never had very accurate timing, but it was the perfect tension breaker. She shook her head in disbelief, caught between a smile and confused surprise.

"Nate!" She laughed. "Are you asking me out? Is this like a best friend for the end of the world type of thing?" Jeannette was actually smiling now. The tear streaks remained, but they were no longer attached to eyes of despair. Nate decided that this could be perfect; he would either run with it or simply play the date request off as a joke he slipped in to cheer her up. He eventually thought it would be best to play it halfway, skirt the edge, test the waters.

"Well, I figured we could talk—it might be a good thing for both of us. You know, to get away from all the bad news." He smiled sheepishly. He was glad to see her still smiling, even blushing.

"Sure, Nate, let's have dinner." She picked up her logbooks. "You come up with where we're going and what time to pick me up." Wiping the tears from her cheeks, she turned and walked away, disappearing into the connecting lab.

Nate hardly noticed. He thought he might float away, and he was actually quite proud of himself for once. He couldn't remember the last time he had asked a woman out. In college, Nate had dated a bit, but even then, he had never been the initiator. He continued to feel high, euphoric, like a high school kid who finally gets the popular girl to say yes to the prom. That was until he clicked on the Internet to kill the rest of the day.

The pictures from Japan had started to filter in. They had found some security images from a couple miles outside the harbor area that were focused on the blast site. He could make out a few masts and what looked like cranes on the time-lapse video, and then suddenly a bright bulb of white light eclipsed the darkness. The white then turned to a huge orange bloom of flame, almost perfectly round, like the fleeting sun just about to set. Slowly, the classic mushroom cloud took shape, and it looked just like the movies or the video from the testing sites at Los Alamos. A rush of wavy heat-filled shock waves started to shake the camera. Nate sat there, watching, his mouth agape. Tremors of fear trembled through his hand, which felt glued to the mouse. A convulsion of terror started in his groin and shot directly up his spine, like an electrical charge, stopping in his hair. Finally the screen whited out and turned to electronic snow, as dust and debris either disabled or destroyed the camera. Then the loop repeated, the lens focused back on the dark, calm, serene harbor area lighted by streetlamps. The second time, it looked much clearer...much more real.

Nate searched through some other videos and still photos. Most were similar to the time-lapse video of the blast; a few showed huge plumes of smoke from farther away. The destruction would have been immense, but everything as of that time was blocked out with dust, soot, and ash. It reminded Nate of a *National Geographic* he had read as a kid, which showed pictures of Mount Saint Helens erupting in Washington state. The ash from the volcano had turned an entire river gray. One website claimed that the bomb had most assuredly originated in North Korea. The North Koreans hadn't even denied the attack; their silence spoke volumes. The report also indicated fires throughout Tokyo had been spread miles away from the site by the wind. Pundits and experts alike were expecting a military response from a UN coalition, which most expected to begin at any moment. The world was already speaking out in full force, condemning the attack; some countries that had even previously sympathized with North Korea were now distancing themselves. Even the Iranians, who had bucked and ignored UN sanctions against North Korea and now had their own renegade nuclear program, were having a "National Day of Prayer" for the victims of the attack on Japan. Nate continued to read; he was completely conflicted between the excitement about Jeannette and the devastating worry and depression over Japan. He turned off the computer and sat thinking about the entire surreal situation. He went to the window and looked out over the trees and road that led down into the center of Middlebrook. It had turned into a "bluebird day," as Nate's father would have said: brilliant sun, two or three sparse puffy white clouds, and the verdant trees and lawn. He stood at the window for what felt like hours, just watching the birds and the few cars that were meandering down the road. It was peaceful, and for the first time in a long time he wasn't waiting for the "car crash."

He walked into the empty waiting room and switched on the television that hung from the ceiling in the corner. He flipped around until he found a cable news station that wasn't in a commercial break. He saw an image appeared of a navy destroyer firing cruise missiles into the air, and then the picture switched to recorded footage of jets taking off from an aircraft carrier under the cover of darkness. Nate read the scroll across the bottom of the picture.

A massive military action is now underway; ships of the seventh fleet of the US Navy in cooperation with Japanese forces have begun sorties against the Republic of North Korea. Land-based stealth bombers have also taken off from airfields in South Korea, Okinawa, and Guam.

Nate sat down in one of the waiting room chairs. The war had started.

EXECUTIONER'S DAY

Deep underground, in a bunker fortified with lead and concrete—impenetrable to bunker-busting smart bombs, conventional weapons, and even small nuclear weapons (barring a direct hit)—the North Korean Leader paced around his makeshift war room.Kim had been moved from the city against his wishes, but his advisor's had insisted. Kim finally relented, the mountain facility had all of the immenities of his presidential palace.

"So the Americans have reacted as we predicted. Their predictability is mesmerizing," Kim said to his chief of staff, who was scribbling notes while watching a monitor that relayed information about the American counterstrike.

"Yes, Dear Leader." He pointed to a map on a table to his right. "So far, the Americans have responded almost exactly as we predicted. They have hit the capitol with cruise missiles from their submarines and warships and have struck against some military targets with guided bombs." The chief of staff looked to the dictator for reassurance that this was as planned.

"Have they destroyed the reactor at Onsong?" This was the crux of their whole operation; without Onsong, Phase 2 couldn't be set into motion.

"No, not yet; perhaps they will save something special for the Onsong facility," the chief of staff answered passively.

"Order more mobile missile batteries to that location, only the obsolete models. Send troops and armor there too. Make Onsong a target they cannot refuse. I want the American commanders licking their lips at the size of the target. I want nuclear waste and any medical isotopes doubled. It needs to be an irresistible satellite signature." Kim walked over to the map. "How badly damaged are our strongest military units?" His concern was making sure they had enough assets left to invade the South when the dust had settled on the entire operation.

The chief of staff stood next to the dictator and looked at the map. "So far the decision to move our elite forces into the mountains has worked. They have been spread out enough not to draw major attention from the American satellites. There have been very few major losses among those units. Our greatest casualties have come from the airfields and the artillery above the DMZ, and specifically our command and control centers in Pyongyang."

Suddenly a tremendous shock wave struck the bunker, knocking chunks of concrete from the ceiling. The intense vibration and seismic disturbance felt similar to an earthquake. The walls shook for two or three minutes, knocking both men off their feet. The lights dimmed and then flashed back on. When the thunder had finally subsided, the room was wrecked. Smashed glass from the computer monitors and paper printouts lined the floor, scattered as if a strong wind had blown through the room. Lumps of plaster sat on the table in the center of the room. The chief of staff rushed to the dictator's aid. Kim had been shaken off his feet and had remained seated against a table leg. "Sir, are you hurt?" asked the flustered chief of staff.

"What the hell was that?" Kim yelled. His hearing hadn't returned to normal; he could barely hear his own voice with the ringing in his ears.

"I don't know, my Dear Leader. I will find out immediately." The chief of staff rushed out of the room, disappearing down the corridor.

Kim stood and brushed the dust off of his black uniform, staggering for a moment before feeling his equilibrium return. The Americans must have targeted the bunker, Kim thought to himself. Making sure others were not around, he moved quickly, checking the hallway then sliding back to the war room. He cleared his throat of the dust and made a brief choking whimper. He quickly composed himself and lit a cigarette. It was an American Marlboro, and they of course had the best tobacco. Importing his smokes had become the biggest inconvenience of the sanctions imposed against his country. He took a long, slow drag, turning the cigarette and watching the burn, then exhaled, his breath shaking out wavy lines of smoke. Where is that idiot? Kim thought to himself. He needed to know if the bunker was still under attack. Had the entrance caved in? Were they trapped? And what the fuck was that rumble? If the Americans had his location, then the whole plan would be put into jeopardy. Who could lead this country but him?

After nearly ten tortuous minutes, the chief of staff burst into the war room. "Dear Leader, I have news!" he exclaimed.

Kim looked back at him with confusion. "What the hell just happened here?" he yelled back.

"Sir, it's the Americans. They've destroyed Onsong! It's just as we'd hoped. That vibration was a shockwave from a very powerful nuclear blast. Perhaps they fired an ICBM from one of their submarines." The North Korean chief of staff smiled. "Sir, the winds are perfect. The Americans have increased the radiation tenfold; a cloud of fallout will soon be blowing to the North, and great amounts of contamination will enter eastern Russia within days."

The North Korean leader took a deep thoughtful drag from his cigarette and grinned. "This is good news. I want the international news feeds monitored. Tonight we will dine and celebrate. I want all my generals who reside in this bunker invited; they shall prepare all of the reports. Let them leave their battle stations for dinner. I want the best food we have, and some of my father's Courvoisier there to boost morale.

Four hours later, at the head of a table in the small officer's mess hall nearly a mile underground a solitary mountain in western North Korea sat the Dear Leader, Kim Jong Un. His generals, advisors, and a selection of military aides lined both sides of the table. Kim stood raising a snifter of Hennessey Courvoisier.

"Today is just the beginning of many great days in North Korea's ascent; we will bring great pride to our homeland. Soon we shall stand among giants in our country's storied history and the giants that had threatened our borders will kneel before us." He touched glasses with the few he could reach. A look of satisfaction had been painted on the faces attached to uniforms of every branch of the North Korean military. Cigar smoke drifted across the room and lingered on the cracked plaster ceiling. Kim sat down and looked around the room, pleased with himself. "If you would, please report our progress in the grand theater of this war for our salvation." He extended his arm toward his general, signaling that he was ready to listen. The man on his right, a commander of the air defense campaign and much too overweight for his tight uniform, stood up. The golden buttons running along his lapel strained to the point of popping. A green belt of fabric struggled to hold in the flab of his enormous belly. Kim thought it pathetic that this man had been allowed to grow fat while his country starved; he sipped from his Courvoisier in disgust.

"Sir, we are filling the skies with flak; our units have even shot down two of the American fighter planes. The enemy has had some modest success and has destroyed many surface-to-air batteries. Also, unfortunately, the American cruise missiles have evaded most of our defenses." The fat man sat back down, and his chair emitted a high-pitched whine as it screamed in agony.

"That may be a blessing in disguise, as your porous air defense allowed the warhead that destroyed Onsong to travel unmolested to impact. Many casualties will be unavoidable; it is the great sacrifice of the people that will lead to our victory. Kim gestured to the next man sitting down the line at the table. "General, what news do you have to report from the border?"

A man who looked like a direct opposite of the first speaker stood to answer. He was tall, skinny, and steely-eyed, with a thick mat of dark hair. He portrayed confidence and pride as he spoke. "Sir, the South Korean and American forces stand at the highest level of alert. They have reinforced five tank divisions along the DMZ, but they haven't pushed forward. In my opinion, they are waiting until the airstrikes have weakened our border defenses. The coalition bombers have targeted our troops along the border. As you know, Dear Leader, your grandfather was a military genius in his own right; he ordered the construction of miles of tunnels in every direction, even under the South Korean border. Our forces have avoided significant damage by moving underground throughout the region. They have bunker-busting technology, but the tunnels are so extensive that they have had little success targeting the heart of our troops and armor."

"So what are the bombers bombing then, commander?" Kim asked pessimistically.

"They have had great success against our many radar installations, and as the general just stated, our antiaircraft positions have absorbed some losses. The Americans are mimicking what they did in Iraq, attempting to soften our antiair and destroy our morale with shock and awe. They expect to have mass surrender on our side, which in my opinion was what Onsong was...more shock and awe. They have demolished some old Soviet-built tanks, but little else. So far, Dear Leader, there is no shock and very little awe." The general sat down, apparently finished.

"What have we intercepted from the televised international newswire?" Kim asked his press and public relations minister, a small man wearing wire-rim glasses and a suit and tie, who was seated to his left.

The man stood and began speaking in a low monotone voice. "My Dear Leader, the world is condemning the American use of nuclear weapons. Russian scientists are predicting that the radioactive cloud will make regions of Siberia uninhabitable. The Russians have many early-warning stations along their coast. They have had to evacuate all of those stations. They are predicting casualties from the fallout, even among some of their soldiers. Hardliners in the Russian government are calling the American strike on Onsong an act of war against the Russian Federation, because of the proximity. Many have called for a return to Cold War readiness, and some have even proposed the reunification of a modified Warsaw Pact. We believe that elements of the Russian conservative party wish to return the country to its Soviet Union status. Our limited intelligence of their military forces indicates that they will have ICBMs and submarines at the highest stages of readiness." The press minister sat down and shuffled papers in front of him. Kim wasn't sure what to believe; the man's job was propaganda, after all. He was essentially a government-sanctioned liar, which was just fine with Kim. Kim had always believed that every lie carried a healthy dose of truth, and if any of the press minister's reports were proven true, it would be great news.

If the press minister was correct, then the Russians were reacting far more severely than even Kim could have hoped. It appeared that everything was coming together exactly as planned. One more phase to go, then God willing, the great fire.

Kim had recognized at least one face out of the subordinates assigned to the bunker with him. He pointed to General Hi Soi and the stack of papers in front of him. The head of North Korea's secret police and cyberwarfare program stood.

"Dear Leader, our French guests have done well with only modest motivation from my team." He placed his hand on a baton hanging from his belt to emphasize what he meant by motivation. "They have created a devastating computer virus, even more impressive than I hoped. They have also cracked the encryption, allowing penetration of both American and Russian Strategic Air Command and their other early warning systems. On your order, my Dear Leader, they will launch the virus, blinding both countries and their satellites. Protocol insures that both countries will assume the other is attacking. The virus will even show various launch signatures blinking in and out from land-based missile silos before crashing their systems completely. If the mutually assured destruction doctrine still holds, both countries will launch on warning. Meaning they will need to fire their missiles so they cannot be hit in their silos. The last radar information that either country possesses will be that the other has launched a full-scale nuclear assault. They will launch their ICBMs. We have also already taken full control of the satellite that operates the so-called red phone system. It connects all communication between Moscow and Washington. If either leader attempts to contact the other to confirm or deny any attack, they will find all links and servers disconnected. By the time they discover that the satellite relay is out of order, it will be too late. The beauty of the digital age is that everything is computerized and connected by satellite. There are no more landlines and, as our French friends say, "Anything can be hacked."

Kim stood and clapped his hands in honor of his generals. "Bravo, gentlemen, bravo. It is a great time to be a North Korean."

Two days later, after mounting political pressure and threatening rhetoric between Russia and the United States, the North Korean dictator gave the order to initiate the virus. Within two hours of that order, the United States and Russia would be approaching a state of war. Less than an hour after that, computer readouts would be in chaos, indicating a massive strike was inbound. It would take less than thirty minutes for both sides to scramble their bombers, and within minutes the first ICBMs would detonate their payloads.

5

SACCHARINE CHARM

Nate walked up the sidewalk to his little brick apartment building. The sun had just set, and there was a slight chill in the air. He had parked on the street because he would be going out soon with Jeannette for their first date and Nate's first date in a long, long time. In an hour and a half, he was due to meet Jeannette at one of the better local restaurants, an Italian place two towns away. Coming out of the stairway, Nate pulled his apartment keys from his pocket and strolled down the short hallway with a bounce in his step. He was excited and felt good; in fact, he couldn't remember the last time he had felt this good. Nate saw a small FedEx package in front of his door. He grabbed the box with one hand and keyed the lock with the other. Once inside, he found a box cutter in his kitchen drawer and cut the packing strip on the top of the small package. Nate pulled out the bubble-wrapped contents, a small black plastic case that was heavier than it looked. This was the box that could harden a cell phone or a laptop against fire, water, or an EMP attack. In the bottom of the package was another small, bubble-wrapped item. It was an SD card that would allow his smartphone to function as a Geiger counter. He set the items back in the cardboard box and walked into the bathroom to shower.

Nate showered quickly and got dressed, spiffing himself up nicely. He took one last long look in the mirror and decided that he had cleaned up pretty good, and other than the butterflies fluttering around in his stomach, he was set to go out.

Nate hopped in his car and drove toward the restaurant. He flipped on the radio, hoping music instead of news would calm his nerves. All hopes of listening to music were dashed when a reporter on the radio began describing how a US nuclear-tipped warhead had been detonated over a facility that was linked to the North Korean device that had exploded in Japan.

Nate might have vomited all over himself if his stomach weren't empty. The reporter continued to recount the international reaction and read a few statements by experts and government officials. All the information began to flow together in a mixed jumble, like some regurgitated word salad. Nate could no longer decipher who was saying what about whom. All he had flashing through his brain was that the United States—his own country—had nuked North Korea in a response to Japan, and now the Russians were livid over the whole situation. Nate kept driving to the restaurant, even more stressed out and anxious than he had been before. The portion of his esophagus that connected to his stomach was irritated with what seemed like a gallon of acid. The butterflies had turned to vultures circling over a rotten piece of rancid roadkill. He was sweating profusely as he pulled into the parking lot of Amoré right on time. Nate found a tee shirt on the backseat and used it to wipe the sweat off his forehead. He walked into the restaurant, and his eyes were instantly drawn to Jeannette, who was sitting at the bar. Nate stopped and watched her for a minute. She looked stunning in a tight black cocktail dress with black high heels; she had even put on makeup. Nate was so used to seeing her in a lab coat or scrubs that she now looked alien to him, but alien in the best way possible. Her dark hair was up in a perfect bun at the back of her head. This exposed her neck, which was at the top of Nate's list of favorite body parts of a woman. The loose hairs on her tan neck led around to her glowing face, which had a radiance that words could not do justice to; it would be like trying to describe the beauty of the ocean if you had lived in a desert your entire life. With no hair in her face or glasses on her nose to distract from her natural elegance, she looked beautiful; just seeing her took away all of Nate's worries.

Amoré was a quaint, darkly lit, Italian restaurant, a split-level design with a clichéd Mediterranean look. Nate walked over to Jeannette without waiting for a hostess or waitress to point the way. Jeannette looked up from her drink and her eyes lit up for a second before her face drifted back to that sad little smile again. Nate could tell just from that smile that she must have been listening to the news as well.

"Hi, Nate," she said softly. "I took the liberty of reserving us a table." Her voice wasn't without sadness, but at the same time the sadness was fleeting. It was almost as though she had talked herself into having a nice night no matter what the circumstances were halfway around the world.

"Hi, Jeannette," Nate said casually. As this was the first date Nate had been on in years, he figured he'd probably forgotten about some chivalrous rule he was supposed to adhere to. Jeannette didn't seem to notice, or else she didn't care that Nate was a bit rusty when it came to these traditions. The waitress, having noticed Nate's arrival, came over and led them to their seats. The restaurant was mostly empty, so Jeannette had been able to pick whichever table she wanted. They sat down at a candlelit table for two, with a white tablecloth and a single crimson rose centerpiece. Their first attempts at conversation were awkward and forced, but as far as Nate was concerned, they could have been worse. Nate and Jeannette talked about the North Korean crisis, which was like mentioning a funeral to someone fighting cancer. After a short time, they both agreed to ignore the subject and avoid ruining the night by allowing it to dominate their thoughts and words.

Nate gave Jeannette the rundown about his childhood, which amounted to small talk, mostly. He told Jeannette about how he had ended up becoming a phlebotomist and made a joke about living the dream. He told some self-deprecating stories about his brief college experience, sticking mostly to the educational aspects. Jeannette explained that she had grown up only a stones throw from an operational Minuteman II missile silo just outside of Wichita, Kansas. She revealed that it had given her a special perspective on the Cold War and how it provided an extra level to her anxiety now. The events unfolding half a world away were sending Jeannette back into a childhood nightmare that she had thought was far behind her. Although she brushed it off like a mere inconvenience, Nate understood how childhood fears could rear their ugly heads in someone's adult life.

Nate ordered the shrimp scampi, assuming it was aristocratic enough to appear cultured yet not sophisticated enough to appear greedy. It was strange for Nate to think so much about his self-image. He hadn't been concerned with what other people thought of him for years—his hair was in dire need of a trim and he dressed in what was comfortable. It had always been about what was easy for Nate.

Jeannette ordered the penne pasta covered with the house specialty vodka sauce and topped with breaded eggplant smothered in mozzarella. The food was very good, and the conversation became sparse but meaningful. Nate and

Jeannette saw sides of each other that they hadn't previously seen.

For a short time, the outside world vanished, and maybe it was the wine, but Nate was genuinely happy sitting in the candlelight with a beautiful woman. After they finished dinner, Nate picked up the tab and walked Jeannette to her car. Nate said his goodbyes and, in lieu of a goodnight kiss, nervously put his arms around Jeannette for a short embrace. She smiled blushingly and thanked him for a very nice night. The parting seemed artificial to Nate, like something that was expected and messy, it didn't match the evening he had just experienced.

Nate made his way back to his car frustrated and alone, kicking himself for being so nervous and immature. He kept playing back some of the stupid things he had said over the course of the evening. No matter how well the evening had gone, he was determined to turn it into a colossal failure. His paranoia and self-loathing always tainted the best days of Nate's life, like a stain on a brilliantly white wedding dress or a bruise on a perfectly ripe apple. Something had been broken in Nate's mind—something that couldn't be fixed.

By the time Nate arrived at his apartment, he was a mess. Between the international calamity and regret over things he should have said to Jeannette, he felt lost. He collapsed onto his bed facedown and hardly moved until the next morning.

Nate called in sick to work. He wanted to avoid the day and, more specifically, avoid Jeannette. He stayed in bed for hours curled in a ball; the previous evening was tattooed to every thought. It was like trying to shake a song that you despise but can't stop humming. He eventually dragged his sorry ass out of bed as the afternoon sun lasered through the window above his computer. Using the remote control, he scanned the television for the most recent news; it was that scab that he couldn't stop picking. Searching through his closet, he pulled out an enormous duffel bag and started filling it with his survival gear: winter coat, three rolled up sleeping bags, and the portable camp stove. He packed anything and everything he thought he could use, including the ammunition left in his gun safe.

The news was more of the same. The Russians had gone apeshit because the United States had used nukes so close to their border and were returning to Cold War relations with the West. They had even closed and abandoned their Washington embassy. The Kremlin had also announced that Russia was planning to boycott the Chicago Olympics in two years. The video footage of a mass exodus out of eastern Russia was heartbreaking. Refugees were transported by any and all means, including train, truck, bus, horseback, and even some on foot. The United Nations was even taking punitive action toward America for using weapons of mass destruction, which broke multiple resolutions adopted by the UN Security Council. It seemed the only allies the United States possessed were the British and the Israelis, who were members of the coalition against North Korea, so their hands were as dirty as anyone's.

Nuclear fallout was drifting farther into Russia, and with each city that had to undergo an evacuation came a Russian politician shouting that things like this wouldn't have occurred if the Soviet Union had remained intact. Phrases like *suitable nuclear deterrent* and *the United States might have thought twice if they still had missiles pointed at their cities* were being thrown about. It wasn't very long before Nate realized that the real worry would be the Russians, not the North Koreans. The Russians had the means to flatten every city from New York to Los Angeles right down to the burbs of Podunk, Connecticut. Nate remembered the story Jeannette had told him about growing up close to an operational missile silo. He wondered if those silos were still armed and ready to fire. A great deal of the nuclear stockpile of both countries had been dismantled or were no longer ready for war. Many treaties and even age had reduced the numbers of useable nukes since the Cold War, but by how much Nate didn't know. The United States held a very potent arsenal, but the military had been streamlined with more tactical weapons and fewer strategic nukes. There still would be a whole lot around though, enough to change life on earth forever. It was mind-boggling to consider that the world could have gone from relatively stable to the brink of epic disaster in less than a week's time. This was all unraveling so fast.

By nightfall, Nate was all packed up and had carried the duffel bag, rucksack, and a few other odds and ends out to the trunk of his car. He could be ready to flee to the shelter at a moment's notice. As he took the steps back up to his apartment Nate was debating whether to call Jeannette and come up with some excuse as to why he hadn't been at work today. Nate sat down in front of the TV, where images were cycling of victims at a triage unit outside of Tokyo. Some people appeared to be badly burned, while others must have been suffering from the early effects of radiation sickness...all of them were simply suffering. These pictures and video clips were mostly from cell phone cameras in a small village adjacent to the blast site. The next video was aerial footage from a helicopter nearing the devastated harbor. Acres of what looked like ancient ruins stood halfway obscured by smoky ash. The ocean had reclaimed some of the harbor, creating a startling juxtaposition of water and fire. It reminded Nate of video he had seen of Japan after the earthquake and tsunami had ravaged the country two years before.

Nate thought back to a similar image that had been stuck in his mind for years. Paper hornets had built a very large nest in a hedge in the backyard of his childhood home. He would sit and watch the hornets come and go, flying off on their missions to collect food for the hive. When Nate's father had found out about the nest, he was furious. His dad claimed he was allergic to bees and hornets, although Nate had never heard him say that before. His old man had tied a dirty red rag around a broom handle. He then doused the rag in gasoline, creating a clumsy-looking torch. Nate's father waited until sunset, when all the hornets had returned to the nest. Nate knew his dad wanted the highest possible kill ratio. As the sun set, Nate was told to wait by the back door with the hose and to only come over if his dad called for him. The old man, who was only in his midfifties at the time, lit the torch and touched the flames to the hive. With a *whoomph,* the nest was instantly on fire, burning with blue and gold flames. Nate could remember hearing the crackle and hiss of the fire reaching the inner chambers of the hive. The sickening sizzle as the fire met moisture was like bacon frying in a skillet. Burning hornets fell from the nest, fighting to survive, their wings flaming as they fell to the ground below. The fire then began to crackle and pop like popcorn as the larva inside the wax chambers exploded from the intense heat. Nate could smell a nutty, burnt, repulsive aroma almost like the smell of burning rope. When the fire had finally subsided, Nate's father called him over to shoot water on the charred bush. Nate remembered looking down on the pile of burned hornets, dead and caked with creosote. A puddle had formed to the side of the bush, and floating in it were pieces of the gray nest that now resembled charcoal smoldered to a soft ash. The images of Japan on the television now reminded Nate of that puddle—oily, slick water with a charred city floating in it.

Nate had fallen asleep in his recliner just as the official casualty numbers were starting to be reported. The death toll in Japan had reached thirty thousand, with double that number unaccounted for. Too many had been injured to even begin counting, and many, many more were homeless or had been displaced. Immersed in another dream, Nate stirred: a female news anchor looked up from her notes with streams of blood flowing from her eyes. She was reporting about a nuclear holocaust. Her desk sat on a bed of rubble and partially melted metal. At her shoulder was a small graphic of a cartoon city that was burning in the night. The newswoman was singing something gleeful, inappropriately gleeful, and Nate couldn't understand the words that were coming out of her mouth as printed dialog in comic book white bubbles.

Nate woke drenched in sweat, with his back sticking to the fake leather covering on his recliner. He was stinking and stiff and, according to the clock on his nightstand, was in serious danger of running late for work. Nate showered and got dressed. Running out the door, he knew it was going to be a rough day.

PYRETTA BLAZE

Kim sat in his bunker he hated the idea that he had to hide just because the bombing had intensifiedThe plan had been even more successful than he had hoped. A toxic cloud teeming with radioactive fallout nearly fifty miles wide by one hundred miles long had drifted over eastern Russia. The Russian parliament had voted unanimously to close its borders and expel the American ambassador as well as all American citizens. The Iron Curtain had been pulled down once more.

Having knowledge of significant tensions between the United States and Russia, Kim ordered the initiation of a cyber worm that had entered the Internet through public servers.

At approximately 6:00 a.m. Eastern time, the Russians' advanced warning systems that monitored the Arctic Circle lit up with heat signatures from multiple missiles en route. The computers told of launches from both land-based silos in the Midwest and submarines based in the North Sea. Similar advanced warning systems at NATO, NORAD, and Vandenberg Air Force Base in California likewise marked launches out of Russia.

With the hotline compromised, the presidents of the United States and Russia were forced to make hasty decisions that would hold the fate of the world in the balance. At 6:30 a.m. Eastern time, the virus wreaked further havoc on both countries' defense technologies, effectively blinding both to any incoming threats. The last image each side saw before their systems crashed was a massive assault on its way. Both presidents responded the same way to the perceived threats: they ordered full-scale nuclear launches on their new enemy.

Within thirty minutes, multiple warheads would enter the earth's atmosphere and impact on military, strategic, and civilian targets.

Kim remained seated and smiled as he realized what he had created. What he hadn't counted on was a single launch from a nuclear submarine stationed off the coast of Japan. The missile had hit the mountain that Kim's advisors had described as an invincible stronghold. The one-megaton warhead had been placed on a massive ordnance penetrator guided missile so powerful that it had collapsed the central elevator shaft and caved in more than half of the bunker. Kim was now beginning to choke on the toxic fumes that were slowly filling what was left of his bunker. His dying thought was the hope that his nation would erect a gold statue of him in the capitol when Korea was the one remaining superpower. Kim's body sat below a mile of earth and rock; it would never be discovered.

Nate finished gathering up anything and everything he could carry on his way out to the car. He had found a fourth sleeping bag at the bottom of his closet—he didn't remember ever buying that many sleeping bags. He decided that they must have come from his parents. Nate's arms were full as he walked outside into a beautifully brilliant spring day. The sky was as blue as it could get, and there was hardly a cloud to be found. Packing the trunk of his car had started to resemble a game of Tetris. Nate moved around jugs of water and the duffel bag and wedged in everything he had carried out.

He drove to work in his typical morning fog; his mind was racing between Jeannette, the thought of war, and his recent bout of nightmares. Nate was so burned out on international news that for the first time in weeks he actually muted the radio before changing the station to a rock channel. He switched around until he found a song he recognized. It was "Tom Sawyer" by Rush, a band Nate had always liked. He hummed along, thinking about what he'd say to Jeannette when he eventually arrived at the blood draw facility. His mood seemed to improve by the mile and by the note, so he reached down and turned up the volume. He began to sing along: "No his mind is not for rent / to any God or government / always hopeful, yet discontent / he knows changes aren't permanent." It felt great to be outside in the air, music blasting, with the sun's warmth drenching his face.

It was 6:45 a.m. He was on schedule to be at work by 7:00 if the single traffic light didn't cause a delay. Suddenly, a loud, high-pitched tone interrupted Rush on the radio. Nate had obviously heard the Emergency Broadcast System tone before; they tested it every so often, especially on the radio. This was different, however. The first words the robotic female voice said was, "This is not a test." Nate's heart skipped a beat or two; he never remembered hearing anything other than the same old recording. He pulled off to the side of the road and stared at the radio as if his attention would increase the speed at which the information flowed. Looking up, Nate noticed other motorists were doing the same thing.

> Any motorists in transit, on foot, or on open ground in the Hartford-New Haven metropolitan area should find a suitable underground shelter in the event of a possible attack. Seek shelter in a low-lying area if available. Suitable shelters include a basement, cellar, or fallout shelter. In the event of an attack and if these places are not available at your location, shelter in place facing away from exterior windows. This shelter should prevent possible radioactive material from reaching exposed skin and eyes. This warning does not suggest that an attack is imminent at this time; please stay tuned to civil defense broadcasts as they become available. This recording will be followed by instructions and the latest on the situation currently threatening your area.

The recording started over from the beginning: "This is not a test," preceded by that singular tone that made Nate nauseous. He was shaking; he had thought he was prepared for this exact scenario, but now that it was happening he knew he had only been fooling himself. He had dwelled on it, obsessed over it, but in the back of his mind he assumed it would never happen. Now his nightmare was...happening.

Adrenaline and panic started to motivate Nate, even if his mind didn't think his body could handle movement. For once, the fight-or-flight response was justified. He pulled his car off the shoulder and onto the road, desperately trying to get ahead of any other traffic. The other cars that had pulled in behind Nate on the shoulder were moving in a disorganized cluster, some heading in the opposite direction, which caused a small snarl on the edge of the street. Nate sped away; he just missed being sideswiped by someone driving on the wrong side of the road. He blew through the stoplight, which was red, ignoring the outrage from the other motorists who must not have heard the alert. The roads were chaotic, with cars speeding left and right while others moved normally. Some drivers weren't reacting; others were freaking out. Through the center of town, pedestrians were running anywhere they could, either to find shelter or because they were simply frightened and following others. In his rearview mirror, Nate watched two cars collide; one of the drivers got out and ran into the closest building. The other driver had been thrown through the windshield, landing on his own hood. The man wasn't moving, and Nate knew that he couldn't have survived the violence of the collision. It appeared that the man's head had been nearly sheared in two down the middle from the windshield glass. Nate was numb; he simply needed to get to his shelter—he couldn't think of anything else. *Just get to the shelter* was all he could think. It occurred to him that not stopping to help people who had been hurt might haunt him later, but he wouldn't be of any use to anyone in his current emotional state.

Thankfully for Nate, the blood draw facility was on the outskirts of Middlebrook, far enough from all of the confusion and panic. He turned up the hill, away from the town center; the road toward the health clinic was empty, so he stepped on the gas pedal. Nate pulled into the parking lot, which contained only one other car: Jeannette's Subaru. He ran toward the automatic doors, not bothering to take any supplies from his trunk. He hoped there would be time later.

Inside, Jeannette was sitting at her computer with headphones on. Nate ran over to her and motioned for her to take off the headphones.

"Nate are you all right?" Jeannette asked with concern. "Were you sick yesterday? You look flushed." She looked back down and continued typing.

"Jeannette we have to get someplace safe right away. The Russians or the North Koreans must be attacking." Jeannette didn't even look up at him.

"Nate, I'm really busy here; there are a lot of walk-ins next door." She brushed her hair from her eyes. Nate glanced next door into the blood draw waiting area, which he had just rushed through. It was empty.

Nate thought maybe she hadn't understood him or that she was confused or something until it clicked in his head...she already knew, but something had snapped inside her and her defense mechanism was creating this wall of denial. She was sitting there ignoring the situation like it was a typical workday. Nate didn't know how to broach the subject, but he didn't have time to consider her delicate psyche at the moment.

"Jeannette, something is happening; we need to get to a safe place. There is going to be a war or bombs or something; they are warning people right here in Connecticut." He walked over and shut off her monitor. Jeannette looked up, puzzled, and stared at him with her head tilted slightly to the side.

"Nate, don't be silly." Something changed as the words left her lips. Nate could see reality creeping in and pushing away the denial. Tears started to stream down her cheeks, rolling off her chin and dripping onto her lab coat.

"I have nowhere to go; my family isn't here. I live in a cheap condo—it doesn't even have a fucking basement," she said through sobs.

"Come with me," Nate said softly. "I need to show you something." He took Jeannette by the hand and led her over to the stockroom door. He opened the door and pushed the boxes out of the way as they weaved their way to the door at the back.

"Nate, what is this?" Jeannette asked.

"Just follow me." Nate opened the heavy door at the back of the storeroom. He flipped on the light and they walked down the narrow stairway. The long corridor was cool and still smelled of fresh paint. They reached the door at the end of the hallway. "This, my dear, is a Nathan Wilder custom-built fallout shelter." He turned the knob and pushed open the door into the large furnace room–slash–office. A weak breeze greeted them as they passed the threshold. Nate walked over and started pulling open the doors of the file cabinets to show Jeannette his stockpile. She smiled a little bit, which Nate thought was a tremendous breakthrough.

"Nate, when did you do all this?" She walked over and stood next to Nate, picking up a can as if she needed to be sure they were real.

"I'm sure I'll have plenty of time to tell you all of that. For now, though, we have to do what we can to secure this place and get everything we can use down here. I'm not sure how much time we have or even if we need to stay down here yet." Nate shut the file cabinets. "I need you to help. You need to get on the web and find out what's coming and how much time we have before it's here." He placed both of his hands on her shoulders, standing square to her and looking into her eyes. "I have some more gear in my car that I need to get, and I want to secure everything so we don't have to worry about something falling on us or someone else coming in here if the shit goes down." She nodded in acknowledgement and Nate could see she had partially pulled her shit together. "We'll meet back down here in fifteen minutes." Nate finished his pep talk and he and Jeannette hurried to get as much accomplished as they could.

Nate popped the trunk of his car and started to load its contents into an empty wheelchair. The parking lot was eerily empty, like the calm before the storm. Not a soul could be seen outside, not even at the urgent care facility, which was usually a bustling hub of activity at this time. No cars were on the road in front of the facility, and Nate could see a line of traffic in the distance that didn't seem to be moving.

A loud, blaring sound thundered through the calm, breaking the silence. It was a civil defense siren, almost like a fire whistle except instead of multiple alarms it was one long, constant horn blast. Nate remembered hearing the town test the trumpeting call of warning as a child; they would do it annually toward the end of the Cold War. The sky was still an azure blue with hardly a cloud, and Nate kept expecting to see something—an army jet, a squadron of attack helicopters, contrail lines from missiles, an air blast nuke, something. The sky was devoid of anything; even birds seemed to be hiding somewhere. The lack of something flying, even civilian aircraft, was unnerving. It reminded Nate of 9/11, when all aircraft were grounded and the skies had an unaccustomed emptiness.

Nate pushed forward with his wheelchair full of water jugs, camping supplies, and the large duffel bag. He pushed through the automatic doors and into the stockroom, where he had to stop and unload everything by hand. After two full trips, his car was empty. Jeannette met Nate in the lower-level hallway carrying a large bottle of water that she had found in the cooler upstairs. "What did the Internet have to say?" he asked, taking the bottle from her. Jeannette looked anxious, like someone had just startled her from behind.

"The Emergency Broadcast System has taken over the entire Internet; I've never seen anything like it. Each site I had clicked on would bring up the same EBS page with clippings from Reuters and the Associated Press at the bottom, along with instructions to take shelter. It's saying that a nuclear strike is imminent. The AP story at the bottom of the page reports that two nukes were airburst over American troops in Afghanistan. The last paragraph was a time-stamped update from Reuters; it said that in response America had fired missiles at Russian military targets from a ship in the Persian Gulf. The last line said that at least a limited exchange of ICBMs against population centers was a certainty and that eyewitnesses from both countries had reported seeing missiles leaving their silos." Jeannette's voice was shaking, and Nate sensed she was fighting to maintain control of her emotions. "Nate, the time stamp on the last report was almost thirty minutes ago." Jeannette opened the door to the makeshift shelter so Nate could carry in the five-gallon jug of water.

They started to arrange the shelter so that nothing could fall on them. Nate noticed that Jeannette had piled scrubs and lab coats on top of the file cabinets. It hadn't occurred to him earlier that she didn't have a change of clothes with her, but the scrubs would do in a pinch.

"There's one more thing I have to do upstairs." Nate started to jog out of the room.

"Nate get your ass back down here as soon as you can; I don't think I can be alone right now," Jeannette said as Nate opened the door to go out.

Nate ran upstairs and started locking every door he could find that led outside. He finished by sealing the sliding front door and locking it with a key high on an automatic panel on the side.

Without warning, an intense, piercing flash from outside lit up the air. Nate instinctively flinched and dove for the floor. It was like a strike of lightning or a flashbulb from an enormous camera. A resonant dull thud followed, coming from what sounded like somewhere above the building. It was like a sonic boom from a jet traveling at high speed. All the lights in the building went out, coating the floor in shadow. Nate ran through every room with an exterior facing window and pulled the shades down as tight as he could. The light outside had changed; it was now blood-red, as if an eclipse had just blotted out the sun and only the red wavelengths could penetrate. Resisting the urge to peek outside and admire the increasingly diseased-looking sky, Nate sprinted into the storeroom and started stacking and pushing boxes in front of the door. He then slid behind the boxes, pulling them toward him as he slammed the door to the stairwell. Nate hoped that the boxes would be heavy enough to add some insulation and keep the door hidden from any undesirable looters who might come poking around for medical attention.

He was halfway down the flight of stairs, feeling around in the dark with his feet, when the steps began to feel like quicksand. The powerful tremor was too brutal to bear as it rattled his teeth painfully. Nate reached for the railing, but it seemed to dodge his grasp like a boxer slipping a punch. His feet were in the air then back over his head as he tumbled down the last ten steps. The walls were flexing and threatened to topple over if the rumble escalated beyond what the structure could sustain. Nate started to gain a very small amount of night vision, which made it seem as though he were falling through space and time with stars shooting past. He hit the landing hard, smacking his forehead on the concrete floor and feeling a pop inside his head like something vital had ruptured. He thought he could feel his brain slam into the side of his skull and ricochet back like a paddleball tethered to its wooden paddle. Blood flowed down his face from a horrific gash that his fingers found with a sharp sting; he desperately blotted at the wound with his sleeve. Nate then feebly tried to roll over and get up on his hands and knees but he had no stability because the ground below him was shaking so violently. He remained at the bottom of the stairs, lying on his back for a moment or two and praying to God the ceiling wouldn't cave in on top of him. There was no sound—it was either too loud or the ringing in Nate's ears had drowned out all other auditory sensation. Pieces of drywall were falling to the floor around him and the vibration seemed to increase with every second. The plaster dust drifting in the air burned his eyes and lungs, and every breath that stabbed through his chest was excruciating. Nate fought unsteadily back onto his hands and knees and knew he wouldn't be able to walk. He began crawling along the floor, moving just in time as a three-foot fluorescent light fixture crashed down to the floor right where he had been lying. It could have been from the shaking floor or the knock to the head, but whatever the cause, Nate began to vomit uncontrollably. He coughed and gagged, spitting phlegm thick with grime on the ground between his hands. It was just the motivation he needed. He braced his hands on the wall, spread out his feet, and began to use his legs like shock absorbers. He had to zigzag his way, bouncing off the walls, but he had made progress to the shelter door. It was like being at sea and trying to run across a patch of ice that was floating on a squalled ocean. His momentum carried him crashing through the door.

The room was pitch black, but he could hear Jeannette whimpering in the dark.

"Jeannette, I'm here!" Nate had to yell at the top of his lungs just to hear his own voice. The roaring was so incredibly intense and the change in pressure had made everything sound wavy and distorted.

"Over here, Nate—I'm on the floor!" Jeannette seemed to be whimpering, but as he followed the sound of her voice and got closer, he realized that she wasn't whimpering but screaming. "Nate where are you?" He stumbled like a drunk, trying to determine her direction as he swayed. Nate tripped over what felt like a mound of sleeping bags against the far wall. He fell to the floor, feeling Jeannette's legs under the pile of sleeping bags. Nate groped his way up to her torso and felt for the rest of her body as the thundering crescendo of vibration reached its apex. They embraced tenaciously in the dark under the sleeping bags, bound by terror and confusion. Jeannette and Nate huddled together, both of them crying without shame or self-consciousness. It was like combat, striving to stay alive and knowing that at any moment the whole building could collapse on top of them. Buildings in the Northeast, unlike those on the west coast, weren't built to withstand earthquakes or seismic activity; this thought continued to cross Nate's mind even as his body was in its fight-or-flight response.

Slowly, gradually, after what seemed like an eternity, the vibration descended. It eventually tapered off, subsiding to a minor tremor like a locomotive pulling away over the horizon. Then it was over—even the tremor was gone. Both Nate and Jeannette could still sense it in their bones, but the floor and walls were still, almost like it had never happened. The only evidence was a long fissure in one wall, the dust in the air, and Nate and Jeannette still holding onto each other, sobbing.

Nate broke the embrace and crawled to the center of the room. He could still feel the buzz in his hands and knees, but it was residual, like your hands feel after hitting an immovable object with an aluminum baseball bat. In the center of the room Nate stumbled on his keys, which he remembered held the small Maglight keychain. He flipped on the tiny flashlight and shined it around the room. The plaster dust lingering in the air made the beam of light appear solid, like a *Star Wars* light saber. The dust that was illuminated by the beam looked like little stars reflecting the light of a giant sun. Nate searched for the yellow plastic battery-operated lantern that was with his camping equipment. He found the lantern in the duffel bag and turned it on, placing it on the desk that sat near the center of the room. The whole room was now dimly lit.

Nate walked over to Jeannette, leaned down, and took her hands to help her to her feet.

"Oh my God, Nate, what happened to your head?" Jeannette asked in a shocked gasp. Nate's hand instantly went up to his forehead and found an egg-shaped swelling that was split by a three-inch gash. Dried sticky blood mixed with dirt, and plaster dust was caked along the side of his hairline down into his eyebrow.

"It's fine; I'm fine," Nate said, shooing away Jeannette's concern with his hands.

"Do you think the world's gone?" Jeannette asked, short of breath.

"We're still here," Nate answered as confidently as he could muster.

"I mean up there," she gestured with a nod of her head. "Could anyone have survived that?" She looked down, hoping to hide her face as much as she could.

"We survived." Nate was trying his best not to sound dismissive, but he felt they should be discussing more important things. He didn't know what they were, but surely there more important words that would apply to a time like this. "I'm sure other people were able to find shelters or were far enough away when those things went off." He put his arms around her again; it just felt right.

"How close do you think those explosions hit?" Jeannette asked, laying her head on Nate's shoulder.

"Jesus, Jeannette, how the hell should I know?" Nate snapped; he immediately regretted it. "I'm sorry, I just...I only know what you know. I'm sorry; this is an impossible situation..." He didn't notice any change in Jeannette; perhaps Nate hadn't been as offensive as he had thought, or maybe she was in shock. "Come on, let's make this place as comfortable as we can." Nate hoped that doing anything other than talking about what had just occurred would help. He released her from the embrace and began sliding his gear against the wall. The black plastic case holding his cell phone had fallen out of the duffel bag onto the floor. Nate thought about the bombs—they could be receiving a fatal dose of radiation and they wouldn't even know it. Did they have hours to live?

He opened the box that was supposed to protect his cell phone from the EMP and placed the phone on the desk next to the lantern. Then he slid his finger across the face of the phone, and it lit up with icons. The phone was operational. It had no signal, and the time and date were wrong, but it appeared to be working normally. The lead-lined box had worked—the cell phone had survived the EMP. Nate touched his finger to the icon that looked like a biohazard symbol. The screen instantly changed to a graph with a series of wavy lines and two separate number readouts. Nate pushed the volume button up and held the phone in the air away from his body. The phone crackled to life with a set of clicks that sounded like a metronome. He walked toward the door and used the phone to trace the doorjamb. The highest reading he found was at the top of the door—that reading was 0.8 rads per hour, slightly higher than the 0.4 rads he found in the remainder of the room. Nate kicked himself for not taking a reading in his apartment before all of this; he had no control factor to compare to. Regardless, Nate knew that even at 0.8 rads, they would be safe for the duration.

"Nate, what are you doing?" asked Jeannette from the area where the sleeping bags were. She was creating a makeshift bed.

"I'm testing the radiation levels in the room; I ordered this thing online that converts a cell phone to a Geiger counter," he said while taking more samples with the phone.

Jeannette looked perplexed, almost as though she didn't believe him. "So you can tell if it's safe down here with your cell phone?"

"That's what it said on the website where I ordered the program," Nate answered.

"And do you believe everything on the Internet?" Jeannette gave him that doubtful, puzzled look again.

"For what I paid for it..." He worked his way to the other side of the room, testing the air as he went. "And it is reading higher at the top of the door."

"So is it safe?" she finally asked.

"As of right now it's safe, but the majority of the fallout probably hasn't come through yet. It's carried on the wind, and we don't know the wind speed or even how far away the blast site is." Nate would have to be vigilant about checking the readings, but he didn't have enough battery reserve to leave the phone on permanently. "I suppose it's also a possibility that there may be a second wave of attacks." Even with Nate's pessimism, Jeannette seemed to breathe a sigh of relief. Just knowing that they were out of harm's way for the time being was enough to relax her slightly.

"So when the hell did you get a Geiger counter and start prepping for the apocalypse?" Jeannette asked with a touch of grateful sarcasm, if there is such a thing.

"It's kind of hard to explain," Nate said. He was reluctant to delve too deeply into his state of paranoia, which, all things considered, was part of the reason they were still alive. "I started to get things together when the whole North Korea thing really blew up...pun intended."

"Well, I'm glad you did, for both of us." She paused. Nate could tell that Jeannette was starting to wonder if it was really better to be alive. "How long do you think we'll need to be down here?" Jeannette asked, interrupting her short period of introspection.

"The website said that in a theoretical nuclear war it would be safe outside for limited exposure after thirty days." They would need to be sure though, and a theoretical war didn't give you radiation sickness. "We'll need to monitor the radiation levels as much as we can, and when it's safe we'll come out."

Jeannette looked shocked. "Oh my God, Nate, thirty days? Do you even have enough food for the two of us? What about water and sanitation? I was hoping you were going to say a week or so!"

"We should have enough food. Water will be a bit tougher, but as long as it stays cool and we ration things we'll be all right. As for sanitation, there's a large plastic sink in the next room; as long as the radiation isn't much higher outside the door it should work as a toilet." Nate chuckled a little. "It won't be pleasant, but the alternatives are even more inferior."

Jeannette frowned at Nate, making no secret about how she felt about the sanitation issue. There were a few large cardboard boxes in the room that had been there before Nate started moving his stuff in. Nate tore off the packing tape on top of the biggest box and unfolded the cardboard flaps, hoping that something useful would be inside. He shined the Maglight in and saw an assortment of office supplies: staplers, paper clips, pens, and reams of white paper. Nate moved on to the second box, hoping for a more useful haul. He again tore off the packing tape and looked in the box. This box contained four large rolls of plastic sheeting like a person might use to protect floors and furniture when painting a room. Underneath the sheeting was a roll of blue painter's tape and a few paintbrushes still in their packages. The last and smallest box also contained painting supplies: a few dust masks, paint scrapers, and a can of paint thinner.

Jeannette walked to Nate and looked over his shoulder as he squatted in front of the boxes. "Did you find anything good?" she asked.

"It's mostly just office and painting supplies that must have been left over from the landlord." Nate shrugged.

After only two hours in the shelter, it was beginning to feel claustrophobic. Nate and Jeannette were both feeling antsy and trapped. They moved about the room making it as habitable as they could. Jeannette had laid out the sleeping bags to make something that resembled a bed. Nate was glad that he had brought four sleeping bags: they could place two on the floor for padding and still have one for each to sleep in. Nate organized a small kitchen area with the camp stove, jugs of water, and a small stack of canned food. There were a few rolling office chairs, and Nate had turned a file cabinet on its side to make a table; the combination would work as a dining area. When they had finished, Jeannette and Nate stood side by side for a few seconds to admire their new home. It would never be ideal, but at least now it looked like an area you could imagine living in.

"Home sweet home," Nate said sarcastically. "So are you hungry?" He picked up a gallon jug of water and splashed a little on his hands, which were pasty white with drywall dust. Then he wiped his hands on his shirt and used the dampness to wipe his face.

"I'll try to eat," Jeannette said as she used the water for the same purpose.

Nate picked up the cell phone and tested the air again, but there had been no change in the radiation level. He dialed a few numbers just out of curiosity, but there was no signal. The phone also had an app that turned the phone into an AM/FM radio tuner. He touched the icon, but it switched to a seemingly endless searching pattern. Either the reception was too poor underground, or more likely the cell towers, the Internet, or the radio stations were no more. Nate realized then that even if there had been radio stations or the Internet, the EMP would have rendered everything inoperable and prevented anything from transmitting.

"So would you like the prime rib or grilled lobster tail?" Nate asked, placing the phone on the wooden desk and reading the labels off of some cans of food.

"I'll take the prime rib, please," Jeannette said with a smile. "I like it rare, just warm in the middle and bloody." She punched him in the shoulder playfully.

Nate took out some pans from his duffel bag and placed them on the wooden shelf closest to the cooking area. "In honor of our first night in our new home, I'll make something special." He opened a can of SPAM with its ready-made key. It looked delicious—pink, slimy, and perfectly shaped like the can it had come in. He cut off two slices and threw them in a small frying pan with a slap. Nate then pushed the red button just below the burner on the small stove. Two clicks and a pop preceded a whoosh of blue flame under the pan. The smell of sizzling meat overtook the smell of drywall and diesel that had hung in the air. The artificial meat product even started to look appetizing as it seared loudly in the skillet. Nate smiled and turned to Jeannette, who was sitting and watching him cook with a grin. He then opened a can of corn niblets and drained the liquid, saving it for later use; they couldn't afford to waste anything that contained water. He dumped the kernels into the pan with the SPAM and mixed it all together with a fork. Finally, he was satisfied that the mixture had been thoroughly heated and began to shovel the concoction onto two plates.

"Bon appetit," Nate said, handing the plate to Jeannette.

"Merci." She took the plate and sat opposite Nate at the improvised table. They had been concerned that eating would be nearly impossible because they had both been fighting stomach

MICAH ACKERMAN

pain caused by stress all day. The smell of the food cooking had changed all of that. By the time the food was finished, they were both famished.

"This is actually really good, Nate," Jeannette said though a mouthful of SPAM.

"You're just starving; right now anything would taste good," Nate answered back.

"It would take a hell of a lot more than twelve hours for my taste buds to accept bad food; I'm usually a very picky eater. Trust me, it's really, really...decent," she said with a light giggle. It was the first time Nate had heard anything resembling a laugh all day, and it sounded really good. The meal really wasn't that bad, and he was actually proud of himself for constructing something edible. They finished and sat relaxing while their food digested.

After dinner, Nate scanned for radiation again. He assumed that the radiation would increase as more and more fallout blew through. The radiation level hadn't increased; it was the same as when he had first checked. He briefly wondered if the phone even worked—the levels should have fluctuated by now. He sat down and started adjusting the settings on the phone while Jeannette volunteered to clean up from dinner. They would be able to use the sink in the next room soon enough, but for now Nate wanted to wait a day or more before opening the door. Jeannette washed the utensils the best she could with the water from the jugs, and they used an empty jug for a temporary toilet. Thankfully, they only had to urinate, and while it was a bit uncomfortable, as long as the other person turned around it was suitable.

The day had turned to evening, and Nate and Jeannette were exhausted physically and emotionally.

"I can barely keep my eyes open," Jeannette said as she sat on one of the office chairs, "but I'm scared to go to sleep."

"I know what you mean. I just want to close my eyes and wake up on a beach somewhere," he said as he set up his sleeping bag on top of the ones that had been spread on the floor. Jeannette followed suit, laying the last sleeping bag out beside Nate.

"I hope you don't mind that I sleep next to you," she said.

"I wouldn't have it any other way," he said, hiding his elation.

"I hope you don't snore," Jeannette joked.

"Not that I know of," Nate responded. They both scooted into their sleeping bags and turned to face each other. He looked into her eyes for a moment, and then they both burst into a giggling fit like kids at summer camp. After the silliness subsided, a startled look of sadness broke across Jeannette's face. It seemed like she felt guilt for having shared that moment of laughter with all that had happened.

"They're all dead, aren't they?" Jeannette said with her eyes welling up. "My parents, my sister, everyone?" Her expression was stoic, numb, but Nate could tell she was dying inside.

"Jeannette, you don't know that." He tried his best to sound hopeful and soothing. "You never mentioned you have a sister." Nate was careful in his phrasing—he didn't want to use the past tense and upset her further.

"She lives in St. Louis; I haven't seen her in a year," Jeannette said, staring straight through Nate like he was invisible. "Nate, it's not like we've had this whole history of deep conversations. Before our date the other day and this whole thing anyway." She waved her arms to indicate the shelter around them. "You only spoke to me when you had to for work."

Nate was embarrassed, but it was true: he was a complete and total pussy when it came to approaching Jeannette. "I guess I'm just shy." Nate cleared his throat, hoping to think of a better excuse. "You always seemed...I don't know...out of my league."

Nate could feel the awkward sound of the statement as it left his lips. It sounded like he was fishing for a compliment.

"Why would I be out of your league, Nate? You're a nice guy with a lot going for you." Now it was Jeannette's turn to feel awkward. She expertly changed the subject. "After college, I drifted away from my family. I was the typical midwestern kid dreaming of the East Coast and begging for any way out of the boonies. I never thought I'd end up in Connecticut, but you know how things go. I went to school and took the first med-tech job I could find; it happened to be here. Plus I have this gimpy mitt...and now I'm thirty years old and the world has been blown apart. Hell, maybe it saved my life; it got me away from those missile silos." The look of despair returned to her face, it was like she had remembered a dead cat.

"Jeannette, we don't even know what happened above our heads, let alone what happened to the rest of the country...and I love that gimpy mitt." Nate was sliding into an unfamiliar role of consolation.

Jeannette sighed as she lay there staring off into space, deep in thought.

"Let's try to get some sleep and see what tomorrow brings; it might not be as bad as it seems," Nate said as he went over and switched off the battery-powered lantern. He felt his way back to his sleeping bag and attempted to get comfortable next to Jeannette. The floor was extremely hard, and the sleeping bags below him didn't soften much of anything.

Nate stared into the darkness. He was on his back facing the ceiling, but he could hear Jeannette's soft breathing next to him. He started to think about all the people in his own life, and it was depressing—the list was very short. Not because of the people he had lost, but because of the lack of people for him to mourn. He had a few acquaintances and some work colleagues, but no real friends and no family. Nate began to drift off to sleep when he was startled to consciousness by Jeannette's stirring. He couldn't remember the last time he had slept in the same room as anyone else, much less right next to someone. Nate concentrated his hearing on Jeannette, thinking her soft sounds might soothe him into sleep, but he noticed she wasn't just stirring, she was weeping softly, choking in the sobs to be quiet on his account. He shifted over and put his arms around her; she accepted his embrace and after a few minutes seemed to fall asleep in his arms. Nate thought to himself how ironic it was that the whole world had to fall apart before he could find a woman who would trust him enough to sleep while he held her.

The next morning, Nate woke stiff and sore. The hard concrete floor hadn't done him any favors, and holding Jeannette all night had been comforting to her but very uncomfortable for him. His eyes felt like they had been glued shut with crusty plaster dust, and his chest felt like an elephant had been standing on top of it all night. He crawled over to the desk that the lantern sat on and pushed the button, squinting as light filled the room and his eyes adjusted. Jeannette was still sleeping calmly, snuggled up in her sleeping bag. Nate took out his phone and pushed the radio icon again. The same thing happened again—the phone tried to connect but the connection timed out after a short period of searching. Any attempt at connecting to the Internet was met by the same error message: "connection has timed out." Nate scanned the room one more time for radiation, but the levels had remained the same. This indicated that either the shielding above their heads had been enough to filter out any radiation, the attack hadn't been as bad as they thought, or the Geiger counter simply didn't work as advertised.

Nate sat on an office chair in the small makeshift kitchen preparing breakfast. He opened a can of fruit cocktail and poured it into two bowls. The syrupy sweet fruit smelled great as he licked the sticky juice from his fingers. Jeannette crept up behind him, having silently awakened while he had been busy selecting a can to open. She put her hands on his shoulders from behind and ambushed him with a peck to the cheek.

"Thank you for comforting me last night; I never would have slept without you, and God knows I needed the sleep, Thank you for all of this Nate, I owe you my life and so much more" Jeannette said as she took one of the bowls of fruit. Nate thought to himself that it was good that one of them had slept well.

"My pleasure," he said as he took his own bowl and began spooning the fruit into his mouth.

"So, Nate, what are we going to do when it's safe up there?" Jeannette said, snuffing out the good mood.

"I suppose it all depends on how bad the attack was. We probably shouldn't hang out around here, if that's what you're asking," Nate said, wiping a stream of fruit juice from his chin.

"That's exactly what I'm asking, but where would we go? And how would we get there? It's not like cars are going to run; even the cars that haven't been blown up will be useless. You saw how bad Japan was, and this, I assume, was ten times worse." Jeannette was dead serious; the gracious kiss and quick smile had been replaced by a more realistic anxiety.

"That's what I'm saying, Jeannette, I don't know how bad it is up there yet. It's still not even safe enough to leave this room. I don't know if there's an area that hasn't been nuked. I would guess a Caribbean Island or somewhere around the Arctic Circle would be all right," Nate said only half-seriously, knowing full well that there would be no means of transportation even if they could leave the shelter. "Let's deal with that when the time comes. For now, we're alive. We can't know anything else until we get some information about the severity of the damage and how much radiation is above our heads." He was trying to be realistic, yet sound hopeful. Jeannette wasn't stupid—there was no way to sugarcoat things and make it all go away.

Nate and Jeannette spent the next few hours making the shelter cozy, but they were limited by the size of the room and the items that they had to work with. A sleeping bag could only be arranged so many ways. By noon, nature was beginning to call on Nate, and the modified water jug would only take care of one kind of output. He decided to take the gamble and open the door to the shelter. With the Geiger counter in hand, Nate took his first steps out of the room. For the first time, the numbers began to slightly increase on the smartphone's display. With each step, the radiation would rise, and when Nate was halfway to the stairwell, the alarm on the phone started beeping. Nate took a step back and used a fork to scrape a line into the concrete floor. The phone's reading was up to 2 rads per hour at that point. Nate figured the cell phone's threshold was somewhere between two and five rads per hour. At that level, they were safe for limited exposure. It was just in Nate's mind, but he felt uncomfortable in the hallway; he turned around, walked back to the shelter, and closed the door. Nate put on one of the dust masks they had found among the painting supplies in the box that had been left in the shelter. He also grabbed a roll of plastic sheeting and headed back out to the hallway.

Within an hour, Nate had fashioned a plastic barrier at the demarcation line that he had scratched on the floor. He stapled the plastic sheeting at the top, bottom, and both sides thankfully the stapler was industrial grade and the staples were heavy gage allowing them to penetrate the hard concrete. He then sealed the edges with tape creating a plastic drape that would hopefully keep the majority of radioactive air on the other side. This would allow them access to both rooms outside the door as long as they didn't linger for hours out there. The broom closet on the one side would serve as a bathroom, and the opposite room, which contained the gurneys and chairs that could be of use with a little creativity, was now available to them.

Over the next few days, Jeannette and Nate took everything they could use from the spare room. They made a double bed by taking the wheels off the gurneys and fastening them together with tape. The extra chairs were used to create a small sitting area next to the bed, where they could sit and talk or relax. The bathroom wasn't even as bad as it had seemed. The big plastic sink actually had a trickle of water that flowed when the knobs were turned. There was no water pressure, but the pump must have been gravity fed or the pipes were long enough to contain a small supply of water. Jeannette didn't think the water was safe to drink, but with a little effort it could be used to wash away their human waste. Nate had even constructed an ugly-looking but serviceable toilet seat out of the wooden planks from the shelving. They had to jump up to get on the boards and had to watch for splinters, but it worked. The worst part turned out to be coming up with sources of toilet paper. But between a few rags Jeannette made from the lab coats and the reams of office paper, they would be in good shape for the near future. All of the ingenuity they had to use to come up with everyday items was a great way to kill time. It wasn't exactly a typical happy little home, but they were making the best of a very bad situation. Sweeping their emotions under the rug had become an important everyday chore, just like finding new ways to create creature comforts from the few items they had in the shelter. Everyone developed their own coping mechanisms; this was no different.

6

SIMON

Simon Huff had lived in rural Connecticut for the last twenty years. His whole life had revolved around his family, which included his wife, Miranda, and their four children. The second most important thing in Simon's life was his church, a small brick building a suburban block away from his own house in Middlebrook, Connecticut. Finding faith had saved him twenty years earlier, rescuing him from a path of self-destruction and selfishness. The church had been an integral part of Simon's resurrection from the depths of filth, and his family had completed his transformation to the light. Now, twenty years later, Simon could be proud of the man he had become.

Reverend Kasper had warned him that the end of days was near. In fact, it had been Reverend Kasper who had told Simon to prepare for the rapture. Simon remembered the sermon that had touched his heart, as if the pastor had meant it only for him. It inspired him so deeply that he dug a shelter in his backyard and purchased a small armory. Even as his neighbors had laughed and mocked him while he tore up the ground with the rented yellow backhoe, he had thought about that sermon. Reverend Kasper had been standing behind the altar wearing his crimson frock, and he spoke the words that had spurred Simon to action:

My children, the rapture is at our doorstep. Too long have we soiled the very name of God, too long has evil been allowed to mingle among us, too long have we stood idly by while the doubters and sinners have cast judgment. This world that God has created with beauty has been crumbling, and these sinners have hastened that crumbling. The signs are here; it is time to prepare for his coming, for his return. Those who have judged will feel his judgment, those who have doubted will doubt no more, and those who have sinned and scarred his earth will suffer his vengeance!"

Simon could recite the sermon word for word; it had been on constant playback in his mind and heart. He thought about it as the bombs fell, and he thought about it now as he lay in safety seventeen feet under the dirt. No one was laughing at him now—no gawking neighbors to cast their meaningless judgment. *It's awfully hard to laugh when you're dead,* Simon thought with humor. Revered Kasper was probably even dead now; Simon would find a way to honor the man who had motivated him to survive.

It had taken Simon and his family seven months to build the bunker: seven months of back-breaking labor for Simon and his two sons. His wife and daughters had even contributed by stocking and decorating the underground sanctuary. It hadn't been an easy job stockpiling enough food and water to sustain six people for a period of months if need be.

He looked up at the hardened soil ceiling above his head. The shelter smelled worse than death. Six people crammed into this dark, dank, tomb no bigger than a large swimming pool—with no running water and no place to bathe. Six people breathing each other's air, choking on the human stink for what had seemed like a decade. The air was thick and steamy; it smelled of mildew, mold, and an earthy, human odor that reminded Simon of rotten meat. He couldn't take this much longer. The kids were mostly grown. The youngest, Simon's daughter Abigail, was twelve. That made things a bit easier; what a nightmare it would have been to be stuck in this pit when the children were youngsters. Simon thought about the dangers almost certainly existed outside the shelter, dangers that were likely far worse than the foul air. He had an ideal imagination for this sort of thing: looters, murderers, and rapists with no law to keep them in check. Reverend Kasper had warned about the fall of society. He had spoken of people who would grow desperate with no moral fiber, no faith in God, and no conscience...people who would do hideous things to survive or simply just take advantage of the weak for their own entertainment. That was why Simon had invested in the armory at the far side of the shelter. He had surprised even himself with the tools one could acquire on the Internet or at the local hunting outfitter.

When Simon deemed it safe outside, his family would eventually leave the shelter. He wouldn't hesitate to kill if his family was threatened. Whatever had been left crawling around out there would be heathen anyway, not worth a moment's deliberation over whether they deserved to live or die. Simon knew their type: the kind of folks who would sell their souls or rob their own mothers for a sip of whiskey. Was it a sin to kill? In Simon's mind, God had already shown them their judgment; he would just be finishing what God had already begun. This work could be as important as rearing children or attending church.

Perhaps this had been God's plan to prepare him for a holy war against the infidels.

Simon smiled in the dark; his children would be warriors in the crusade to help God rid the world of the vermin that had survived the fire. He would use charm and intellect to rebuild the flock; he had always possessed a talent for political persuasion, and if that persuasion didn't work he could always fall back on force. Numbers would count for something in this new wasteland—numbers and firepower. If half the world or more had already perished, then a gang of six healthy souls, six well-armed healthy souls, would be a force to be reckoned with. A combination of strength and intelligence would be the way forward, and Simon had always believed that to deal with flies you would need honey as well as a flyswatter. It was better to have them come to you than to chase them around the room. Simon's children weren't soldiers, but they could learn. The two eldest, Thomas and Jed, were strong and willing, while the girls, Abigail and Katherine, while young and naïve, were enthusiastic. The girls would need to be watched carefully. Abigail was twelve, but Katherine was fifteen and slowly becoming a young woman. The sickness that was outside would be drawn to them like dogs to a bone; they would likely be the targets of any demented mind that they would come across.

Simon sighed and twisted in his blanket; he hadn't found sleep since the radio had cautioned him that the bombs were coming. He didn't know how long his family should remain buried in the backyard; they could be still receiving doses of radiation, which he knew nothing about. He would wait for a sign before venturing up to the surface. The attack had been very intense; at times he had wondered if the bunker could sustain the shaking that had followed. What would be left up there was anyone's guess.

Simon drifted in and out of sleep, and soon he was enveloped in a dream.

He was back in that flophouse as a much younger man. He sat on a urine-drenched couch cooking a sizzling amber liquid on a spoon, feeling his breath escaping slowly in a cold shiver of want. Simon could sense himself sinking into the torn tweed couch as each arm was tied off with a tourniquet. The walls were stained black and brown, and the air stank of fecal matter and butane. The two hands that had been tying the tourniquets slid out of sight between the plaid, foul-smelling couch cushions. He looked down at the tourniquets, which were meaty, bleeding intestines dripping with yellow bile. Simon couldn't move, and he wasn't sure he wanted to. The hands returned at the end of long arms that seemed to be track-marked and bruised skin stretched over bone. Four hands in all waved in front of his face, each taunting him with a fat syringe full of the maple-syrup-colored liquid. The syringes all had blinking green neon lights on the side that spelled out the word GOD. Simon tried to scream as the needles punched holes into the crooks of his arms. The plungers on the syringes depressed on their own and the tourniquets popped off with a sickening wet snap, like a locker room bully whipping a wet towel. He felt the rush as the narcotic shot throughout his veins and followed their spiraling road map to his heart. A warm, tingling sensation began in his balls and flowered outward to his feet, making him convulse in ecstasy. Simon could hear hymns all around him; it was the pipe organ from his small church. The couch had become a hard, wooden pew shiny with lacquer. He sat and listened, alone and much older.

He woke in a pool of his own clammy sweat; his boxer shorts were wet with something else. Simon felt around in the dark for the cloth pouch that hung from the side of his cot. His hand soon found the tattered, leather-bound Bible. With his other hand he found a pen flashlight that he had stashed for just this purpose. The Bible was well-worn with dog-eared pages and smudges where the oil from his fingers had built up. The binding had been broken, and the stitching was strained from holding the pages to the spine. Simon thought back to an idiom his mother had repeated over and over: "A Bible that is falling apart often belongs to a soul who isn't." He believed that now more than ever—the world had fallen apart, yet Simon felt confident, even reinvigorated.

He shone his light the best he could, wedging the penlight between his front teeth and wrapping his lips around the cylindrical tube. Simon flipped straight to the back of the Bible, Revelation—it had always been his favorite, even before the bombs had fallen. He had read it many times since that morning: the seven signs and their corresponding seals, John the revelator and his warnings, saints, sinners, horses, trumpets, and locusts. It all had been foretold with such imagery, and to think he would see it all.

Morning must have come while Simon had been reading, because the most reliable clock in the shelter, his wife's circadian rhythm, had chimed. She rolled over on her cot, which was located about three feet from Simon's own. He could barely see her in the weak light thrown off by the small flashlight. Miranda was a stocky, meek woman whose self-esteem as much as anything else had encouraged Simon's feeling of superiority. Miranda had a round cherubic face and short black hair that she kept tied back tightly in a bun. She looked over at Simon with her eyes reflecting in the light. "Did you sleep at all, my dear?"

Even after twenty years of marriage, she remained sheepish in Simon's presence.

"I'm fine," Simon snapped, not wanting to have to explain why he hadn't slept yet again. "Wake the children," he ordered her sternly. "I have something to discuss with them." He swung his feet over the side of the cot, his bones popping as he stood. He walked over to the Coleman lantern that had been hanging from one of the beams he had used to buttress the shelter. He struck a match and lit the lantern, which filled the dirt-walled room with orange light.

Simon's four children sat around him at the table, hazy from sleep. "As you know the rapture has come," Simon said to them. "It is the end of days that your mother and I have been preaching to you about. We have explained the scripture to all of you at one time or another. Now the end could come in days, or it could come in years, but we are certain that the time has begun. The divine wheels are turning. This world is finite; it always has been, but at least now we can see the finish line." He searched the faces in front of him, wanting to be positive he had thoroughly grabbed their attention. "We must prepare ourselves for the violence that will surely follow. The heathen that have survived this nuclear storm will behave as animals. They will scramble and crawl, scratch and claw, rape and murder without fear of consequence or repercussion. Think of this shelter as the mighty Ark, and think of yourselves as Noahs. It may be the end, but God does not want us to suffer. He has shown us the way, but there are many obstacles to come before he blesses us with our call to his Kingdom. Hell has come to this land, and Satan's agents of evil are on the prowl. We can no longer rely on prayer alone, for this too must be God's will. We will earn our places at his side." Simon's eyes were unyielding; he hoped to scare his teenagers into order and obedience—it had worked before. Fear, in Simon's opinion, was often the most effective motivator. "We will brace for God's war to come to our doorstep. There is no magic in this world that will spare us from this atrocity." He wanted to sound like George C. Scott firing up the troops in the movie *Patton*. "I want every one of you to be proficient with firearms. Even you girls. No mercy will be shown to you, and you shall grant none. In fact, you may be the most desired prey." Simon locked eyes with his youngest, Abigail. He wanted to be sure that she knew he meant her. "We will train every single day that we are confined to this pit. Then, when it is safe outside, we will train there. You will learn to kill, because they will not hesitate to kill you...or do worse to you girls."

The children knew not to speak while their father was giving instruction. Doing just that had ended badly for them on more than one occasion. Simon had no qualms about showing them what a belt was good for aside from holding up pants. He considered himself a tireless worker when it came to the molding of young minds.

By the time Simon had finished giving his missive, it was time for breakfast. The children were grateful to be free from the grip of their father's eyes. Miranda had begun cooking powdered eggs and rehydrated bacon on the propane burner that was the shelter's stove and means of heat. It was something of a luxury to have meat without refrigeration, but Simon had been smart—he had gone to every army surplus store in the area and bought up all the dehydrated meat and jerky he could afford. The family would need lots of protein to remain strong while waiting for the fallout to clear. Eating had turned out to be a tremendous chore, not because of stress or the bland, preserved quality of the food, but because the shelter stank to high heaven. The smell permeated into everything on their plates; it would taint even the best meals Miranda could cook. The smell of excrement was bad, but the worst thing was the ammonia coming from their urine fermenting in the toilet hole. Simon had dug a latrine pit in the floor of the far end of the armory, beyond the family's sleeping area. They had been using lime to dilute the stench, one scoop after each use, but the lime was running out. They had to reduce the amount they used, Simon rationed the lime down to one scoop every six days. That would mean a week's worth of shit and piss sat untreated at a time.

The family had finished eating, and Simon had ushered them into the armory, which was really a long, dirt-walled extension of the main shelter. Simon had found the design for the shelter on the Internet. It was similar to what many people in England had built in their backyards during the blitz of World War II. The shelter had one main room with dirt floors and patchy drywall—Simon hadn't ever finished hanging all the drywall—and a solid dirt ceiling buttressed with wooden beams holding back a couple thousand pounds of soil, roots, plywood dividers, and loose traprock. Fine-mesh chicken wire had been rolled across the ceiling as a retaining screen to prevent loose clumps of dirt from dropping on their heads. It wasn't airtight, which was a good thing, because he hadn't been able to afford an automated ventilation system. Simon had built vent pipes at all four corners with air filters made from charcoal fish tank water filters.

The armory, which was about the size of a large walk-in closet, consisted of four gun racks, two mounted on each wall. The racks were filled with a variety of small arms, mostly hunting rifles, shotguns, and a selection of handguns. The crown jewels of Simon's cache were two mail-ordered Bushmaster AR-15 assault rifles. The AR-15s were semiautomatic, but they could be converted to fully automatic with the right conversion kit, which Simon hadn't had time to acquire. He wanted to avoid any serious legal scrutiny, and fully automatic firearms of that type had been outlawed in Connecticut. If he had ordered the conversion kits, it would have thrown a red flag up on the Internet. Simon had already been concerned that simply ordering the rifles had put his name in a special book that Big Brother maintained on so-called radicals. He knew that his civil liberties had been eroding slowly over the years, and he wasn't about to give up any more freedom.

Simon stood at the racks, matching guns to the children based on size, weight, and recoil. The lighter weapons with less kick were passed to the girls, and the heavier weapons, including one of the Bushmasters, were given to the boys.

By the end of the day, he had taught the children to load, sight, and clean their weapons. He had them squeeze the triggers of the unloaded guns, explaining the importance of breathing and squeezing as opposed to jerking the trigger.

"In the army or at the police academies, they would tell you to make sure of your target before you pull the trigger. That you can't take back a bullet after it's left the barrel." Simon locked eyes with his children. "I'm here to tell you all that in this Godforsaken world, that's bullshit. I want you to shoot first and ask questions later; we don't have the luxury of making sure a stranger is a threat before we fire. You should assume anyone who is trespassing or approaching you means harm...and I want you to shoot to kill. Nothing is more dangerous than a wounded animal." Simon pulled his oldest boy, the twenty-year-old Jed, in front of him. "A kill shot is any shot that hits the head," he put his hand on Jed's face; "the torso," he moved his hand from Jed's head across his chest down to his stomach, pausing to point out the lungs, heart, and liver; "and the throat, which is a good place to aim, especially if you are in close quarters." Simon cupped his hand over Jed's throat, and a frightened look emerged on Jed's face.

The day had been a roaring success; Simon's children could now defend the shelter and protect themselves aboveground if necessary. His family was evolving; they were learning to survive and thrive among the many obstacles that God would test them with. For the first night since the nukes, Simon slept without a stir.

7

PRUSSIAN BLUE

After three weeks in the basement of the blood draw facility, Nate and Jeannette had accepted and even grown accustomed to their situation. Every day had become a routine, just like before the missiles had done their damage; the routine had simply morphed from work and home life to survival and searching for constructive ways to kill each day. They had passed the time playing cards, which Nate had made from cardboard boxes neatly cut for size and illustrated with number and suit. He had even used his passable artistic skills to draw face cards with kings and queens that vaguely resembled Jeannette and himself. Jeannette had also used her time creatively, writing in a journal that detailed each day of their lives in the shelter and what had forced them there. Nate had become quite handy at designing and building useful items from the sparse supplies within the shelter and the adjoining rooms. He had fabricated two suits from plastic sheeting and duct tape that would hopefully keep the majority of radioactive particles from reaching their bodies when they eventually went outside. He had also constructed a chandelier of flashlights, which he hung in the center of the room. Although Jeannette's contributions were more for entertainment and to improve their environment than for function, she too had been busy. She had used the box of painting supplies to paint a full landscape mural on one wall. It showed a field with a pond, a few scraggly trees, and some cows. It was the kind of mural you might find in a grammar school or rural community center, but it added color to the drab and lifeless walls that had felt like they were closing in.

In addition to their arts and crafts projects, Nate and Jeannette were in a more stable place emotionally. The first week in the shelter had been dominated by grief and denial, but even those feelings were difficult to hold on to when they weren't even sure what they were grieving for. The lack of information and separation from the real world had left them in a kind of melancholy limbo, where crying for the dead seemed false because they had no news of who had survived or who hadn't. By the second week, there were still moments of mourning, mostly at night when the lights were turned off and the silence wrapped its knuckles around their necks. Nate felt imprisoned deep inside some chamber in his own mind, fighting to hold onto reality and be the rock that Jeannette could cling to. During those periods of silence, something fundamental changed in Nate—he would lie awake at night listening to Jeannette weeping softly and promise himself that he would be the one to hold it all together for both of their sakes. The anxiety, panic, and paranoia had melted away and been replaced by a fierce loyalty and determination to make this world an acceptable place for her. He soon began to mold his emotional state around Jeannette's mood: if she needed a shoulder to cry on, Nate would provide it. If she wanted to be alone, Nate would find a task in some corner of the room away from her to distract his attention. Each morning he would scan Jeannette for any sign of pain just as he would scan the room for any sign of radiation. Jeannette was strong—she didn't necessarily need Nate's doting, endless consolation—but she was also smart enough to know that he had needed to be the caregiver and that if he spent too much time focused on himself the facade of strength would crumble. It was in this way that they had saved each other, as neither would have made it through those first few weeks alone.

As the days passed, their affection for one another grew. They had become emotionally dependent on each other. The physical aspects of their relationship lagged behind, but human need and proximity soon trumped any reservations they had. Nate believed that their predicament couldn't be the only reason for love, that whatever blossomed must occur naturally and not simply because he may be the last man on earth.

Nate could feel sleep leaving his body and had the feeling he was being watched. He opened his eyes to see that Jeannette had already turned on the flashlight chandelier, lighting the room. She had returned to bed and had been lying there watching him sleep. She slid closer to him and kissed him deeply. It was not their first kiss. In fact, they had danced around awkward, clumsy make-out sessions like infatuated teenagers. Nate pulled away and looked into her eyes for a moment.

"Nate, why do you always pull away every time I try to show you some affection?" Jeannette said, giving Nate a frustrated look.

"I don't know, Jeannette, I just feel strange," Nate said, doing his best to shake off his morning fog.

"Strange how?" She had Nate cornered, and even though this conversation had been building for days, Nate wanted to avoid it entirely.

"I don't know; I guess I feel like I'm taking advantage of you." He couldn't quite find the words that best described how he felt. "I feel like you aren't *choosing* me, I'm just your only option. If we were to get together, I'd want it to be something that would have happened without all of this." He sat up and gestured with his arms to indicate he meant the shelter around them.

"Nate, that's fucking stupid," she said with a small laugh. "I'm an adult; don't you think I know what I'm doing? Or is it that you think you're so irresistible that simply being alone in a fallout shelter is enough to get you laid?" She chuckled again.

"That's not it; I'm..." He didn't have an answer that wouldn't sound too self-deprecating, and the last thing he wanted was to sound like he was feeling sorry for himself.

"How do you know this wouldn't have happened anyway?" she asked with a sober expression. "Nate, I like you for you; it wouldn't matter if the world were the same as it was before the bombs."

Unable to think of any more excuses, Nate finally just made the decision to go with it. He placed his hands on her cheeks and leaned in, kissing her softly. The kissing expanded into heavy petting. They both remained fully clothed, as the topic of sex had come up before. The biggest obstacle to a consummation of their relationship was the lack of adequate birth control in the shelter. Jeannette had been deathly afraid of becoming pregnant, and the thought of bringing a child into this doomed world was enough birth control for both of them. The question, though, was whether that fear could ward off temptation long enough for it to be safe outside. Historically, the threat of conception had never been an adequate deterrent to animal lust. For now, the duo was happy to act like hormonally challenged adolescents and fill their days with cutesy flirtations and hour-long face-sucking sessions.

A constant, friendly debate between Nate and Jeannette had been building to a crescendo. The question was about the time at which it would finally be safe enough to leave their nest and take advantage of the remainder of the building, including the ground floor. Nate felt that prudence and a conservative timetable would be best. He felt there was no need to push it when it concerned their health. There would be nothing to lose by waiting a little longer. Jeannette argued that it would never be completely safe and that they would soon need supplies, information, and the freedom to move around more than a few steps in any direction. She was being affected more by the cabin fever than Nate and was ready to take the risk if it meant having windows to look outside and the rooms above to move around in. They had eventually reached a compromise that they would carefully walk upstairs, checking the radiation levels as they went, in two days. The plan was to scavenge the upstairs for any supplies, get an idea of how stable it looked, check if the windows and doors were intact, and retreat to the shelter at the first sign of danger or high radiation levels.

That night was one of the nights Nate had come to dread. Jeannette had spent the night dwelling on the past and in and out of sobbing fits. It had all begun when she started thinking about all the animal species that would now be extinct because of the nuclear war. Nate had tried to play the optimist, explaining to her that places like South America and Africa should have been spared any major damage. The only way Nate knew to console her was to tell a story from his youth, something about himself that would show vulnerability.

"My father was an anxious man, probably a high-functioning schizophrenic "He took me to this cabin he rented in upstate New York every deer season," Nate said, sitting on the floor and leaning against the wall next to Jeannette. He still hadn't had the guts to tell her about his own mental health issues. Even after their time together in the bunker Nate was still self-conscious, afraid he'd say or do something wrong. A neurotic like him couldn't change overnight.

"So I'm upset about all these beautiful creatures being wiped off the face of the earth, and you want to tell me a story about deer hunting," Jeannette said, wiping the tears from her cheeks with the back of her wrist.

"Just bear with me...please?" Nate said.

"OK, go on."

"My father and I drove up one afternoon. It was a Friday, and we left Connecticut as soon as I got home from school. I was probably twelve or thirteen years old—pretty young, but old enough to know that my old man was one weird dude and that all dads weren't like him. The drive was mostly silent; my dad wasn't much of a talker even when he was feeling normal. He was so introverted...always in deep thought."

"Sounds like someone I know," said Jeannette with a slight brightness painted on her brow.

"Yeah, I get some of that from him." Nate was just glad to see her mood improving. "We had hardly said anything to each other, no father-son bonding or happy camaraderie. About an hour into the drive, my dad starts to get really nervous. He is sure that the car behind us is following him. That it's some government vehicle that has been sent out to track him down. I should mention that he always had some conspiracy theory that people from some secret agency were watching him and wanted to bug our phone or whatever they do. So anyway, we drove along, and the whole time he had one eye on the road and one eye on the rearview mirror. He became so convinced he had a tail that he started swerving from lane to lane trying to lose the car behind us. It was a black sedan, like one of those old cop cars." Nate stopped, trying to think of the model of car he was talking about.

"Crown Victoria," Jeannette said, interrupting Nate's thought process.

"Yeah, Crown Vic, right. Anyway, it didn't change lanes but stayed behind us for at least a half an hour. He even had me questioning whether it was someone chasing us or spying on us. He almost killed us both pulling over to the side of the road. When the car passed, it was some eighty-year-old purple-haired lady who could barely see over the steering wheel. She was probably following us because it was easier to see our car than to see the lines on the road. My dad was so freaked out that we booked a room in the closest motel and spent the weekend eating pizza and watching football. The whole time we were in that motel room, my dad sat by the window looking out into the parking lot." Nate finished his story and looked down at Jeannette, who had snuggled up and laid her head in his lap.

"So the moral of the story is that your dad was crazy and so am I?" she asked, with enough humor to keep from insulting Nate.

"No, the moral of the story is that things aren't always what they appear to be. Sometimes your mind can make things into a whole swirling mess when it really isn't as bad as it seems. We know that the bombs fell from the shaking ground and the fluctuation in the radiation levels, but we don't know that it's a nuclear wasteland outside. We don't know that all of those species are dead, and we don't even know that a whole bunch of humans are dead. Nature is very resilient," Nate said.

Jeannette gave Nate a puzzled look. "Have you ever heard the Khrushchev quote that in the aftermath of a nuclear war the living will envy the dead?" she asked morosely.

"Yes, I've heard that," Nate answered.

"I just hope that's not true." Tears were welling up in Jeannette's eyes again.

Nate wasn't entirely sure how to respond. He knew what she meant and why she felt the way she did, and he actually agreed with her to some extent, but what good did it do to let each other crumble under mounting dread? That was what Nate's whole life had been until now and he was sick of it. There weren't a whole lot of choices: either they had to make the best of what they had or they could curl up and die. The only positive of the latter would be that they would be together. He would need to remain pragmatic about the situation until Jeannette could join him in reality.

Two days later, Nate and Jeannette pulled the plastic coveralls over their clothes. The plastic suits were tight-fitting and hot, wicking in body heat and moisture. Nate duct taped their sleeves and ankles and pulled on the plastic hoods that he had attached to the back just below the neck. The opening in the face was the only area where skin would be exposed to the outside air. They each put on the dust masks they had found with the painting supplies, which would cover their mouths and noses, hopefully filtering out any large particles. They also had rubber dishwashing gloves, which had been stashed in the room with the sink they'd been using as a toilet. Nate had even made little plastic booties to fit over their shoes that could be taped to the cuff at the leg. After they had finished suiting up, they stood back and admired each other.

"You look like a Russian cosmonaut about to be launched into orbit," Jeannette said with a muffled giggle through her dust mask.

"Well, at least we won't be dragging a shit ton of radioactive molecules back down to our home," Nate answered coldly, killing the humor. Nate picked up his smartphone—which was useful only as a Geiger counter—and put a clip of ammo in the Glock nine. He slid the top of the gun back with a click, pulling a round into the chamber, and slipped the handgun into the suit's plastic waistband.

"Why are you bringing that?" Jeannette asked in a disapproving tone.

"Because we can't be sure that a squatter or a looter didn't break in and isn't hanging out upstairs," Nate answered.

Jeannette seemed satisfied with Nate's justification for the handgun and picked up the duffel bag, which they had emptied out to fill with anything useful they might find upstairs.

They were both excited to be leaving the confines of the room they had been cooped up in for three weeks. Nate led the way, shining a flashlight ahead of them. He opened the door and walked toward the plastic barrier that had separated the usable area from the area they had deemed unsafe. Nate popped the staples from one side, creating a gap big enough for them to slip through yet small enough that it wouldn't be too hard for them to close off upon returning. He held the Geiger counter in front of him as he walked and slipped through the plastic. Jeannette was close behind carrying another flashlight, the duffel slung over her shoulder.

The hallway was pitch black, and plaster dust still hung in the air eerily like a fog. The ground was littered with small pebbles of plaster and the light fixture that had fallen during the nuclear attack. It felt like the surface of the moon: foreign and dark. Nate half expected a serial killer to pop out and slash them like something from a horror movie. It was cold, and Nate smelled a musty, metallic smell even through his dust mask.

"Hold this," Nate said, handing the smartphone to Jeannette. "We're holding at 1.5 rads; if that alarm starts buzzing, let me know." He then pulled the handgun from his waistband and climbed the stairs, holding the light in one hand and the gun in the other. Jeannette was a few steps behind, carefully trying to maintain her balance without using the handrail. Nate stood on the top step, placed the flashlight under his armpit, and twisted the brass doorknob. At first, the door wouldn't budge. Nate almost lost his balance and fell back into Jeannette, which would have sent them both careening down the steps. Nate pictured himself piled up on top of a badly injured Jeannette on the dark landing at the bottom of the steps. His hands were slimy with sweat inside the rubber gloves, which only added to the feeling that he had been using someone else's hands to turn the knob. Nate remembered the boxes full of gallon jugs of cleaner he had pulled against the door on his way down to the shelter. He lowered his shoulder and simultaneously turned the knob and rammed into the door with as much strength and leverage he could garner. The door slid open about a foot—not enough to slide through, but enough to give him a foothold for balance and end his teetering act on the top step. Nate repeated the process, ramming the door with his shoulder and pushing his weight forward using the foot of floor space as leverage. The boxes tumbled forward with a tremendous crash as Nate's momentum carried him stumbling into the storeroom. Nate clenched, bracing for impact with the floor, and inadvertently pulled the trigger on the pistol as he landed. Thankfully the safety was engaged and the gun simply clicked as the trigger hit the metal mechanism that blocked the hammer.

Nate stood up in the storeroom, his feet aboveground for the first time in more than three weeks. He looked back at Jeannette, whose eyes told Nate that she had been fighting back laughter as she watched him struggle with the door and his own balance. Other than the toppled boxes, the storeroom looked identical to how Nate had left it. They waded through the fallen boxes to the end of the storeroom; Nate held his breath, hoping they wouldn't end up opening the door to a disaster movie. He pushed the door open, entering the blood draw area. Nate was relieved to see that it appeared empty and undamaged.

Daylight flooded in from a cracked window on the far side of the room. It wasn't sunlight, but it gave the room enough of a glow to steal away the darkness. Everything seemed orderly, and Nate allowed himself to hope for a moment that perhaps the attack hadn't been as awful as it had seemed. Maybe the fact that they had been in the cellar during the attack had magnified the shockwaves of very distant blasts. It would be possible (although unlikely) that the intense vibrations had traveled underground and had simply reverberated back and forth off the concrete walls like an echo in an underground cavern. Of course, Nate wasn't used to wishful thinking, and the pessimist in him quickly took over. He strolled over to the cracked window with Jeannette just behind him. He pulled the ripcord on the brown slotted plastic blinds. All hope quickly dissipated like air forced out of a squeezed accordion. Nate heard Jeannette gasp; even through her dust mask the sound matched the feeling in his own mind. Nate turned and saw that her hands were over her mouth. She was choking in a sob and the tears were starting to stream down her face. Nate could feel his own eyes welling up with grief. He turned his gaze back to the window, which was spider-webbed with cracks.

The view outside was ghastly, almost surreal. From the slightly elevated window, the landscape resembled a long-dead swamp covered with a dusting of fluffy, off-white snow. There were no leaves on any of the trees; even the evergreens that always kept their needles through the winter were barren. Half of the trees were broken off or devoid of limbs; it looked like a hurricane had flattened the small wooded valley. Everything was coated with a gray and white ash that seemed to stick like dirty confectioner's sugar. A low fog hung two or three feet above the ground as if someone had turned on a giant smoke machine. The fog only added to the desolate atmosphere. Plumes of thick, black smoke wafted upward like tiger stripes across the horizon. The color of the sky was purplish gray, as if a monstrous thunderhead had enveloped the sun and covered the earth, ready to dump a flood on the diseased land. Unlike a thunderhead, the cloud cover wasn't approaching or moving away...it was everywhere. The light that did penetrate was strange and lacked the feeling of warmth that the sun had always supplied. Nate could see scattered dead birds, some above the ash, some just below it, with a wing or a few feathers breaking through the small piles of ash. It could have been the health care worker in him, but the word that kept coming into his mind was *infection*. Everything looked infected, infected with a blight of ash and soot.

"What's the rad count?" Nate asked Jeannette softly, the words cracking and chirping from his mouth.

She looked down at the device in her hand. "It says 3.5 rads per hour." Jeannette looked jaundiced, and Nate wondered if she might vomit. She was shaking, and the hand that held the Geiger counter trembled steadily as she held it out to him.

"OK, we need to hurry up. We've wasted enough time here and prolonged exposure wouldn't be safe," Nate said as he started to scope out the room for anything they could use in the shelter. What he really wanted to do was hold Jeannette, hold her until the memory of the outside world faded from his mind, but he was right, they needed to get a move on. They took as many things as they could carry: extra batteries, staples, a few odd tools, lab coats, instant coffee, and a jug of hand soap. Jeannette found the jackpot: a large cardboard box full of toilet paper. They unpacked the box of toilet paper and put it into the duffel bag along with Nate's haul. He had noticed that the water cooler in the waiting room had a full ten-gallon jug of spring water on it. He went over and heaved it off the plastic frame. From the waiting room, Nate could see the foyer and the two automatic sliding doors that led outside. Both doors had large mazes of cracks in the safety glass, where rocks, bricks, or debris had been either tossed against them by the shockwave or by human hands. The door looked to be locked and unbreached; a drift of ash about a foot deep had blown against the door, where it sat undisturbed. Nate could see out to the parking lot, which was now a cracked canyon of asphalt. A small structure across the street that had been a machine shop was partially collapsed and missing a large portion of its roof. The whole area looked like it had been trampled by a herd of gargantuan elephants.

Nate returned to Jeannette, lugging the heavy water jug in both hands. He had stashed the flashlight and the gun in his waistband. A look between the two was all the communication they needed to know that it was time to hurry their collective asses back down to the dungeon.

After returning to the shelter, shedding their protective body condoms, and restapling the plastic barrier, Nat and Jeannette went to work stowing the items they had gathered upstairs. When they had finished, they sat down at the small table in the kitchen area to talk. It had been shocking and depressing, but not entirely unexpected, to see the wreckage of the exterior world. The small view that had tortured them was only a tiny glimpse of the overall devastation. Both knew that the areas even closer to the ground burst bombs would be far worse. "If it's that bad here, and this area didn't even take a direct hit, I can't even fathom what the rest of the country looks like," Jeannette said solemnly. She had been the first to speak and break the tension burning their insides. "Where do you think the closest target was?" Jeannette looked at Nate like he would give her some relief from the weight they both felt.

Nate took a minute to think. He was far from an expert on Cold War Soviet missile targets or whether those Cold War-era targets were even still viable. "I'm sure the sub base in Groton was one of the military targets, the Coast Guard Academy is there as well, so it's like two birds with one stone. That doesn't even take into account General Dynamics, Electric Boat, and the other installations there and in New London. They build the Sea Wolf nuclear subs, which would be considered a first-strike weapon. It's the most appealing target in Connecticut. That would be about fifty miles from us." He stopped trying to remember the other likely targets, which he had once checked out on the Internet. "New York City, of course, which is a civilian target as well as financial and industrial, that's about seventy miles from us. Possibly Hartford and New Haven could be civilian targets—they are less than thirty miles away, but then again they aren't exactly high-profile cities." Nate thought about the flash of light he had seen before retreating to the shelter that morning and how much time could have elapsed. He had never been good at those time and distance word problems. It was also possible that the initial blast had been an airburst nuke blown in the upper atmosphere for the EMP effect, which knocked out the grid.

"But Nate, those places are all so far from here. The damage here was so severe, I just can't..." Jeannette's voice trailed off into a sob.

"So..." Nate ignored the sob, hoping that she would get lost in conversation rather than misery.

"So, the way the environment looked outside, it appeared as though..." Jeannette couldn't get through a sentence without breaking into tears. "It seems like a bomb must've landed close—maybe only a few miles from here?" She closed her eyes and was silent. Nate reached for her and she brushed him away.

"That's what I was talking about when I said the cumulative effect of the bombs. If a shitload of megatons fell on New York, Philly, Boston, hell, all the way down the East Coast, that radiation would be carried on the jetstream through our area. That's a lot of fallout. We'd have seen thousands of rads per hour here at the peak." Nate certainly wasn't a nuclear physicist or an expert on fallout, for Christ's sake he hadn't didn't even have any real knowledge about weather patterns. "The only thing I really know is that if a bomb fell within a few miles of here, we'd be dead. That doesn't even take into account the size of these explosions; we aren't talking about the bombs that ended World War II. We're talking about weapons that are light years more powerful than anything that has ever been used before. Everything that hit south and west of us will be carried here... all that ash outside, which could have been from as far away as Detroit or from the missile bases in the Midwest." As soon as the words left Nate's mouth, he regretted them. He had been riffing and wasn't thinking about Jeannette's family or where she had grown up. Her face turned an ugly shade of red, and for a moment Nate wasn't sure if she was going to burst into more tears or punch him in the face. "Jeannette, I'm so sorry; I wasn't thinking." She put her hands to her face.

"No, Nate, you're right. That's a lot of radiation. It will be a miracle if anything survives." Jeannette put her hands back up to her face and, with her elbows on the table, rocked mechanically back and forth. She stayed this way for what felt like an eternity to Nate, he tried to comfort her, to hold her, hoping it would be cathartic for both of them. Each time he went to her, however, she pushed him away, and Nate could sense that he was only making matters worse.

Jeannette slowly slid her hands down her face, exposing her bloodshot eyes. She exhaled slowly, and when she spoke she had completely changed the subject—a trick Nate had always used to divert the anxiety and depression away from the issue bearing down. "Nate, what do you think you'll miss the most from the world, from civilization?" Jeannette was studying Nate's face, but it seemed like more than just curiosity; it seemed like this might be some kind of test.

"You mean besides people?" he asked, searching his mind for an answer that didn't sound shallow.

"Yeah, besides the people you cared for," Jeannette replied quickly, not allowing Nate a moment to procrastinate.

"Hmmm." Nate stroked his chin, feigning a look of intelligence. "Honestly, I'll miss the Boston Red Sox and Fenway Park; I'll miss fishing on opening day weekend, the one day I loved in April. I'll also miss sushi and of course my shitty little car, which has probably fallen into the abyss in the parking lot." Nate could feel the mood in the room lighten considerably; he even thought he saw a small, sly smile. Everything had been all doom and gloom, but that was broken by the playful sentimentality of the question. "So, Miss Inquisitive, what creature comforts are you going to miss the most?"

"Let's see...I'll miss Starbucks Coffee. I know it's expensive, but it's damn good coffee. I'll miss going to the movies on the opening night of some must-see pop culture phenomenon. I'll miss my bathtub. It was such a great tub...deep, and I could get the water really hot. Sometimes I would lie there for hours, just soaking..." Jeannette jokingly mimicked Nate, stroking her own chin.

"Tell me more about this bathtub. And don't leave out any details, especially the part about your lack of clothing." Nate showed Jeannette a serious face that only looked serious from the outside; inside he was laughing, and he could tell she was too.

"Nate, I think you're being fresh," she said with a sensuous smile that caused a great disturbance in the force...the force that resided somewhere below Nate's belt buckle. "I'm going to miss being able to fly off to the Caribbean on a whim, or hop on a plane and fly out west to see my..." Jeannette couldn't finish. Sheer heartbreak had painted itself on her face again, returning like a cancer that had been in remission, only to rear its ugly head stronger and more malignant than before. Nate wished he had some kind of magic emotional chemotherapy, something he could say or do to make it all better, but the only thing that would help her was time. The one thing they had a wealth of was time. "I mean—" she tried to speak, only to have her head return to her hands. She appeared to be weeping soundlessly. Nate moved his chair next to her and placed a hand on the back of her head, massaging her scalp soothingly.

"Jeannette, sweetheart, you have to stop doing this to yourself." Nate was finding it easier and easier to slide into his consoling shoes. Jeannette took one hand away from her face and placed it on Nate's own hand softly. Nate could feel the moisture from her tears with his hand. She kept her hand there for a moment before suddenly grabbing his wrist and tossing it away forcefully.

"No, Nate!" She glared at him with a rage he hadn't seen before. "You need to stop doing this. You're always playing the strong one; you act like this is something happening to me, like this is something that I need to get over. Guess what Nate? It's happening to both of us, the whole fucking world is gone, blown away, toxic. Millions of men, women, and children are dead, gone, disintegrated in seconds." Tears flowed from her eyes as she yelled into Nate's face, but her voice didn't waver. She even took it up a decibel. "I liked you better when you were whimpering with me; at least then I knew you were human. You act like you didn't get enough hugs when you were a kid, or your dad didn't play catch with you. I'm sick of being this whiny little bitch that you feel sorry for; I feel so alone, even though you're right there. What kind of person barely even grieves when the whole world is falling apart? Are you enjoying this? I mean— what the hell is this shelter anyway?" As quickly as the tirade began, it stopped. Nate didn't know how to respond, where to begin, or even if he wanted to. He felt sick to his stomach, wounded. He was stunned and felt like a fool for being the comforter, for trying to be the strong one. His devastation must have been obvious, because Jeannette got up and walked over to the far corner of the room, where she leaned against the wall and slid down until she was sitting.

After nearly ten minutes of silence, Nate had composed himself enough to approach her. He walked over and stood above where she was sitting. "Jeannette, the truth is I didn't have anyone. I can't say I know how you feel because I don't. I didn't have a family out there somewhere; I mean I could cry over some plants or animals...hell, I could cry over the Red Sox. But I kind of think it's just as sad if not sadder that everything's gone and I had no one—what does that say about me? I've had a crush on you since I first saw you. The one person I deeply cared for is right here, so no, I can't whimper with you, because you're alive and that's what matters to me." Nate was trying his best; something he had always lacked was tact and timing. He felt like he should have told her from the beginning about the anxiety, the paranoia, the hours of obsessing, but now it would only seem like an excuse.

"Nate, I'm sorry, I'm so sorry. I don't know why I said those things to you; I didn't mean them. You have been there for me every step of the way, and you were just trying to be sweet. I don't know what came over me." Jeannette stood up and wrapped her arms around Nate. She brought her face up to his and kissed him deeply, passionately. Then she whispered in his ear, "You actually think I didn't know that you had a crush on me, you dumbass? You could hardly say hello without blushing."

Before Nate realized what was happening, they were making out, and for the first time legitimately undressing. They had clumsily made their way to the bed, mouths attached for the entire journey. Nate caressed her naked body with one hand while moving on top of her. He explored her curves with his mouth, moving from her neck to her navel. The heat and lust was insanely intense, Nate had dreamed, pictured, imagined this moment for years. He was trembling and nervous, and soon they were in the throes of ecstasy. Nate was moving with as much precision as he could find in his awkward body. Neither of them had been virgins, but they fumbled with each other like they were, and it all felt so new. Nate had always heard that women had to have a deep emotional bond, perhaps even love to enjoy sex, but men just needed a warm body. He decided that whoever had said that was full of shit, because this experience was so far beyond the worthless conquests of his college days. They were making love, birth control or not, nuclear war or not. Nate wanted this moment to last. For once he knew what it felt like to give yourself to someone, to give pleasure and have that gift returned twofold. Nate had remembered reading that anxiety and pleasure could not exist on the same plane. Whoever had written that knew their subject matter, because Nate could feel the stress and anxiety melt away as he melted into Jeannette. In his own opinion, he performed admirably.

8

DRAWING BLOOD

Simon must have calculated wrong somewhere along the line while stocking his fallout shelter. After three full weeks underground, he was faced with the reality that he would be forced to cut his family's food rations in half or else risk running out entirely.

By Tuesday of the fourth week, Simon had decided that the time was right for the family to try their luck back in their house aboveground. The combination of the lack of adequate food supplies and the buildup of ammonia and methane filling the bunker was forcing them out. Simon would have preferred to stay another week to make sure that the air above would be safe, but he had no way of measuring the air quality anyway. The air up above had to be safer than the atrocious smell down below. Simon called to his oldest son, "Jed, I need you to get two handguns from the armory." He pulled Jed by the arm away from the lessons he had been teaching the younger children.

"Can I ask why, Father? I was right in the middle of help-ing Abby with her long division," Jed questioned timidly, fol-lowing his father out of the living area. The eighteen-year-old still feared his father, even though he was now a man himself. Simon assumed it was respect that caused Jed's skittish behav-ior, but he would've been just as pleased to know it was fear. He thought fear of God was a good thing to instill in a child, and to those children Simon should be God.

Simon's body temperature seemed to rise with each addi-tional minute he dwelled in the hot, swampy, and rank shelter. He had been losing his patience with the shelter and with his wife and children. He felt like control was slipping away, and to regain that control he'd need to be in a more comfortable environment. He snapped at Jed, "Just do what I told you, you little cuss. We're getting out of this Godforsaken cesspool. I'm going to need you to go above with me to make sure the house is secure enough for the family."

After pocketing two handguns, Simon and Jed walked back to the living area. His teenage children were all sitting around a large table that Simon had built using two sawhorses and a top made from painted plywood. Miranda was doing her best to pick up the lessons where Jed had left off.

"Jed and I are going up. If everything looks safe enough we will summon you all," Simon said to Miranda.

"Shouldn't we discuss this, hon?" Miranda said in almost a whisper.

"Since when do I need your permission to do anything?" Simon shot back with a stern look that he had practiced over the years and saved just for her. Miranda instantly turned her head down, breaking the painful gaze.

Simon climbed the ladder that had been bolted through the sheetrock and hung down from the front side of the sleep-ing quarters. He climbed to the top and paused, looking down at Jed who hurried over and climbed up a rung or two. Simon then slid the iron rod that worked like a deadbolt across one side of the three-foot-square metal hatch. He could hear some kind of debris shift and then slide off the top as he forced open the hinged metal hood. As Simon continued to push the lid and climb, gravity soon took the hood of the hatch all the way open, and it slammed into the ground with a thud. Ash flew up in a dusty cloud; the ash was gray and had the consistency of fine sawdust as it hung in the air around the folded open hatch. Simon took two steps back down the ladder and spoke to Jed: "Bring up two bandanas with you."

Jed disappeared into the shelter and a minute later came back carrying one scarf and one bandana. Jed climbed the ladder and handed the two items to his father. Simon took the bandana and wrapped it over his nose and mouth, tying the ends behind his head while teetering on the ladder. "Wrap that thing around your face like this; it will keep the majority of the dust out of your lungs," he said in a muffled voice, motioning to Jed's scarf.

Simon stepped up the ladder, emerging halfway out of the hole into the outside world. The air smelled musty and burnt, like someone had put out a major house fire with a lot of water, leaving behind creosote and mildew. He felt like a phoenix rising from the ashes, and though the air smelled strange, it was still a mile better than it had been in the bunker. His head cleared just from having the freedom to breathe without choking on the smell of human waste. The entire world had been coated in fine, milky ash. It took a few moments for Simon's eyes to adjust. The sky was a dark gray twilight, although it was only ten in the morning, but it was brighter than it had been in the shelter. The world around him appeared to be black and white, like he was looking through a filter that caused everything to lose its color. The sky was gray, the ground was white, and the trees stood black between the two. Even things that had color, like Simon's car, had been faded to a dark, muted shade beneath the film of ash. It reminded Simon of a 1950s television show that was shot in the late fall after the leaves had fallen—the bare and sickly trees looked like shadows of threatening aliens ready to reach out and grab.

About thirty feet away toward the road, lying on what would have been the sidewalk, was an ash-covered corpse. No flies buzzed around the dead mass of flesh, and the only reason Simon knew it was a human corpse was the hand reaching up toward the sky frozen in rigor mortis. The temperature seemed to be around the low fifties, which would be on the colder side for early may, but not outside of the average range.

Simon climbed up out of the hole and stepped on the ground, feeling a slight resistance under his foot as his shoe pushed up a small cloud of ash. With every step, a small poof of ash followed him. He looked over at his two-story house, which was caked from roof to foundation with the stuff. The first thing Simon noticed was that the addition had completely collapsed in on itself. Simon, Jed, and Thomas had built the addition themselves to provide two extra bedrooms for the girls. Even with the damage, however, the Cape Cod–style house was in remarkably good condition, far better than what he had feared when they had felt the ground shaking as the missiles fell. Looking around the street and toward the neighboring houses in the small suburban cul-de-sac, Simon saw that most people hadn't been so lucky. It appeared that every other house was now a pile of beams, clapboards, and rubble.

"Come on, son, what's the holdup?" Simon called down to Jed.

Jed slowly emerged out of the hole in the ground like a groundhog testing the air after a long winter. He deliberately moved his hands, avoiding the ash as he pulled himself free from the metal hatch. Jed's head spun around like it was on a swivel as he took in the decimated surroundings. His face was full of fear and apprehension. "Father, is it safe to be out here? I mean, is all this ash still full of radiation?" His soft voice was garbled by a trembling fright and the scarf tied tight over the lower half of his face. Simon didn't have the answer, but he'd be damned if he was going to look clueless to his oldest son.

"We don't have a choice. We're running low on food and water. I'm sure most of this stuff is inert—probably just city ash carried by the fires. God knows that shelter is becoming intolerable; he'd give us a sign if it were unsafe up here." The answer was vague and indirect, but there was some truth in it. Simon didn't know much about radiation. He didn't know how much they could be exposed to or how long it would take for fallout to decay.

Simon and Jed trudged along to the house, stepping over downed branches and tree limbs and kicking up a dusty, ash path as they walked. The ash they kicked up hung loosely in the air for a few seconds before finally settling back to the ground. Simon wondered as he walked if there was any local or state government left. Would there be rescue stations, aid drops, refugee camps...or was the government destroyed and useless? The buildup to the attack and the actual bombs had all happened so damn fast; it hadn't been like the Cold War, which had simmered for years, with people giving instructions about what to do if the nukes actually came. This time only the very intuitive had had time to prepare. Thankfully, Simon had been one of the intuitive ones. He drew his gun and walked up the steps to the back door of his house.

A few feet away from his father, Jed stood with his eyes locked on the wreckage of a play structure Miranda and Simon had bought for the children when he had been eleven years old. The bent metal swing set and twisted slide looked like some hipster's idea of a modern art masterpiece; to Jed it represented the last vestige of his youth, a place where he could run to escape the wrath of his father. For some reason, Jed was fixated on it; he couldn't pull his eyes away. It was the ultimate insult of this wasteland, a worse torment than any rotting body or neighborhood house turned to rubble. Down in the shelter, Jed had been encapsulated by a hard shell of denial, not fully understanding what had happened above. Outside in this reality, that hard shell was becoming cracked and covered with ash, much like the backyard of his youth.

Simon opened the storm door of the white two-story cape that had been his family's sanctuary for the last two decades. He held the gun out in front of him, scanning the dark kitchen for any signs of movement. Simon had no doubt that whatever had survived in this barren world would be dangerous and desperate, probably starving. Some light had been coming in through the cracked windows, but hardly enough to illuminate the other side of the kitchen. Simon flipped the light switch next to the door frame out of force of habit—he was fully aware of the lack of electricity. The shelter lights had gone out even before the worst of the bombs had hit. He felt his way down the hard linoleum countertop to the drawers. The third drawer down was the family's junk drawer, full of miscellaneous kitchen utensils, screws, batteries, rubber bands, bread ties, anything that didn't have a designated location. Simon remembered the red plastic flashlight he stored there; he had last used the flashlight under the sink when he was cleaning the drain trap. He reached in and fumbled through the odds and ends until his hand found the cylindrical plastic body of the flashlight.

He flipped on the light, expecting to see some ghostly apparition ready to pounce on him. Instead what he saw was his kitchen, which had looked like someone had thrown a grenade in it. The mess was extraordinary. Every cabinet stood open, and glass and dinnerware had smashed on the floor in front of each one. The refrigerator was wide open, and the smell of rotten food and mildew washed out the burnt ember smell in his nose. Containers of dry food, cereal, oatmeal, and flour had fallen from their cabinets and split open, spilling on the counter and covering the floor below. Simon couldn't decide if the kitchen had been ransacked by a looter or if all of this had happened during the seismic shift caused by the nukes. Simon needed to think. He assumed that if a looter or squatter had attempted to get a free lunch, they'd have taken the dry food, broken packaging or not. He also began wondering what had happened to Jed. The boy had been waiting outside for a long time, and Simon was feeling creeped out. Simon carefully backpedaled to the back door, weaving his way around the broken dishes and trying to keep from making a lot of noise. If there was a squatter in the house, Simon wanted the upper hand by being on his home turf and using the element of surprise.

He glanced through the storm door that led out to the backyard; the glass was covered with a pasty film. It was like looking through a bottle of milk. Jed was out there standing a few meters from the fallout shelter; he looked like he was in some sort of trance. He was staring into space with glazed-over eyes, and his face was drawn and pale. The cliché rang true that he looked like he had seen a ghost. Simon was about to open the door and call over to Jed, at the very least to shake him out of his funk, when he heard a strange, rhythmic crackling sound. He wasn't sure why he hadn't noticed it before, but the more he concentrated his ears the more persistent the sound became. He crept quietly back through the kitchen following the sound, which seemed to be coming from the living room. The living room, or family room as Miranda called it, was attached to the kitchen by a short hallway stenciled with ivy and flowers. Simon tiptoed his way through the short hallway, and with every step the rattling sound rose up and then fell, only to start over again. His heart was pounding. The noise was familiar, but he couldn't quite place it—the sound was like somebody running a stone over a washboard, but sloppy and wet like a bubbling fish tank. He would take a step or two then stop and listen for the sound again. Finally Simon was at the threshold of the living room. He cocked the gun, slowly sliding the slide on the top of the pistol and holding it as the spring pulled the bullet into the chamber. Simon had tried to be silent, but the gun made an audible click, and he held his breath, wondering if the unidentified sound would stop or change. He listened intently, but the sound hadn't changed its monotonous taunt: "rrrr pp tt," then it would pause for a moment and come again, "rrrr pp tt." Simon shone the light all over the room, checking the corners. There was nothing that seemed out of the ordinary. He hadn't seen any movement, and there had been no change in the strange noise. He moved the light around, trying to hone in on the sound. Finally, he saw something odd on the floor: a pile of clothing or blankets that seemed to be the source of the sound. He thought for a second that perhaps an animal—a raccoon or a skunk—had found its way into the living room and made a nest on the floor. "Oh, God, please don't let it be a skunk. I can't take any more acrid odors," he whispered to himself as he walked toward the lump of fabric. The sound was definitely coming from under the mound, and as he got closer he realized that the clothes weren't empty. A man of about fifty was lying on Simon's living room floor, wrapped tightly with what looked like every blanket in the house. The man only became visible as Simon got closer. He was bundled from head to toe, with only a small circle of his face exposed to the air. The face was filthy, slathered in a mixture of blood, dirt, and ash. Simon could see where portions of skin had peeled away like a monstrous, festering sunburn. The man had been snoring heavily, immersed in a deep sleep or possibly a coma. Simon's opinion was that the squatter had probably been on drugs or drunk and had passed out. The noise that had drawn his attention to the man was a clinking, raspy snore of a stranger a thousand miles away in dreamland.

Simon's blood began to boil; he could feel his blood pressure thumping in his temples as the rage banged against the inside of his head searching for a way out. How dare this low-life befoul Simon's home, his palace, the place where he had reared children? His fear of running into a squatter had turned to anger and hatred. Simon walked over to the center of the room and grabbed one of the tweed cushions from the sofa. The man probably would have slept there if it hadn't been easily visible from three different doorways. He placed the cushion on the dirtbag's face, mounting him in the process, and pushed down with his hands directing his entire body weight into the man's skull. The man woke and kicked out, bucking like a wrestler on the verge of being pinned. Simon quickly reached for the gun, which he had placed on the floor next to the man's head; in one fluid movement he brought the gun up against the cushion. The man, who was larger and stronger than Simon, had begun to panic and attempted to roll out, but Simon had too much leverage and the blankets kept the man confined. He squeezed the trigger twice, firing into the cushion, which acted like a silencer. The sound of the shots was still loud enough in the enclosed room to echo off the wall loudly, making Simon's ears ring with agony. Two small snakes of smoke seeped from the gunshot wounds in the couch cushion making the air smell like cordite and burnt plastic. The man's feet had been shuddering and suddenly stopped as the nerve endings gave up the last of their electrical impulses. Simon kicked away the cushion, revealing what was left of the man's face; it had been caved in from the bridge of the nose to the lower jaw. A bloody mess of gray matter, skin, and pulverized bone remained where his eyes would have been. Simon placed the couch cushion back over the gore, thinking he shouldn't have ruined a perfectly good cushion on this piece of humanized filth. He picked over the body, checking the empty pockets for some kind of identification; it would have been an awful shame to waste the bullets on a neighbor.

"Father!" Jed, who must have heard the gunshots, suddenly appeared at the living room entryway. Simon pointed the flashlight at him to indicate where he was.

"Jed, help me move this body," Simon said, wrapping the blankets back over the squatter.

"Father, who is that?" Jed said, pointing at the corpse.

"It's some thieving vagabond, just like I thought," Simon said, grunting as he shifted the body so it was completely covered. "Jed, this is the kind of person I taught you to prepare for. Thankfully, I got him before he got us, and you didn't have to take care of it this time." Simon was out of breath. "Now get over here and help me; we don't want your sisters to see this mess."

They picked up the body, Simon at the head and Jed at the feet, and dragged it out the front door and down the steps. They dropped it on the sidewalk that led up to the house. Simon thought it would be a fine warning to any other strangers that his house wasn't a hotel or soup kitchen. "That's that," Simon said, brushing off his hands on his jeans.

"Father, you're just going to leave this poor man's body here to rot?" Jed asked pleadingly.

"Same old Jed," Simon chuckled. "Always wants the puppy to come home with him. If I had a pike, and if this man had a head to place on that pike, I'd rather do that than leave him here to rot." Simon turned and walked back into the house. Jed lingered for a while looking at the roll of blankets that encased the stranger. He then looked down the street. Nothing moved; there was no sign of life anywhere, just dying trees, falling houses, and ash...welcome to adulthood.

9

AFTERBIRTH

Nate and Jeannette had started spending more and more time aboveground. After a full month in the shelter, they were now whiling the days away upstairs. Nate was still apprehensive about breaking the imaginary seal of the front doors. The radiation level had stabilized, but he was still concerned about toxicity in the ash and dust blowing around. There had been a few days of steady drizzle, but Nate was waiting until they saw a good, hard rain to wash away the toxins before he was entirely convinced that danger had passed.

Jeannette had been killing time in the lab studying field medicine from the selection of medical encyclopedias and journals. Her theory was that the world had changed and that she would need to evolve or else be rendered useless. Not that she thought there would be a new job in her future, but survival would be a job in itself. There wouldn't be much benefit as a medical technologist in this hostile environment, but there would be a demand for people who could treat wounds and illness. It would be harder for any opportunistic person to hurt or kill her if the person thought she could save his or her life. She had already read through everything on triage, severe burns, and of course radiation poisoning. It's amazing what you can learn when you have nothing else to do besides read, study, and practice. She spent a lot of playful hours wrapping Nate's imaginary wounds with clean bandages and rubbing balm on his imaginary burns. She was impressively dexterous considering the birth defect in her left hand. Jeannette was smart enough to know that she couldn't teach herself to be a full-fledged doctor, but she also knew that she and Nate could help a lot of people, even without official training or a medical license.

Nate spent his days making the building more like a home. What items they lacked he would build or even invent something that could serve as an approximation. During this time, they were the happiest they had been since the missiles had unleashed their warheads on the Earth. They had settled into a routine that had continued unabated for days. They would mark the time by crossing off the boxes on the calendar with a big red X, like a death-row inmate. On a Tuesday morning in early June, that tranquil routine was turned on its head.

Nate was sitting behind the desk in the reception area tinkering with the smartphone and trying to find a way to charge it using D batteries. Jeannette was in the lab writing notes and highlighting passages in a textbook called *Pathology in the Third World*.

They both were startled out of the hypnosis of their work by a loud, clattering crash. The sound had come from the sliding glass doors in the foyer. Nate drew the handgun from the top drawer of the desk and hopped up to investigate. Outside the door, through the silt and cracks, he could see a woman attempting to smash through the safety glass with half of a broken red brick. The woman was dressed in long flowing rags, and greasy, matted black hair hung from her head in clumpy strips. She would hurl the brick at the glass, then walk over and pick it up, only to walk back and throw it again. The heavy glass would dimple and crack in long zigzags, but the brick never completely broke through. Nate watched the woman repeat the process again and again; soon Jeannette was standing at his side viewing the circus. Behind the woman, sitting in a red Radio Flyer wagon was a second woman wrapped in a dirty, light blue blanket. The second woman hadn't moved from the wagon to help her friend with the glass assault; she just sat there like a prop in some strange play. The woman in the wagon looked much worse for wear. Her hair looked like it had been hacked off with a dull razor blade, it was wispy and aside from some thick patches at her ears was transparent at the top and back. The visible parts of her scalp and face were red and peeling, as if she had fallen asleep in a tanning bed. Her thick winter coat was caked with muddy ash, and her pants looked wet or stained with brownish liquid. Nate didn't want to think about what the source of the liquid was.

Jeannette whispered to Nate as if the women could hear them through the door, "We should let them in; they look desperate." She put an arm around Nate's shoulders.

"You've got to be kidding; we don't know anything about these people," Nate said, hoping he didn't sound too harsh. Jeannette stepped forward to get a closer look; she was holding a cup of water in one hand and took a sip nonchalantly. Based on where they were standing and the caked spatter of dirt and ash, Nate figured there was no way that the two women could see inside the building. The woman who appeared to be the stronger of the two kept picking up the brick and flinging it at the glass with astonishing force. "Jeannette, I know you want to help these women. You have an endless supply of sympathy.

I want to help them too, but at what cost?" Nate put some effort into talking Jeannette down, but he knew in the end she'd get her way; it wasn't worth a battle.

"What cost would there be, Nate?" Jeannette knew exactly what buttons to push.

"They could be covered in radiation!" Nate was losing, and he knew it wouldn't be long before he was opening the doors, but he persisted anyway.

"If they're covered in radiation, that's all the more reason to get them inside." Jeannette said as she took another sip of her water.

"Well, they could be feral," Nate said half-heartedly.

"Feral, Nate? You think they're *feral*? Just open the fucking door."

"Maybe they're carrying disease?" Nate said, exhausting every possibility he could think of. He felt a bit like the glass door and Jeannette was the brick pounding relentlessly into him.

"Nate, we worked with blood for a living every day." Jeannette was already moving toward the door. "Every day of your life, you stick needles in people's arms that could have hepatitis or other blood-borne illnesses, and here you are afraid of a couple of people who really need our help." Jeannette was more than halfway to the door when Nate stopped her.

"OK, OK, but let me open it," Nate said, rushing ahead of Jeannette. If one of the women had a knife, he wanted to be the one she'd have to deal with. Nate scooted over to the door, keeping the pistol in plain sight. He banged on the door with his fist to get the woman's attention; she was bent over reaching for the brick again. "Hey, how can we help you?"

The woman saw Nate and quickly put her hands together miming prayer and mouthed the words, "Thank God." Then she went to the wagon, said something to the other woman, and pulled her over closer to the door. Nate twisted the metal knob on the bolt lock and slid the door open about six inches.

"Please," the woman said as soon as the door opened.

"Do you need some help?" Nate said thinking that it was beyond obvious that they needed help, but Nate wanted to be clear that he meant them no harm.

Out of breath from throwing the brick, the woman spoke quickly; she sounded to be in her early twenties, but in her condition she looked much older. "We were hoping to find some medical supplies; and I couldn't get the wagon across the broken parking lot to the clinic, my mother is very sick." The woman had been shaking violently. Nate couldn't determine if it was from prolonged exposure to the elements or from fear. Right away Nate knew that these two women were not a threat, at least in terms of physical violence. The younger woman's nose was running in a small stream of snot over her lips. Nate thought she had probably once been very attractive; she had sharp, high cheekbones and bright eyes.

Jeannette stepped in front of Nate and slid open the door a foot further; a pile of ash mounded up in the track. "My name is Jeannette, and this is Nate," she said to the woman.

"I'm Denise, and this is my mother Joanna. She can't walk; I'm not sure if she can even stand right now." She turned and looked down at her mother in the wagon. "Can we come in? It's cold out here and my mother is very sick," she asked timidly, never taking her eyes off the gun that Nate cradled in his right hand. Nate saw her eyes and he immediately put the gun in the belt of his jeans, embarrassed.

"I'm sorry, please come in," Jeannette said empathetically.

Denise hobbled over to the wagon, picked up the handle, and pulled her mother into the foyer through the doorway. The second woman, who had been introduced as Joanne, sat in the wagon looking like a giant in the small children's toy. Her arms and legs were hanging over the sides, and she slowly pushed with her feet as her daughter pulled her forward. Nate thought the wagon looked awfully unstable and a whole lot less than comfortable. Once they were inside, Nate quickly slammed the sliding glass door closed and turned the lock. He walked behind the reception desk and found two surgical masks. The phlebotomists used the masks while drawing blood during cold and flu season. Nate strolled over and handed Jeannette a mask. The mother, Joanne, didn't look healthy at all. Her complexion was blotchy and red in the light, and she was emaciated, her eyes sunken deep back into her skull and encased in heavy purple bags. She was moaning softly, and Jeannette put on a pair of nitrile gloves, bending down to the woman. "Joanne, how are you feeling?" Jeannette asked in her most professional but compassionate voice.

The daughter, Denise, answered for her. "She's been too weak to talk since this morning. She hasn't eaten or taken in any liquids; before that, she couldn't hold anything down. She's had bad diarrhea and bruises all over her body. We left the place we were staying at to try and find help when she wouldn't talk this morning." Denise bent down and stroked what was left of her mother's ragged hair. Joanne grimaced in pain as her hand went over one of the raw spots.

"Nate, help me get her out of this wagon." Jeannette said taking Joanne under the arm. Joanne grimaced again and a low gurgling sound came from her gut. Nate took Joanne under the other arm and they counted to three and lifted her from the wagon. Joanne let out a whimper and Nate saw that her eyes were shut tight as they lowered her onto the carpet. The woman seemed to ease up once she was lying on the floor.

"Jeannette, I'm going to run down to that spare storage room and get a couple blankets and maybe a pillow from our room. Are you all right here for a minute or two?" Nate asked, already moving toward the doorway back to the blood draw area.

"Thank you, Nate, that's just what I was thinking. Can you also bring us some water?" Jeannette answered, picking up Joanne's arm and taking her pulse.

"Not a problem," Nate said and walked quickly out of the room.

"Denise, what have you and your mother been doing since the bombs? Did you have shelter? How long did you wait before going outside?" Jeannette, who hadn't had any experience triaging patients in an emergency situation was shooting off questions without waiting for an answer.

Denise looked at her mother lying on the floor, then back at Jeannette. "We heard about the Russian attack on television, when that emergency tone thingy came on. I was visiting my mom's condo in the town center; I don't live around here. We grabbed all the food and water we could carry and went down to the cellar of the condo. Well, it's really more of a small boiler room than a cellar. When the missiles exploded, it shook the walls and floor so hard..." Her eyes went blank, and Jeannette could see she was shivering; obviously the experience had traumatized her. When she began to speak, it seemed to be from some far-off place. Her voice was trembling. "All the water pipes burst, and the power was out. Then the small boiler room began to flood. We stayed as long as we could, but the water was so cold; within an hour or so it was up to our knees. We knew we had to leave, but there was no place to go." Denise spoke in long, drawn out gasps, as if she was breathing the words instead of speaking them. She had a thick Long Island accent, which made everything sound surreal, like was discussing a mafia hit. "So we went back upstairs to mom's condo, but all the windows were busted." She pronounced windows *wind-ers* and water *waddah*. If the story hadn't been so sad, Jeannette would have found it rather cute. "We hung blankets over the windows and tried to seal off the holes the best we could, but after a few days we ran out of water." She was interrupted by Nate returning with the blankets, a cushion, and two large cups of water. Denise took the water and drank deeply, finishing one cup in a long slug. She took the second cup and sipped on it as Nate and Jeannette set Joanne up with the blankets and cushion. Jeannette began palpating the woman's abdomen. She scrunched her face like she was troubled by what she felt, Joanne's face contorted in pain when Jeannette pressed on the area a second time.

"Go on, Denise. So what happened after you ran out of water?" Jeannette asked, distracting the girl's attention away from the examination of her mother. Denise took a huge gulp of water, as if the memory of them running out had made her thirsty. "After we ran out of water, we had to leave. We walked down the street; the ash was falling like snow, it was a few inches deep. There were some dead bodies just lying in the road—some people who had had car accidents, some just lying there." Nate remembered the car accident he had witnessed and mentally kicked himself for not helping. "We went into the library. It was empty, but the door had been left unlocked. We stayed there for...I dunno how long...there was food and water there, enough for a while." She took another sip of water and sat on the ground next to her mother. Nate thought he might be able to get some more useful information out of Denise, so he took up the questioning where Jeannette had left off.

"Denise, did you see any other people—any firemen, or police, the army maybe? Anyone who might be here to help the town or bring in supplies?" Nate was quickly realizing that potable water would be the lifeblood of this wasteland; it would be the currency of the local economy.

"No, we didn't see anyone here to help," Denise answered.

Joanne began to moan loudly. She suddenly sat straight up, looked at Denise, and said in a terrified, creaking whisper, "They're coming for us, Denny, we have to hide—your father told us to hide if they come." As quickly as she had sat up, she lay back down on the carpet.

"She must be hallucinating; it's a symptom of radiation sickness and post-traumatic shock syndrome," Jeannette said. She adjusted the blankets to make Joanne more comfortable. Nate would have to wait to get answers to any more questions.

Jeannette stood and waved her hand to Nate and Denise, indicating that she wanted them to go into the receptionist's area. She whispered, "We need to talk; let's go in the back for a minute." They all walked through the door to the blood draw area. Jeannette deliberated about how much she should tell Denise about her mother's condition. She decided to lay all the cards on the table and let them fall where they may. "Denise, your mother has radiation sickness and she's severely dehydrated. I'm not a doctor and neither is Nate; she needs a hospital. I've been reading about this, but there's only so much I can do with what we have here. She's going to need IV fluids immediately, electrolytes, iodine, and if we could get it, Prussian blue." Jeannette made eye contact with Nate, hoping he was getting the message.

"What's Prussian blue?" Nate asked.

"It's a type of blue dye that doctors in the sixties found out binds with radioactive particles in the intestines so they can be expelled as waste." Jeannette answered. She looked at Nate again. "We don't have any of those things here." Nate knew exactly what Jeannette was thinking and finished the sentence for her in his head. *But they do next door.* That would mean suiting up, going outside, walking next door to the clinic, breaking in, and locating the equipment and medicines that Jeannette needed. Denise interrupted Nate and Jeannette's seemingly telepathic conversation.

"Can you save my mother?" Denise asked, looking directly at Jeannette; she knew that if Joanne could be saved it would be on Jeannette's shoulders.

Nate knew what his role would be without a hospital, and he started to think about the logistics. There was no transportation, and the closest hospital was almost twenty miles from the blood draw station. It would take days to walk there, and that would mean dragging Joanne through ash and who knew what other dangers. Then if they could even make it to a place that could help, there would be the very real possibility that the hospital would not be operational; or if it was operational it might be overrun. Joanne was in no condition to be moved, even if the world hadn't become a nuclear wasteland.

Jeannette looked back to Nate and spoke to Denise. "We'll do our best, honey, but you need to prepare yourself. The radiation sickness might be too far along, but that doesn't mean we can't make her more comfortable, and it's definitely not too late to help you. If your mom has radiation sickness, there's a good chance you do too."

• • •

Jeannette stood in front of Nate, helping him tape up the plastic suit. She had volunteered to go, but Nate had come up with an excuse: that he couldn't take care of Joanne if her condition deteriorated any further and Jeannette was not there. With each piece of tape Jeannette put around his ankles and wrists, the anxiety level inside Nate's mind increased. The air outside was probably safe enough for limited exposure. After all, the girl and her mother had made it to the blood draw facility. The radiation outside would have decayed significantly, but that ash would still be full of all manner of toxins. "So, Nate, you know what you're looking for, right?" Jeannette asked. They had already gone over it twice, and she had given him a list, but she wanted to be sure. It would really suck for him to go all the way over there and come back only to have forgotten something important. Nate thought Jeannette was acting like he would be venturing a mile undersea, when in reality he was strolling through the ash and dust to the building next door. "I want you to get an electrolyte-heavy IV solution; iodine tablets or liquid; Vancomycin, Cipro, or any other broad spectrum antibiotics; Bactrim or any other antibiotic ointment for burns, that would include silver nitrate; sedatives; painkillers or any analgesic or anti-inflammatory that's strong; and anything else you think we could use." Nate repeated the list back to her from rote memory, something he had always had a knack for.

"Jeannette, I think I've got it," Nate said with a little frustration. He was already getting irritable in the claustrophobic plastic suit.

"Yes, and you're not getting yourself hurt in the process," Jeannette smiled and kissed him on his exposed cheek. "Are you sure you don't want me to come along?"

Nate returned the smile, thinking how lucky he was to have been stranded in this place with her. He could have been alone, which would have made everything exponentially worse. "I can handle this; plus you need to look after our guests." Nate hoped his voice hadn't sounded like he was suspicious of Denise and Joanne.

With a quick embrace for Jeannette, he walked out the foyer and slid open the glass doors. His first step outside was like stepping out onto the moon; the ground softly crunched under the sole of his shoe. Nate looked down at the small pile of ash he had stepped in; it resembled what is left over after a camp fire has burned itself out. Nate walked a few steps toward the health clinic, he had gowned up inside the plastic suit he had made; he also had a flashlight, figuring it would be dark in the clinic. On his back was the biggest knapsack he had, and in the plastic cinch belt around his waist was the Glock, just in case a looter had camped out in the clinic. He had the flashlight in one hand, and in the other he carried an eighteen-inch crowbar that they had found in the janitor's closet in the basement. Nate walked slowly across the ash-covered asphalt of the parking lot; he didn't want to trip in the fresh potholes. It took Nate nearly thirty minutes to navigate his way through all the crevices and fissures that were left behind from the violent shaking when the bombs had detonated. Some of the cracks actually resembled small canyons, up to twenty feet wide and at least six feet deep, one of which had partially swallowed Jeannette's Subaru.

Nate arrived in front of the health care clinic already out of breath. It was his first trip walking more than a few feet in a month, and the combination of the thick air and breathing through a painter's mask had sapped all of his energy. He could hear the faint rumble of thunder in the distance. It had been constantly overcast outside, but even with the persistent misty drizzle it hadn't looked like they had any significant rain since the nukes. The automatic doors, which were identical to the doors at the blood draw facility, were spattered with gray and black wet ash. The ash had mixed with the misty air to adhere itself to the glass like paste. The fogged glass was opaque, impossible to see through no matter how much Nate rubbed with his rubber-glove-encased palm.

He took the crowbar and managed to wedge the flattened tip between the two doors. He reared back using all his weight and the leverage of the bar, but the door wouldn't budge. Nate wasn't strong enough to break the lock; all he did was bend the metal sheeting around the frame an inch or two. He had tried to get into better shape in the bunker by doing push-ups and sit-ups, not to mention his active sex life. In combination with his recent sparse, rationed diet, Nate had lost nearly ten pounds and gained some muscle. He had to rethink his entrance plan. He knew he couldn't simply break the glass; he had watched Denise throw a brick at the same type of glass twenty times or more with no luck. It was safety glass and was probably bulletproof, made to spiderweb without shattering. That thought process brought him to the round keyhole lock. The glass was bulletproof, but the lock surely wasn't. Still, Nate worried that shooting the lock would cause the bullet to ricochet back into him. Nate settled on standing about ten feet back at an angle and shooting the lock to avoid a ricochet.

He took the gun from his belt and backed up four large strides diagonally, aimed, and fired. A loud ping and a bright spark jumped from the metal just above the lock. He cocked the gun again, this time adjusting his aim for the recoil, and fired. Nate heard the same sound, but this time when he looked at the lock he saw that it had been punched out in one solid cylinder. He walked over to the door and slid it open with one fluid push, quite pleased with himself for getting the door open without blowing off his own foot.

Nate walked into the waiting area. It was dark, and shadows danced on the floor. He flipped on the flashlight. The layout of the urgent care clinic was nearly identical to the blood draw facility that had become his and Jeannette's home. From the outside, both buildings resembled boxlike retail outlets, but inside they looked like every other doctor's office on the planet. The biggest differences were that instead of a blood draw station, reception area, and lab, the urgent care clinic had exam rooms, a small pharmacy, and a nurse's station. There was no evidence that anyone had been inside since they had last been open for business. The place had sustained much more damage than the blood draw clinic. The carpet was wet and squishy, and the air smelled of mold. Each step Nate took caused a sickening suction sound. At some point the sprinkler system must have turned on or have been ruptured. Water dripped from above and the fiberglass ceiling tiles were stained coffee brown with black spots from mildew. Huge sections of the tile had caved in, revealing fiberglass insulation and a maze of wiring. Three-foot-long fluorescent light fixtures had fallen and smashed down, spreading thin, eggshell-like glass all over the floor.

Nate slid behind a wooden half-door to the area where patients would have been first examined. The treatment area was long and rectangular, with a new stall every couple of feet. In the center was an island where elongated computer monitors stood so doctors could review x-rays and still stand within earshot of the nurses. The far end of the rectangular room had collapsed into the foundation. It sloped down at least fifty feet, where the concrete cellar walls were visible. Between the two levels were exposed pipes and ductwork. The ground water had come up through the cracked concrete and had pooled at the base of the collapsed floor. It looked like a giant had stomped down on the whole rear end of the building. Steady streams of water were pouring through the ceiling above the damage the sprinkler system must have been gravity fed as well. The entire room was cold, damp, and dark. It gave Nate a serious case of the willies. He half expected to hear a Theremin playing a creepy series of notes any second, all that was missing was the cobwebs. It reminded Nate of a movie he had watched once about an abandoned insane asylum that was haunted by the crazy patients who had been tortured or given unnecessary lobotomies. The aseptic white walls coupled with the wires hanging out like tentacles could have been a set in that horror movie.

Nate shook off the jitters and wandered around the portion that looked safe, checking the doors and rooms. In a small cordoned off area he found a glass door with red stenciled letters that read Pharmacy. He didn't need to shoot the lock this time; he used the pry bar and smashed the glass above the silver knob. He reached his arm through the opening he had made in the glass, avoiding shards that hung down like fangs. Grabbing the interior knob, he turned it to pop the lock. The door opened to a slender closet, much like a kitchen pantry. The walls were lined with shelves that held all manner of medical supplies. Sitting on the floor at the back of the room was the pixis unit, which was a four-foot-high chest of drawers with a keyboard and monitor fixed to the top. The drawers would be sealed, but Nate knew right away what they contained: alphabetized drugs. The unit was set up so that a doctor or nurse would punch in a confidential password and the medicine they requested would be dispensed at the bottom. It was like a vending machine for junkies. The problem was the computer on top; it was used to accept a password then calculate the amount and type of drug prescribed and by whom. The computer would prevent any theft or even abuse by the staff. The problem was that without power, even if Nate had a usable password, the computer wouldn't work. He approached the machine and hastily started to spear the crowbar into the tops of the handleless drawers. After about twenty whacks at the gap above the top drawer, the crowbar caught. It pushed through the thin crack separating the cover of the machine from the drawer; the bar was buried three inches into the composite cabinet. Nate simply pushed forward on the exposed end of the crowbar, and he heard the clasp that kept the drawer closed break. He then wedged his fingers into the gap and pulled the drawer open. The drawer consisted of twelve slots holding foil bubble packs of pills. He read the labels and took what he needed, now with the top drawer open the drawer below it was easy to pry. He simply repeated the process. It was full of liquid vials of medication; again, Nate took whatever he thought Jeannette might need. The third drawer was full of syringes, varying sizes of needle attachments, and clear plastic tubing. The final drawer contained full IV bags; he placed everything into the knapsack and started examining the shelves. By the time the knapsack was full, Nate had found everything Jeannette had requested and some other items that he thought would come in handy, including a box of condoms.

Nate walked across the parking lot feeling like a conquering hero, his chest was filled with pride that he had accomplished a dangerous mission. He looked up at the sky and began to feel like he might be able to get along in this damaged world.

10

MEMORABILIA

For the first time in twenty-nine days, Simon was able to sleep in his own bed, under his own roof. A lot of work needed to be done to make the house habitable again. It seemed like every piece of glass in the house, including the windows, was now in a million tiny slivers. He had cut himself three times picking up glass off the floor, and the family had filled four five-gallon buckets with all the shards. It had been very time-consuming, but it was cleaning, and over the years Simon had become a per-fectionist—he enjoyed cleaning. If only the vacuum cleaner had worked it would have only taken a couple of hours. Simon had covered the windows with plastic and weather stripping and, when that ran out, with old bedsheets and thumbtacks.

Now that the house was in living condition, Simon lay in his bed staring at the ceiling. He was exhausted, but it felt like he was even too tired to sleep. His head was swimming with thoughts of the past and apprehensions about the future. He was feeling things he hadn't felt in years, and none of it was positive. The torment of addiction had returned. It seemed as severe as it had been the first few months after getting clean. It wasn't so much that he wanted to use; he wouldn't put himself through that again. It was more about memories. The tastes, the smells, the pleasure, the whole ritual of getting his fix haunted him like a nightmare. Simon wouldn't even know how to get dope with the way things were now, and he was so out of practice. Still, he couldn't get that damn shit out of his head; it was like having a toothache and constantly touching the abscess with his tongue, only to feel the sting again. He wondered if this was a test from God. Simon felt hypocritical being a man of the lord yet dwelling on thoughts of opiates.

The worst thoughts he couldn't shake were about the horrible acts he had committed to facilitate his habit. Could he be feeling guilt or the pangs of an infinitesimal conscience? Simon didn't think so. He didn't believe in guilt, because he believed everything was as God had planned. If he had hurt someone or stolen, it was all a symptom of the evil that had eventually turned him down the path of God. It had been a means to the end, and the end had been his faith; he could never regret anything that had brought his faith with it. Everything had been worth it, because finding that higher power had cured Simon. It was the most addictive fix of all.

The memories were tough to bear though; it was like being haunted by yourself. Simon remembered a night when he was in his early twenties. It was before Miranda, before the children, and before he had found the church. It was during a time when he would try any vice to numb the memory of his childhood and drunken father, who used to brutally beat his mother. Simon had broken into his parents' home. His mother was asleep in the bedroom, and he had cleaned out her jewelry box and took her "rainy day" money from the jar on her dresser. He had all the funds he would need to get high, so he tiptoed his way out of the bedroom through the living room. Walking through the living room, he heard the familiar foghorn snore of his father passed out drunk on the sofa. Simon remembered his eyes filling with a red rage and most of all vengeance. He had wanted more than anything to pay his father back for all the abuse and humiliation; it would be his way of self-medicating.

Simon could see the faint glow of his father's cigarette still burning between his fingers; the long, flaky ash seemed to teeter on the end of the small cherry. A bottle of his dad's high-test rotgut sat on the coffee table, an arm's length from his sleeping father. Simon picked up the bottle, thinking he could take a swig or maybe smash it over his father's ugly face. Alcohol had never been Simon's flavor of choice, but he knew how irked his father would get if he drank it. He looked at the bottle and then turned his attention to the blanket balled at his father's feet. He spontaneously poured half of the bottle all over the blanket, and then he trickled a little on the arm of the couch, the carpet around it, and the top of the cushions sticking out from under his father's body. Thinking back, Simon remembered the devil himself taking over his body at that moment. He told himself he was just going to scare his father, give him something to think about. He pulled out the lighter that he used to cook dope, a cheap, blue Bic Flip-it. Even in memory, Simon could see his thumb on the metallic wheel that used friction to produce the spark. He flicked the lighter and watched the blue and orange flame dance; he watched that flame for a long time before touching it to the booze-saturated blanket. The fire rose quickly; it spilled off the blanket and ran up the arm of the couch like water spreading over a smooth surface. In seconds, his father was encircled in fire. Simon ran for the door, taking one last look back at his dad, who was now awake and screaming in confusion. Their eyes met for a moment, and when his father suddenly stopped screaming, Simon could see in his dad's eyes one emotion: understanding.

He never saw his parents again. Simon had heard from a distant cousin that his father had survived with third-degree burns over 90 percent of his body. The strange thing was that Simon believed he had evened the score; he wasn't sorry. The problem was that he couldn't get the damn image out of his head. He had never told anyone the story, not even Miranda. She would occasionally ask him about his parents, and he told her they were dead and he hadn't had a happy childhood. Simon had always expected the police to knock down his door, but it never happened; he figured his father either hadn't told the truth or couldn't. Miranda had been a good wife and was the mother of his four children, but their marriage had always been a closed book. Simon wasn't interested in giving her a history lesson on his life. Of course they were amicable, for the children if nothing else, but they had never shared deep conversation, even when he was courting her. They acted like roommates with a mutual investment rather than lovers.

Simon sighed and turned his head to look at his fat wife fast asleep next to him. He wondered what the future would hold for his family; tomorrow he'd take Jed and Thomas to explore the town center, two miles from the house. They would need to stop at a few houses and scavenge for food and water. He also wanted to see if anyone from the church had survived. He would need to take stock of what they were up against; would there be law and order? If there wasn't, he meant to provide it. If it was a time for survival of the fittest, Simon fully intended to be the fittest. If it was a man eat man world out there, then he would be eating well.

• • •

The next morning Simon woke at dawn, even though he hadn't remembered falling asleep. No one else in the house was awake yet at least not that he could hear. Simon sat on the edge of the bed tying his boots; he had picked up the shitkickers two months ago but had never put them on. They were shiny black Doc Martens, and something about them made Simon feel like a commander in the military. He looked in the mirror. With the boots, he stood a few inches taller, and with his black debloused cargo pants, he looked like a black ops commando.

The house was cold—not unbearable, but cold. Simon hadn't seen the sun since the bombs had fallen. He shuffled downstairs; the two boys, his good little soldiers, sat waiting in the den.

"Boys, it's time to go," he said, using his best drill sergeant voice.

Jed stood up first; he was a big bull of a boy with a strong back but a weak constitution. His size and strength made Simon proud, while his teddy-bear-like presence made him cringe. Jed had his mother's face, round and doughy, and his father's intense eyes. Some interior aspect of Jed scared Simon; he thought there was an outside chance that Jed would one day snap and murder him in his sleep. That thought made Simon wonder if homicide was hereditary, but if that was what it would take to make Jed a man, so be it. Simon was always willing to sacrifice for his children.

Thomas, on the other hand, was a squirrelly kid, all piss and vinegar. Thomas would jump off a bridge if Simon requested it, but at the same time, Thomas made no effort to hide his hatred for his father. He was a quiet kid, thoughtful and introspective, but he also had a temper, and Simon loved the aggression he saw when that temper showed itself. Simon thought to himself how funny it was that two brothers growing up in the same household could be so different.

Simon and the two boys packed their backpacks with water, extra ammo, a hunting knife, a few scraps of food, and flashlights for scavenging dark houses. The plan was to walk to Main Street, the center of Middlebrook, and see if they could find out any news of the outside world. They would also need to find out if there was any organized authority in power and check on the church to make sure it was still standing. If the church was intact, there was a reasonable chance that Reverend Kasper was still alive. He would have a grasp on the state of the congregation.

Simon and the boys strode out into the stale morning air; they stepped over the body that was lying on the front walk. He gave Jed a stern look, letting him know that to talk about the dead man with Thomas was forbidden. The dark sky had just started to lighten; the eastern horizon had a cloudy, dull indigo hue, slightly brighter than the revolting dark gray above. Simon led the way with his six-volt hand lantern punching holes through the inky, dawn darkness. The air was thick like an invisible pea soup fog that they couldn't see, but they could feel it in their lungs. Simon walked quickly; he and the boys kept their eyes and ears open for any sign of movement. Both boys were armed with lever-action deer rifles from Simon's armory; he carried the Bushmaster assault rifle. After what had happened with the squatter, Simon wasn't ready to take chances. If it weren't for the bandanas wrapped over their mouths and noses, the three of them would have resembled a father/son hunting party.

Under the hush of dawn, the cul de sac looked peaceful and sleepy. It seemed like an ordinary morning just before sunrise... if you could ignore the fact that the houses all looked like they should be condemned. A fine, grainy coating of ash covered the street, making their footprints visible all the way back to the house. The light breeze blew dust devils up off the asphalt, where they swirled and fell. Simon scanned the ground for any other footprints, but the ash had obviously shifted in the last few days, erasing any trail like a shaken Etch-a-sketch.

"Father, should we search some of these houses?" Thomas asked, his voice muffled by the bandana.

"No, son, we don't want to carry the extra weight until the walk back home," Simon replied, as he stopped for a moment to sip water from a jug in his backpack. He kept shining the flashlight around and behind them to avoid any surprises.

"Father, where are all the people? Surely some have survived," Jed questioned as he passed the water bottle to his brother.

"I'm sure some have survived, but that doesn't mean they aren't sick. Some souls are probably poisoned and dying; perhaps some are starving or dehydrated. Not everyone had the foresight to prepare like we did. There could be ailing people in these houses right now, suffering from radioactive sickness." Simon pointed the flashlight at the row of houses across the street as if there might be a set of eyes peeping out from one of the broken windows.

"What is all this ash from? Is it because of the explosions?" Thomas asked timidly.

"I think some is from the explosions and some is from the fires that the explosions caused. Remember, whole cities—heck, whole countries were burned," Simon answered, kicking up a cloud of dust in a pile of ash that looked like volcanic sand. "Enough with the twenty questions, boys, we have to get going," Simon said coldly.

By the time they reached Main Street, a light rain had started, creating a gritty, sticky paste on the road. The sky had brightened, but the sun was blocked by a thick layer of pallid clouds. At the base of Main Street was a four-way stoplight. One of the roads on the right led to a fork, and one direction of the fork led up a long hill to the industrial park, which held the health clinic and post office; the other road off the fork led south out of town. Middlebrook town center was basically one long road of two-story structures that were commercial at street level and residential on the second floor. At the far end of Main Street was the town green, surrounded by municipal buildings, the Chatwood Library, Town Hall, and the Middlebrook Volunteer Fire Department. The rest of town consisted of farmland, two schools, and rural suburban plan housing. The only police presence in Middlebrook was a resident state trooper. Simon couldn't remember his name, but if anyone had information about what, if any, government had survived, it would be him. That, of course, was assuming the trooper himself had made it through.

Simon and the boys carefully walked down Main Street, seeing more and more signs of human activity. Footprints left in the ash crisscrossed the road and sidewalk, heading in different directions. They followed a pair of scuff marks off the street onto the sidewalk, like they were tracking wild game. A majority of the brick buildings weren't badly damaged, but the glass showcase windows of the storefronts had been. Shattered glass covered the sidewalk as they approached a deli where Simon had often bought lunch. The Middlebrook Deli had catered a church picnic just this past year; Simon had placed the order. It was difficult to tell if the deli had been looted or if the damage had come during the nuclear attack. Simon was peering through the broken display window when he glanced up and saw a man carrying a metal pail across the street.

"Hey! Hey, you with the bucket!" Simon yelled, leveling his Bushmaster in the direction of the stranger. The man was startled and started to run without a look in Simon's direction. "Hey, don't be afraid we just want to talk!" he called lowering the rifle but the man kept up his pace in the opposite direction. Simon thought he recognized the man from around town, but it was difficult to say for sure, because the man hadn't been facing him. Simon didn't want to chase the man down, but he needed some basic information. "Stop or I'll shoot!" Simon yelled. He had no actual intention of shooting, but it was the only way he could think of to get the man to stop. It seemed to work; the man froze in his tracks and placed the pail he had been carrying on the ground. He held up his hands like he had been caught fondling the blue ribbon sow at the county fair.

Simon trotted over to the man, who was standing in the middle of Main Street.

"I don't have anything to steal, and I'm very sick," the man said. He looked like he was scared shitless, shifting back and forth like a toddler who had to piss. "You wouldn't want to eat me; I'm very sick," the man said again. He was skin and bones, wearing a blue mechanic's coverall that was caked with dirt and ash. His hair was shaggy and his face was covered by a badly neglected beard. Simon's jaw dropped—had this man really been worried that Simon and the boys might eat him?

"Sir, we just want to talk. We've been cooped up in a shelter on the outskirts of town since the bombs dropped," Simon said in the most pleasant voice he could muster. He pulled a packaged granola bar from his backpack and handed it to the stranger. The man dropped his hands and looked at Simon strangely, and then he took the granola bar. He ate the bar in three big bites, hardly bothering to chew what had made its way to his mouth. "Who would eat you?" Simon asked the man, who seemed to relax a bit.

"We've heard rumors about bands of men who have been taking people once they run out of food." The man licked his fingers. Jed pulled a small water bottle from his backpack and handed it to the man. Simon shot Jed a disapproving look.

"Who's we? How many people are here in town?" Simon asked.

"There's fourteen of us holed up in the basement of the fire department. It's one of the last places that have a little water. It seems like a few people trickle in everyday, they are either emerging from shelters when they run out of food or coming from the outskirts of town like you guys," the man answered. He must have assumed the threat had passed because he reached down a picked up his empty bucket.

Jed chimed in, "What about the store shelves or scavenging nearby houses for food and water?"

"There isn't a real grocery in Middlebrook. Everyone used to drive to Merseyside and hit up that big box supermarket. All we have is Creighton's Convenience, and we've taken what we could there. A lot of the canned goods have already been cleaned out," the man answered.

"What about the houses?" Thomas questioned.

"People feel strange breaking into their neighbors' houses, especially when most are occupied by rotting corpses. Everyone is scared of catching something; some of us are already sick, and all of us have weakened immune systems from a lack of food and clean water. A girl took her sick mother up to the health clinic yesterday and she never came back. People are scared to travel too far, and nobody knows how much radiation is out here." The man looked beaten down, like he hadn't slept in weeks. He spoke quickly.

"This is survival. People need to get over their fear of dead bodies if they want to keep from becoming one," Simon retorted. He was growing frustrated; he had been hold-ing out hope that some kind of order had been maintained. "There must be more survivors. What about the police or the National Guard? Surely there must be people left who can set up aid stations or who can hold these cannibals accountable. Who's your leader?" A lightbulb went off in Simon's head—perhaps God's plan wasn't for him to exterminate these people, perhaps he was meant to shepherd them through this catastrophe.

"We haven't seen anyone like that in Middlebrook," the man stated. "There was a resident state trooper in town before everything happened, but we haven't seen him. Somebody at the firehouse said he was run over by a truck after the sirens went off, but we haven't come across a body...at least not his body. We don't have a leader; everyone is helping each other, and like I said, more and more people have trickled in every day. Everyone around here was pretty scattered, and if you haven't noticed, the buses aren't running." Simon thought the man had some balls to be joking around when he had just been stopped at gunpoint by three strangers. "Listen, why don't the three of you come to the firehouse? I'm sure you'll get more answers there than I can give you," the man said, gesturing for Simon and the boys to follow him.

They followed him down Main Street. The light rain and ashen sky made everything seem bleak, but in Simon's brain the wheels were spinning. He thought about how strong and charitable he was, the perfect leader for these wayward souls. Simon could feel the inebriation of power, and he hadn't even met these people yet. He would usher them through this difficult hour, and for that they would thank him, God does work in mysterious ways.

"My name is Bystrek, Paul Bystrek," the stranger said to Simon as the four men shuffled down Main Street in the midst of a torrential downpour. They followed Paul into the firehouse, a sprawling one-story municipal building with a red brick facade and a tattered American flag on a bent flagpole. Next to the front entrance were three hulking white bay doors. The glass windows on the doors had been smashed and covered with green plastic tarpaulins and duct tape. The four men entered the garage area, which still contained the town's bright red fire trucks. As a young boy, Simon had been enthralled by fire trucks, the giant red beasts with reflective high-gloss paint. He noted that these trucks reflected under three rows of track lighting hanging from the ceiling.

"There's power here?" Simon asked. Jed and Thomas trailed a couple feet behind; they seemed to be awed by the fire trucks too. They arrived in a small area at the back of the bay that contained three private offices. One of the offices had a small placard on the door that read Fire Marshall in gold letters.

"The lights are powered by a generator; diesel, I think." Paul pointed to a bank of switches lining a panel on the wall. "We keep the lights running for a few hours during the day, and we turn on the exterior lights at night. Like I told you, we've had a couple new people trickle in each day. Some of those new survivors have told us they came because they could see the floodlights at night," Paul said as he opened the door at the back of the first office. The door led to a stairwell that descended to a rectangular room that resembled a high school cafeteria. Cots had been arranged against the closest wall, and the far wall contained rows of lockers behind a wooden bench that ran the length of the room. At the far end of the room was a series of lunch tables, and it appeared that a kitchen was through a doorless archway beyond that. The room had stark white walls, and the hard linoleum floor shined with black and white checkered squares that left Simon feeling like he was walking across a giant chess board. A group of men and women sat around a table far in the back corner. The group looked like a PTA meeting for the homeless; they were all scribbling notes, yet they sat dressed in dirty clothes and some of the faces were in desperate need of some kind of ointment.

An elderly gentleman who appeared to be wearing pajamas and brown slippers stood from the group and examined Simon and his boys from afar. When the old man eventually spoke, he had a deep voice with a slight lisp. He sounded like a cross between Richard Nixon and Elmer Fudd. "Good work, Paul; you have found more survivors." The man smiled in a welcoming way, showing a mouth full of gleaming white dentures. "I'm so glad to see our numbers swell; it's such a blessing. My name is Roger Wilkinson, and I was once the tax collector of this great town...that was before all of the senseless destruction." Simon thought to himself that if this guy was running the show, the town was far more desperate for leadership than he could have imagined. Roger introduced all the men and women at the table, nine in total. He went on to tell Simon of all the progress they had made in the last few weeks—securing the firehouse, sealing the broken windows, starting to fix the radio, and having each survivor take responsibility for one aspect of everyday survival. They had begun taking stock of their assets and were trying to begin the process of functioning like a town again. Roger also discussed threats that faced everyone, including a group of mysterious road agents. He even told Simon about the two women who had made an attempt to travel to the health clinic yet never returned.

The agenda for the day was to wait for the storm to pass then send out two search parties. One search party would head in the direction of the health care clinic in an attempt to find out what had become of the two women. The second search party would strike out in the direction of Simon's residence, check as many houses as they could for survivors along the way, and then retrieve Simon's wife and daughters. They could return and fetch their belongings later, but everyone agreed that getting Simon's family to safety was imperative. Simon would need to make a decision as to which party he would accompany; he would volunteer to lead, of course, and would send the boys with the other group. A vision had begun to form deep in the interior jelly of Simon's mind—he was marching across the land carrying a sword, a stunning beacon of hope. He was followed by a herd of people, leading them to the light through this darkness. His leadership would emerge in this firehouse, on this day.

11

THE ORPHANS OF TIME

Denise began to tell Jeannette and Nate everything she knew about the state of the town since the attack. Her mother lay in the waiting room on top of a gurney with intravenous fluids being fed into her arm; she was still unconscious.

"After about a week at the library, we were out of water, so my mom and I went out. The first place we checked was the firehouse across the street. There were people there, like six of them; they had supplies they had found at the firehouse—emergency rations and such." Denise spoke like she was close to exhaustion, very slowly with long pauses to drink water.

"Did anyone at the firehouse have any information from outside? Like did they know how close the bombs hit or if any place was spared from the attack? Someplace we could all go to get away from this shit?" Nate asked, relaxing in the reclining chair he had formerly used for drawing blood. Jeannette frowned at Nate for his use of profanity.

"A man at the firehouse—I think his name was Russell—was trying to fix a shortwave radio that was attached to one of the fire trucks. He thought that if he could get his hands on some parts he could get it working," Denise responded.

"So there were six of you at the firehouse when you left to come here?" Nate said, watching Jeannette get up and go check on Joanne in the waiting room.

"No, there were six when we first got to the firehouse, but more people came in before we left to come here. One man's name was Bob; he came from outside of the town center, from one of the farms. He said there are dangerous people wandering the countryside; they are hurting people and robbing them. He told us that on his way to town he hid in a chicken coop and watched these men go into a house. Then he heard gunshots and screams. After a while, they dragged a woman out and took her with them. He said they were really rough with her; one man punched her in the face when she wouldn't stop screaming. We asked Bob why he hadn't tried to help the lady, and he said there were four of them and they had guns. He just laid low until they left." Denise finished her story as Jeannette walked back into the room.

"Here, take these," she said, handing a blister pack of pills to both Nate and Denise. The blister packs contained iodine hydrochloride and Prussian blue tablets. Nate could tell by the look on Jeannette's face that she didn't have any good news about Joanne.

"How is she?" Nate asked Jeannette. Denise looked at Jeannette intently, with palpable anxiety.

"She has a high fever; I think she's in a coma. It may be too late for the antibiotics to work. She also has a lot of edema, which would mean her kidneys are likely shutting down. There just isn't much we can do, even if there were a hospital or a dialysis machine we'd..." Jeannette stopped midsentence, realizing that Denise wasn't taking the news well at all. She began to sob, her nose and eyes wet with grief. Jeannette walked over to where Denise was sitting and got down on her knees so she was at eye level.

"Honey, let's just give it some time and let the medicine and fluids work. This isn't over yet," Jeannette said as she took a tissue from a box on the desk and delicately wiped the tears from Denise's face. She handed Denise another fresh tissue for her nose.

Once Denise had cleaned her dirt-streaked face and brushed the hair from her eyes, tucking it behind her ears, Nate could tell she was much younger than he had originally thought—probably seventeen or eighteen years old.

That night, Jeannette made up the reclining blood draw chair with a blanket, sleeping bag, and pillow for Denise to sleep in. Nate and Jeannette had agreed that it would be best for Denise to sleep close to her mother while they slept downstairs in the shelter. They both instructed Denise to fetch them immediately if her mother's condition changed in any way. It would also give Nate and Jeannette a chance to talk in private now that their situation had evolved. The night was quiet; Denise was curled up in the draw chair humming softly to herself, and Joanne was in the waiting room making a strange, scary gurgling sound as she lay unconscious.

Nate turned down the sleeping bags on the two attached exam tables that had been their bed for weeks. Jeannette walked over to him, wearing one of Nate's Depeche Mode T-shirts and white cotton panties with pink roses. "Nate, what are we going to do? I'm really worried about Denise," she said empathetically.

"There's not much we can do; I think we all know you're doing everything you can," he said, lying down on his side of the jury-rigged double bed.

"Nate, Joanne is dying. Her organs are shutting down. I'll be surprised if she makes it through the night. Denise is just a girl; she can't be much older than sixteen, and she's going to be devastated. She can't survive out there on her own," Jeannette sighed, climbing under the sleeping bag next to Nate and snuggling up in his arms.

Nate knew exactly what buttons Jeannette was trying to push, and she was becoming insanely accurate. "So what you're saying is if and when Joanne dies we should take Denise in?"

"Nate, I don't think we have a choice." Jeannette's words were somber, but Nate knew that some part of her was happy to have another project to fix.

"What about the people down the hill at the firehouse? She was with them longer than she's been with us; maybe they have some kind of survivors' bond. How do you know she'd even want to stay here with us?" Nate bit down on his tongue, knowing that Jeannette didn't care about that and had already made up her mind. "Maybe she wants to be on her own. It's a different world now."

"She needs someone to take care of her. Girls her age aren't capable of making decisions like that."

"She seems pretty self-reliant to me—she got her mother all the way up here by herself," Nate said, but Jeannette was steadfast and stubborn.

"She needs someone to take care of her, Nate," repeated Jeannette.

"Jeannette, she's hardly a kid anymore. Don't you remember when you were her age?" Nate replied. Jeannette cringed at his statement. Nate wasn't against the idea entirely, but someone needed to play devil's advocate, and he wasn't ready to submit that it had been fated.

"Because she's going to be sick! Very sick!" Jeannette snapped angrily, getting up on one elbow and piercing Nate with fiery eyes. He suddenly realized what exactly Jeannette had been implying. He felt utterly stupid. Denise's path since the bombs was identical to her mother's—the same mother who was upstairs playing blind man's bluff with death himself. He thought about it: how long would it be before Denise began losing her hair by the fistful? Or until she had ulcers all over her pretty face?

"Do you really think she's been exposed that much?" Nate asked, knowing the answer. He quickly intervened before Jeannette could scold him again. "She's young and resilient; why don't we ask her how she feels—ask her what she wants to do?" He thought for a moment. "That's if her mother doesn't pull through." Nate felt like a father who had just granted his daughter permission to stay out late on a school night.

"Nate, you sure do drive a hard bargain," Jeannette said, giggling as she snuggled back in against Nate's warm chest.

Thunder clapped above the building and reverberated loudly, even down in the fallout shelter. It was the first real storm in over a month. Nate pictured the rain washing away the rest of the ash—a complete radioactive enema, erasing all the decaying atoms and leaving behind a clean and shining valley of wildflowers. Without a doubt, it was an overly optimistic daydream; the most Nate could realistically hope for was a little sunshine. He got up from the bed and turned off the lantern on the desk in the center of the room, then he lay back down next to Jeannette, who had been picturing something far darker: a deluge of radioactive rain poisoning the already diseased landscape. Both Nate and Jeannette drifted off to sleep listening to the ominous rumble of the storm.

Jeannette was walking down a sterile white corridor, an endless row of hospital rooms on her left and right. Her hand was holding something cold, heavy, and slippery; she glanced down and saw a Civil War–era surgical bonesaw. The handle was slick with congealing blood, and the teeth of the saw were gummed up with pink gristle and yellowish shards of cartilage. On her right in the hospital room, a man rose to a sitting position, two bloody stumps jutting out from his blanket where his legs should have been. Flesh and a jagged portion of femur protruded from his hastily hacked wounds. "You took my legs..." the patient said softly. Jeannette continued to walk, looking into the next room. Another man lay there, his torso and face badly charred with radiation burns. The man began to thrash and scream as Jeannette rushed into the room to help him. She grabbed his shoulders to push him back onto the bed and felt his skin sloughing off under her hands as she struggled to hold him down. "I need some help here!" she howled, only hearing her own voice echo off the walls over and over. A doppelganger of Jeannette hurried into the room. It was like looking in a mirror, but instead of wearing a T-shirt and cotton panties the pseudo-Jeannette sported a butcher's apron with rose imprints in blood. Pseudo-Jeannette squatted down and picked up the bonesaw from the floor at Jeannette's feet. She began sawing at the man's legs in long strokes. Blood began to spurt in fountains and puddle on the floor beneath the exam table. Jeannette's double turned to Jeannette and in her own voice said, "You have more patients; better get cooking, Jeannie." Then she smiled, a look that scared Jeannette more deeply than the amputation taking place in front of her. Jeannette backed out of the room and started to run down the corridor, but the rooms didn't change; each room contained a bizzarro-Jeannette performing some heavy-handed crude surgery. Most of the patients looked like they had been horribly burned; they were all in excruciating pain. After what seemed like hours of running, Jeannette found the end of the wing and peered through two sliding glass doors. The view was of the parking lot outside the blood draw facility; a line of patients in various states of distress stood under an orange sky. Flies buzzed around the queue of people waiting; some of them had maggots crawling on their faces.

Jeannette woke with a shiver. Her mouth tasted of pennies, as if her brain had overheated, melting a few wires in the process. She looked over at Nate, who was snoring softly, and put her arms around him. For the moment she felt safe. Jeannette listened to the thunder for a while before drifting back to sleep.

• • •

The next morning, Nate could feel a black pall fall over the blood draw building. Bad tidings had been ushered in with the heavy rain. Jeannette and Nate had been woken by a tearful, incoherent Denise. She had urged them upstairs to the waiting room, where Joanne had passed away at some point during the night. Nate unhooked the IV lines and covered the bluing corpse while Jeannette tried her best to comfort the inconsolable sixteen-year-old. In the end, the only thing capable of pacifying Denise was a tablet of Valium. While Denise faded into a sedative-induced sleep, Jeannette and Nate debated the best way to responsibly dispose of the body. The heavy, monsoon-like rain would make outdoor burial difficult at best. There was no easy answer; even if they had a shovel to dig a suitable grave, the rain would make that chore nearly impossible. They decided to push off the decision as long as possible, at least until they could discuss it with Denise.

That afternoon, Nate, Jeannette, and the brokenhearted Denise sat in the lab and danced around the issues at hand. "Denise, honey, we are so sorry. Is there anything we can do to make you more comfortable?" Jeannette asked, sitting across from Denise. The teenager sat still with bleary and bloodshot eyes; she hadn't spoken since waking from her slumber. Nate brought her a cup of water, which she nursed slowly as she gazed off into space. "Denise, I know you don't know Nate or me very well, but I want you to know that you can stay here as long as you want." Jeannette reached over and picked up Denise's hands as she spoke. Nate could sense the tension in the air; it was like a weight pushing down on all three of them.

Jeannette looked up at Nate before getting to the quandary at hand. "Denise, we need to do something for your mom. I know this is difficult, but it's not safe for us if her body stays where it is."

"My mom wanted to be cremated," Denise said, breaking her self-imposed vow of silence.

"What, honey?" Jeannette replied. She had heard Denise perfectly, but she wanted to press for details.

"My mom wanted to be cremated and have her ashes spread in the ocean," Denise said, glancing up at Nate.

"I think we can manage cremation," Nate added somberly. "But we'll need to wait until the rain slows some."

Jeannette stood, stretching her back; Nate thought she looked spent, like she was partly blaming herself for Joanne's death. Joanne had been Jeannette's first real patient, and even though she had been beyond help when Denise had brought her in, it seemed to Nate that part of Jeannette felt she had failed.

"You need to be careful, Nate; that rain might be toxic, and anything you burn that has been irradiated will put the particles back into the air. You're going to have to find something for fuel in here."

"Yeah you're right" Nate said, "I remember reading something about that."

Nate spent the afternoon waiting for the rain to stop and breaking up a few waiting room chairs to burn under Joanne's body. He looked down at the stiff corpse wrapped in a sheet; it was the first human corpse he had ever dealt with up close. It wouldn't be his last, he knew; this new world was going to be a world of loss, a world full of orphans of time. About an hour before dark, the rain finally slowed to a light mist. Nate and Jeannette wrapped Joanne's body in a blue moving blanket they had discovered in the lab closet. They tied the blanket tightly with rope and then slid newspapers and magazines from the waiting room under the rope so that they would be pinned against the body. They then carried the body, with Jeannette at the feet and Nate at the head, out to the small alley between the blood draw building and the health clinic. Nate had already piled up the wood from the broken chairs in a makeshift pyre. When Denise was ready, they doused the blanket and paper with paint thinner they had found in the bunker, soaking everything thoroughly.

"I think we should say a few words. Denise, would you like to begin?" Jeannette asked softly. It was the first time Jeannette had been outside the building in more than a month; it seemed fitting for this new world that the reason was a funeral.

Denise spoke haltingly. "My mother...everyone always complains about their parents, but for me...my mother was my best friend." Denise couldn't continue—she lost it completely, falling to her knees on the wet, ashy ground. Jeannette went to Denise, embracing her and helping her up from the ground. Tears streamed down Jeannette's face as she tried to wrap her arms around Denise. Denise turned to Nate with a blank look on her face and said, "Just light it." She broke free of Jeannette's grasp and ran out of the alley with her head down. Nate heard the sliding glass doors slam shut. He bent down, struck a wooden match, and touched it to the blanket covering the body.

It caught fire immediately. Plumes of thick, foul-smelling, black smoke wafted up between the two buildings. As Jeannette and Nate walked away, Nate turned back to see the black smoke decorate the white walls in shadow.

12

THE FIREHOUSE

Back inside the blood draw facility, the somber vibe matched the dismal weather outside. Since the cremation, Nate had been busy gearing up for the walk to the firehouse. Curiosity had been eating at him ever since Denise had mentioned the place. They also would soon be desperate for food and clean water, and of course Nate still yearned for news from the outside world. Sooner or later, they were going to run out of supplies, and Nate thought it might be a decent idea to scout out some local sources. Jeannette was in the lab attempting to soothe Denise, who Nate figured would be bereft for quite some time. Nate hadn't told either of them what he was planning. Jeannette had begun treating Denise for radiation exposure, which was as good a distraction as any for them both.

He entered the lab wearing his heavy Gore-Tex coat with a rifle slung over his shoulder. He had forgone the plastic suit this time, figuring that the environment was likely as suitable as it was going to get. Besides, the plastic suit was becoming a hassle and had already begun to rip. "Jeannette, I'm going to go check out the firehouse. I'll see what I can find out—see if there might be help coming from the military or at least locate a source for clean water and food."

"Nate, are you sure that's a good idea?" Jeannette asked. She had been reading from *Gray's Anatomy* and was sitting next to Denise, who had fallen asleep.

"Today's as good a day as any; we need to see if we can get a better idea of where we stand. And who knows? Maybe they've got that radio working," Nate said.

"So how long should I wait before I sprint down that hill with guns blazing to rescue you?" Jeannette snickered sarcastically, but her grin vanished as Nate pulled the handgun from the belt at the small of his back.

"I don't think it's a bad idea for you to hold onto this, just in case." He handed her the pistol. "Do you know how to use it?"

"I think I can figure it out without severely injuring myself," Jeannette said.

"So give me an hour to get to the firehouse, an hour to scope out the scene and talk to the people there, and then an hour to walk back."

"It won't take you two hours in travel time, Nate. It's less than two miles down the road."

"But who knows what condition the road is in or what obstacles might hold me up along the way?" Nate looked down at the watch on his wrist. "It's two o'clock now. Let's say that if I'm not back by five you should start to worry. If it starts to get dark, just sit tight. I don't want you wandering around out there at night." Nate didn't want to sound patronizing, but at the same time he knew that Jeannette was eager to get outside; he didn't want to give her a good excuse.

"OK, big daddy, the little women will stay here and take care of the chillin; we'll have supper on the table when y'all get home," she said acerbically, with thick layers of offended sarcasm.

"When you accuse me of being misogynistic, don't use a Southern accent. You don't want to endorse the stereotype," Nate countered with equal smugness.

"I'm not accusing you of being misogynistic, I'm accusing you of being a male chauvinist. It's a subtle but important difference. I still think it's stupid of you to go out there alone, but I'm not your mother. Just be back before dark." Jeannette spoke the last part exactly like a mother giving her teenage son a curfew. Nate couldn't understand why Jeannette was acting so snippy—either she truly had anxiety about him being out there alone or she wanted to be included. Either way, it was a side of Jeannette that Nate wasn't accustomed to yet.

Nate took his backpack, which contained a small amount of water, his flashlight, and some extra shells for the rifle. He slid open the glass door and slid it closed behind him, making certain it was shut tight. The rain had slowed again; now it was just spitting from the definition-less clouds. Part of Nate felt exhilarated to be outside, progressing forward; the other part felt like he was neglecting his duty. The whole building had begun to feel like a prison, and getting out felt like a work furlough or conjugal visit. He was going to take advantage of it.

Nate walked through the damp, mushy ash past the small industrial park next to the health care buildings. The plain, square white structures stood empty like molars in a giant mouth; they had once held machine shops and Internet mail-order warehouses. Though they may have seemed strangely out of place in rural Middlebrook, the businesses housed there provided much-needed employment for the blue collar workforce of Middlebrook. For Nate, the walking wasn't as difficult as he imagined; the only obstacle was the occasional Volkswagen-size potholes sunk deep in the road.

Walking freed Nate of the walls he had been inside and also allowed his mind a chance to reflect on the past month. He thought about the morning, the cremation, his time with Jeannette in the shelter, and how everything had so drastically changed—how *he* had changed. It was like he had entered the fallout shelter as a lowly, paranoid caterpillar, and the shelter had been his chrysalis, so that now he was emerging as a butterfly...well, maybe something a tad more masculine than a butterfly. He had seemingly undergone a complete metamorphosis—from an anxious loner to someone who could be depended upon by a woman and now a teenager. He still wasn't completely confident and had moments of panic and even sheer terror, but at least he felt like he had been built for this, built for survival. Nate knew his life, though; he knew his history. Every time he seemed to have a solid grasp on the present, the future would come along and cut off his balls. Nate changed the channel in his head, trying to concentrate on the road in front of him.

The road was blocked by a fallen telephone pole. The pole had broken off five feet from the ground and now lay across the road. Behind the pole was a long line of cars, all of which had been abandoned, or at least they had been abandoned by the living. Nate stepped over the telephone pole, avoiding the downed wires. Of course the wires were benign, but even so, Nate felt uncomfortable even stepping near them. The vehicles were a different story; his curiosity brought him right alongside the first car. The air must have become unbreathable quickly, he thought, as he peered into the sedan that stood idle in the road. A rotting corpse lay curled in the fetal position on the back seat. The lonely cadaver had tried to shelter in the car or had simply crawled into the back seat to die. Its skin was drawn tight to the bone, and a pile of gelatinous brown goo sat on the seat next to the corpse's torso. It reminded Nate of pictures he had seen of the "bog people" who had died thousands of years ago and been found perfectly preserved in a peat bog somewhere in Europe. He became fixated on the face of the victim, which had been frozen in time with a look of panic that Nate knew far too well. The air smelled of char and sulfur, but a far worse odor had made its way through the closed car windows—the smell of death. The line of cars had been washed clean by the rain, but tiny lumps of plastered ash had formed rings on the ground around the wheels.

Nate moved on and fought to keep his eyes from the interiors of the cars. The first corpse's face had already burned itself into his mind as vividly as a color photograph; he knew it was the type of image that would haunt his dreams. He paused at the next vehicle, whose door was open, and he had a thought: he hadn't ever had the chance to try the ignition in his own car. What if the EMP *hadn't* wrecked the wiring in cars? Maybe it was just the grid that was affected. He reached his hand inside the driver's side door of the silver SUV and grabbed the key hanging from the ignition. He held his breath and mentally crossed his fingers and toes. The key turned with a click, but nothing else happened. The car had become a two-ton monument to Detroit and the past. Nate closed the door and continued down the road, occasionally glancing into the stalled autos, hoping to see something he could use. Some of the scenes inside the cars were horrid; he tried not to look, but it was like driving by the scene of an accident. A whole family had died in a minivan like some twisted, morbid picture of the worst family vacation ever. A man whose lips were pressed to a gap in a slightly rolled down window, his hand still on the wheel, petrified by rigor mortis. Nate closed his eyes but he could still see the desperate, decayed faces and the fearful look that would remain on those faces for eternity. He finally stumbled to the end of the line of metallic tombs, bent over, and dry heaved. He turned and looked back; the traffic jam stretched for nearly a quarter of a mile up the hill.

At the bottom of the hill, Nate came to a fork in the road. One direction led south out of town, and the other continued toward Middlebrook center. Nate followed the road in the direction of the town center to a four-way intersection. The town's lone stoplight was dancing in the light breeze; one of its support cables had snapped, leaving the stoplight off kilter. It appeared to be in danger of crashing down at the next heavy wind gust. Nate took a left onto Main Street. He walked down the small median in the center of the road, scanning the buildings and storefronts on both sides. Most of the structures had severe damage—smashed-out windows or swayback roofs. The stores were all family run and consisted of boutiques, a frozen yogurt shop, antique dealers, and two restaurants. Few of the buildings would be useful for scavenging, but the pizza parlor and convenience store might have supplies Nate could use. At the very least, there should be bottled water and scattered canned goods, depending on who had scavenged there first. Everyone in this world would need to get accustomed to finding new sources of sustenance, and that would include scavenging houses and businesses, some limited hunting (depending on which animals had survived), and eventually farming. The hope would be that some farmers had well-insulated barns that had kept small numbers of livestock alive. Those animals would most likely have some contamination, but some level of contamination might have to be acceptable for breeding stocks.

Nate continued to trounce along, taking a mental inventory of stores that looked promising for finding water on the return trip. Through the drizzle, Nate could hardly recognize the firehouse; he used the library, an unmistakable stone building, as a landmark. The library stood directly across Main Street from the Middlebrook Volunteer Fire Department. Both buildings bordered the town green, which was at the farthest end of Main Street. Nate was standing about two full football fields from his destination. The air seemed to hang in smoky tendrils in front of his face, like he had passed through the aftermath of a forest fire.

He began to see signs of human existence: perfect shoe prints outlined in gray had been left in the wet ash at his feet. Some had been distorted or washed away by the rain, but most were mirror images of rubber-soled shoes. The zigzags in the ash appeared random, leading in all different directions, but the trail's destination could have been erased by the rain. The whole place felt like a ghost town, like Tombstone, Arizona, without the sand. He expected to see a tumbleweed crossing his path at any moment. The last time Nate had been on this street, it had been bustling with life; now it was deserted and dead. The street itself resembled an enormous ashtray or some bombed-out third-world shithole. The entire area would have been condemned in Nate's past life.

As he walked, he could see the firehouse standing alone like a beacon of hope shining in a pasture of death and decay. As he got closer, the building distinguished itself from the neighboring structures immediately. First off, Nate noticed that there appeared to be power to run lights of some sort. Secondly, the broken windows had been patched with tarps; even the large garage bay windows had been covered with heavy, clear plastic or green tarps. The shards of glass that covered the sidewalk in front of every other building were conspicuously missing at the firehouse. Someone had worked hard to sweep up the shards, removing the hazard for anyone passing by.

Nate wasn't sure whether he should knock on the door or simply stroll in and announce himself. He didn't want to risk being shot as a looter; he didn't know these people, and more importantly, he didn't know their state of mind. They could be scared shitless of anyone walking by, or they could be thrilled that others had survived. He walked over to the closed garage doors and wiped the hardened film of ash in a circular motion, creating a small circle to peer through. Nate could see two men inside; one was up on a fire truck taking off a fixture of some kind with a socket wrench. The other man was sitting at a table with the guts of something electrical splayed out before him. Nate knocked loudly on the wood paneling below the plastic window. The man who had been sitting at the table looked up; he was soldering components together. He smiled at Nate and then stood and rushed over to the garage door.

"Come in the front door—to your right!" he yelled through the plastic, pointing to the door he meant. Nate walked over to the door that was below a floodlight fixed to the brick facade and turned the knob. He entered a small foyer. Framed pictures and plaques hung from the cream-colored wall. On the opposite side of the foyer hung a mounted, stuffed moose head with Christmas ornaments hanging from its enormous antlers. The man who had waved Nate inside emerged from a doorway on the left. He was a big, boisterous man with huge white teeth and a generous smile. He reached out and shook Nate's hand with a grip strong enough to make his fingers crack audibly.

"Hiyah there, I'm Bob Halloran." The man's enormous hands enveloped Nate's like a gorilla snatching a buzzing mosquito from the air. Bob looked to be about six-foot-five, Nate thought, and he seemed as thick as he was tall, but sturdy, like an interior lineman. He had a 1950s military-style flattop haircut and wore a red and black checkered flannel shirt. He spoke in a booming baritone voice, saying, "We're so glad you made it, young fella!"

"My name's Nate Wilder," Nate said with a smile. Nate felt a kinship with Bob almost immediately; it was something he hadn't experienced in a while. Nate handed Bob his coat, shaking off the chill and wetness. "I work—or worked—up the road at the blood draw facility. My coworker and I sheltered there through the worst of it."

Bob looked surprised, but the welcoming good cheer continued. "Oh, that is great news; we're starting to put together quite a little group of survivors here. The problem is that no one has any medical training, and some of us have been pretty beat up, been through hell in the last few weeks. Actually, we had a couple women here, a mother and daughter. They went up to your clinic; the mother was in real bad shape," Bob said, ushering Nate farther into the room.

"Yeah, Denise and Joanne," Nate said. "They showed up on our doorstep a little while ago. Unfortunately for Joanne, it was too late to help, but Denise is still there getting treatment from my coworker, Jeannette." Again, Nate could see the look of surprise on Bob's face.

"Well, that's really too bad about Joanne; I knew her from around town; she was a real nice lady. We just lost a married couple; they were outside when the heavens came down," Bob said plainly. "Let me introduce you around. We actually had a search party due to go track those ladies down, but at least now we know. Nate, I'm so glad you're here. Follow me."

They walked past the door through which Bob had entered the foyer. Nate looked through the open door into the main garage area. Four red fire engines were gleaming under the fluorescent lights. Nate could hear the rumbling of a generator, which answered the question about the lights he had forgotten to ask. He could still see the other man sitting on top of the second fire truck; the man had a large toolbox next to him and was rummaging through it. "What are you guys working on in there?" Nate asked, pausing as they passed the door.

"We're cannibalizing a radio from engine twelve. We finally got a signal yesterday, just static, but at least we know the thing turns on. Russell, the gentleman up on the truck, is taking the antenna off the hook and ladder. That should give us the megahertz to reach anywhere in the state, maybe beyond. Russell was a computer engineer back in the world; he figured out that the EMP—do you know what an EMP is?" Bob interrupted himself with the question.

"Electromagnetic pulse, yeah, it's why everything electronic is fried," Nate answered quickly.

"Right, that's what they tell me," Bob said as they reached the moose and took a right down a stairway. "Russell figured out that the EMP had fried all the wires and blew the fuses; anything with complex wiring or a microchip is as useful as a rock. The only way to get anything to work is to bring it all back to analog and replace the damaged parts. Hell, if we can find an old car, we might get it running, but most vehicles have computers nowadays. They don't make 'em like they used to." Bob realized the irony of the statement and smiled as he said, "Well, I guess right about now they don't really make 'em at all." He gave out a hearty laugh.

"So do any of the survivors you were with have radiation poisoning?" Nate asked, thinking about what Jeannette had said about being useful in this evolving world.

"Ayup, I figure we all glow in the dark now. Some had it worse than others—puking, loose teeth, swollen glands—and I told you about the married couple that passed away."

The two men reached the bottom of the stairs and opened a door to a large room that looked like a cross between a locker room and a small gymnasium. A handful of people were milling around between rows of cots. At the opposite end of the room was a group of long, brown cafeteria lunch tables. Nate was blown away by how many survivors were here; he counted at least ten, and there seemed to be twice as many made up cots with blankets or luggage sitting on them. Obviously some people were out of the building, perhaps gathering supplies or searching for more survivors. The whole place seemed well organized, and Nate felt a renewed faith in society and its ability to come together after tragedy. Bob led Nate to the back of the room by the tables and introduced him to some of the survivors.

Nate was impressed; Bob explained that the main group had been subdivided into smaller crews of three or four. Each small group had been assigned a job that would aid in the community's survival. One group was sent out to search for survivors (he explained about the group that had been preparing themselves to go up to the health clinic); they were finding more and more survivors every day. Another group was sent out to the surrounding houses and stores to scavenge for anything the group could use. The third group Bob listed was the construction crew; they were working on surrounding buildings to clean up any hazards like broken glass, collapsed roofs, etc. The idea was to turn those buildings into temporary housing. Finally, Bob told Nate about his group, the tinkers. Their charge was to fix whatever machinery or electronics they could, such as the radio. They were also responsible for keeping the generator running. Groups had been assigned based on a person's skill set and what he or she was trained to do before the bombs.

Bob walked over to a small group of men who looked like they were preparing to go outside. Nate could see them talking for a moment, and then Bob walked back to Nate with a dejected expression.

"Nate, I thought that was the group going up to the health clinic, but it wasn't. The group that was supposed to go to the clinic just left; I don't know how we missed them. Maybe that's a good thing—they can bring your friend and Denise back here where it's safe." Bob spoke as though he were apologizing to Nate. It wasn't a huge deal to Nate at first; the group of men could save him a trip back up to the blood draw facility, get

Jeannette and Denise, and be back by dinner. The more Nate thought about it, though, the more he began to worry. What if Jeannette was frightened and pulled out the gun? What if she thought the search party was there to harm or kidnap her and Denise?

Nate was about to tell Bob that he should attempt to get to Jeannette before an accident happened when a man burst through the door excitedly, yelling for everyone's attention. It was Russell, who was trying to catch his breath. He looked like he had just been told that his wife was unexpectedly pregnant.

"Everybody, come quick! Upstairs...I can't believe it...come quick!" He was bent over breathing heavily. Everyone stopped what they were doing and gathered around Russell, waiting for an explanation.

"Upstairs—I hooked up the radio for the first time, and we got a signal! Somebody answered me!"

13

MISUSED

Jeannette sat across from Denise sipping hot tea in the lab. Over the course of their stay, Nate and Jeannette had determined that the lab was consistently the warmest room in the building. For whatever reason, probably the insulation, it held in any available heat. In this case, it was body heat and the heat thrown off by the portable camp stove that Jeannette had used to heat the tea. Jeannette had hoped that spending some time alone with Denise would help them bond on some level.

"Denise were you in school around here?" Jeannette figured that getting to know each other and what they were like before Armageddon would be the best way to break the ice.

"No, I was just here visiting my mom for spring break. My parents are divorced; I live with my dad on Long Island. I go to East Islip High School there," Denise answered, seeming only partly interested in the conversation. She had been staring off into space for most of the day and simply played along with the small talk to humor Jeannette. Jeannette didn't blame her. In fact, she thought Denise was in relatively good shape, considering that they had cremated her mother a just a few hours ago.

"So, what's up with you and Nate? Is he your husband or something?" Denise asked, doing her best to sound interested.

"Well, Nate and I are a couple, I suppose. Nothing is official or anything, and no, we're not married, but I trust him with my life. He's a little goofy, but he's also sweet and dependable." Jeannette spoke with pride and fought back a smile when she thought about Nate. She knew Denise was still reeling from the death of her mother and was careful not to break the somber mood with an inappropriate smile. Jeannette sympathized with Denise; after all, they were probably all orphans now. But she also knew that learning to deal with death quickly was going to be an important part of surviving in this world.

The day slowly slid by, like a snail sliming its way up a hill. Jeannette did her best to comfort Denise, but the conversation was awkward and sparse. Finally, Jeannette relented. There was no use pushing Denise if she wasn't ready to talk. "Denise, it's all right if you want some time alone; God knows I would if I were you."

Denise took a few moments to respond. "I'm sorry, Jeannette. I'm just so drained and don't feel like talking. I just miss my mom and dad is all."

"I understand completely; just let me know if you need anything." With that, Jeannette got up, walked over to Denise, and covered her with a blanket. Denise relaxed a bit; she was sitting in a chair and using a cardboard box full of lab chemicals for a footstool. Jeannette walked into the blood draw room and went to the window for a look out at the gray, depressing sky. She scanned the sloping road through the picture window at the back of the room, hoping to see Nate. The window was spotted with caked white ash, giving everything a frosted look. The stark, naked trees and empty industrial buildings made the whole scene resemble a bombed-out Bosnian winter. Out of her peripheral vision, Jeannette noticed movement. It was pretty far away, but she definitely saw something move. She focused her eyes on the spot as much as she could and picked out a solitary figure emerging from the mist. Jeannette's heart swelled— Nate was returning home. The figure was crouched slightly, moving cautiously, as if stalking some invisible prey. Jeannette could see his rifle held out in front of him, ready to shoot if necessary. Then the man stopped and held up a closed fist. He turned and waved, and a second man materialized out of the mist, then a third and a fourth. Anxiety and fear crawled into Jeannette's throat, making her want to gag...like she had swallowed a gulp of curdled milk. The four men were walking in a diamond pattern toward the blood draw building. The group was in some kind of military formation; it reminded Jeannette of the Vietnam War movies her father used to watch, with a point man followed by his platoon. The men were too far away from Jeannette to see their faces. She didn't know what to do. Were they marauders looking for loot or victims? Was it Nate bringing help? Had the army come to Middlebrook? Whoever it was, Jeannette wasn't about to take any chances of being seen. She squatted down, keeping only her eyes above the windowsill and being very careful not to make any sudden movements.

Jeannette crawled out from under the window and quickly turned off the battery-powered lamp, filling the room with shadowy darkness. She didn't think anyone would notice the change in light from the outside. A little light still came in through the windows, which allowed her to move around without bumping into anything. She made her way into the lab, making certain to avoid passing in front of the window. Denise was still sitting in the chair, but she had discarded the blanket, which lay on the floor at her feet. Jeannette looked around for the gun, she wanted to protect herself and Denise even if it meant killing a stranger. Hers eyes searched and As Jeannette looked closer, she could see that Denise was cradling the handgun in her lap. Jeannette had absentmindedly left it on the lab counter.

"Denise, what are you doing?" Jeannette said from the doorway. Denise jumped. She hadn't heard Jeannette enter the room, and she turned with a startled look. She picked up the gun and put the barrel to her temple.

"I don't want to live in this disgusting world anymore," she said with no emotion. Jeannette didn't know what to do; she had a group of men advancing on the building, and now she had a teenager threatening suicide.

"Denise, I know it seems hopeless, but you just have to get through this," Jeannette begged nervously, trying to find some way to defuse the situation.

"You're damn right it's hopeless," Denise snapped.

"Honey, things will get better. You're going to get through this; you'll find someone who loves you...you'll fall in love. Things might not be as bad as they seem, the whole world can't be a devastated mess like this. We don't even know the extent of the damage, who knows maybe only a couple of areas got hit, You need to put the gun down."

Denise didn't budge. She stared at Jeannette with eyes full of anger. "I'm all alone...the world is shit...we'll all probably die anyway. I'm just speeding up the process."

"Give me the gun, Denise. There is a group of armed men coming up the hill. I don't know if they are here to hurt us," Jeannette said, hoping that the men might be a distraction.

"Do you think I care? I wanna shoot myself, and you want me to worry about some assholes hurting me?" Denise screamed.

"That's not what I'm saying, Denise. I'm saying that there are assholes coming and I want to protect myself. You're holding our only weapon!" Jeannette yelled back. She thought that tough love, or at least selfishness, might work. Jeannette had no real experience with teenagers except for memories of when she had been that age.

"Who's coming? Are you sure it's not Nate?" Denise said. At that moment, Jeannette knew that she had been successful in preventing the suicide. Now she needed to worry about the men.

"I don't know; I don't think it's Nate. They looked suspicious the way they were creeping up the hill. I think we should hide. If it is Nate, he'll call out," Jeannette said, approaching Denise slowly to get the gun. Denise sat there looking unfazed, but she had lowered the gun slightly. It was now pointing at the side of her neck.

"Oh, God," Denise said, bursting into tears. "I can't take this."

"I know, honey. We can have a long talk later," Jeannette said, taking the gun and hugging Denise all in the same movement. For the first time, Denise thoroughly returned the embrace, sobbing into Jeannette's shoulder. Jeannette stood up and helped Denise to her feet. "We have to hurry; they'll be at the door any minute." Denise was still crying softly when Jeannette half-led, half-dragged her into an equipment closet on the far right-hand side of the lab.

"Shouldn't we hide in the cellar? Maybe the area where you and Nate sleep?" Denise whispered with a sniffle.

"No, there's no exit downstairs. If those men search down there we'd have nowhere to run; we'd be cornered," Jeannette whispered back into the pitch blackness of the closet. She could feel the moist heat coming off Denise and hear her breathing, but she was blind in the darkness, which only amplified the anxiety.

They stood, trembling with fear, for what felt like an eternity. The warm carbon dioxide from their exhalations made the closet stuffy and humid. It felt like a coffin. Jeannette began to think that the closet had been a really bad idea. She felt like she had to get out, like she would suffocate if she didn't. The worst part was that they had no idea where the men were. They could have passed by the building entirely—their target could have been the health clinic. Just as Jeannette was about to open the door to check where the men were, she heard a loud thud followed by the distant clank of metal on metal. She could hear yelling too. It seemed far away and muffled, but it was definitely yelling. Jeannette focused her ears and tried to hear what the men were saying.

"I hear someone talking or yelling," Jeannette whispered.

"Yeah, I hear it too," Denise answered softly.

Jeannette cocked the pistol and held it in front of her with shaking hands, then she felt for the safety and pushed the small, hard button. She had had a quick lesson on gun use from the late-night security guard, Marty, who would walk rounds between the two facilities. One night when Jeannette was working late, he had stopped in to check on her. He was a sweet guy, a retired cop, and Jeannette was fond of him. That night, Jeannette asked jokingly, "Can I see your gun?" He responded by taking the pistol out of its holster and handing it to her. Marty had explained how to hold the gun, how to aim it, and how to click off the safety and cock it.

Denise heard the click of the gun. "Jeannette, they could be friendly," she whispered.

"They could be," Jeannette replied, "or they could be rapists or murderers, or both."

Jeannette could hear talking and footsteps through the door, but they were too muffled to understand or to identify the intruders. One thing was certain; the men were now inside the room. Jeannette was horrified, both for herself and for Denise.

Suddenly the voices got louder; Jeannette could tell that the uninvited guests were now very close to the closet door. She pressed her ear to the door, holding her breath.

"Look, someone's been here recently," Jeannette heard one of the men say.

"Yeah, this looks more like a living room than a lab. This tea is still warm," a second man answered.

"There's also warm water on the stove," another said. Jeannette remembered the water she had boiled for the tea; she hadn't used it all.

"Hello?" one of them yelled out. "Hello, whoever is here, we're not going to hurt you." The men were silent for a second or two, listening for a response. Jeannette held her breath again, thinking her terrified exhalations sounded like a freight train.

Finally, Jeannette heard one of the men clearly say, "I don't think anyone's here; maybe they're next door at the other place."

"Yeah, Simon, let's get out of here. It'll be dark soon, and I'm freaking starving. Let's get back to the firehouse before those crazy dudes come out."

Denise heard that they were from the firehouse and burst from the closet. "We're here!" she screamed, like it was a surprise party and she had jumped out to surprise the lucky guest of honor. The men had turned to leave, but when they heard Denise they rushed to her. One of the men recognized her right away. "Denise, thank God we found you! Let's get you girls to the firehouse where it's safe and have some dinner." Jeannette insisted on staying, she was worried about walking off before Nate had returned, especially with men who she had just met. They could all walk down to the firehouse when Nate returned if that was what they all decided. Some small part of Jeannette wasn't ready to trust anyone yet.

14

THE TRANSMISSION

Nate followed the group up the stairs and into the garage. They moved quickly, and by the time Nate reached the fire truck a small crowd had gathered in a circle around the table on which the radio sat. Russell spoke again into the CB: "Please say again—we can barely hear you."

Eventually, a crystal-clear voice boomed through the receiving speaker. "Middlebrook, we read you. This is Sergeant Dickerson of the Maine National Guard. Over." The gathering of people around the radio burst into a raucous cheer. They were all buzzing, and Nate couldn't help but smile, though he wished Jeannette was there to share the joy. Russell turned around in his seat in front of the radio and yelled.

"Everyone be quiet! I need to hear this." There were a few more murmurs from the crowd, but they petered out quickly. "Sergeant, this is Russell Colvin. We're here in Middlebrook, Connecticut. Are you all the way up in Maine? Over."

"Well, Russell, I sure am glad to hear from you. My unit is on patrol here in New Hampshire. You must have one hell of a radio. Over." The murmur began again. Everybody had their own idea of what Russell should say, and some people began shouting out those ideas.

"Yes, sir, there's like twenty of us here in a firehouse. We've fixed up the radio. People here want to know if you can get down here to help us. Over," Russell replied.

Nate could hear the sergeant speaking to somebody on his end before coming back on the radio. "Russell, that's a negative. Those assholes must have really had something against Boston, because they hit that area with enough nukes to make it hot 'til the next ice age. We're mostly on foot working south, but we ain't gonna make it that far; our orders are to check into Augusta in a week. Maine was mostly spared, and the recovery effort is being quarterbacked from there. Augusta is the center of the universe now, and they don't want us anywhere south of Concord 'til they can reinforce us next week. Over."

"So what the hell are we supposed to do?" Bob asked no one in particular.

"Sergeant, what should we do? We don't exactly have it made down here. Over." A rumble of agreement spread across the concerned group like a rash.

"Middlebrook, the way I see it you have two choices," the sergeant said. "You can sit tight, keep yourselves alive, and ride out the winter. Rebuild what you can until we can get to you. Or you can attempt to make it to Maine. We'll be resupplying up and down this area for at least the next month. Humanitarian aid is starting to be trucked in from Canada." There was a long pause of radio silence before the sergeant came back on. "Keep in mind, you'll need to give Boston or any other hotspots a wide berth if you decide to head north. Also, just so you're warned, the roads aren't exactly secured. Over."

Russell had to speak over the rumbles from the group behind him. "Sir, do you know where else around here has been hit? We may need to know where these hotspots are. Over."

"Yeah, Augusta got a satellite image from the Canadians. The Russkies hit New York City real hard, the sub base in New London, some area in the sound called Plum Island, Hartford, Albany, and some other area in upstate New York, we think maybe Buffalo. The whole country's a real mess, but I know we hit 'em back just as hard. A lot of soldiers were overseas, in the Middle East and such, and their boats are coming in all the time, so we're organizing our forces to try to save as many states as we can get to. We've even had some communication with the West Co—" The sergeant was cut off midsentence; the transmission had turned into a wall of static.

"Sergeant...Sergeant Dickerson, are you there? Over," Russell asked desperately into the black handheld receiver.

"What the fuck's going on?" someone in the crowd yelled.

"I dunno—I think we lost him. Sergeant Dickerson, are you there?" Again there was no response, only static.

Immediately a furious conversation started; it boiled down to one question: *Should we stay or should we go?*

• • •

It was a week before a town meeting was called; there simply had been too much disagreement to get anything done, especially a quick decision about abandoning the town to travel north. Simon had asserted himself as the dominant figure helping the two factions come together to find a democratic solution. The town politics reminded Nate of high school, with the popular alpha kids attracting the needy outcasts like seagulls drawn to a dump. Over the course of the week, Simon had also moved into a leadership position for the community, which was desperately in need of a cohesive voice. It had seemed like a great idea at the time to name Simon interim chairman of the community. There were few objections.

Nate had returned to the blood draw facility to fill Jeannette in on the news. They spent the night of the radio transmission back in the blood draw building, but later that week they moved down to the firehouse. They really craved community, and it seemed that more and more survivors were coming in every day.

The night of the town meeting, everyone was ushered downstairs in a chattering mob. People took their seats at the tables in the rear of the basement. Each instinctively sat among the factions of people who agreed with his or her own point of view. One group of people had decided that the best thing to do was try to ride out the winter in Middlebrook and rebuild. It was only May, but everyone was concerned about the winter, it's something ingrained in New Englanders that goes back hundreds of years. The spring is "Fat City"; rivers teaming with trout and game would be abundant, but they always knew that the ice and frost are right around the bend in the seasonal roller coaster. The other group was vehement that they should all cut their losses and migrate to Maine; it was the only way to survive. Nate and Jeannette remained neutral; they had discussed the issue ad nauseum and had come to the conclusion that the decision wasn't so black and white; both sides had points that could be argued favorably.

A group of people stood up, went to the kitchen, and returned to serve dinner. They dished out bowls of canned beef stew and rock-hard hunks of bread. Simon stood and said grace, and everyone began eating. While they were eating, Simon stood again and began the debate.

"This is America, and in the American tradition of democracy, I feel we should have a vote on whether we choose to make the pilgrimage to Maine or remain here in Middlebrook to salvage the town and make the best life we can." Simon clapped his hands together and rested them on his stomach. "Before we vote, we shall have an orderly open discourse, discussing the benefits of each path. I understand that there have been private discussions about this all week. It is indeed a stressful decision, but I think if we are open and honest and keep our heads, we will come up with the right choice." He finished his speech and sat down to eat the rest of his dinner. Nate wondered who had died and made this guy the end all be all of Middlebrook and thought maybe it would be better if the vote was for whether or not he should lead.

Bob Halloran, who was quickly becoming one of Nate's best friends in the community, stood and started the debate. "I think we should pack up what we can carry and head north. There isn't enough food or water to get us through a cold winter," he said, smiling his friendly smile.

A grumbling chorus came from across the room, where Joe Conway stood and threw in his two cents. "I don't think that's realistic; the travel would be on foot, and we can't even begin to understand the dangers that are waiting on that road." He turned and nodded his head toward his two children, who were neck deep in beef stew. "I have a family. We can't expect the little ones to walk all the way to Goddamn Maine." Joe sat down incredulous and obviously irritated.

Simon stood immediately. "Please, people, let's keep this civil. There is no reason to take the Lord's name in vain."

Bob stood again. "But how will we survive the winter here? There isn't any fuel to heat this place through the cold, and you know burning wood is dangerous. Plus, like I said before, sooner or later we'll run outta food and water. You don't want your kids to starve, do you?" Bob sat back down. It all reminded Nate of a parliamentary debate in England where the members of parliament stood up in front of the magistrate, spoke, and sat back down. It seemed so formal.

Simon rose to his feet and slowly paced behind the line of people seated to his right. His eyes slid up and down the upturned faces before stopping to speak. "How many people are in our group now?" he asked. Without waiting for an answer, he continued, "-Thirty six. We are building something here: a community. If everyone works together and we gather all the food, water, and fuel to burn, we can make it through the winter, but we'll have to work together. More and more survivors are trickling in daily. By summer we will have Main Street reconditioned and full of families. Help will come, but I'm not sure we even need it. Just to get it on record, my vote is that we stay and rebuild our beloved Middlebrook."

Nate felt dizzy; his conscience was acting out a good cop/bad cop routine. He couldn't decide for himself if he wanted to stay or make the trek to Maine, let alone stand and give advice to others about what they should do. The one thing he did know was that Simon's line of surviving through the winter was complete bullshit. The resources in this town were finite, and if there wasn't enough they'd all die. Nate waited for a lull in the debate and stood, keeping his eyes focused for any objectors. He was anxious; public speaking was hardly one of his strengths. "Why does it have to be all or nothing?" Nate asked. "I think we can all agree that Middlebrook is a place worth holding onto, yet we don't have enough of the everyday necessities we need to survive indefinitely. We know about Connecticut winters—we've all seen more than a few. They can be harsh, with a foot or more of snow cover all winter, or they can be mild, without so much as a flake of snow. On the other hand, civilization seems to be stationed in Maine right now. Joe was right; it's not realistic to move the whole community to Maine. We have too many people who would be vulnerable on the road. However, we could make a list of volunteers, a list of the strongest, most able people, with skills that would be useful on the road. That team of volunteers could move quickly, hopefully reaching Maine in weeks and bringing back supplies, information, and help in general." Nate could hear the nervousness in his own voice, and the silence that followed his spiel compounded the problem. Standing still and hearing no feedback from the group, Nate awkwardly continued, "No one wants to abandon Middlebrook, but we can't rebuild and thrive without some kind of outside assistance. This town has never been self-sufficient, even in the best of times. We do have community here, but we're still a part of this country, aren't we? Don't you want to find out what happened to the rest of it, the president, what happened to your out-of-state relatives, everything that having a lifeline would mean?" It occurred to Nate that everything he had just said was at least partially bullshit, but he also understood that the need for information from outside was trumped only by the need for safety and sustenance.

Bob was the first to speak as Nate sat down in embarrassment; he felt like he hadn't influenced anyone with his argument.

"I think Nate has a point. Even if this scout team finds a paradise in Maine, we can't be sure that the road there is safe. If we send a smaller advance team, they will be able to travel quickly and travel light without putting families in peril," Bob said, and he sat down, nodding at Nate with a smile.

The group murmured with their alliances and family members for a few moments before simmering down. Simon stood and waved his arms to quiet his audience like the host of some Elks Club award dinner. "Middlebrook, we have a choice to make tonight." He paused to heighten the effect, enjoying how the group seemed to hang on his every word. Nate found this sanctimonious, melodramatic, and totally cliché. Simon, on the other hand, looked like he was savoring the respect, and he smiled, knowing they had resigned themselves to his leadership. Even if his leadership had come by default or act of God, it was the positive reinforcement that Simon yearned for. "The choice we make tonight will impact our lives forever. The options have been placed before us. The first option is to stay here and rebuild this town, all hands on deck, surviving on our own merit. Option number two is to pack up what we can carry and travel as a town to Maine. Now we have a third option, which would be Nate's option: to send an advance team of scouts to Maine to determine if it's safe on the road and see if Maine is even suitable for us, and of course to bring back supplies and information. We shall vote by secret ballot. If everyone would please write their choice on the slips of paper being passed out." Simon nodded to his wife, who got up and started handing out small slips of paper. Nate was impressed that Simon had the ballots ready. Once everyone had finished writing, the votes were placed in a shoebox at the center of the head table.

Everyone was allowed to mingle around the room making conversation about the future, about Maine, about Middlebrook. Nate and Jeannette picked each other's brains about how they had voted; the vote was their first act as full members of this postwar community. Nate glanced over at Simon and Russell, who were separating the small white pieces of paper into three piles. One of the piles was at least twice the size of the smaller two. Nate, for all his apprehension and apathy, was actually excited to hear the outcome.

Simon called the meeting back to order. He began, "The town has spoken, and although the choice wasn't unanimous, the vast majority was united as one." Simon was increasing the schmaltz factor with every word. The whole scene felt to Nate like an awards ceremony at the Benevolent Order of Christ. The cheesy buildup was far too much for the situation, but Nate could feel the group's anticipation swelling, and he was likewise on pins and needles waiting for the verdict.

"The group has decided that the best course would be the compromise Nate proposed. Of course, that means we need a pool of volunteers for the journey north." A brief, vocalized cheer and applause followed Simon's announcement before he hushed everyone back to a dull roar. No one will be forced to go or forced to stay. Nate, will you be choosing your team?" Simon said, looking Nate in the eyes.

Nate couldn't believe Simon's audacity. Yes, he had come up with the plan, but it had only been a suggestion. He turned to Jeannette with stunned disbelief; she seemed to be as shocked as Nate. "I wasn't aware that I had volunteered to go," Nate said, completely flabbergasted. He instantly regretted it; he should have exuded confidence.

"You wouldn't have suggested something for the group that you weren't yourself willing to participate in, would you, Nate?" Simon asked with a heavy dose of condescension.

"That's not what I meant," Nate said, trying to spin some damage control. "I just meant that I wasn't sure I'd be best suited to go, much less lead the journey." He tried to think quickly; there would be no easy way out of this.

For the next two hours, Nate canvassed the group while doing his best to avoid Jeannette in the process. Finding volunteers who were eager to walk to Maine wasn't as easy as Nate had hoped. Bob Halloran was the first to join up; he was quickly becoming Nate's right-hand man in this whole endeavor. By the time Nate had come up with seven willing and able volunteers, it was nearly midnight. In the end, he had to really sell the trip. Everyone agreed it was a grand idea, but when it came down to who would actually journey outside the friendly confines of Middlebrook, the unlucky souls who could be guilted into it were the only volunteers.

The entire community, aside from Nate and Simon, had bunked down for the evening; even Jeannette had retired to her cot. Nate was sitting at one of the tables across from Simon discussing the journey to Maine.

"Did you put together your posse?" Simon asked with his slick, used-car salesman pitch, which was starting to grate on Nate's nerves like fingernails across sandpaper.

"I think we're set; I just want to talk this over with Jeannette before we lock everything in stone," Nate answered, tilting his head toward Jeannette, who was sleeping on a cot on the other side of the room.

"Well, that's something I wanted to speak to you about." Simon paused as if he was about to dish out some really sorry news and had been bracing himself for the response. "I don't think it's wise for both of you to go on this mission. You are the only two people here with any medical training. I understand that the two of you are close, but if someone gets hurt or sick in town we'll need someone who is trained to help. You also don't want her life to be in danger out there on the road...do you?"

Nate wanted to concoct an excuse as to why Jeannette would be needed on the road, but unfortunately, what Simon said actually made sense. Still, Nate couldn't shake the feeling that Simon was using Jeannette as an insurance policy to make sure Nate and the group would have every reason to return. It would work, too, because Nate knew that he couldn't stomach this life without her.

"You'll need to be back before the first snowfall. Travel will be difficult enough in perfect weather, let alone with winter storms to contend with," Simon said, breaking the moment of awkward silence.

"Do you think there's any chance we could get a car running? It would cut down on the travel time significantly," Nate said, joining the discussion again.

"I doubt that would be possible, especially within the time-frame that we'd need it. That isn't even taking fuel into account; any car we could get running would have to be an antique, and those beasts aren't exactly environmentally friendly, if you get my drift," Simon sighed.

"I imagine most of the roads are blocked or destroyed any-way," Nate added.

Around two in the morning, Nate collapsed on his cot next to Jeannette. It had been a long day and an even longer night. It was the first time Nate and Jeannette hadn't gone to bed at the same time, and he missed their goodnight routine. Nate lay awake listening to the snoring and tossing and turning of his fellow refugees in the firehouse basement. That's what they had all become...refugees in their own town. Nate thought about the pilgrimage he was about to take. They had agreed to depart in two days—enough time to plan a route and prepare supplies for the long journey.

The road north would be hazardous in so many ways. They had no idea what would be waiting for them on the open roads—desperate people, starving survivors. Nate knew that human nature would dictate what they would do to survive. He had seen enough postapocalyptic science fiction movies to know that rape, murder, and even cannibalism were possible in the most dire circumstances. He also thought about the walk. It would be time-consuming and physically exhausting. They would be limited to back roads to avoid "hot spots," such as major cities like Boston. Stealth would be important too, or at least trying not to draw attention to themselves. If only there was a better way to travel—something faster, more efficient. Then just before sleep, an idea came to Nate...bicycles! They could collect enough bicycles from around town for everyone on the team.

15

THE ROAD WARRIORS

The next day started with a series of dull concussions that shook the ground. A buzz of speculation spread around the community like a case of the chicken pox. Some folks wondered if it was another attack or if a deadly invasion force lurked over the horizon. By midmorning, the consensus among the brain trust was that a fuel station or power plant had somehow caught fire and exploded. Perhaps the firestorm still lingered beyond town, or a freak lightning strike had ignited the fire. As unnerving as the sonic reminder of destruction was, the group moved forward with their daily tasks. Assigned groups began heading out to scavenge supplies, while others returned to the infantile stages of rebuilding the surrounding structures. Nate requested that the scavenging groups keep their eyes out for adult bicycles that appeared to be road-worthy.

Jeannette began setting up a triage and treatment room in one of the offices on the ground floor of the firehouse. Starting with the children, she began cleaning scrapes and bruises that had either never healed or were healing poorly. She soon realized that medical supplies would need to be transported from the health clinic to the firehouse. She couldn't keep working out of the small first aid kits that hung on the wall, and the adults would need to be treated for various issues, from radiation burns to intestinal distress.

Nate spent the day shuttling supplies from the clinic and blood draw station to the firehouse. From the top of the hill on which the draw station sat, Nate could see thick black smoke on the horizon. It was difficult to see through the gray, low-hanging air, but it was there, like a black scab on the overcast sky.

Nate made three trips back and forth hauling medical supplies for Jeannette. He loaded a garden cart with the bandages, antibiotics, and various other items she had requested. He intended to have a long conversation with Jeannette about his inclusion in the trek and the fact that he needed her to keep her ear to the ground while he was away. He simply hadn't had the time yet. Nate would wait until nightfall, when he and Jeannette would spend their last night together...at least for a while. He finished his last trip and sat in the firehouse garage waiting for Jeannette to complete her exams.

As the afternoon wore on, the scavenging crews started to return with the bikes they had found. It started with two or three, but by the time darkness began to appear in the eastern sky they had accumulated an assortment of mountain bikes and ten-speeds. All of the bikes were adult size, and most were in perfect shape, taken from sheltered garages. One or two of them needed to be lubed or have the wet ash cleaned off their chains. A few of Nate's travel companions worked on the bikes, preparing them for the road. The bicycles with the thick, treaded tires would be the most useful for riding on the gritty, sand-like ash that coated everything. Even the ten-speed street bikes would be useful, especially for the hills and valleys they would have to traverse. Ken Sandberg, who had been a real estate agent before the world went down, and Thomas Huff, who happened to be Simon's son, sat on the floor in front of the line of bikes fastening assorted attachments to their chosen rides. Some were holsters to hold firearms, others were racks to hold bags of supplies. The additions would help carry water and food, which was a major issue—they could search buildings along the way, but having a small stock would be essential.

It was after five o'clock in the afternoon when Nate and Jeannette started the hike up to the draw station. They had agreed that it would make their last night together special to spend it in the shelter, which would always be their true home. Nate started the conversation. "You know, I'm supposed to be leading this endeavor up north."

"Yeah, Nate, I was there. I just wish we could have talked it over before you locked yourself into something so dangerous," Jeannette said, watching the purple and black sky darken incrementally as they walked. "I was kind of hoping you'd back out or convince some other sucker to take your place."

"How could I back out?" Nate said stoically. "The whole thing was my idea, and I know how to survive outdoors. I grew up camping and hunting with my dad. This trip is as much for us as it is for the town. We won't survive without help. It's not like I've always wanted to travel to Maine. If I could choose I'd rather it be Barbados." Nate forced himself to smile; he really didn't want to go any more than Jeannette wanted him to.

"Nate this is hardly some family camping trip; it's a wasteland, and that wasteland is occupied by badasses surviving on that road...surviving off of idiots who take travel lightly." Jeannette turned and looked Nate in the eyes. "These people at the firehouse, and you and I for that matter, don't realize how sick we all are or how sick we're going to get."

Nate looked at Jeannette incredulously. "I feel fine; all the people I picked are in tip-top shape."

"Nate, most of us have been exposed to harmful levels of radiation. Some people are starting to lose teeth and hair. I saw two cases of nausea and diarrhea, and those were children. I've seen symptoms that lead me to believe we all have some level of PTSD—what a surprise...who would have thought a nuclear war would be traumatic?" Jeannette said sarcastically, but the scowl never left her face. "What if you get sick on the road? What if the symptoms hit you in a week and you can't function? What if your little expedition takes you through a hot zone?"

Nate hadn't given his own health much thought. He also hadn't noticed any severe cases of radiation sickness, other than Denise's mother and a few members of the community who had skin lesions. He had seen a few broken bones, bumps, and bruises, and he had assumed they were the extent of the community's health problems. "I don't know about any of that, Jeannette, but the thing is, we have to try to make it. None of us will survive without outside help. Don't you also want more information about what happened? What was hit and what wasn't, or if any government exists out there? If there's any chance of things going back to the way they were?"

Jeannette stopped in her tracks and said in a soft, somber voice, "What difference does it make?"

"You can't really believe that," Nate snapped. "Don't you care what happened to the rest of the world? You have to believe it can come back!" Nate was raising his voice now.

"We've been bombed back to the stone age, Nate. Do I care about the people who did this to us? The people who have known this could happen since the end of World War II? No, Nate, I don't care about them!" Jeannette raised her own voice even louder: "I care about survival. I care about you. Don't you fucking get it? I just found you, and now I could lose you without even really knowing you."

They walked for a minute or two in silence. Nate felt a mix of emotions: he was angry, he was confused, but the feeling that kept nagging at him was love. He hadn't felt more in love with Jeannette than he did at that moment.

"Jeannette, I swear I'll make it back to you, but I have to try to get us help—for you, for me, for all those people in the firehouse. I don't want to simply survive; I don't want to have to worry whether tomorrow is the day we'll run out of water," Nate said.

"No, Nate, you're trying to justify something that has no justification. There's no suitable justification for nuclear war. What do you think you'll find out up there? I know you well enough to know that you're trying to solve some kind of mystery."

"That's not true; you know that's not true. We can't survive without—"

"I know, Nate, you told me already," she said, sighing heavily. "I think it's fucking crazy to go out there when we're surviving here. I think you're a dumbass, but no one can ever accuse you of being selfish. I hate everything about it, but I understand why you feel you have to go," Jeannette said. It was the first time Nate could remember her giving in to anything. She had always been so Goddamn stubborn, but that was part of why he loved her.

They continued to walk, weaving their way through the dead cars full of their dead cargo. The parking lot from hell still affected Nate no matter how many times he traversed the road; it was like a punch in the gut seeing all the death. The smell and the metallic caskets were an assault on the senses. Nate glanced over at Jeannette sadly and saw that her face was streaked with tears. He reached out and grabbed her hand, pulling her into his arms. He held her for a long time as they stood in the gruesome maze of rotten cars.

Arriving at the blood draw station felt like returning home after a month-long vacation. It hadn't felt that way when Nate was simply gathering supplies, but now with Jeannette it felt like home. The memories of a better, simpler time, when it was just Nate and Jeannette, were spilled all over every room they entered. Down in the bunker, where they had spent the better part of a month in close quarters, the feeling was so intense that it was like they were an elderly couple returning from a nursing home to the house they had built and lived in all their lives. Nate cooked some canned food on the small camp stove while Jeannette told him about her first day as the unofficial town doctor. They reminisced about the early days in the shelter, when they had been so new to each other...strangers, really. They laughed about the hijinks among employees back in the day, when the draw station was no more than their place of employment. Jeannette even taught Nate some basic first aid that he could use on the road.

After dinner, they retired to their makeshift bed and lay together, spooning and kissing, just enjoying each other. Very few words were spoken, but looks were exchanged that said more than words ever could. Nate started to feel a panic attack brewing; he had the dreadful thought that this would be their last night together. They stayed that way, lying next to each other, for what seemed like hours, until Nate could feel Jeannette breathing deeply as she slept. He carefully got up from the bed and snuck over to the desk as quietly as he could. He took out a roadmap he had found at the firehouse. Using a red Sharpie, he traced the route from Middlebrook to the Maine border. It would be a slow, winding journey through back roads and small highways, but it would bypass most of the major population centers. The route would allow them to avoid nuclear pitfalls like Boston and the Connecticut coastline. Nate traced the route as it paralleled the Connecticut River and skirted the I-91 corridor. It took him longer than he had anticipated. Finding a passage around Hartford was the most painstaking, but if they kept to the west he figured they should be all right. He drifted off into thought as he traced the thick red line on the map. He had assumed he'd be the one taking all the risk and heading forward into danger, but as his mind wandered, his thoughts congealed around Jeannette. She'd be trapped in this community full of strangers with the constant threat not only of outside psychopaths but of desperate men inside the town. Jeannette was the strongest woman Nate had ever met, and she could take care of herself. That thought kept replaying in his mind like a record skipping constantly at the same part in a song. A group of horny men surrounding her with lust in their eyes was almost too much to bear. If Jeannette were attacked or, worse yet, raped, who would be here to stop them? Who would watch over her? Who could Nate trust to be Jeannette's protector in his stead? The answer came from the last place he would have thought. As much as Nate disliked Simon, he knew that Simon's Calvinist ways would prevent any unruly behavior. For all of Simon's faults, the one thing he could count on was Simon's rage for order.

Nate finished the map, and though he should have been bushed, he knew his body and—even more so—his mind were light years from sleep. He began packing for the trip north, filling his largest camping backpack with clothes, cans of food, extra ammunition, a sleeping bag, and his hunting knife. His cell phone, which would again serve as a Geiger counter, was at the firehouse taking a charge from the generator. He would need to use the phone sparingly, of course, because that charge would need to last from Middlebrook to Maine on bike. He finished packing all the things he felt he could carry relatively easy.

Then he sat down to make a list of items his crew would need before they left town. As soon as Nate's pen touched the paper, however, he knew it wasn't a list he was writing, but a letter to Jeannette. He wrote all the things he hadn't had the balls to tell her or hadn't had the chance. Nate wrote a paragraph baring his soul, folded it, and walked up to the chair he had watched Jeannette sit in for days reading her medical books. He placed the folded paper on her seat and looked around the darkened room. He began to feel overly sentimental. What if he never returned? Tears rolled down his face, and suddenly he felt like he would never be able to leave Jeannette. The times they had spent there after the bombs were the most important of his life...that was what the letter said.

• • •

Nate's team of seven cyclists gathered in front of the firehouse. They had loaded all of the supplies they could safely carry onto their bikes. The scavenging crews had been extremely successful, and Simon had donated the guns and ammunition. The advance team (as it was being called by the community) consisted of Nate; Bob Halloran; Simon's son Thomas; Ken Sandberg; Morty Heffernan, the high school physical education teacher; Carl Drew, a farmer from the outskirts of town; and Carl's girlfriend, Donna Nguyen.

The remaining forty or so community members had assembled to see the group off. Nate looked over the crowd; there were a lot of new faces. He wondered how many more survivors would make their way to the firehouse while they were on the road. People would wander in from neighboring towns, and the scavenging crews were still coming across survivors who had been holed up in their homes since the first hours of the attack.

Jeannette pushed her way through the crowd and walked up to Nate, throwing her arms around him in a hug that was so intense it was almost painful. Nate held her as tightly as he could and noticed that others were hugging their goodbyes as well. Nate felt like a soldier shipping off to war, and in a way he was. Jeannette whispered into his ear, "You better come back to me."

Nate swallowed hard and whispered back, "I promise."

She pulled back slightly so their eyes were about a foot apart, locking eyes with him, and for the first time she said those three words: "I love you." All at once, Nate's heart exploded and his legs were frozen to the ground. He couldn't go...he couldn't leave her...not like this.

His mouth found a way to work out the words, "I love you, too." It was all so cliché. Nate wished he could have thought of something more original to say, something poetically epic. He had finally found love, and here he was leaving it behind by choice. Jeannette was right—Nate was, in fact, a dumbass.

The six men and one woman mounted their bikes like a group of cavaliers mounting their noble steeds. Simon strolled forward out of the buzzing crowd, parting the community like Moses parting the Red Sea. "Let us bow our heads in prayer," he shouted over the rumbling murmur of the crowd. Nate could see he was preparing a sermon. "Lord, we ask that you watch over our brothers and sister, who shall make this pilgrimage on behalf of our community. Let them walk boldly through the valley of the shadow of death, let them fear no evil, and if they shall fall, please embrace them in your loving arms." Simon brought his hands apart, palms facing the sky, as if he were checking for raindrops. "And Lord, bless this town. If we have offended thee and fire and brimstone was our punishment—please forgive our trespasses. Give us the strength to complete your work and to create a new society, a more loving and honest place in your image. Amen."

Nate could have done without the last part, but he figured the more luck tossed in their direction, the better. After all the farewells were complete, there was nothing left to do but pedal away. Nate's mind started racing; he could hear that second voice in his head, the voice of anxiety and panic. He had begun to sweat; what if the reason he had overcome his anxiety was Jeannette? What if the road north brought with it all the paranoia, the panic attacks, and the cloud of dread that had weighed down his entire life before the bombs? Nate took one last, longing look at Jeannette; she looked as apprehensive and depressed as he felt. Then he said something really cheesy: "Regulators, mount up!" And off they pedaled north into the gray mist.

16

FEEL THE BURN

The road was cluttered with debris, abandoned cars, and downed trees, making travel treacherous and slow going. The one visual aspect of the roadside that Nate couldn't shake was the leafless trees. They stood lining the road like a parade of skeletons looking down on the group as they pedaled by. The leafless trees were nothing new to Nate in this new landscape, but they presented an image that he couldn't get used to. Every surface was covered by a brownish-gray film; rain-saturated ash stuck to everything like glue. The cracked road was barely visible through the scum. Their bicycle tires carved thin ruts in the ash, leaving seven weaving lines behind the group as they swerved to avoid the obstacles. They passed house after house. All were dark and empty, and some had doors wide open where the scavengers had entered them. The scavengers would leave the doors open to indicate that those houses were the ones they had already searched for food and survivors. Occasionally they would pass corpses lying in the road, not just human bodies, but dogs, cats, squirrels, birds, and even what appeared to be a deer.

The first couple of miles passed as easily as Nate had hoped. He was riding a high from hearing Jeannette profess her love and the adrenaline from being on the road. Considering it had been years since he had been on a bike, Nate felt surprisingly limber. The pace was slow, but shockingly, the oldest member of the group, Bob Halloran, led the pack. Nate could feel the tingling burn in his calves and the chafe in his asscrack, but it was nothing he couldn't push through. He could already see the benefit of the bicycles. Not only were they making better time than if they were walking, but the exertion made them less likely to talk, so they were nearly silent. Other than the long, thin trails the bikes were creating in the soot, there was very little sign that they had moved through the area at all. They had eaten up three or four miles in the first thirty minutes. The slow progression only became frustrating when they looked back and realized they could still see the taller structures in Middlebrook. The scenery was depressing, but not unexpected; everything was gray, bleak, and broken. There were no signs of life, no movement on the roadside...or anywhere else for that matter. Nate kept thinking that something had to have survived out here—maybe some animals that were hidden away in their dens when the strongest clouds of fallout blew through. Not only was the lack of life disheartening; it was also creepy. It reminded Nate of walking through a graveyard at night. He might be perfectly safe, but the atmosphere still scared the shit out of him. He wondered how many streets in America now looked like this one. How many dead graveyard neighborhoods were there?

Every few miles, the group had to stop and scrape the clay-like ash out of their tire treads. The first conversations among the riders began at these stops. They all felt the same way:

that they would need to feel each other out before any bond of companionship could be formed. As the leader, Nate knew he should expedite the process by breaking the ice.

"All right everyone, I know it's tacky and totally like the first day of school or something, but I think we should all introduce ourselves to each other and maybe say a thing or two about who we are." Nate hated the idea—it felt forced and childish—but he also felt it was completely necessary. The group would need to depend on one another, and how could they do that if they didn't know each other?

"Let's not," Carl Drew said in a snarky tone. Carl was a farmer who had agreed to come along only if his girlfriend Donna could come too.

"On that note, Carl, I think you should go first," Nate replied with a snarky smile of his own.

"Nate, it's a small town. Most of us know each other already," Bob added.

"Just humor me." Nate had forgotten that most of these folks had known each other for years. He was the only outsider.

"Fine, Nate," Carl chuckled. "My name is Carl Drew, but most of you know me as Eggers. Everyone calls me that because I have the biggest chicken farm in Middlebrook. If you've had a bacon, egg, and cheese or an omelet at the deli, then you've had my eggs," Carl finished with a satisfied look of pride. He was a short, stocky man, but his stockiness wouldn't be confused with fat. Muscles rippled under his shirt with every movement.

"Very good, Carl, you get an A+. How about the little lady?" Nate asked, feeling very much like a grade school teacher.

"OK, my name is Donna," the tall, Asian woman who had been riding with Carl replied. She had beautiful dark hair, which was tied back with a red scrunchie. "And if you ever call me *little lady* again, I'm gonna cut your nuts off," she said, giving Nate a look that could melt paint. "I'm a mail order bride from Cambodia," Donna said with sincerity, like she was quoting the cost of a Wall Street stock. All six men looked at Donna, appalled, and quickly turned away. She burst out laughing. "I'm just busting your balls," she said, and everyone laughed nervously. "Seriously, my family moved to Connecticut when I was very young. I always loved farm animals, so when I met Eggers online, I thought *What the hell*. I work...worked at the library." Thankfully, the mood of the group seemed to have lightened considerably. They had moved together into a tight circle, and most had smiles on their faces. Nate knew you could tell a lot through body language.

Nate turned to the youngest member of the group, who was the only one not in the circle. Thomas Huff stood off to the side, scraping the grime out of his back tire with a small stick. The young man must have felt Nate's eyes, because he looked up nervously. "Uhh...my name is Thomas, Thomas Huff. My father is Simon, the new mayor."

"Wow, that takes balls," Eggers said, interrupting Thomas.

"Take it easy, Eggers; you know what the kid means," Bob snapped in his thick New England drawl.

"No, Bob, I won't take it easy. There hasn't been an election since the boomers, and this kid's dad is proclaiming himself mayor of Middlebrook," Eggers said angrily.

"I just meant that he's been helping with leadership since it all happened," Thomas said. The kid was trembling with fear, and Nate thought he might've been fighting back tears. Maybe this was what Jeannette had meant when she mentioned symptoms of PTSD; perhaps people were becoming overly sensitive. Nate tried his best to stem the tension before he had an argument or a crying kid on his hands.

"Thomas, no worries," Nate said warmly.

"Yeah, kid, no worries," Eggers repeated. "I'm sorry, I was just bustin' stones. I guess I'm a little tense." Nate couldn't determine if Eggers was being sarcastic or sincere, but either way, his remark seemed to ease the tension.

"Eggers, you're the biggest asshole," Donna said, looking at Thomas with a genuinely warm smile that Nate was grateful for.

"I'm Ken Sandberg," Ken said, like he had been reading Nate's mind that the subject needed to be changed quickly to break the deafening silence. "You guys might recognize my face from the real estate signs in front yards around town." Ken was a handsome man in a TV game show host kind of way. He was in his late forties and had perfectly trimmed hair and a manicure.

"Yeah, we've been seeing your face a lot around here," Morty said.

"Well, the economy went to shit; we've had to move a huge volume of foreclosures," Ken answered apologetically.

"That's not what I meant," Morty replied with a smile. "Property values have *really* gone into the shitter. I mean, look around—the whole neighborhood's gone to pot." Morty laughed as he spun around holding his hands out. Everyone looked at the ash-covered, dilapidated houses and instantly got the joke. Nate knew that people sometimes dealt with trauma through humor, and this was exactly that.

"My name is Morty Heffernan, and I grew up here in Middlebrook. I've been the PE teacher at the high school for the last twenty years. I know most of you, and that's why I'm here. All I've ever known is this town, and I'll be damned if it's gonna die on my watch. If there's a way to help them live a little longer, for this town to survive, I...I just had to do something." Morty had put things back into a clearer perspective, and his emotions were raw and exposed. He had to be about fifty, but he was probably in better shape than most men half his age. Nate thought he looked just like every gym teacher he had ever known: dressed in a matching track suit and new sneakers.

Bob stepped forward. "My name is Bob Halloran." The whole conversation was beginning to remind Nate of a group session at an AA meeting. "Everyone knows me, so I'm not gonna bore y'all with the details. I've had a good life because of people like y'all and Nate. If it takes risking what life I have left for the younger generation, then..."

OK, let's not get too sentimental here; you're depressing me," Eggers blurted out.

"All right, I think everyone's said their piece, now let's get moving," Nate said before anyone could start singing "Kum Ba Yah."

"What about you, Nate?" Donna asked as the rest of the group nodded in agreement.

"Fair enough," Nate said. He had been hoping to avoid the speech, but turnabout was fair play. "My name is Nathan Wilder, and everyone calls me Nate. I sheltered in the blood draw facility and have lived in Middlebrook for ten years. I never really got to know many people; I guess I was just a loner."

"So you're a doctor?" Morty asked.

"Not exactly, but I do have some medical training." Nate didn't want to delve too deeply into the past or explain why he had worked in Middlebrook for so long and didn't know anyone.

"We need to get moving; I want to cover some ground before dark," Nate said, getting on his bike.

The team seemed rejuvenated as they mounted their bikes after the short break. Nate had hoped to be past the town line by sunset...or what they now considered the sunset, seeing as they hadn't seen the sun for so long. He thought it would be too discouraging to spend their first night on the road within the city limits. Nate had left his watch with Jeannette so she could take pulses. The group had to estimate the time of day, as the vale of dark clouds seemed to erase the existence of time. Nate began to keep a lookout for suitable, relatively secure shelter. Even though they wouldn't be stopping for the night yet, it would be helpful to know what kind of structures might be available. He was already concerned about the sleeping arrangements; it would be prudent to sleep in shifts, with someone staying awake as a lookout. They hadn't seen a single living soul, but who could tell what might come out at night? The group would need to be vigilant, even if it meant just watching the bikes; losing even one bike would slow them to a crawl. It was a testament to how tired he was that he had already begun to think about sleep. Breathing the dusty, polluted ash couldn't be good for their lungs either; he thought perhaps some of the energy that had been sapped from him was due to the poor air quality. He pulled to the side of the road to let Ken and Eggers pass and took a shirt from his pack. He tied it over his mouth and nose, and almost instantly the filtered air felt better in his lungs. He saddled back up and pumped hard to catch up to the others. He wished he was in better shape; every extra push of the pedals created a fire in his calves. As Nate caught up, the group saw the shirt tied over Nate's face. They stopped, gulped water, and made their own cloth masks.

The group settled in for the night in an abandoned bank with an enormous hole in the roof. They probably could have pushed on further, but it had started to sleet lightly, and the conditions were miserable for riding. Sleet in late spring could do strange things to a person's internal seasonal barometer. The hole in the roof had its benefits and drawbacks. One benefit was that the group was able to build a fire indoors, and the hole allowed the smoke to drift out without asphyxiating them all. The drawback, of course, was that the sleet and cold wind drifted in through the same hole. They built the fire out of broken-up office furniture, and they found plenty of now-useless paper to start it with. Morty pried open one of the teller drawers, and they had all kinds of fun being pyromaniacs with twenty-dollar bills. Bob pocketed a couple thousand dollars in mixed bills, saying, "Hey, you never know—we might need something to trade for supplies, and money might still have some value up north."

The first night on the road passed without incident. They were all dead tired and sore all over, and even the wet carpet in the bank wasn't enough of a deterrent to their exhausted bones. Twenty miles from Middlebrook and hardly a bump in the road; they were on their way.

Nate rolled out of his sleeping bag to the sound of Bob building up the fire. "Good morning, Chief," Bob said cheerfully as he held a disposable lighter to a wad of dollar bills sticking out from underneath a smashed wooden chair.

"Do we really have time for a fire?" Nate asked groggily.

"I thought it would be nice to start the day with a warm breakfast, maybe a cup of hot Joe." Bob pulled a Ziploc bag of instant coffee from his pack and held it up to show Nate proudly.

Nate sat up and looked around; the bank had been full of inky shadows when they had set up camp the night before. Now he could see that it was a fairly typical small town bank, with three teller stalls, a tall counter, an area to wait in line, and a drive-up window. The customer area had two tall cubicles where customers could stand to write their deposit and withdrawal slips. The group had broken off the top frames of the cubicles to use for firewood. The roof of the bank had collapsed inward at the drive-up window, creating the hole in the roof. It must have been a weak spot in the design of the structure that had caved in during the rumble from the nukes. The walls of the bank appeared to be painted a pasty yellow, but water damage had baptized the yellow in with brown stains. Debris had been blown in through the hole in the roof, leaving a collection of dead leaves and ash scattered behind the counters. It was amazing how quickly the elements had tarnished the interior; it looked like decades of damage instead of two months.

All of the others were still asleep, snoring away in their sleeping bags. Nate scooted over next to the fire. The warmth felt like being reborn, breaking the chill of the air and waking him up better than any cup of coffee.

"So, what's on the menu, Bob?" Nate asked, wiping the sleep and grime from around his eyes.

"Instant coffee and instant oatmeal," Bob answered sadly.

"No pancakes, eggs benedict, and bacon?" Nate joked.

"Only what we could carry, my man, and we're gonna need to find more food as we go." Bob dumped a liter of water into a foldout saucepan designed for camping. "Nate, do you worry that we haven't seen any signs of people, living or dead?"

"Well, we have seen a few corpses scattered along the roadside and in cars," Nate answered, and then he started thinking about Bob's question. The truth was they hadn't come across many bodies; not even close to an amount that would add up to Middlebrook's population before the bombings.

"I know about the few corpses we've seen; but there still should be more people, alive or dead." Bob had begun pouring packages of instant oatmeal into the steaming water.

"My guess is that a lot of people died in their homes. They would have watched the news and taken shelter inside. But when the bombs fell, a lot of windows were shattered, so they would have been exposed. Some people probably gathered their loved ones and waited for death so they could die together. Some people probably tried to flee in their cars." Nate remembered walking down the hill by the blood draw station—the faces, the smells, the families. The whole atmosphere and overall tragedy seemed to be welded in some spot in Nate's brain.

"Yeah, I know the scavenging crews are still finding quite a few bodies in the homes. I suppose you're right, Nate. I reckon it's just cause I can't wrap my head around the fact that the community at the firehouse is all that's left." Bob looked down at the ground for a moment, avoiding Nate's eyes.

"That's the best answer I can come up with, buddy," Nate said. He really didn't have a good answer; he was trying his best to avoid conspiracy theories. After Bob woke the rest of the group, they ate breakfast and got back on their bikes under the gray sky, which was exactly the same as the last three weeks.

After the first mile, Nate wasn't sure he could keep pedaling. His legs were so sore and stiff they felt like they had been dipped in bronze. He tried to push through the pain, not wanting the others to see he was in trouble; by the second mile, his legs had loosened. They rode down a long, rural road lined with stone walls and fields. It looked like the area had once been a vineyard or a farm; now it resembled a rolling, snow-covered meadow. All of the vegetation was dead and looked like it would crumble to dust with any pressure. The ash looked similar to a dusting of snow. It swirled up in tendrils that looked like mini-tornadoes as the wind blew. Little piles of white dotted the fields at different intervals, and scattered dead crows surrounded each pile. It didn't take Nate long to figure out what the piles were. They were dead farm animals—sheep, cows, maybe horses. The amazing thing was the crows that littered the ground around each carcass. The crows must have survived the fallout but died when they fed off the toxic carrion. It was another reminder of the harsh reality of this diseased land, but the fact that the crows had survived to feed on the dead animals gave Nate hope that some species other than humans had made it through the fallout.

"So, who knows where we're going?" asked Ken, who was leading the group as they came to a four-way intersection.

"I have the road map in my pocket, but I'm positive we keep going straight here," Nate said as he pulled up next to Ken and skidded to a stop. Down the road, Nate saw why Ken had stopped. A pile of charcoaled wood was smoking and smoldering about five hundred feet up the road. The pile of charred beams had once been a house that was now burned to the ground. Only a few blackened beams from the frame stood smoldering like a forgotten campfire left to burn itself out.

"I thought you might want to avoid that," Ken said, pointing out what Nate had already seen. Donna and Eggers rolled up behind, followed by Bob, Morty, and Thomas.

"Yeah, so it's a burning house. Could have been from a lightning strike from the storm last night," Morty said, panting for breath as he poured water from his mounted water bottle onto the bandana that covered his mouth.

"Well, in my experience, a lightning strike doesn't hang people," Ken said, pointing to a long, cylindrical object hanging by a rope from a tree in the front yard of the house.

"Holy shit!" Eggers added with equal parts shock and disgust.

"Nate, what do you suggest we do?" Donna asked.

Nate had been trying to peg their location on the roadmap. Taking the crossroad would bring them closer to Hartford, a known hotspot, and away from the highway Nate had hoped would lead them to the Massachusetts border. Going the other direction, west, would take them on a course that backtracked most of their journey so far.

"I don't see any reason to deviate from the plan, which would be to continue straight ahead," Nate said, hoping he hadn't shown any doubt in his choice. "That person won't be bothering us," he added glibly.

"It's not that person I'm worried about," Ken replied.

"Yeah, what if whoever hung that guy is still hanging around down there?" Eggers threw in his two cents.

"Listen, if we veer off course every time we see a dead body or roadside carnage, we'll never make it to Maine. But maybe we should unholster our guns…just in case," Bob said, acting as the voice of reason as usual.

As the group closed the distance to the smoking ruin Nate could see the cylinder hanging from the tree take shape. It was definitely a body. They stopped in front of the house and looked up at the morbid form hanging from the tree. It was a man who looked to have been about forty years old, but it was difficult to tell much else. His face was bloated and disfigured by the swelling, and it was a ghastly shade of blackish purple. He was hanging by an orange outdoor extension cord, the kind you would use on your leaf blower or hedge trimmer. The first thing Nate noticed was a yellow piece of paper sticking out from the man's belt. A knocked-over chair that had been used to get the man up off the ground and into the noose lay in the ash just below his dangling feet. Nate righted the chair and climbed up on it to retrieve the folded paper.

"EEEEEWWWWW! Don't touch it!" yelled Eggers with a childish laugh. Nate stepped back down off the chair, opened the letter, and read it to himself.

To whoever finds my body:
I would be much obliged if you would please give me a Christian burial. My kids, Jason and Samantha, died four days after those assholes blew up the planet. I buried them in the root cellar, because Sharon said it wasn't safe to go outside. Sharon was my wife. She died two days ago. She had been so sick, and she wanted so much to be with the kids. I didn't have the strength to bury her. I've been so tired of fighting them off, but there were too many of them, so I burned the house. I don't know if they were after us or the house—now they get neither. I think God will understand. After all, he allowed everything to happen. We'll be in a better place. I hope this message finds

someone with a kind heart. The thought of hanging in this tree to rot is unkind.
Thank you.

Sincerely,
Thomas Kerman

"Cut him down," Nate said as he put the folded paper into his pocket.

"What did it say?" Morty asked.

"It's a suicide note," Nate answered, looking for something to dig with; he noticed a shed out behind the ruins of the house.

"What did the note say, Chief?" Bob asked as he stood on the chair, sawing at the extension cord with his pocket knife.

"He's asked for a proper burial. His wife and kids were dead; that's why he burned the house. I guess he couldn't take it anymore," Nate said to Bob softly. He didn't want any arguments from the peanut gallery about giving a "Christian burial" to someone who had committed suicide, especially from Simon's son Thomas. Nate walked out to the small shed and found a few shovels. He had always been sensitive to the issue of suicide. It wasn't that Nate had ever come close to killing himself, but people with mental health issues sometimes feel a kinship for their own brand. It's like knowing what the absolute worst case for your disease is.

A memory came flooding back to Nate; he had been a senior in high school. For the senior trip, his class had taken a bus to Washington, DC. They were on their way to the National Zoo, having just left their hotel, when the bus stopped behind a long line of traffic. As they approached the cause of the delay, the students started yelling and pointing. A man was on the outside of a bridge, high above the street they were traveling on. When the other students saw the man and the police talking to him through a bullhorn; they all rushed to the closest side of the bus so they could have a better view. Many of them pulled down their windows and were waving and cheering through the gap. They all began to chant "Jump! Jump! Jump!" while laughing happily. All of them but Nate, that is. He had never found out the fate of the man on the bridge, but it was the other students' reaction that had always stuck with Nate. The easy answer was that they were just kids and they didn't know any better—they didn't understand the gravity of the situation. Nate had always thought it was more, though—an almost primal demonstration of the lack of compassion that exists toward suicidal people and, to a lesser extent, people with mental illness. That lack of compassion could lead to anything, whether it was cheering as a fellow human being plummeted to his death or even nuclear war.

They buried Thomas Kerman in a shallow grave next to his house. Morty constructed a cross from two tree limbs cut from the very branch the man had been hanging from. He drove the cross into the ground at the head of the burial mound. Thomas even said a short prayer for the stranger who simply couldn't take this world on his own. There was no debate about the mortal sin of suicide or why they were taking so much time away from the road for a stranger. Nate wanted to think that, at least among his group, ideals were changing and anyone could be driven to their end by this Godforsaken world. He preferred to think that among this group of travelers, who had all been driven so close to the end themselves, there was compassion. This small act of kindness brought them closer together than any first day of school introductory routine.

They got back on their bikes and pedaled away from the smoking house in silence; no one looked back.

17

GRAY DAY

In the basement of the firehouse, Simon called the community meeting to order. In the days prior to the departure of the advance team bound for Maine, Simon had sensed a rift brewing between those who believed in him and those who trusted and believed in Nate instead. Imagined or not, Simon would need to quash any dissension in the ranks. His opinion was that this vacation to Maine was foolhardy; action isn't the answer to every problem, and reducing the number of able-bodied men in the town could leave them all vulnerable. The only positive of the trip was the absence of Nate, whom Simon had considered a threat since the first day he met him. Simon had also had the foresight to send his son Thomas to watch over Nate and to keep the mission on track. He had had a long father–son chat with Thomas, explaining the nuances of town politics. He had reminded the boy never to be too trusting and especially not to grow too fond of his newfound traveling companions. He assured him that those idiots would leave him for dead if it suited their interests. The kid was too strong-willed and gullible for his own good; he could be taken advantage of, and Nate would try his best to do just that. Thomas had always been a momma's boy, but he desperately craved his father's approval; Simon understood that and used it to his advantage. The kid had always taken the extra step to please Simon, and this trek was a prime example of that. Simon had asked Thomas to volunteer, and although the boy detested the idea of leaving his mother and sisters, it had been Simon's request, and Thomas was determined to make him proud.

Simon strutted to the front of the room, where he had set up a small podium after the dinner tables were out of the way. He stood behind the podium, savoring the pageantry of looking down on the men and women of the community—his community—as they took their seats. The community had grown to more than fifty members; some kept guard in front of the firehouse, but most sat in front of Simon. Some of the people no longer slept in the firehouse, having moved to neighboring buildings, but they still attended the community meetings. Keeping everyone warm and fed had become a daunting challenge, but Simon had met that challenge head on as he had done with every other challenge he had ever faced.

"I've called this meeting because I think it's imperative that all of us share in the decision-making process. We have come so far since that horrible, dark day of destruction. I wish you could all feel the pride I feel in each and every one of you. We have great plans for the future, and I hope that tonight I can show you where we are going." Simon took a long sip from a glass of water that was on the table beside him. "I wish to begin with what we have accomplished in the last week. As all of you know, seven brave souls, including my youngest son, are on the road as we speak. They are risking their lives to seek aid for this great town. Our scavengers have found enough food to fill our entire pantry." Before Simon could continue, the crowd stood and applauded. He gestured for them to temper their enthusiasm by waving his hands downward. "Our technical staff has restored the hand-pump for the well out back. The groundwater is still too contaminated to drink, of course, but after boiling and proper filtration, it can be used for washing. Our security team has pushed abandoned vehicles into the road at four crucial entrance points to the town center. The entire town of Middlebrook now resides in one block. This will make it easier to defend our most precious resource...our people. No one will be allowed in or out of the roadblocks without permission." A grumble of disagreement began among the seated adults that grew to individual shouts. Simon acted confused and feigned an expression of innocence. "Please, please, everyone. It's for our own safety and protection." Simon desperately wrangled for control of the raucous crowd. "And," he shouted, "and it's only temporary!" With that, the crowd finally started to calm down.

"Please, as I said, it's only temporary; we will only need these security measures until we're sure what exactly we're up against."

A man stood from the middle of the crowd. "And how long will that be?" He yelled bitterly. A murmur of agreement rose from the crowd.

"Sooner or later, some very undesirable people will show up, and they'll want our supplies or, worse, they'll want our people," Simon answered back.

The same man, whom Simon recognized as Mr. Bystrek, stood again and fiercely stated, "You know, we've been hearing about these supposed bad guys since Gray Day." *Gray Day* was the slang term the community had begun using to refer to the nuclear attack. "I haven't seen any evidence that they're even out there." The man turned to look at the crowd. "Have any of you witnessed these boogie men?"

Simon ignored the interruption from the agitator. "As soon as we are in a better position to handle *any threat,* we will reopen our streets and allow community members to come and go as they please." Simon took another sip of water and read off the notes he had prepared. "Let me continue. Russell is currently working tirelessly on converting the oil burner in the firehouse so that it can safely burn a variety of fuel sources. We will assign a new scavenging crew to siphon fuel oil and gasoline and collect clean wood and coal from around town. Remember, we are limited to wood that hasn't been exposed to radiation." Simon was feeling better now that the crowd had relaxed. "Our next order of business is from our resident health expert, Jeannette Leach. Jeannette has proposed some steps to help us stay healthy. She believes that the corpses in the area pose a significant health hazard—that they need to be taken care of. I know we have moved the majority of corpses outside of our block, but she thinks we should burn or bury all the corpses we come across. So I have proposed creating a special unit to respectfully remove and dispose of all the bodies they can find. Jeannette suggests that we also should come up with a better method of sanitation. Everyone has been using the three porta-potties out back, which we have been dosing with lime, but apparently that's not adequate. If anyone has any ideas for a solution to our sanitation problems, please see me after the meeting. I know we have architects, engineers, and former plumbers among us, so if any of you have an idea that helps make our lives better, please, don't hesitate to make suggestions." Simon had read his entire list of accomplishments and new proposals. He had agreed to open the floor for public comments or questions, and as much as he despised the idea, he needed to play the role and all that it entailed.

"Does anyone have anything to add or any questions?" Simon asked loudly. It was uncomfortable to constantly have to raise his voice, but without electricity there was no microphone, and he couldn't justify running the generator just to amplify his voice.

The bald man in his late forties who had been Simon's bane throughout the meeting stood up. Paul Bystrek, who had been part of the scavenging crew and who Simon had never heard utter a word before the meeting, shouted, "I'm still hung up on this prison camp concept. We've survived since Gray Day without barricades. Now all of a sudden we need to be protected from ourselves?"

Simon felt exhausted by the constant references to the road blocks. Why didn't these people realize that it was absolutely necessary to keep out any intruders?

"Mr. Bystrek, I've told you that it's only a temporary solution. My security team recommended it to make their job easier." Simon had given his best answer, and he was growing exasperated, but the crowd seemed to agree with Bystrek, which Simon worried could become a major wedge. Simon couldn't risk his leadership position over something so stupid. "Anyone who wants to go outside the roadblocks can come to me and I will happily write them a pass."

"So now we need a pass? Maybe we should have numbers tattooed on our arms too so you can keep track of everyone!" Bystrek said sarcastically.

Simon laughed nervously. "Mr. Bystrek, I think you are exaggerating the situation just a bit. This is simply a temporary security measure, and it's in the town's best interest." Simon couldn't repeat himself anymore; it was becoming painful. "Are there any other questions or comments that *don't* concern the roadblocks?"

Bystrek must have been as frustrated as Simon, because he sat down in a huff. Simon was happy to accept the stalemate. The meeting broke up for dinner with a murmur of disgust from the community. Simon was thankful that no questions had been asked about his security force. The security team had been trained and selected in private by Simon himself. The fact that it existed was an open secret—it was public knowledge that Simon had armed a group of ten men. The group had been drilling and taking target practice while the others were out scavenging or working on tech projects. After dinner, Simon retreated to his room. He had moved into the fire marshal's office soon after asserting his leadership. He had carried a cot up from the basement and positioned it on the side of the room away from the large pine desk that was the focal point of the small office. It was now a multipurpose room that served as Simon's office and bedroom. Some of the townspeople probably considered it odd that he slept upstairs in the office while his wife and children slept in the basement. Simon's excuse was that he didn't want to disturb anyone while he was working hard for the town and burning the midnight oil. The added benefit was the appearance of self-sacrifice by Simon and the thought that if the basement was adequate for the leader's family it was adequate for all.

Simon replayed the meeting over in his head. Perhaps Bystrek had been right; the murderous cannibals had never materialized as Simon had thought they would. Maybe it wasn't so bad out there. Maybe the cities had never emptied out, with hordes of criminals fleeing to the rural areas. It didn't occur to Simon that people could be out in the wasteland relying on each other instead of preying on the vulnerable. Simon knew human nature too well; he was convinced that sooner or later the town would be invaded. In the morning, Simon would go to his church and find out what had happened to Reverend Kasper. If anyone could help Simon with leadership, it would be the good reverend. His congregation had had about twenty-five parishioners. Simon couldn't believe that not a single one had made his or her way to the firehouse.

He blew out the candles that he used as his main source of light when the generator was off. They were trying to conserve fuel, so they had rationed its use for emergencies. He found his cot in the dark and lay down, still in his "official" clothes and shoes. Simon liked to sleep with one eye open, ready to go to work for the town at a moment's notice. He wondered if the community knew how much sacrifice he had given everyday. It didn't matter if they did or not. Simon knew that generosity was in his nature—he had always been a giver.

Simon was driving the bus for the Teen Weekend Summer Retreat. He was listening to the girls sing happily while occasionally glancing at them in the three-foot-long rearview mirror. They were singing a melodic, joyful tune with strange lyrics and a familiar refrain. Simon focused on the lyrics as the girls reverted back to the chorus: "Simon Huff can't get it up, so he smiles and flirts while he peeks up our skirts. Simon Huff can't get it up, he wants us to touch him while he drives the bus. He likes it to hurt cause he's a sick pervert." The bus suddenly began to change; the seats became brown and bench-style, like a bus from the 1970s. Simon was no longer driving the bus; he was now a passenger. He looked down at his hands, the hands of a ten-year-old. His Osh Kosh B'gosh overalls were saturated with urine. The teenagers were still singing, but as Simon turned in his seat to look at them, he saw that the girls were wearing clothes from the '70s—tube tops and sleek jeans with flared cuffs. The song was the same, however. "Simon Huff can't get it up, so he smiles and flirts while he peeks up our skirts." Simon could feel the tears running down his cheeks; all the teenagers were laughing hysterically. Even the bus driver, who Simon remembered from fifth grade, was giggling and smiling at Simon. Simon kept trying to tell himself not to be a baby, to toughen up and be a man, but the tears kept flowing.

Suddenly, a girl was sitting in the seat across from him; she was dressed like a cheerleader. She turned with a ferocious look and shouted, "They'll never follow you, Simon! You're just a pathetic bus driver; you couldn't lead a dog to a bowl of Alpo." She slid toward the aisle, and Simon thought for a second that she was going to hit him. "You can't lead them, Simon; even your own children won't follow you. The only fucking people who will follow you are the passengers who ride behind you when you drive the bus." The cheerleader was screaming at the top of her lungs, her eyes burning red with hatred. Simon could feel the heat pouring off her. "You're just a pathetic bus driver!" Simon willed his ten-year-old body to rise. He needed to do something, anything, to get out of the path of the hate spewing from the cheerleader's mouth. He turned to the girl and shouted, "I don't drive a bus anymore, you bitch!"

Simon woke and sat straight up on his cot. He said to himself out loud, "I don't drive a bus anymore." He repeated it again, a little more quietly, to assure himself. "I don't drive a bus anymore, you bitch."

The downward spiral had started.

Simon had walked for nearly thirty minutes, and he still hadn't reached the church. He had been sidetracked twice by community members he had come across working on various tasks. The community was buzzing with excitement, because Russell had managed to get an old farm tractor running. They were now able to tow deserted cars out of the street, and with a trailer attached, they could move bulk supplies into the center of town.

He had left the center of town for the first time since he had moved his family to the firehouse. He had forgotten how truly devastated the outer roads had looked. He passed the used book store and the middle school, which resembled a dilapidated crack house on the wrong side of the tracks. A tree had fallen into the left side of the building, tearing out a huge section and exposing a classroom on the second floor. All the windows had been smashed, and the holes looked like black eyes glaring out from the front facade. Simon knew the small church that was so important to him was just past the town cemetery next to the middle school. The area felt desolate, lifeless, and hollow, like someone had used a huge auger to bore out his town. The ash-covered ground was ugly enough, but the spots where the ash had blown away, leaving brown spots of dirt and dead grass were just as grotesque. It left the lawns looking like they had unholy polka dots.

Simon had feared the worst walking past the graveyard; part of him expected the church to be flattened. As he turned the soft twist in the road, however, he saw the church standing in its impeccable glory. It appeared to be virtually untouched. Some of the stained glass windows were smashed in, but the white clapboard structure was completely pristine. Simon smiled and increased his speed. He held out hope that someone from his congregation might be alive inside, having sheltered in the church. He hurried up the front walkway, searching for footprints in the ash, but the white double doors looked as though they hadn't been opened in weeks. He still held onto the hope that Reverend Kasper would be inside, offering sanctuary to whomever needed it. He pounded on the white double doors with his balled fist. Then he put his ear to the door, but no sound came from the inside the church. He banged again, hearing the knock echo inside the building. There was a strange smell in the air, something faint that Simon couldn't quite place. He turned the heavy brass knob and pushed the door open into the church.

The air inside was stale; it smelled of dust, and he detected a slightly wet, fishy smell, almost like seaweed. The sanctuary looked normal, a long aisle with lacquered wooden pews lining both sides. Porcelain statues displaying the stations of the cross hung on the walls below the stained-glass windows. At the far end of the aisle was a white wooden altar elevated on a riser. Four-foot brass candlesticks stood on both sides of the altar. Behind the altar was a life-size crucifix that Simon had always thought was disturbingly graphic. Everything looked as Simon had remembered, except for one odd thing: sitting on the pews were purses and jackets, as if their owners had placed them there and had to leave in a hurry. He couldn't understand why these objects had been hastily left behind. He walked down the aisle to the front of the church; on the left side of the altar was a door to the basement. The basement was used for church gatherings, bingo, and Sunday school. Simon opened the door and was instantly hit with a stench that sucked the wind from his lungs. The odor was easily identifiable now: it was the smell of decaying flesh. He ran down the stairs, stumbling as he hit the bottom, and burst through the basement door.

He had found his congregation. Men, women, and children sat slumped over the long tables they had used for church dinners. At first glance, Simon wondered if they had all sheltered together and succumbed to radiation. Maybe the church was drafty and the fallout wasn't stopped by the walls and foundation. The corpses were badly decomposed, and Simon gagged as he tried to breathe in the foul, oily air. These were all people Simon had cared for so deeply, and now they were all dead. The biggest question on his mind was why had they all come here... and when? Did they all run to the church when they first heard the sirens? He examined the room as much as he could stomach, and he noticed that the one thing all the corpses had in common were the rows of empty Dixie cups in front of each body. Simon walked over to the table and picked up one of the cups. It was empty, but the inside was still stained red from whatever had been in it. Simon put the cup to his nose and smelled its interior. Behind the smell of death that filled his nostrils, he could smell something else: almonds. It was cyanide. He had read about that faint odor many times in his detective novels. They were all dead, and this wasn't an accident—it hadn't been caused by fallout, it was suicide. He looked up from the cup and saw the corpse of Reverend Kasper at the back of the hall. Something changed in Simon's head. A red tornado of hate and loathing began to swirl inside him. He felt like a parasitic worm had tunneled into his brain, and the worm was now laying eggs of violence. They had all moved on to God's Kingdom, and he hadn't been invited. He felt like the congregation had done him dirty, like Reverend Kasper had fucked his wife and left the sheets for Simon to scrub.

The rage made him robotic—as if the cruise control button had been pushed somewhere deep in his core. Voices spun around inside him arguing with each other; one of the voices was the cheerleader. The next few moments seemed to happen in stages, like vacation photos through a slide projector. First, Simon found himself outside. He had broken the lock off the utility building behind the church. Next, he was carrying a red five-gallon can of gasoline down the basement steps. Then he was dousing the floor, the corpses, and even the cheap altar upstairs. He poured gas on the tapestries, the pews, and dripped a long line down the aisle and out the church doors. Before he had even grasped what he was doing, he had touched the flame from his Zippo lighter to the long liquid wick. Blue flame ran in a straight line into the church, as a howling scream of fire gobbling up lacquered wood hit Simon's ears. The crackle and pop of the heat eating oxygen and fuel was like a symphony of combustion.

Simon was pushed back by the heat as the fire ate its way up the walls, fully engulfing the church. He turned and walked back toward the center of town. Something fundamental had changed in his psyche; he was cognizant of that fact, but he was in no hurry to do anything about it. He could taste the hatred, and he knew the only thing that could be a salve to his wounded heart would be blood.

18

PASSED LIVES

Jeannette's office had begun to resemble a hospital exam room. She had posted a sign-up sheet for appointments in the basement, and nearly every community member had signed up to be checked over. The one-month crash course she had taken in emergency medicine had prepared her for some of what she had seen, but not all. The town's people all thought of her as a doctor, and she wasn't about to freak them out by explaining the truth. If they had a better option, things might have been different; besides it wasn't like she could be prosecuted for practicing without a license these days. Her first patient of the day was an elderly gentleman who had been having breathing problems from all the ash floating around. Jeannette listened to his lungs through a stethoscope, and although she did hear some rattling, they sounded relatively clear. She diagnosed him with bronchitis and gave him some antibiotics and a surgical mask to wear when venturing outside. She sent him on his way with a smile.

The next patients were supposed to be a mother and her ten-year-old daughter, but when Jeannette went out to call them in, she found a slip of paper taped to her door. She went back in the office and read the note. It was from Simon.

Dear Jeannette,
I know your thoughts must be with Nate right now, but I hope this won't affect your work here. The community must come first, even though we miss our loved ones traveling to Maine. We all have to pull our own weight if we're to thrive. Also if there are any patients you consider to be contagious, I think you should come to me with your diagnosis. We want to avoid panic in all scenarios. You must keep in mind the fact that the world has changed. I know it's not what you're used to.
God Bless You.
Simon Huff, Town Magistrate

Jeannette had always assumed Simon was self-absorbed but basically harmless. Even when Nate had told her, "Something just isn't right with that guy," she had written it off as Nate's anxiety in hyperdrive. Jeannette bit down on her lip. Who the hell did Simon think he was? Jeannette called in her next patients, but she found it hard to concentrate.

She warmed the circular disc of the stethoscope and placed it on the mother's back, just below her shoulder blades. At first, Jeannette didn't hear anything alarming. "Take a deep breath, Gina," Jeannette asked as she slid the stethoscope to the other side of the woman's back. As Gina took her second deep breath, Jeannette heard a slight catch in her breathing. It sounded like air was being trapped and then releasing with a slight whistle in the bottom of her lung.

"So what is it?" Gina asked with concern.

"Just a second," Jeannette answered pleasantly.

Jeannette motioned for the little girl, Amy, to jump up next to her mother on the exam table. Amy smiled and climbed up on the wax-paper-covered table. She was exceedingly cute but rather skinny. She had long, dirty blond hair and big brown eyes that were very dark, like chocolate icing on a vanilla cupcake. Amy looked like she hadn't slept in days—there were large, dark circles under those gorgeous eyes. Most of the town, including Jeannette, probably looked like Amy. A good night's sleep was a rare commodity.

Jeannette listened to Amy's chest and noticed the same slight rasp in her breathing. Her heart rate was normal, but the rasp concerned Jeannette.

"Amy, do you cough a lot lately?"

"A little," Amy answered softly.

"She's been coughing a lot at night," Gina said.

The girl didn't have a fever, and other than the hitch in her chest and the fact that she looked thin, she appeared healthy enough.

"I think both of you have a bronchial infection from the ash. I'm going to give you some broad-spectrum antibiotics and some iodine tablets to help protect you from any radiation." Gina looked alarmed at Jeannette's recommendation.

"I also want both of you to wear these when you go outside," Jeannette said as she handed Gina two surgical masks. She walked them out to the main bay of the firehouse. "Gina, just keep an eye on the coughs, and if either of you experience symptoms like nausea or vomiting, come see me immediately."

Jeannette had been extremely busy all afternoon. She was running low on surgical masks, and although she had thought she had enough antibiotics to last, they were going fast as well. The symptoms ranged from psychosomatic abdominal pain to the early stages of long-term radiation sickness. On top of the multiple ailments, five new citizens had been found on the roads in the southern part of Middlebrook. They were all severely dehydrated and must have been much closer to ground zero of one of the nuke blasts. They had walked from an area closer to the Connecticut coastline—close enough to the Groton Sub Base to receive an unsafe amount of exposure to radiation.

She would also need to make time in her busy schedule to hit up the health clinic for more supplies. There were items that Nate hadn't found that she could really use, especially one particular item for herself—a home pregnancy test. Jeannette wasn't convinced she was pregnant, but her last period had been before the fallout shelter with Nate, and that was more than two months ago. She knew that stress and weight loss could cause menstruation to stop or become irregular, but she wanted to be sure. Jeannette had been through this before; it had been one of the reasons she had left the Midwest. During the summer, just after graduating high school, she had become pregnant. One abortion and some extremely pissed off parents later, and she was on a plane to New York. It was a horribly scarring ordeal that she lived with to this day, but bringing a child into this devastated world was a terrible option. At the same time, Jeannette had sworn to herself that she'd never have another abortion, no matter what the circumstances were. Besides, it wasn't as though a Planned Parenthood clinic was right around the corner anyway. At least this time she had been in love with the man she was sleeping with.

Jeannette allowed herself to imagine having a child with Nate and smiled. She thought about him out there on the road and said a small prayer for his safety. "I miss him so Goddamn much," she said aloud. She had never told Nate about the real reason she had left Kansas; she didn't want to burden him with that baggage any more than she wanted to look like damaged goods. Jeannette knew that Nate wouldn't care about that—hell he would probably have comforted her for it. Jeannette thought maybe it would be worth telling Nate just to be back in his soothing arms. She had kept herself exceedingly busy, but time still crept by like she was a kid waiting for her birthday. "Please let him come home in one piece," she said out loud, "and here I am talking to myself like a fucking schizophrenic." She laughed, and even that sounded a little crazy. Then she thought how amazing it was that love could change you so profoundly; it was like a mental illness. Jeannette had a few more patients to treat; she made up her mind to hike up to the health clinic after that.

When she wasn't seeing patients, Jeannette felt like she was drowning in loneliness. Her only friend in the community was Denise, who had been keeping busy by teaching the youngsters their ABCs. Although Denise and Jeannette seemed to have an unbreakable bond, the age difference caused some awkwardness that prevented them from becoming true confidants. They still chatted every night, and Denise knew Jeannette missed Nate, but sooner or later Denise would find a love of her own. It's human nature in times of crisis even teenagers find companionship. Jeannette hated feeling depressed, but there wasn't much she could do about it. She feared her depression would last until Nate was back in her arms.

It was early afternoon when Jeannette decided she had seen enough patients for the day. She put on her jacket and taped a note to her door saying that exams would resume tomorrow morning. It would be a refreshing luxury to leave the firehouse; she'd been cooped up there because of Simon's strict edict. Edict or not, Jeannette would be going up the road today. Jeannette made a beeline for the front door. She didn't want to get distracted by any community members asking her if their scabs looked infected. She took a surgical mask from her coat pocket; it was one of the last ones she had. The coat had been acquired from the lost and found box at the library. Jeannette zipped up the coat and pushed through the exterior door onto the sidewalk. She walked to the side of the building to find the garden cart that Nate had used to fetch supplies. It was sitting against the building, but it looked like someone had been using it recently. Three roughly used car batteries sat in the wooden cargo area. Jeannette heaved the batteries out and stacked them next to the building.

She paused before pushing the cart forward on to Main Street. The skies were gray, but what else was new? The drab conditions fit her mood perfectly. Jeannette wondered if perhaps she was hormonally challenged by a first-trimester pregnancy. It would be quite a lot of work to push the cart the entire two miles to the health clinic, and then the return trip would be even harder with a full cart. The entire walk down Main Street, her thoughts were dominated by Nate and her own feelings of isolation. She felt like the town pariah even as she took care of every wound, every sickness within the community it seemed that friendship or even having someone to talk to was as hard to find as a sunny day—she started thinking that she should have insisted on going with Nate. She knew it wouldn't have been impossible to talk him into it. As much as she loved Nate, he had always been a bit of a pushover.

She hadn't really been paying attention and nearly walked right into one of Simon's roadblocks. Four cars had been pulled end to end; together they created a nearly impenetrable barrier. She looked back over her shoulder and realized that cars now blocked off access to the street at the alleys between buildings and any other entrance onto Main Street. This created the feeling of being walled in. It did feel like a prison, and even though she wasn't totally against the idea of keeping bad guys out, she didn't like it. If Simon was nothing else, he was efficient. Main Street had become one long fortress, as Simon and his minions had been busy with their new tractor.

Three men with rifles stood on the other side of the road-block. They had been busy laughing it up and passing around a cigarette, which was an expensive commodity among the community members who smoked.

Jeannette casually strolled up to the roadblock. "I'm the town doctor; I need to get essential supplies from the health clinic," Jeannette stated, hoping she sounded official.

The men spun around with their guns pointed in Jeannette's general direction. "No one in or out without Simon's permission," the man who appeared to hold the highest rank said. "Do you have permission to leave the community?"

"Simon wasn't around, and the supplies are essential. He left me a note, so he's probably on some important business," Jeannette pleaded.

The guards begrudgingly let Jeannette through a small space between the cars. She walked away shaking her head at how confined they had become, all in the name of a security threat that hadn't even materialized. Jeannette thought of Nate with every step. As she was passing the area Nate had called the parking lot of death, she saw that most of the cars had been moved off the road, while others were missing entirely. There were no bodies around anymore, which she considered a good thing; there was a chance that the lingering bodies could start an epidemic of cholera, or worse.

Jeannette arrived at the health clinic completely exhausted. She filled the cart with all the supplies she needed, including the pregnancy test. She hadn't known that the health clinic had been so thoroughly destroyed and wondered why Nate had never mentioned it. She pushed the cart out of the building and looked over at the blood draw facility. It had been their home together for more than a month. She pulled the cart over to the facility and placed it in front of the building. She slid open the broken glass doors and walked inside. It was dark, but the window let in enough ambient light to see without tripping over anything. She walked behind the reception desk, the area where Nate had sat on so many days and worked on his inventions. Her eyes welled up and she choked back a sob as she walked into the lab, the area she had worked and had spent so many days before and after Gray Day. Her chair was right where she had left it. She had grown to love the chair, and she walked over to sit down and have a rest. In the chair was a folded piece of paper with her name on it. She hadn't remembered seeing it before; she picked it up and started to read.

To my dearest Jeannette:
I've never been great with words, especially words that describe my feelings. I guess I'm the typical man in that regard. I know that you don't agree that it's necessary for me to take this trip, but I can't take the risk that the snow will come and I'll have to watch you starve. I'd never been in love before I met you; I know all the clichés have been said before, and I wish I had words that could make you understand how I feel about you. You're the best thing that's ever happened to me, and I'd rather live in this mess of a world with you than live in a perfect world without you. I will do everything in my power to make it home to you. Just know that if I don't, it wasn't for a lack of trying. I will love you forever.
Nate

"Yeah, he's not great with words," Jeannette said as her tears fell onto the paper. She folded the note and put it in her pocket. She didn't know if reading it had made her miss him more or had made her feel better, but she knew in her heart she would read it many times again before he came home.

Jeannette pushed the cart back down the hill; it was much easier going downhill than it had been going uphill. She thought of Nate and wondered what he was doing on the road. Was he still alive? Did he think of her as often as she thought of him? She rounded the corner onto Main Street, looking forward to getting back to the firehouse and going to sleep. She saw the roadblock ahead of her, but it looked different. Now there were five men standing in front of the cars instead of three, and one of the men was Simon. She thought about turning and running the other way for a moment; the last thing she wanted to do was talk to Simon. But she made her way to the roadblock, where two men stood on each side of Simon holding rifles. As Jeannette approached, they lowered the rifles and aimed them at her. "What the fuck?" Jeannette said. The feeling of having a gun pointed at her was enough to scare the shit out of her, even if she was pretty sure Simon wouldn't allow anyone to be shot.

"Jeannette Leach, you are under arrest for the crime of breaking curfew without permission," Simon said smugly with an insane grin. Jeannette could tell that something had changed in Simon; something in his eyes worried her deeply, and for a moment she fully believed he might actually have her shot.

"Simon, you know I was just getting medical supplies for the community," Jeannette said. She could hear the fear in her own voice.

"That may be true, but we can't have everyone running off all willy-nilly anytime they damn well please." Simon was grinning again, a sick, strange grin that reminded Jeannette of an evil carnival clown. Jeannette had also never heard him swear before or even use a minor curse word like *damn*.

"Simon, this is insane," Jeannette said, horrified. Simon looked like he was angered by that remark, but then his face contorted and returned to a grin.

"Boys," he said. The guards looked at him questioningly, and then two of the men lifted their guns to their shoulders.

"OK, OK," Jeannette said. "What do you want from me?"

"You will be placed on house arrest until a time when you can be sentenced properly," Simon said with sincerity, but the grin was still plastered below his nose.

"What does house arrest mean? It's not like you have those ankle bracelets," Jeannette said nervously.

"It means if you leave the firehouse, even for a minute, you will be shot...dead." Finally, the grin changed to an expression of satisfaction. The men surrounded Jeannette, and two of them grabbed her under the arms as they walked her back to the firehouse. Simon looked through the garden cart full of medical supplies, which Jeannette thought was another odd move. He then ordered one of the men to push the cart to the firehouse. Jeannette recognized one of the guards as Jed, Simon's oldest son, but the other ones she didn't recognize or didn't remember seeing before. They all walked toward the firehouse. Jeannette couldn't believe what was happening.

19

THE BLACK SWARM

Nate's group of cyclists had made great time, and he was thrilled that they were finally about to reach the highway that would take them north at double the pace. It felt like late afternoon to Nate; they had been riding all day, but the gray sky had shown no indication of darkness. The number of abandoned cars had increased steadily the closer they got to the highway, and as they pedaled around a bend in the road, they saw an astounding sight. It appeared to be an endless line of cars, all facing north and blocking both lanes. A heavy steel Jersey barrier on each side of the road ran parallel to the blacktop, and with no shoulder or bike lane, riding on the side of the traffic would be impossible. The line of traffic stretched as far as they could see, where an overpass obstructed their view beyond. It appeared that they would have to ride single file down the center line of the road.

"What is this?" Bob asked, straddling his bike just ahead of the stalled-out cars.

"It looks like some sort of mass evacuation. I guess when these people heard the reports or sirens they tried to get out of dodge," Nate answered.

"I guess they didn't make it," Eggers said from behind Nate.

"There's a smaller version of this heading south out of Middlebrook on the way to the clinic," Nate said, trying to think of a way to circumnavigate the mess. Some of the cars appeared empty, but most had corpses, either in the seats or spilled out onto the road. The corpses were in varying states of decomposition, and the smell began to waft over the group.

"Oh, God, it stinks," Eggers said, holding his nose and wrinkling his face.

"Damn right it does," Ken said, pulling in behind Eggers.

"So do we go around or go through?" Bob asked as Thomas and Donna skidded to a stop.

"Well, going around would mean backtracking at least a couple of miles. I don't even remember the last crossroad. That's probably why the snarl is so bad here," Nate said as he pulled the roadmap from his pocket. He traced his finger along the thick red line until he found their location. "We just passed Burrbury. That overpass is route 8, the interstate. The on-ramp should be just on the other side of that bridge. We need to get on that interstate; it's the only major thoroughfare on this side of the state. It will take us through Massachusetts and almost all the way through New Hampshire." Nate folded the map and put it back in his pocket.

"What about another ramp farther up the line?" Thomas asked timidly. Even after several days on the road he was still a bit uncomfortable with the group.

"We'd be dealing with the same problem. It would involve backtracking miles, and even if we found another exit it could be the same situation with the traffic," Nate answered.

"Y'all heard the man, we're pushing onward. Everyone mount up," Bob said, sounding like a cross between a cowboy and a Maine lobster fisherman.

They all hopped on their bikes with Nate leading the way. It was slow going—the cars on either side meant they had to ride slowly and in single file. The most time-consuming aspect was the obstacles. It seemed like every fifty feet there was a body or a piece of luggage lying in the three-foot gap between the cars. The most disgusting chore was picking up the bodies, which were stiff and resembled not enough leather stretched across bone. They still stunk and were gooey even after two months in the elements. They had nearly reached the overpass when the conversation began—it was easier to simply walk the bikes than to keep getting on and off to clear the path.

"I was out feeding the hens when it all began," Eggers said, referring to the attack. "I heard the sirens; Donna was inside watching the news."

"I had been watching everything unfold," Donna added. "The Russians were livid. I guess when we nuked North Korea the bomb we used was too big—it was overkill. The fallout was carried right into Russia by the wind." She looked like she was trying hard to accurately remember those last few hours of news. "The Russians were angry, but the news said we sent millions in aid and had agreed to pay trillions in damages. It seemed like they had worked things out. Then something must have gone wrong, because that emergency broadcast thingy came on." Donna spoke like she still couldn't believe it had happened.

"That's when I ran into the house and we started to move supplies into the root cellar." Eggers pronounced *root* like "rut." "We had used that cellar to store canned vegetables and pickled eggs."

"Ugggh, loads of pickled eggs," Donna chimed in.

"Anyways, we stayed down there for ten days," Eggers said. He turned to Nate. "How about you, what's your story?"

"Well, for me it all started a week or so before the bombs." Nate remembered those days, and it wasn't a fond memory. "I was addicted to the news—sucking it up like a junky—but at the same time it was freaking me out in some kind of duality I can't really explain. Anyway, I just had an awful feeling. I...I...really can't explain it. I started stocking the basement of the blood draw station." Nate tried to remember everything and conceal his mental state at the same time. "I found Jeannette at work, and we hid out there for a few weeks." Just saying her name brought out a deluge of emotions. He couldn't bring himself to utter another word, no matter how petty. Nate's thoughts must have been splayed out all over his face, because the others sensed it.

"You better watch out, Nate, women are more dangerous than a shock fence in a rain storm," Eggers said with a smile.

"Shut the fuck up, Eggers," Donna said playfully and smiled compassionately at Nate. "Ignore this asshole."

"The mouth on you girl," Eggers said.

"Yeah, the mouth on me will bite your head off, and I'm not talking about the one attached to your long-assed neck," Donna retorted. *She could bust balls with a group of sailors and make them blush,* Nate thought to himself.

"Love is bullshit," Ken said bitterly. "It only comes with two endings: years of boredom or years of pain." Ken looked like he was lost in memory, his eyes focused on some point ahead of the group. "Yeah, maybe I'm cynical," Ken said, breaking into his moment of introspection. "Divorce will do that to you."

Within an hour, they had reached the bridge. The traprock that extended from the roadside up under the bridge was littered with abandoned suitcases and the corpses of people who had sheltered under the bridge after giving up on the traffic jam. The stench under the highway was unbearable, so Nate and the others increased their pace until they had cleared the overpass. Once they had come out the other side, another depressing sea of traffic led up around the semicircular on-ramp. A more surprising sight was the three men rummaging through a station wagon fifty feet ahead on the right. Nate stopped and turned to Morty: "Do you see those three guys up there or am I imagining things?" Two of the men had opened the rear door of the station wagon and were digging through what looked like luggage. The third man was standing watch outside the car, looking around.

"Yeah I see 'em. Do you think they're dangerous?" Morty asked, pulling a handgun from the holster on the crossbar of his bike.

"I'd like to try and avoid finding out the answer to that," Nate said carefully as he watched the men to see if they had spotted the seven riders. Nate knew that the numbers favored his group and they were well armed, but he wanted to avoid a fight at all costs. He didn't want any of his people hurt by these guys, and he didn't know whether the three individuals had friends waiting around the corner.

"Morty, ask Bob if he can come up here," he said, leaning his bike against a car and watching the others do the same. Nate wanted to have a quick council with his top adviser, but the whole crew had gathered around Nate like a football huddle around its quarterback.

"So what do we do?" Donna asked nervously.

"I say we take 'em out," Eggers said forcefully, with a look of anger that Nate had never seen in him.

"We can't just 'take 'em out,' Eggers. For all we know they could be fathers scavenging for their children," Bob whispered as though the men could hear him, even though they were far beyond earshot.

"Better safe than sorry. Ken has the deer rifle; with that scope we could take care of them before they even know we're here," Eggers said. But as he turned to point at the men, they realized it was too late. The three men had seen Nate's huddle and were now having a huddle of their own and pointing at them.

"Well that idea is hot, no pun intended," Eggers said with a sarcastic smile, a look Nate had grown accustomed to.

"Guys, make sure your weapons are ready. Let's go talk to them. Maybe they have some information that would be useful to us. Just keep quiet about Middlebrook—the last thing we want is to broadcast that there's a secure, well-stocked town forty miles up the road," Nate said, taking his own nine-millimeter from his pack. The seven bikers left their bikes leaning against the cars and began walking toward the men. The men broke their huddle and likewise began walking toward the group. The two factions met about ten feet apart; the three men were ragged looking, grungy, and worn. They looked like extras in a *Mad Max* movie. All three were covered with cuts, bruises, and infected-looking open sores. Their hair was matted and greasy, falling out in spots that revealed raw, bare red patches of scaly scalp. They were all dressed nearly identically, with a cross between biker leather and winter ski clothes. The other thing Nate noticed was that each of them wore a black cloth armband about three inches wide tied tightly between the elbow and shoulder.

One man was carrying a wooden baseball bat with a six-inch nail driven through the barrel. Nate wondered if the nail was for intimidation purposes or if it actually had a functional purpose. Another of the men, who had dyed-blond hair (what hair remained) and Elvis Costello glasses, was carrying a large iron pry bar. The third man looked like he had taken a spin in a clothes dryer and walked with a limp; he was obviously wounded and appeared to be holding a flare gun. The pistol was overly large with a wide barrel, but the giveaway that fired flares was that it had been painted blaze orange.

The two groups stood staring at each other in silence, like two bullies sizing each other up on the playground. The man in the glasses placed one end of his pry bar on the ground and leaned on the bent end. "Well, if it ain't the Hell's Angels," he said, looking over Nate's shoulder at the bikes leaned against the cars.

"And you must be the Three Stooges," Eggers shot back.

"Now that we've got the introductions out of the way," Nate said, attempting to ease the tension before Eggers picked a fight. "We're headed north and we just want to get through this mess of traffic without any trouble. We don't know you fellows and we didn't mean to startle you. We come in peace." Nate thought a direct and honest approach was the best course.

"What's up north?" the man with the modified baseball bat asked.

"That's our business," Eggers snapped. Nate wished Donna would elbow him so he'd shut up.

"We heard there's a National Guard troop up north and they might be offering help," Nate said quickly so they wouldn't get too bent out of shape from Eggers's jabs.

"Ain't nothin' up north. There ain't nothin' nowhere 'cept what you been seein': rottin' gluebags and ash," the man with the glasses said, sounding more apathetic than hostile. Nate wasn't sure what a gluebag was, but he assumed the man meant a decaying corpse.

Bob stepped forward and asked, "How far north have you guys been?" The three men looked at one another suspiciously.

"We've been up to the Mass border and back," the sickly guy with the limp answered with a certain amount of pride.

"Do you have families or a camp nearby?" Nate asked, hoping the men had more innocence in them than it had first appeared.

"And what's with the black armbands?" Eggers added before the men could answer.

The men again looked at one another very suspiciously, like they weren't sure how to answer or how much information to give out. "What's this—twenty questions?" Glasses asked accusingly.

It was the man with the bat's turn to reign in his subordinate. "Take it easy, Bug." He spoke directly to Nate as if the others weren't there. "Families? We don't have any families to speak of. We've been living off the road since the world went to shit. The armband just means we're in mourning for the millions of dead people," he said, shooting the man with the glasses a sharp look that made him choke in a giggle.

"Listen, we just want to get through here without any trouble," Nate said, ignoring the suspicions he had about the men. He did want to get through, and as quickly as possible. Nate didn't trust a thing about these men, but he also knew how quickly the conversation could explode.

"Not a problem. We don't own the road, but there's people out there that think they do." The man with the baseball bat backed off; he wasn't hiding his warning, but Nate knew he was hiding something.

Before long, Nate's group of cyclists had mounted their bikes. Bob led the group and Nate took the rear so he could make sure Eggers wouldn't be the last one alone with the vagabonds. They began to pedal ahead and had reached the start of the on-ramp when Nate stopped to look back. The sight was alarming: the men weren't scavenging cars anymore. One man was squatting down and the other two were stooped over, pointing and talking. They were examining the long, thin tire marks in the ash, the tire marks that would lead all the way back to Middlebrook.

• • •

Nate and his band of ten-speed heroes had passed the Massachusetts border two days ago. They seemed to be flying now; the highway had been a Godsend. Even when there was traffic congestion, the bike lane always allowed a passage to circumnavigate the forgotten vehicles. Nate was pleased about the progress they had been making. The scenery hadn't changed. In fact, Massachusetts seemed even more desolate than Connecticut, if that was possible. The roadside consisted of dead trees, rundown strip malls, and decrepit fast-food joints that at least allowed the group to restock canned food and potable water. As the group pedaled along, Nate thought about how athletic his legs had begun to feel. The soreness had abated, and he rarely felt the lactic acid burn in his calves anymore. He thought about Jeannette daily and longed to be with her every night; he hadn't ever had the feeling of want as badly as he did. It was like the desperation he used to feel to be free of a panic attack, only this desperation was the best kind.

Nate felt the incline increase as the bikers climbed yet another sweeping hill. Bob, who was riding beside Nate, groaned loudly. "This hill looks like a pain in the ass, buddy," he said, flipping the gears on his mountain bike. Nate couldn't believe how strong and durable Bob looked on the bike. He was a big man and he handled the bike with immense agility.

"Yeah, but at least there should be a long downhill glide on the other side," Nate said, hoping he sounded more enthusiastic than he felt.

"I'll race yah to the top, pardner," Bob said gleefully.

"No, I think I'll take this one slow," Nate answered.

"We've been takin' 'em all slow," Bob scolded sarcastically as he pumped the pedals.

Thankfully, the road was mostly free of ash as it had all been blown from the elevated highway, but the hill was just as onerous as it had looked. Most of the group gave up trying to ride it and were now walking their bikes. Nate was determined to stay on his bike, and by the time they reached the apex, the only other member of the posse still riding was Donna. They both stopped at the top and congratulated each other, sharing a celebratory bottle of water. They were standing at the top sipping water when Donna abruptly gasped.

"Nate, what the fuck is that?" Nate was standing about five feet away, yelling encouragement to the walkers. He limped over and joined Donna; his legs had started to cramp up. Nate hadn't bothered to look down to the bottom of the downslope, but when he finally did, he understood Donna's gasp.

The bottom of the hill appeared to be a dumping ground for corpses. Decomposing bodies were littered in every direction on both roadsides. Mingled with the bodies was what looked like strewn garbage, almost like a dump truck had spilled its cargo of rubbish and death. The bodies stood in stark contrast to the gray ground, and the more Nate looked the easier it was to tell just how many there were. Other bikers joined Nate and Donna at the top of the hill.

"What the hell is that?" Morty screamed in shock.

"It looks like a dumping ground—" Nate said, but Morty interrupted him before he could finish.

"No, that," Morty said. Nate turned and noticed that Morty's eyes were staring upward instead of downward like the rest of the group. He was looking at an area about fifty feet up off the side of the highway to the left. At first glance, Nate didn't see anything out of the ordinary except a cell-phone tower, something they had come across often throughout their journey. He focused more closely on the tower, which was slightly bent like a crisscrossed metal Leaning Tower of Pisa. Then he saw it. About halfway up the tower a man had been crucified, his arms spread out in a bizarre stigmatic pose. The man was tethered at the wrists and ankles with what appeared to be barbed wire. Nate couldn't be sure from a distance, but the slight state of decomposition led him to believe that the corpse was relatively fresh.

"I ain't climbin' up there to cut him down," Eggers said with his usual vulgar tact.

"How did he even get up there?" Ken questioned with an expression of disgust.

"They must have used the ladder on the side of the tower. The guy was prolly already dead," Bob replied solemnly.

"You guys need to see what's at the bottom of the hill," Donna said, pulling everyone's attention away from the blasphemous spectacle. The group collectively walked toward the downhill slope of the highway. They stood with their jaws dropped, gawking at the morbid mess below. No one spoke for a moment.

"You think it was radiation?" Morty finally said.

"No, they're on top of the ash," Nate said softly. "And they're too piled up to have died of radiation sickness. It's more like they were...tossed there."

"Maybe there were more of them and some got away. Couldn't it be some type of radiation zone held in by the valley? Maybe the ones that got away put that guy up there as some type of warning," Ken said, as if he needed to convince himself the scene had some kind of innocence.

"Yeah, real nice warning," Eggers said acerbically.

"Well, I think it's easy enough to find out," Nate said, pulling the smartphone from his front pocket. He hadn't turned the phone on since Middlebrook. He had hoped to conserve the charge just in case they were forced to travel closer to the out-skirts of Boston. "I want you all to wait here; I'll wave you down if it's safe," Nate said, hopping on his bike.

"You sure that's a good idea, buddy?" Bob asked with his usual fatherly concern.

"I've got the Geiger counter; if the alarm goes off I'll turn around immediately," Nate chirped, starting to glide away slowly. There would be no need to pedal, as the downhill momentum was enough to carry him all the way to the base. Nate held the Geiger counter out to his side while keeping one hand firmly gripped to the handlebars. He had almost arrived at the corpses when it became blatantly obvious that radiation hadn't killed these poor souls. He was getting so sick and tired of seeing dead bodies. There was blood on the road and on most of the bodies. Some of the deceased had large, gaping craters in their heads or torsos. Nate didn't need to be a genius to ascertain that these were the most likely sources of all the blood. The familiar smell of rotting carrion filled his nostrils; it had become an odor he had grown accustomed to, a fact that he hated. He stopped his bike and put the cell phone back in his pocket. Then he paused before waving the other bikers down. A very odd sensation came over Nate: pure, clear, anger. He didn't want to see this anymore. He was tired of coming across displays of death. He hesitantly waved down his friends, and for a second he thought about the word *friends*. That was exactly what his companions were: friends who he wished he could spare from the deplorable sight.

The group ambled among the bodies playing detective, and theories began to emerge about what had occurred. There was no prejudice: the cadavers included men, women, and children, young and old. Most were slashed, stabbed, or had their throats slit from ear to ear. A few had large bullet wounds—mostly the men, who had probably tried to fight back. Some of the corpses, mostly the women, were naked. The colorful objects that Nate had originally thought were garbage were actually clothing that had been either ripped from scattered packs and suitcases or ripped from the bodies of the women.

"It looks like these poor people were heading north like us," Donna said sadly,

"Yeah, some kind of exodus," Ken said, picking up one of the open suitcases.

"Hey! Come here!" Eggers yelled, drawing his gun. "We've got a live one!"

They all ran over to the high brown grass that resembled straw ready to be bailed. On the treeline off the side of the highway was a badly injured man lying at Eggers feet. The man's legs were severely twisted nearly in a complete spiral below his waist. His pants were torn and burned, exposing a gash where a sharp white bone protruded from his skin. The man was moaning but conscious; he had pissed himself, leaving a dark, wet stain around his zipper.

"Water, please, water," he croaked, with a voice so dry that it made Nate thirsty. Nate bent down and poured some water into the poor man's mouth. His hand grabbed at the bottle and Nate let him take it. He gulped it down greedily.

"What happened here?" Nate asked.

"It was the Black Swarm," the man said, panting for breath. "Kill me, please, you need to kill me. I can't feel my legs...I'm dead already...just kill me," he begged.

"What in hell's name is the Black Swarm?" Morty asked urgently.

"It's...a road gang. Evil fuckers. They go from place to place killing, taking the women, taking whatever they need." The man struggled to speak and took another gulp of water.

Donna knelt down next to the man, wiping his head with a rag from her back pocket, then pouring more water onto the rag and holding it to his brow.

"What do you mean they go from place to place?" Nate asked. He was now concerned about Middlebrook.

"There are at least thirty of them in this group, more in other states on other roads. They wear black armbands. It takes a lot of food to feed that many guys. Lots of water, too. I heard they got a home base to the west, outside of Albany." The man groaned loudly. "So they send out scouts in every direction. Maybe these scouts are on their last legs, injured or sick, so the leaders, the stronger ones, push em out, say if they find a settlement or stockpile, they'll bury 'em proper, maybe take care of their family if they got one." The man was speaking in starts and stops, making him hard to follow. "These scouts, they got walkie-talkies, long-range ones that the home base fixed up. They find a place that is ripe for the pickin' and call in the closest gang, the soldiers." The man coughed and then winced with pain. "It's a network, like a hive—that's why they call it the Swarm." The man kept talking quickly, like he was trying to get all the words out before the pain shot through him again.

"Who are these people?" Ken said, sounding disgusted with his fellow man.

"Some of 'em is escaped cons, or bad dudes anyway. Others just want to survive. They're like locusts. They use up the goods and then move on." The man was pale and sweaty; Nate wasn't sure how much longer he'd last. "I been lyin' here for two days since the attack. You gotta kill me; I ain't gonna make it. That old bitch had a hand grenade; I didn't see that one comin'."

Nate instantly realized they weren't talking to a victim. "So how come you know so much about this Black Swarm?" Nate asked, not even attempting to conceal his suspicion.

"Because I'm one of 'em," the man said, reaching into his pocket in agony and pulling out a black armband, which he promptly threw in Nate's face. Donna jumped up from her position of compassion, and Eggers cocked his pistol and pointed it at the man's head.

"Eggers, wait," Nate said quickly, before Eggers could blow the shitbag's head off. "How far south would they go?" Nate asked loudly.

"It all depends on where the scouts call in from. Listen man, I don't know anything else. Just kill me."

"How far south would they go?" Nate could feel his blood pressure rising as he yelled. The man was silent, but he looked up at Nate with a look of pleasure, like he was enjoying shining Nate on. Nate lost his temper; all he could think of was Jeannette. He kicked the man in his twisted legs, but the bastard didn't even flinch; he had been telling the truth and was apparently paralyzed from the waist down. Nate knew the man's spinal cord must have been severed at the lower back. He put his foot on the man's stomach and bore down. The other members of Nate's group looked on in horror. The man howled in agony. Nate was starting to lose his shit, all he could see was Jeannette's face on one of those naked bodies. He lifted up his foot ready to stomp down.

"OK, OK, just wait," the man said pleadingly.

"How far south would the gang go?" Nate asked again, this time calmly, his knee was still raised above the man's gut.

"All the way to the coast," the man said.

Nate closed his eyes and turned around. He stood and thought for a moment, facing away from his own disapproving friends. Nate turned back around, looked Eggers in the eyes, and nodded. It was all Eggers needed; he walked over to the man, leveled the gun, and fired. A squirt of blood sprayed into the air, followed by a trickle from the quarter-sized bullet hole in the man's head.

20

THE FALL

Simon felt like he was ready to break. He had become fragile, like the anger had been tearing out huge chunks of his intestines. It was ten o'clock at night, and he should have been trying to get some sleep, but he closed the door to his office and sat down behind his desk. "That know-it-all bitch—someone needs to be made an example of. These ingrates...all I do for them. All I want is a little credit," Simon said to the closed door. He stood and paced behind his desk. Stopping, he picked up the monitor off the desk and hurled it at the wall, screaming out, "Suicide's a mortal sin, you bitch!" The monitor smashed against the wall, pulling the cable out from the useless desktop computer. He walked over to his cot and sat down, trying to calm the jumbled conversation in his head. He had always been so calm and collected, stoic in the face of adversity; now he felt unraveled. For a moment he forgot who he was. He had lost everything that had connected him to God, only he hadn't lost it—it had been stolen. His head began to rock back and forth with some uncontrollable muscle spasm. He placed his head in his hands to stop the motion, but it didn't help. It was like he was having a seizure, only the seizure was confined to his neck. His lips were buzzing like he had just eaten a spoonful of cayenne pepper.

There was a knock at the door. He tried to compose himself; someone must have heard the monitor hit the wall or fall to the floor. Simon stood from the cot and a rush of blood pumped into his brain, causing a dizzy spell. He stumbled over and began picking up the pieces of glass and plastic spread along the floor. "Just a minute," Simon yelled hoarsely, in a voice that vaguely resembled his own. The door swung open. "I said just a—" Simon looked up and saw his wife standing in the doorway. She waddled forward, quietly closing the door behind her.

"Simon, we need to talk," Miranda said in her mousy voice. Simon thought how sick she made him feel, how useless she was, like the computer monitor he was picking up from the floor. She wasn't even good for making children anymore.

"What do you want—can't you see I'm busy?"

"Simon, you haven't visited with your daughters in weeks; you have Jed out there day and night guarding those roadblocks; and worst of all, you sent Thomas away without even telling me."

This was all he needed: a family guilt trip to add to the stress. He felt the grin return to his mouth. It was the happy face...his happy face. Simon stood holding the monitor cable in his right hand, the grin plastered to his face like a tattoo. Before he even realized what he was doing, the cruise control button was pushed again. He threw the cable over Miranda's head and pulled her close, spinning her around as he crossed the cable over itself. Miranda desperately tried to flee, but she was caught by surprise, and her struggles only tightened the rubber-covered copper cable around her throat. They fell clumsily. Miranda was facedown on the floor now, but Simon had fallen directly onto her back. He pulled back with all the strength he could muster. She did her best to roll out from under him, but Simon had practice keeping his weight centered like he was riding a bull in the rodeo. Miranda's face started to turn maroon, then a ghastly shade of purple, and thick white foam flowed from her mouth onto the floor. Her eyes bulged from her skull like a telescope-eyed goldfish, protruding way beyond the normal limit of the human head. Simon could feel the life slip from her body as she slowly stopped struggling, giving in to her fate.

"Sleep tight, Randi," he said with one feeling—exhilaration.

Simon stood and looked down at his dead wife; his first thought was that she wouldn't be easy to move. He pulled the green wool army blanket from his cot and rolled up the body the same way he had with the squatter who had invaded his territory. He didn't know how he was going to dispose of the body, and he didn't even care. For the time being, he felt peaceful. After a couple of minutes of finally thinking with a clear head, he dragged the six-foot steel gun safe out from under his cot. One by one he took all of his guns and placed them on the desk. Then, with an incredible amount of effort, he picked up Miranda's body and forced it into the gun safe. It was a tight fit—he bitterly thought to himself that he wished he had a shoehorn—he had to sit on top of the safe to get it to close. He snapped down the clasp and padlocked it. He would move the body soon if he had the chance; if not, he could deal with the smell. He slid the gun safe back under his cot. Simon looked at the guns. He wasn't sure what to do with them. Then he thought about it for a moment and said out loud, "This town needs an example." He carried the guns like a load of kindling out to the garage bay, which was completely empty. Most of the community would be down in the basement sleeping or getting ready for bed. Simon looked around. He knew what he wanted to do with the guns, but he was now sure how to do it. Then he saw the lockers along the walls. The community had used up the lockers in the basement, so some of the men had moved the fire boots and coats out of the lockers upstairs so they could store clothing and personal effects. He read the names along the lockers. They were written on masking tape in blue magic marker. Eventually, he found the name he had been searching for: Bystrek. Simon carried the guns over to the locker and stashed them, closing the door when they were safely tucked away.

He went back to his office and laid down on his cot. He thought about what he would do over the next week. He would need more soldiers. He had twenty loyal members of his security force, but was it enough? He'd ask Jed to recruit more able-bodied, like-minded strong lads. He would also need to call a town meeting—someone had stolen his guns and they would need to get to the bottom of it.

• • •

It took Simon two days to organize and schedule the town meeting. Jed had found six more men willing and able to help defend the community's integrity. He called the meeting to order at six o'clock. The throng of citizens had just finished eating dinner. Simon walked up behind the podium. "I have called this meeting to order because we have some very unfortunate news. My dear wife, Miranda, has gone missing. I have recruited six new members of the security team to help search for her, but I feel her absence is related to another troubling development." Simon looked around the room; the community was hanging on his every word with concern on their faces. "Some troubled soul has broken into my office. They ransacked it, breaking the computer on my desk and stealing all of my precious guns. As you know, I have been supplying the security force with weapons and ammunition from my own stock." Simon looked over at his security team standing along one wall holding their rifles casually. "My security force has performed a meticulous investigation, and we found that the guns, unfortunately, were taken by one of our own community brothers." A surprised gasp escaped from the seated assemblage. Simon nodded to his foot-soldiers; they walked behind the seated community. "It pains me to say that we recovered the guns from the locker of Mr. Paul Bystrek."

"That's not true; it's complete bullshit," Bystrek stood and shouted, but it was too late. The security team had already surrounded him.

The crowd erupted. One individual yelled, "We need a trial!" Another yelled, "Hang the bastard!"

Jeannette sat in the back of the room and put her head in her hands.

Simon stood at the podium, admiring the chaos. His security team bound Bystrek's hands behind his back with white plastic zip ties. The security group walked among the crowd of community members, many of whom were now standing. The security team didn't hide the fact that their guns were ready to be fired if need be. The atmosphere was sinister and dark; the whole room seemed to be enveloped by a mix of hysteria and confusion.

Simon stepped closer to the podium. "Calm down, everybody, please. We have come to a verdict!" Simon had to scream over the rumble of angered citizens. As soon as Simon said *verdict,* Jeannette stood up and left the room, which Simon ignored, but the rest of the crowd quieted to hear this "verdict."

"We don't believe Mr. Bystrek had any accomplices, but if anyone would like to come forward, we would be happy to listen to your side of the story." Simon paused, knowing that there wasn't a chance in hell anyone would step forward. "If there are no objections, Lieutenant Huff, will you please read the verdict."

Jed walked over to the podium. "Mr. Paul Bystrek will be hanged by the neck until a time when he can no longer trouble our beloved community." Jed walked back and joined the security force, which was stationed at different intervals throughout the crowd. The crowd erupted again, but it was short-lived. One man stood and yelled, "You can't do this!" for which he quickly received a rifle butt to the stomach. The rest of the crowd looked shocked and scared. They quickly sat down and silence enveloped the room. Many could be heard weeping openly, both men and women.

"I hereby conclude this meeting of the Middlebrook town government," Simon said, and he walked out of the room followed by his security force.

The next day, Simon walked back from the town green; Paul Bystrek's body was now swinging from a hundred-year-old oak just west of the town hall. He had ordered his security team to execute the dissenter in private, as there was no reason Simon could think of why women and children needed to see the untidy business. He finally felt like he had true power—control over the community and his own mind. It was a beautiful morning for another overcast gray day. Simon would be meeting his first lieutenant Jed at the roadblock at the head of Main Street. Simon was pleased his security team was working like an efficient piece of machinery, and Jed was taking to leadership like a gold medal slalom skier takes to snow. "He sure takes after me," Simon said to himself gleefully. The key to leadership wasn't God or sugar, it was using an iron fist to throw an uppercut to your followers.

Simon met Jed at the roadblock, admiring how he'd become a man right under his nose. He was tall and blond, just like

Simon, and he was thriving in a world that very few were able to thrive in. If only Simon's own father had been so attentive and giving, not easy—for there could be no mistaking Simon's generosity for coddling or going easy on the boy—but giving, yes definitely. Jed walked closer to his father. *Yes,* Simon thought, *best not to have a warm conversation in front of the men.* Out here they weren't father and son, they were general and lieutenant.

"First Lieutenant, all quiet on the eastern front?" Simon asked with a smile.

"Dad, where's Mom?" Jed asked harshly.

"I told you, son, she's missing."

"I thought that was all part of that asshole Bystrek thing," Jed said accusingly.

"Watch your tone, soldier," Simon remarked sternly.

"Dad, where is she? Mom never lea—" Suddenly, Jed's head exploded in a spray of blood and skull fragments. The gore covered Simon's face, and he picked a portion of Jed's scalp off his nose. Jed's headless body stood for a moment before tumbling to the ground in a heap. Simon couldn't think—he didn't understand what had just happened.

"Everyone down! We've got a sniper!" one of the security team yelled while taking cover behind one of the cars that made up the roadblock. The security team started firing back in the direction of the shot. Bullets flew in every direction, some pinging off the car or shattering windshields and car windows.

Simon stood dazed; he could hear the bullets screaming past his head, and he could feel the air part as the projectile came within inches of his head. The yelling and chaos churned around Simon, but he was frozen. He felt the grin start to form at the corners of his mouth—this was how it had to be. Simon drew his sidearm and started firing wildly. The shots seemed to be coming from a group of trees between two of the storefront buildings. Simon crawled on his hands and knees behind a bullet-pocked car; he used it for cover as much as he could, but the incoming fire was too intense. Soon, his fifteen-shot clip was empty. Simon stood and walked back to the firehouse, he needed to get more ammunition. As he walked, bullets hit the ground around him, but he knew that soon the angle would be too extreme for the snipers to get a clear shot, and it would look cool to his men if he didn't panic. The rest of his security force was running up the street to join the battle and rescue the four pinned-down guards. Simon looked back; his headless son was splayed out on the ground, the silver car behind him covered in blood. His security force was putting forth a valiant effort. Simon would return with more guns, maybe tell that know-it-all bitch he had told her so, suicide was indeed a mortal sin. "Wait a minute, that doesn't make sense," Simon said to himself, but the grin told him it did make sense, perfect sense.

21

BUGS ON A WINDSHIELD

Jeannette stood in her office staring at her packed duffel bag, which was sitting on the exam table. She loved helping people, but she could do that anywhere, perhaps even Maine. It was time to leave. Everything Nate and she had loved about the town had gone to shit. Simon had gone mad, and this whole scheme with Paul Bystrek, who seemed like a sweet man even though Jeannette hadn't known him well, had been nauseating. She was kicking herself for not forcing the issue with Nate one way or the other—if he had stayed, he might have been able to prevent this catastrophe, or if she had gone with him they could've lived in Maine, safe and sound. Which brought her thought process to another issue: how would she find Nate between Middlebrook and Maine? She sat down at her desk, not knowing what to do. She couldn't stay in this fucked-up town the way it was, and she couldn't leave and risk Nate coming back to this mess with her gone. If only Simon didn't have so much damn control; how could the members of his security force simply give in to his craziness? Jeannette didn't believe for a second that Simon's wife was really missing or that Paul Bystrek had really stolen a bunch of Simon's guns for some unknown purpose. She knew about mind control and groupthink, like how Hitler turned a whole nation on to his idiocy, or how cults recruited members, but this seemed even more absurd. Simon wasn't even that charismatic. Maybe those boys on his thug force were just so scared and desperate to survive that they'd follow anyone who gave them some power.

Jeannette pulled open the bottom drawer of her desk and took out the Glock Nate had left for her. Maybe she could get to Simon before he caused any more trouble. Jeannette held the gun in her hand and started daydreaming about pulling the trigger and the look on Simon's face as the bullet left the muzzle.

Without warning, a series of gunshots came from outside the firehouse. For a second Jeannette thought she might have accidentally pulled the trigger, but the gunshots weren't close; the sound had definitely come from the street. Jeannette got up from her seat and went to the door; she heard them again. It sounded like firecrackers—a lot of firecrackers. What the hell was going on? Was the whole place imploding at once? She stuck her head out the door and saw two people running for the basement. Another man was hustling up the stairs and out into the garage; he was carrying a rifle in one hand and a box of ammo in the other.

"Hey," Jeannette yelled, getting the man's attention. "What's going on?"

"The town's under attack! There's people hurt, you're going to be needed," the man said, opening the door to the street. "Oh, and somebody better tell Simon; he might still be in his office." The man raced out the door. Jeannette could hear the loud gunshots echo through the open door into the garage. It sounded like World War III out there, Jeannette thought, although she was pretty sure World War III had already happened. The last thing she wanted to do was go tell Simon that everyone needed his expert leadership. She walked over to his office door, which was only two doors down from her office. Yellow and black caution tape crisscrossed the door. Jeannette wondered if he would even be in there with that tape over his door, he liked for things to appear orderly, and the tape made it look like his office was a crime scene. Then she remembered the "break in." His office could have been a crime scene, and now she had an excuse to knock on the door. She picked up the gun and placed it under her belt at the small of her back, as she had witnessed TV cops do a thousand times.

She banged on Simon's door, but there was no answer. She waited a second or two and knocked again. Still no answer; she looked down and saw that the lock appeared to be broken. For a split second she thought maybe someone *had* broken in and stole the guns. She pushed open the door, breaking the caution tape. "Hello?" she said, but the office was empty. "Uggh!" she wailed, as a putridly thick smell punched her in the nose. Jeannette backed away from the doorway. Something had definitely died in that office; she had a naive thought that maybe a raccoon or something had gotten into the heating duct, but then she mentally smacked herself. "Simon's wife," she said out loud.

"Simon's wife what?" a voice behind her said. Jeannette shut the door and spun around in terror—she knew the voice well.

Simon was standing in the garage next to a fire truck; he had just walked in the door from the street. "Simon's wife what?" he said again.

"Simon, what did you do?" Jeannette said reaching slowly behind her back for the handgun.

"I strangled her, and I'm gonna do the same to you, because suicide's a mortal sin and you killed my Jed." He wasn't making any sense, and that scared Jeannette, but the lunatic grin absolutely petrified her.

Jeannette pulled the gun. "Simon, don't come any closer, I have no qualms about shooting you," she said, aiming the gun at him. But Simon didn't stop—he didn't even slow down. "Simon, don't!" she said, thinking he was way off the guano farm. Maybe he wanted to die. Simon kept walking; he was almost on top of her now. She pulled the trigger, but nothing happened, just a depressing click. Jeannette stumbled back, giving her a little more time before Simon had her in his grasp. She quickly slid the slide on the top of the gun, but it pulled back and snapped closed quickly, there was no shell to engage.

"Do you really think we'd let you have a loaded gun in your desk while you're on house arrest?" Simon giggled.

"Oh, fuck!" Jeannette yelled. "Help me! Somebody help me!" but anyone who could help her was already outside busy with the gunfight or off scavenging. Even the children had moved their daily lessons to the library a few days ago. Simon grabbed Jeannette by the back of the head; he had a handful of hair in his fist. Jeannette could see tears in his eyes, but there was no grief. They were tears of hate. His breath smelled like a dragon fart, and a horrible growling sound seemed to come from somewhere behind his Adam's apple. Jeannette punched out at the sound, but the punch was off and hit him in the side of the neck. Simon cocked his arm back and Jeannette watched as his fist crashed down right between her eyes. She heard a violent crack; then excruciating pain erupted from the bridge of her nose out the back of her whiplashed head. Her eyes welled up with water, and she could feel the blood trickle down her septum. She swallowed a thick load of snot and blood and swung her own fist balled around the pistol in a whipping motion with everything she had. Jeannette felt her knuckles explode as her fist hit the side of Simon's head. The weight of the gun in her hand intensified the blow, but it also crushed her fingers agonizingly against the handgun's grip. He stumbled back, confused, and appeared to be appalled that someone would have the gall to hit him back. It gave Jeannette just enough time to slip his grasp. She painfully lost a handful of hair and probably some roots in the process, but she was free. She turned and ran, but there was nowhere to go. If she headed toward the street she would run right into Simon. She smashed through the door to the basement and ran down the stairs, using the banister to slide, her feet barely touching the ground. Jeannette crashed through the door at the bottom of the stairs, praying that some of the cooks were in the small kitchen. She could hear Simon on the stairs. He was in no rush—she had nowhere to go. She was trapped.

Jeannette didn't know what to do; she couldn't hear anyone working in the kitchen, and her nose was gushing blood like an aquarium with a bullet hole. She could hear each of Simon's footfalls pound the linoleum steps as he slowly made his way down the stairs. Her heart was pounding. "Think, think, think!" she said loudly. Simon had begun to hum softly; it was a strange tune that Jeannette didn't recognize or much care about. She needed to do something, and fast. Simon's foot hit the landing and Jeannette ran for the kitchen. The small cubbyhole of a room was dominated by a silver commercial-sized stove. She followed the kitchen back into a curtained pantry, but there was nothing inside but wall to wall canned food. She thought about pelting Simon with cans of soup, but if she missed she'd be right back where she had started—in a fist fight. She hurried the two steps back to the kitchen. The fluorescent lights reflected off the high-gloss white walls—at least the generator was on, she thought while scanning the walls for anything she could use as a weapon, it would have been even worse for her in the dark. Jeannette could hear Simon's twisted humming grow louder with each stride as he crossed the long room that had housed the majority of the community. *Why couldn't someone be here now?* she thought. Then she saw the perfect weapon: a heavy butcher's knife was hanging from a nail by the stove, she wondered why she hadn't seen it coming in, but realized a plastic guard had hidden it from the doorway. "It's beautiful," she said softly and grabbed it from the wall. She prepared herself; the humming was right at the kitchen door.

Simon stepped into the room, and Jeannette held up the knife, thinking some intimidation might help. "Where's your cheerleader outfit?" he asked, grinning like he had just lost his virginity that morning.

Jeannette gave him a clueless look and then charged him with the knife, running at him with every ounce of strength she could muster. Simon instinctively put his hands in front of himself to block the knife's penetration into his chest. The blade went through his hand, stopping at the handle, and blood poured to the floor as the two struggled to gain leverage over each other. Simon had one hand on Jeannette's wrist, while the other was now attached to her knife.

"You know, if you kill me you'll go to hell," Simon said desperately, trying not to faint from the sight of the knife through his hand.

"No, I'm pretty sure I'm going to heaven, because I spent your reign here—in hell," Jeannette said. She could feel that Simon's grip had become slick with blood. She pulled downward as hard as she could, and the knife cut a straight line from his knuckles to his palm. The knife slid out and she swung it instantly, catching Simon across the throat. The knife must have been sharp, because it cut through the tendons of his neck, his windpipe, and his jugular in one swipe. Simon collapsed to the ground, gasping and gargling. Sprays of aerated blood flew from his mouth as he coughed out his last breath, his mouth and lips painted crimson. The blood pooled around Simon's head and spread quickly, like a spilled gallon of milk.

"I don't believe it," Jeannette said in awe. She had never killed anyone, and it wasn't an event she took lightly. She threw the knife down on Simon's body and walked out of the room as quickly as she could; there was no urge to look back. She ran up the stairs screaming for help, hoping someone was in the garage. Two of Simon's security team looked up and saw her covered in blood. They rushed over to her, catching her by the armpits as she collapsed into their safety. She spent the next twenty minutes explaining what happened. At first, the two men looked at her like she was insane—Simon wouldn't have gone crazy like that. But Jeannette sensed that they had seen it in his eyes previously. She showed them his body and explained about the man who had suggested that she try to find Simon. She told the guards that she had gone into his office to warn him that there was shooting in the street and how he had startled her when he came in through the door. Jeannette even told them about the grin, and together the three of them discovered the origin of the smell in Simon's office. Of course it was Miranda's body. They believed her after that.

Two more men hobbled into the garage. One had a gunshot wound in the foot and the other had been shot through the shoulder. Jeannette rushed to their aid and quickly had them patched up and resting in her office. Over the next two days, the standoff in the street continued day and night. Jeannette slowly became the saving grace of Simon's security team as she stitched, removed bullets, and stopped profuse bleeding on three more men. The town was under siege; the unseen enemy had dug in all around Main Street, and it was all hands on deck as men and women armed themselves and protected one another, defending the firehouse fiercely. The enemy was strong, but the people of Middlebrook were willing to give their lives for their home, and some of them did. No one seemed to notice that Simon was gone, or maybe they simply didn't care. They were fighting for their lives, fighting to protect their families. The mess in the basement kitchen was cleaned up; Simon's body was placed in the alley next to the firehouse and cremated with the bodies of his wife and son. Simon's daughters took their mother's death extremely hard and blamed their father for it, but Denise and Jeannette were there to console them. After all, they would always be a part of the community.

The gun battle in the street wore on. It seemed to come in waves, with bullets flying for an hour, then nothing for two. No one knew who the attackers were or what they wanted, and no one wanted to find out either. Middlebrook was cut off; the invaders could simply take their time and starve them out. The pantry was well stocked, but the food wouldn't last forever, and neither would the ammunition. By the third day, the shooting had slowed considerably; the intruders had either lost their will or were surprised that someone had the nerve to fight back. Or maybe they were simply biding their time until more targets presented themselves—Jeannette thought it was probably the latter.

22

LIVE FREE OR DIE

Nate turned to his friends. They all stood silently, staring at the broken vagrant with the hole in his head. Eggers holstered his gun without a word. Donna was covering her mouth with her hand; Morty looked at the ground like he had lost a contact lens. It wasn't the supportive scene that Nate had hoped for. Perhaps friends were more fickle than Nate had thought; he hadn't had many over the years to know for sure. Bob walked over to Nate and threw an arm around his shoulder, reassuring Nate in the validity of human contact.

"You did what you had to do, buddy; I know it was hard for yah," Bob said loyally.

"Hard for him? I'm the one who shot the fucker," Eggers said sternly.

"Shut up, Eggers. You've wanted to roll someone since we pulled out of Middlebrook," Ken snapped. Donna and Morty fought back smiles, and after a moment Eggers smiled too. Soon they were all chuckling. Even Thomas was standing off to the side, smiling.

Nate stood in front of his group of cyclists quietly deliberating. They had a real dilemma on their hands.

"Nate, what's up?" Bob said, noticing Nate's demeanor.

"We need to think seriously about turning back toward home," Nate said. He could feel the anxiety slithering up his spine like an unwelcome relative who's overstayed his welcome.

"Why?" Ken asked with confusion, but Bob knew instantly.

"Because Nate thinks that group of hooligans is headed there," he said, looking to Nate for confirmation.

"Those three guys we ran into back at that line of dead cars had black armbands," Nate said, as the battle began in his head. He didn't know whether the group should keep pushing forward at all costs or try to get back to Middlebrook before something really bad happened there. "I think those guys were the scouts this lump of shit was talking about," Nate said, kicking a plume of ash at their mangled informant.

"But Middlebrook has to be fifty miles south of that pileup. You really think those three douchebags will make it that far? Plus we're halfway to Maine, maybe more, and I ain't goin' back empty-handed. Hell who says they could even find the place? There must be a hundred small towns that could have food between here and there," Eggers said passionately.

"It wouldn't exactly be like finding a needle in a haystack, Eggers. They can just follow our tracks in the ash or call in their gang to do it," Nate said.

"I don't know, Nate—that sounds pretty improbable. You're talking about those dipshits following tracks in the ash fifty miles—ash that is shifting and blowing around constantly," Ken said. "That's a long walk, and if they called their gang in, the gang would need to travel even farther. Besides, its not like Middlebrook is even a straight shot from there."

"If they get to Middlebrook, my dad will make that gang wish they were never born," Thomas said proudly, shocking the group not only with his comment but the fact that he had even joined in the conversation. "We have to go on; we've come so far."

"So I suppose it's unanimous—we keep to the plan," Nate said cautiously.

"Yeah, stay the course," Eggers said with a chuckle.

The bunch mounted their bikes and pedaled north away from the massacre, away from Middlebrook, and for Nate, farther away from Jeannette.

• • •

The refugees walked in groups of ten or twenty; they were huddled together for safety and comfort. Some carried children, and some carried possessions that were dear to them. The aggregation of pedestrians had started close to the New Hampshire border. Nate and his cohorts were mostly ignored by the exhausted throng of men, women, and children. At first, Nate worried that someone would attempt to snag their bikes, but most of the emigrants hardly even looked up as they rode past. About an hour ago, the cyclists had stopped and asked a haggard but friendly family where everyone was walking to. They had told them about Camp American Phoenix, a huge refugee camp the military had erected outside of Manchester. Nate and his group were elated; they wouldn't have to ride all the way to Maine, and Manchester was less than a day's ride away. They pedaled through the night, and as the sky brightened in the east, they could see the immense green tents and floodlights of the camp. The location looked like a former fairground; it was at least a mile long and nearly as wide, and surrounded by a seven-foot-high chain link fence with a toll booth–style entrance. In front of the entrance was a crowd of refugees waiting to be processed. Lines of eighteen wheelers were parked outside the fence, and four large gray Sea Stallion helicopters sat on a strip of blacktop beyond.

Nate's group of bikers stopped at the back of the huge line of evacuees and high fived like children celebrating a touchdown by their favorite team.

"I can't believe it, buddy, we made it!" Bob said, hugging Nate so hard that he thought his lungs might burst.

"We're not done yet!" Nate said, but he couldn't keep the smile from his face either.

"What are those flags painted on the sides of those trucks?" Morty said with a jubilant curiosity.

"Looks like..." Bob said, squinting "...Canada, China, Israel, and the Brits."

"How did they get them running?" Thomas asked.

"I don't know, and I don't care!" Eggers said joyfully.

"Prolly came down from Canada. Maybe the EMP wasn't that bad up there," Bob replied.

They left their bikes leaning on the fence and waited in line for four hours, but the time passed quickly and happily. They were all exhausted, and the waiting was the most relaxation they'd had in more than twenty-four hours.

As the group drew closer to the front of the line, Nate could see a long table at the entrance. Behind the table, four soldiers sat writing in huge logbooks. Nate could hear a female soldier asking questions to the group in front of him. "How many people are in your party? Does anyone in your party have any wounds, injury, or illness?" Then the next soldier took each refugee's name, date of birth, and where they had come from.

After receiving the answers, each soldier would scribble something into the logbook. It was all very official and orderly. Once the processing was completed, groups were split up: anyone who had health problems was directed toward a triage unit, and the others were sent to the housing director with a package of C-rations for each person.

Nate got to the table. "How many people are in your party?" the female soldier asked in a drained and monotonous voice.

Nate interrupted her questioning. "Listen, we're not staying. We have urgent information for Sergeant Dickerson of the Maine National Guard." It was only a little white lie, but Nate was desperate—they couldn't waste time hanging around a refugee camp waiting to catch some head honcho in the john. "There are people in danger, and he needs to know about it."

The female soldier seemed frustrated and pushed her chair back from the table, saying, "Whitaker, take over; I have to take these people to see the colonel." She turned back to Nate and said, "OK, follow me and don't get lost. That means stay with me." The soldier got up from her seat and introduced herself: "I'm Lance Corporal De La Rosa...let's go."

Nate turned to his crew and said, "All right, guys, let's go. Stay tight; don't get separated." They waded through the mass of refugees past two long tents the size of a football field and down a well-trodden dirt pathway; it was like Main Street of the tent metropolis. Refugees and soldiers were working on various tasks inside the cloth shelters. The two largest green canvas structures looked to be full of casualties, like a MASH unit near a battlefield; IV bottles hung from poles standing beside occupied cots. Beyond the two large infirmaries were a series of medium-sized tents the size of small houses, and past that Nate could see a city of smaller tents that stretched for what seemed like miles. They walked through the sea of people to the entranceway of one of the medium-sized tents. The flap that served as a door was closed.

"This is Colonel Champlain's office. I hope it goes without saying that you need to be on your best behavior. Champ does everything by the book, and this isn't exactly kosher," De La Rosa said before she turned and faced the closed canvas drape. "Champ, I have some people who need to speak with you. They say it's urgent priority."

A feminine voice sang out from the tent, "Send them in." De La Rosa opened the canvas flap, with Nate and Bob on her heels.

"The rest of us are going to wait outside," Donna said with an embarrassed smile. Eggers, Morty, Ken, and Thomas all nodded in agreement.

"Cowards," Nate said acrimoniously, but with a grin.

Nate and Bob followed the corporal through the tent's opening into a small office. The interior was light years from what Nate had expected. It looked like it could have been taken out of any insurance company. A large desk was positioned on the hard dirt in the back, file cabinets lined both walls, and a large picture of President Everett hung on the support pole in the center of the room. Behind the desk was a woman who looked to be in her midforties. She had light brown hair that had been tied back in a ponytail. She was wearing a neatly pressed blue uniform with metallic black bars on the lapel.

"How can I help you?" she asked in a pleasant voice.

"My name is Nathan Wilder, and this is Bob Halloran. We've traveled here from Middlebrook, Connecticut, because we spoke on the radio to Sergeant Dickerson."

"Dickie left three days ago on patrol; his unit has been working tirelessly to open up new routes here and eradicate the Swarm," she said. "So how can I help you? We're extremely busy here."

"Our town of Middlebrook is desperate for help, the winter is coming and we may not have enough food and water to make it through," Nate said.

"Mr. Wilder, many communities are in dire need of help."

"I know, but—" Nate started.

"But we have reason to believe that a massive attack from the Black Swarm is imminent," Bob said quickly, meeting Nate's eyes as he spoke.

"Do you know this for sure?" the Colonel asked. Her interest had been piqued.

Nate and Bob looked at each other again and spoke nearly in unison, "We're sure." Nate didn't want to lie, but all he could think of was Jeannette sitting in the basement of the firehouse milking the last drops of soup from a dented can. It was a strange thought.

"Would you know how to find your town by helicopter?" she said, picking up the phone on her desk.

"Doesn't the GPS work?" Nate said, but the colonel ignored him; she was already speaking on the phone requesting two helicopters for a four-hour round trip.

Nate and Bob walked out of the tent with smiles on their faces. Donna was sitting on Eggers's lap on a stump next to the tent, and Morty, Ken, and Thomas were mingling with a group of soldiers, who couldn't have been older than teenagers, on the other side.

"We're in business," Nate said joyfully.

"What do you mean?" Donna asked as the others gathered around.

"They arranged for two helicopters to fly us to Middlebrook. One of them will be full of supplies, and the other will carry us and six heavily armed members of the newly reinstated Force Recon," Nate said.

"They're Special Forces—real badasses," Bob said with pride.

"How the fuck did you manage that one?" Eggers asked with surprise.

"We told her that we have reason to believe Middlebrook may become the target of a large Black Swarm attack," Nate answered, sharing another glance with Bob. "Come on, we have to get over to those helicopters."

"Nate, that's something we want to talk to you about," Morty said. He had an apologetic look on his face. "Ken, Thomas, and I are gonna stay here. You're gonna need somebody to keep the pressure on to get supplies to Middlebrook through the winter. Plus, we've met some people who say they can get us enlisted."

"Enlisted?" Bob asked, confused. "Morty, you're almost fifty; Ken, you're what—forty-two? Since when do they enlist old farts?"

"Gee thanks, Bob," Ken sneered.

"They need everyone they can get—even old farts. We have a country to rebuild," Morty said.

"What about your family, Thomas? What about your dad?" Nate asked, looking at Thomas.

"It's time for me to live my own life. Plus I think my dad would be proud. It's not every day that you get to be a part of something so important," Thomas answered.

"Wait a minute," Eggers said. "You guys rode bikes all the way here from Connecticut to save our town, and now you're gonna abandon it?"

"We're not abandoning it; we just think this is the best way we can help," Ken said.

"Maybe you guys could come back, you know—stay up here for a few weeks and then hitch a ride to the firehouse?" Donna pleaded.

Bob smiled. "It's their lives, and it might not be such a bad idea for them to stay. I'm proud of you guys," he said, walking over and shaking their hands, which evolved into a Bob bear hug for each man. Nate did the same, telling them how much he appreciated the fact that they had risked their lives next to him. Eggers and Donna followed, with only a minor snickering remark from Eggers.

"Well, I guess this is goodbye then," Nate said sadly, and they parted ways. Nate turned back and gave the three a sarcastic salute as they walked toward where they had last seen the helicopters.

23

DREAM SEQUENCE

The helicopter flew high above the desecrated ground. Nate looked out the small window at the gray planet below; it looked like a moonscape, like somebody had replaced the earth with a gray hunk of used charcoal. Donna, Eggers, and Bob had already fallen asleep in the back cargo hold of the colossal Sea Stallion helicopter. The inside of the craft reminded Nate of a subway car, with seats facing the wrong direction. Nate was seated next to Assistant Commander Anfernee Tollison, an officer in the special forces from Detroit. Commander Tollison had been stationed in Germany during the nuclear attack; it had taken him more than a month to get back to the states. Nate tried not to be a pest, but he desperately wanted information about what exactly had happened. Not that it would change anything or make things better—he just needed to know the details for his own sanity.

"So, start from the beginning: what exactly set everything off?" Nate asked. He had to raise his voice to a yell to be heard over the thunderous rotor and engine. Nate wondered how anyone could sleep through the racket.

"You know how we nuked North Korea?" Tollison said. "Well, that fallout drifted into Russia."

"Right I know all that, but—"

"Yeah, but did you know that the Russians nuked us because of some fucking computer virus?" Tollison said. "We nuked them right back, but it was all a virus in the DOD software or something."

"Holy shit; you mean to tell me no one even intended to blow up the planet?"

"No, that's not really it. I guess the virus told the spooks that an attack was already underway. Everything got all fucked up," Tollison yelled. "I don't think anyone really wanted to nuke anyone. Except of course North Korea—we meant to nuke them."

"So was it the North Koreans who planted the virus?" Nate asked as loudly as could.

"No one knows for sure, at least as far as I know."

"So who got hit?" Nate asked.

"Every major city from here to California," Tollison answered.

"What about other countries—was anyone else involved?" Nate was thinking about Paris and London. He knew that during the Cold War, Europe was in the same boat as the Americans.

"Nope, everyone else stayed out of it; just a couple hundred nukes lobbed between us and Russia. That's why we're starting to get humanitarian aid from around the world; I think all those countries felt like they owed us from decades of foreign aid."

"What about our government? Did the president survive?" Nate asked.

"Not really; we've had to start from scratch. Washington's gone, of course, and Air Force One crashed on the way to some secret bunker. I heard the president was on board." Commander

Tollison pulled his headphones up to his ears and leaned back in his seat. It was a message to Nate that he was done talking.

Nate sat quietly, thinking about everything he had just heard. He had so many more questions, but Tollison was now bouncing to his music, and Nate didn't want to piss him off any more than he may already have. Nate sat back and thought about Jeannette; he prayed to God that she was still alive. He needed to see her face, to feel her warmth, to be home. He slowly drifted off to sleep, lulled by the same rhythmic pounding he had cursed minutes ago.

"Lock and load!" someone yelled. Nate bolted up in his seat, dazed from the short nap. He could hear loud pings smacking into the rotor.

"What's happening?" Nate yelled to the commander.

"We're taking fire!" Tollison yelled back, pulling the slide on an M249 machine gun.

"Where are we?" Nate yelled.

"Right over your fucking town!"

The helicopter swung hard to avoid the ground fire, and Nate caught a glimpse out the window. It was Main Street. An exploded car sat smoldering in the middle of the street. Nate could see men running on the outside of the storefronts that lined the road. He began to panic. They were already there; the Black Swarm had already taken over the town. "Shut up, just shut up; you don't know anything yet," he whispered to himself. But part of him knew that Jeannette was dead; there was no way she would allow herself to live with what the Swarm would do to her. "Just do something!" Nate yelled to himself. Tollison looked over at him strangely.

"We can't do anything until we land!" he yelled back.

"I know where there's a landing pad!" Nate yelled. "It's away from the center, away from the small arms fire."

"Where?" Tollison yelled.

Nate directed him to the health clinic's helicopter landing zone; they had used it when a bad accident had occurred in Middlebrook or if someone was in cardiac crisis. Tollison relayed the information to the pilot through the mouthpiece attached to his helmet. On the way to the landing zone, Nate explained as best he could the setup of Main Street: how the firehouse at the far end had been the Community's home and that anyone outside of Main Street was probably an enemy. Within minutes, the helicopter was landing next to the clinic. The men unloaded along with Eggers, Donna, and Bob; everyone was armed with light machine guns.

"I want you to cover us from the air. Seek and destroy. Kill all those motherfuckers outside of the main street. I don't want to get my ass shot off. Use the minigun!" Tollison said through his headset to the pilots of the helicopters. The six special forces team members, along with Nate, Donna, Eggers, and Bob, backed away from the choppers as they took off flying in the direction of Main Street.

"Double time toward the fighting!" Tollison yelled. And the group started off down the long road into the center of town. They kept up an exhausting pace somewhere between a run and a jog. Nate wondered how they could do it for so long; he could feel his side splitting with an intense case of the stitches. He pushed through the pain, keeping a picture of Jeannette's face in his mind every time he felt a painful twinge. Force Recon led the way, but Nate and his friends weren't far behind. Biking through three states had left them in better shape than even Nate could have hoped. They passed the hill down to the fork in the road; Nate could see that the asphalt had been cleared of the dead cars, which was an ominous sign. Perhaps the Black Swarm had moved the cars somehow for easier access to the next town. He could hear gunfire up ahead. The group took shelter behind a row of cars that had been setup to block off Main Street. The sound was deafening. The only thing to ring through the gunfire was the "tink, tink, tink" as empty shells landed on the rooftops. He could hear the helicopters overhead making long, strafing runs with their enormous guns. The buildings on his side were hit with projectiles that seemed to take out a whole brick with each impact. Nate looked through the car window; he could see blood ahead on the street and what looked like a couple of bodies lying in front of the firehouse.

"Look, Middlebrook is fighting back!" Eggers yelled. At first, Nate thought that maybe the Black Swarm was shooting at the helicopters, but then he saw the two men in front of the firehouse. They were kneeling beside the building with rifles, firing across the street. Nate didn't see any black armbands.

"I'm going to help them!" Bob yelled. And he ran out from behind the car in the direction of the firehouse.

"Wait!" Tollison yelled, but it was too late—Bob was already fifty feet up the road, ducking into an alley and firing his gun wildly in the direction of the attackers. Tollison spoke quickly into his headset. "Hammerhead, we're moving in." He then turned to his men. "OK, I want covering fire; we go two by two." He then turned to Nate, Eggers, and Donna. "You stay here," he said sternly.

"No problem," Eggers said in his usual sarcastic tone.

Watching the Recon Force spread out was like watching a professional ballet ensemble perform *Swan Lake*. They glided between buildings, firing as they went. Nate was in awe. They coordinated their movements with the choppers to devastating effect. Nate wondered how anyone could have survived their persistent onslaught—firing and moving, firing and moving. The problem was Bob seemed to think he was one of them. He burst out into the street, firing like Rambo at a gap between two buildings that seemed to be the enemy's stronghold. He started yelling, "Come on, you mothafuckas!" Nate even chuckled for a second, until Bob's hip started to shoot blood like it had its own machine gun. Bob crumpled on the ground, howling in pain. Nate couldn't take it anymore. He ran out from behind the car, firing as he went. He must have looked pretty stupid, because no one was firing back. The shot that hit Bob was the last gunshot they heard from the direction of the trees. The pressure that the Recon Force had put on must have been too fierce and too intimidating, because the street quieted all at once. Either all of the invaders were dead or they had been scared off by the attacking helicopters.

Nate rushed to Bob's side. He was lying in the street bleeding profusely from a huge crater in his hip the size of a dinner plate. Nate slid to the ground at Bob's waist; there was so much blood. Bone and muscle was exposed, along with the femoral artery, which was squirting blood rhythmically like a lawn sprinkler. Nate ripped off his own shirt and placed it on the wound, applying as much pressure as he could, but it was nearly impossible to get a grip with all the slick wetness. Nate looked up to see the Recon Force sweep into the gaps between the buildings to secure the area. The street was quiet except for Nate's grunts of frustration and exertion. He pushed as hard as he could, but the bleeding just wouldn't stop. The shirt was saturated in seconds, as Bob was being exsanguinated.

"Bob, stay with me," Nate said desperately. He could hear Donna crying behind him.

"What the fuck!" Eggers yelled. Nate looked up and saw tears streaming down his face.

"Bob! Bob!" Nate yelled, but he was bleeding out...there was nothing Nate could do. "Stay with me, dammit!"

Bob opened his eyes slightly. "It was a good run, buddy," he said softly. There was no Bob behind the voice.

"Bob, don't die on me," Nate said, and he could feel the tears on his own face. Bob opened his eyes again and looked into Nate's eyes.

"Nate, I just want you to know that Jeannette...Nate! Nate!" He turned his head with his last bit of strength and whispered, "It's time to land..."

Bob was shaking Nate awake. "Come on, buddy! We're home; it's time to land." Nate looked up at Bob, who was standing above him. "We're gonna put down behind the firehouse. Commander Tollison says it looks pretty calm here. There's a car burning on Main Street, but it doesn't appear to be—" Nate stood up and hugged Bob as hard as he could. He was confused; the dream had been so vivid.

"Whoa, take it easy there, cowboy. You're gonna break an old man." Nate was so overjoyed that he nearly kissed the big oaf, but he didn't want to seem completely crazy.

The helicopter landed without incident. The townspeople must have heard the choppers coming in, because they flooded out the back of the firehouse and stood cheering. The scene reminded Nate of a documentary he had watched about the fall of Saigon. It was like they wanted to get out, to go somewhere, before the rest of the world crumbled down around them. The crowd of ragged human wreckage threw their arms into the air, straining toward the approaching helicopter. It was like they were reaching for God, reaching for the sunlight that had been absent for months. It was sad, chaotic, and gorgeous, all at the same time. Nate's legs were wobbly. The helicopter had landed, but he could still feel the motion in his soul. The hatch separated, the top half swinging up and the bottom half turning into a set of stairs. He could feel the anxiety again, but for once in his life it was the good kind of anxiety, the kind you feel when you're there for your mother, holding her hand as she passes away. The kind you feel when you first see the woman you're going to love for the rest of your life. The kind you feel when that woman finally relents and your lips meet for the first time. Nate could see Jeannette standing in the front row of the crowd; his heart began to pound. She looked thin and had two dark black eyes, like a raccoon wearing mascara. She was beautiful. The entire trip replayed in his mind from the moment he had pedaled away from her to flying above the wreckage of this lost planet. Nate didn't know if it would ever find its way back. All he knew was that he had found his way back to Jeannette. He ran down the stairs, nearly breaking his legs on the pavement as he ignored the rotors spinning above his head. It felt like this had all happened before—like déjà vu. *Maybe this is what home feels like,* Nate thought. He rushed into her arms, holding her tight. It felt incredibly good to be in her embrace, the place where he belonged. She was sobbing deeply, and Nate didn't hold back. He cried like a baby. Then he turned to her and asked, "Did anything happen while I was gone?"

That's when the shooting started...

If you enjoyed this book please sign up for my mailing list at http://www.micahackerman.com/mailing-list.html Stay tuned for the second book in the "Wormwood" series and for my second novel "The Third Gender" coming late summer 2014. Thank you for reading.

Made in the USA
Charleston, SC
20 May 2014